Jules Wake's earl be
a writer came at the age of ten. was
diverted by the glamorous world of PR, but eventually the
voices in her head persuaded her it was time to sit down and
write the novel she'd always talked about.

Her debut, *Talk to Me*, came out in 2014. Since then she has
published a dozen bestselling cosy and contemporary romance
novels as both Jules Wake and Julie Caplin.

juleswake.co.uk

 twitter.com/juleswake

Also by Jules Wake

From Italy with Love

From Paris with Love this Christmas

Escape to the Riviera

From Rome with Love

Covent Garden in the Snow

Notting Hill in the Snow

THE SATURDAY MORNING PARK RUN

JULES WAKE

One More Chapter
a division of HarperCollins*Publishers* Ltd
1 London Bridge Street
London SE1 9GF
www.harpercollins.co.uk

This paperback edition 2020
2

First published in Great Britain in ebook format
by HarperCollins*Publishers* 2020

A catalogue record of this book
is available from the British Library

ISBN: 978-0-00-832365-3

Printed and bound in Great Britain by
CPI Group (UK) Ltd, Croydon CR0 4YY

This book is dedicated to my Great Aunt Hilda who at 105 is an inspiration to us all

Chapter One

I picked up my pace, clutching my travel mug of coffee – there was no way I could start the day without a hit of caffeine – my heels click clicking like runaway castanets as I joined the midweek tide of people pouring along the path with ant-like efficiency, all headed towards Churchstone station and the daily commute to Leeds.

I listened to the sharp, staccato beat of my shoes. To me they said, quick, precise and well-organised. And just because I wore high, sexy designer shoes (Russell and Bromley thank you; who can afford Jimmy Choos?!) I wasn't like all the bitch bosses in romcoms. They were high but not super high, and made from supple, polished black leather. As sexy shoes, went they were workmanlike but expensive. I think shoes say a lot about you. I wanted people to know that I, Claire Harrison, had got where I was through hard work and intelligence but I still had class and style. Shoes have nuances and with this pair, I'd nailed it. Just like the meeting I was headed to. I'd worked all weekend to get this presentation to within an inch of perfection.

Mentally, I ticked off my list. Presentation done. Boardroom booked. Team briefed. The truth was, I'd been working for weeks on this meeting and had clocked up many a sleepless night. Reorganising the audit team was a huge responsibility and I was just praying I'd got it right and wasn't creating an opening for a couple of redundancies. My promotion to partner depended on this and surely by now I'd jumped through enough hoops. Unfortunately, they just kept piling more on my plate, as if to test at what point I'd give in. They'd have a long wait.

On the personal front, I'd texted my sister an ambiguous 'maybe' in response to repeated pleas to help her this weekend, booked a long-overdue dental appointment and seriously considered phoning the doctor to arrange a smear test. All in all, my to-do list was nicely full of ticks and just as I was congratulating myself, everything came to a sudden halt. With a start, I slapped a hand over the top of my coffee cup and stopped abruptly because an older woman with a dandelion clock of white hair wearing a sunshine-yellow tracksuit, Day-glo pink trainers, and a silver lamé messenger bag slung across her chest darted out of the lane on the right, cutting across the main path only to disappear down the opposite track. Thankfully, despite slopping wildly, my coffee stayed put and hadn't dripped all over my brand-new kingfisher-blue suit, worn with a crisp white shirt designed to say I'm chic, stylish and extremely competent. Or at least that's what I hoped it said to my bosses. Phew no spillage. Near disaster averted.

Unfortunately, even as I was congratulating myself, it

seemed the woman's sudden appearance had startled several wood pigeons pecking desultorily on the grass verge and with a cacophony of outraged squawks and a flurry of feathers, they clumsily took flight, heedless of the commuters hell-bent on reaching the station for the seven-twenty train.

The man in front of me stopped dead and then, in order to avoid the pigeons, the stupid idiot took a step back doing a *Matrix*-style back-bend manoeuvre, sending the tails of his fine wool suit flying. In some sort of slow-motion panic, I registered this as he tried to dodge one of the birds, adding a twist at the last minute that brought him face to face with me, or rather, coffee cup to coffee cup.

The refillable cups collided, a spout of brown liquid shooting up into the air. And what goes up must come down. We both glanced up with quick, horrified fascination and then there was no time to dodge the inevitable downflow of hot, wet coffee.

The splash hit my beautiful white shirt dead centre, right above my cleavage, liquid seeping through and puddling in between my boobs. Brown stains blossomed with inexorable progress, bleeding out over my chest across the front of my white shirt. Shit. Shit. Shit. I did not need this today of all days.

'Oh my God!' I cried and glared up at him. 'You idiot.' Why the hell hadn't he had the presence of mind to hang on to his bloody coffee?

He was trying to stroke the coffee away from his own white shirt, completely oblivious to what he'd done, and then he glanced up at me, his eyes zeroing in on my damp chest.

'Idiot? Me? Why weren't you looking where you were going?'

'Me?' I asked, now rummaging one handed in my shoulder bag. I had some travel tissues in there somewhere.

'You went into the back of me. In a car, it would be your fault.'

What? He had to be flipping joking. 'You reversed into me. Look at the state of my shirt.' I let out a 'Grrr' noise out of sheer frustration. My shirt was absolutely ruined. And why was he glaring at me as if this was my fault.

Wow, he has unusual eyes, a kind of golden green.

Who cares about his effing eyes, Claire? What is the matter with you?

Given the circumstances, that was a completely inappropriate observation. Since when did I go around checking out men's eyes? I gave up on that sort of thing a long time ago. A girl can only suffer so many disappointments. My career was enough for me; besides, lots of men couldn't hack it. Couldn't handle that I was more successful than them.

'Shit. I've got a meeting with the board in an hour's time. Look what you've done.' I glanced down at my coffee-stained shirt.

He pulled a hanky out of his pocket and began rubbing ineffectually at his chest, which made me bite back a quick smile of amusement. Couldn't he see that his shirt, like mine, was toast? 'And I've got a meeting with the Vice President of Commercial Banking in an hour's time,' he snapped back, those unusual eyes flashing with fury.

'And I'm presenting to the CEO who is coming up from London,' I retorted as I shook out a tissue to mop up the worst of the liquid, now cooling and pooling with an uncomfortable tickle between my breasts.

'Good for him. Are you attempting to play my-job-is-bigger-than-yours? Because I can assure you, my meeting is pretty important.'

'Just like a man to assume his meeting must be more important than a woman's.'

Oh God, I've been down this road so many times.

'Not at all.' His eyes narrowed as he said a touch snootily, 'I'm just observing that my meeting is very important and that I'm now going to be on the backfoot if I go in looking like this.' With surprisingly expressive hands, he flicked them downward to make his point.

'I've been preparing for this meeting for weeks,' I snapped back, my heart starting to thud with the realisation that this really was a disaster. This meeting was supposed to show the big wigs that I was the ultimate professional, totally in control, and knew exactly what I was doing. The swan gliding without effort and not the puddle duck swimming for her life.

For a brief moment, we both stood examining ourselves and each other, surveying the damage, horribly aware of the curious looks of the other commuters and then we both carried on our pre-programmed trajectory towards the station, mopping ourselves as we went. He with a large hanky and me with a succession of tissues.

I winced as we fell into step together. At least I'd got off lightly. Only my shirt was ruined, perhaps thanks to the small shelf of my boobs – useful for once – which had taken the brunt of the coffee downpour. Unfortunately for him, there was a stain right down his crotch. That stain wouldn't be coming out any time soon. That really was a disaster.

'Where do you work?' I asked.

'What?' he asked shortly with an angry glance my way, as if to ask what the hell did that have to do with anything.

5

'Where do you work?' I asked again, even more irritated. I was trying to be helpful.

'Beechwood Harrington,' he snapped out.

'No,' I said a little more gently. 'I meant the location. Is there a shop near where you work, like an M&S or something?' I nodded to his trousers. 'You could buy an emergency...' My voice trailed off as he looked down and his eyes widened in horror. He muttered an epithet under his breath.

'This is a six-hundred-pound Armani,' he snarled. 'Marks & Spencer doesn't cut it in my line of work.' He checked his watch and I could see him doing the same rapid calculation I'd just done. Was there time to go home and change?

'It's better than nothing,' I returned. 'I was trying to help. Find a solution. Have you got time to go back home and change? Or you could phone someone?'

'Phone someone?' He didn't need to look quite so incredulous.

'Yes, like in your office. I'm going to phone my PA – she comes in later than me – and ask if I can borrow another shirt or something.' Ros, my fantastically reliable and awesome assistant, lived in the city and absolutely refused point blank to arrive at work a second before she had to – she had school-aged children that had to be dropped off – but was a trojan for every second she was at work.

'What?' He looked at me as if I were completely mad.

'It's a solution.' I was big on solutions; in fact, most of the time that was my job.

He gave a short mirthless laugh. 'Hmm, I can just see myself in Chas's suit. I'm a thirty-two waist. He's at least a forty. Oh, let me see, Gav, he's five foot ten. Half-mast trousers are all the rage in my office.'

I looked down at his legs, and up and up and up. He must have been at least six two. He had long legs, really long legs, a slim waist, broad chest, and wide shoulders. My mouth went a little dry. If he hadn't been so grumpy, he'd have been seriously hot. Especially with those gorgeous eyes against his dark skin, which were now studying me with a slight hint of amused condescension. I think I might have been ogling. Feeling a blush streak my cheeks, I hurriedly said, 'Have you got hand driers in the loos? Maybe you could rinse your shirt out… dry it off in the gents.'

With a glower he shook his head. 'Any more bright suggestions?'

'I'm only trying to help,' I said with an indifferent shrug. It was his problem after all.

'It would have helped a lot more if you'd been looking where you were going.'

God, he was like a dog with a bone. 'Don't be so ridiculous. You're being childish. What's the point of going over old ground? What's done is done and now you need to find a solution. If you're not interested in my very sensible suggestions, that's your loss.'

I was pleased to see my words shut him up rather neatly. As we hit the edge of the park and the familiar station sign loomed into view on the other side of the road, I pulled out my phone.

'Hi Ros, it's Claire. Sorry to bother you so early. Yes. I'm on my way. Can I ask a huge favour? I've had a bit of disaster. A spillage… yes… coffee everywhere. Please can I borrow a clean shirt? White?' I asked with more hope than belief. 'Okay. I didn't think you would.' I laughed out loud at the very thought of it. 'Do you have a colour that anyone might

7

describe as pale?' Ros favoured patterns and bright colours. 'I know,' I responded to Ros's snort and observation that her impressive double-D accommodating shirts would drown me. I'm a comfortably average thirty-four B. 'But I'm desperate.'

'Thank you, I owe you... not that much.' I laughed at her suggestion that she was given the rest of the week off. Ros was nothing if not forthright and ballsy.

'Handy to have such an accommodating PA,' observed the man rolling his eyes.

'Jealous?' I asked sweetly, now that salvation was at hand. He ought to be; Ros was worth her weight in gold, and the rest. She was a diamond among PAs and my absolute rock.

'It's just a question of hiring the right sort of people.'

The man snorted rudely. I shrugged again. For God's sake, I'd tried to help him but if he was just going to be sarcastic he could sort himself out.

'I have an excellent PA,' he retorted, 'but I don't think my legs will do justice to one of her Reiss skirts.'

We flashed our travel passes and headed down to the platform in perfect synchronicity, my quick strides matching those long legs.

As usual at that time, it was crowded. He came to a stop in the one clear area and I was buggered if he was going to have it all to himself, so I stopped there too. There was room for us both despite his scowl at my proximity. Ignoring him, I began to scroll through my messages on my phone.

Damn, my sister wasn't taking no for an answer.

Don't give me that I'm working crap. It's Saturday. Even Wonder Woman gets a day off. Tell me you've got something better to do.

My sister Alice was not one for subtlety. I sighed. I was knackered. The last thing I wanted to do was spend a Saturday trimming her sodding hedge. It was horribly overgrown, took up two sides of her garden and I really needed to go into the office. Maybe I could fob her off to the following Saturday. I was so behind, having been given yet another project to sort out. That was the by-product of being good at your job and good at finding those pesky solutions. You ended up with everyone else's problems and had to solve them when someone else threw in the towel with the deadline imminent. Going into the office at the weekend meant I could get loads done. Gritting my teeth, I wondered if I ought to offer her the money to pay for a man to come in but I'd already paid for my nieces' school dinners and their summer uniforms this month. Not that I minded, but every now and then Alice would get on her high horse and accuse me of throwing my money around to 'buy people'.

Thankfully, the arrival of the train dispelled my thoughts on the best solution for Alice's hedge and I realised that my new friend and I had boarded the same carriage, snagging the last available seats which were, as bad fortune would have it, bang opposite each other. He plugged himself into his phone and I pulled out the sheets of my presentation to go over my points one last time, making sure I had committed all the figures to memory, absently tugging at my clammy shirt to pull it away from my chest. Damn. It was guaranteed that my best M&S Rosie for Autograph bra was ruined and, to add insult to injury, I'd bought four pairs of matching knickers, at a ridiculously expensive price.

With a shake and a rattle, the train pulled out of the traditional Victorian station with its painted white wrought-iron and pretty hanging baskets, sliding away from the view of industrial yards and workshops into open countryside in a matter of minutes.

I sneaked a few glances at the man across the way. If he weren't such an arrogant git and didn't have such a pissed-off expression on his face, I might have thought him quite good looking with his almost golden skin and the unusual coloured eyes, which were heavily fringed with lashes most girls would envy. The severe haircut didn't suit his thick black glossy hair but I liked those dark heavy eyebrows that framed a very attractive face with a square, almost movie-star, chiselled jawline.

As if he felt the silent study, he glanced up and glared at me. I dropped my eyes to his crotch; that dark stain across the waistband and down his mid-grey trousers really was quite unfortunate. I shot him a small smirk. Okay, so I wasn't being very nice but all my attempts to be helpful earlier had been rudely rebuffed.

His lips hardened and he stared at me. A hard stare. Shades of Paddington. Well, two could play at that game. I would stare back at him until he dropped his gaze. Unfortunately, he was made of sterner stuff and held my gaze without a trace of self-consciousness or any sign of backing down. I stiffened and sat a little taller, which made his lips curve very slightly with a touch of derision, as if this were some small sign of weakness. I took this as a direct challenge and lifted my chin. I raised an eyebrow, which gave me what I knew was a haughty air. Ros had told me off on more than one occasion for using this, saying it made me appear horribly superior, which I thought wasn't necessarily a bad thing.

He raised one of his eyebrows as if to say, *is that the best you've got?* It was almost cute. He was almost cute. A little ping of recognition went off in my chest. I very nearly caved and smiled at his sheer arrogance and self-confidence. He was gorgeous and he knew it, but… no; I forced my mouth to firm into a straight, uncompromising line. He really did have the most amazing eyes and at the moment I had carte blanche to study them. It was rather liberating. The colour was almost sea green but with a touch of whisky. Now his cockiness had been replaced with sheer determination. Again, I nearly crumbled. I could almost see the testosterone boiling up. He was hell bent on winning this challenge. Well, so was I. I quirked my lips in an answering satisfied smirk, as if I knew something he didn't. As I did, I was aware of the older man sitting next to him putting down his paper and tuning in to the show. It was like a domino effect, and now, in my peripheral vision, I could see the other commuters one by one turning to watch the silent battle of wills.

Oh dear God. What have we started?

There was a heavy, charged atmosphere in the carriage and my skin prickled in awareness of the glances flicking back and forth between me and this random stranger. I felt the flush heating my cheeks which made the cocky git smile, his wide mouth curving up to reveal a flash of white teeth. Nice mouth.

Oh yes, go the whole hog Claire. Imagine what it would be like to kiss him because that's really going to help.

Yes, very nice mouth. His lower lip is full, sort of biteable…

Seriously. I'd really said that in my head. I was really thinking that. I sank my teeth into my own lips, imaging it a little too vividly.

From the sudden flicker of his eyes, I must have given myself away. He was a hunter. The sort that thrived on the chase. My heart fluttered, an honest-to-God flutter, and almost as if he sensed it, his eyes narrowed.

Oh heck, what is he thinking now? Does he know?

Does he know that I'm imagining bad things, inappropriate things? Wholly-inappropriate-on-a-packed-train things. Like taking that white shirt off.

I sat up smartly. This was not train behaviour. It wasn't normal behaviour. Certainly not *my* normal. Despite all this weird stuff going on in my brain, I held his gaze.

It hadn't been too difficult at all at the beginning to see exactly what he was thinking.

I'm going to win. I'm going to beat you. I'm going to grind you to dust under my superior staring skills.

Now he was warier and – I was pleased to see – a little bit impressed.

Yeah, sunshine. Not so arrogant now, are you?

He does have lovely eyes though…

The train pulled in to the next station and new people crowded into the carriage. One man was even grabbed and held back by a passenger to prevent him standing in front of us. Everyone was watching us, craning their necks to keep us in their eyeline. Oh God, we were the star attraction on board. There was no way either of us could give way now.

And the cockiness was back – he'd also realised that we were the centre of attention. I was conscious of the bated breaths around us against the backdrop of the noisy rattle of the train.

God, he's sure of himself.

His eyes bored into mine and there it was again, the tiny trip in my pulse. This was quite sexy. A power of wills. I parted my lips and just touched my upper lip with the tip of my tongue. I saw the answering glimmer in his eyes, a fractional movement of his muscles. He'd noticed all right. I shot him a sultry smile which did more harm than good because his eyes widened ever so slightly, and if I hadn't been staring so intently at him I wouldn't have seen it.

Bad move.

This man was not backing down from a challenge and now I'd ramped it up. No, he wasn't going to give way, not now I'd added sex into the mix. His brows rose again and he gave me a mocking smile, with enough kilowatts of sexiness to knock me back into my seat.

Whoops, big mistake. Huge.

But a thrill of adrenaline burst through me; I felt edgy and alive. Aware of my body. Aware of the sexual buzz that thrummed through my veins.

With a sudden jolt, the train came to an abrupt halt, sending the people hanging onto the rails pitching forward. A woman in a lightweight pale blue mac lost her handhold and tumbled forward, almost landing in his lap. Instinctively he glanced her way, his hands moving to steady her.

Ha! He'd lost. He looked away first. When he turned back to me, I gave him a small grin of triumph and with a lift of my brows, shuffled my papers and made much of going back to my presentation as if he was no longer worthy of my time. I was dying to sneak a peek at him but the challenge had been won. There wasn't going to be a rematch. I ignored the voice in my head, all for being fair and honest, arguing the case that my victory was by default.

A few minutes later, after the train lurched forward again, it slowed into Leeds City station. Standing up, startled a little by a burst of regret, I waited until he raised his head and met my eyes.

'Good luck with your meeting,' I said with a victor's smile and sauntered off the train.

I'd never noticed him before on my morning commute in the last six months of walking across the park to the station. Churchstone was a relatively small place, with a population I was sure I'd read somewhere of only thirteen thousand people – a hell of a lot smaller than I was used to, given the nearly half a million that lived in Leeds, where I'd spent the previous six years.

Part of me wanted to turn back and see where he was but I resisted. Would I ever bump into him again? Although, I could do without the 'bump' part. I glanced down at my coffee-stained chest and groaned inwardly.

Halfway down the platform, I felt a prickling down my back and a second later he pulled level. My heart leaped at the sight of his dark, handsome face.

'I'd have won if it hadn't been for the interruption,' he said.

'Ha, you'd like to think so.' I felt a burst of pleasure. 'Only losers look for excuses.'

'Excuses?' he all but spluttered. 'She fell into my lap.'

I shrugged, biting back a grin, as if to say, *not my problem*.

'Are you always this contrary?' he asked as we mounted the stairs.

'I'm not contrary,' I said indignantly. 'Most people think I'm lovely.'

Surprising me, his mouth curved into a sudden grin which did the whole clichéd transform-his-face thing, but it really did. Those eyes really were something and he had the most perfect teeth, except the bottom ones crossed each other very slightly.

'Okay, prove it.'

'How am I supposed to do that?' I asked.

Like a magician with a quick sleight of hand, he produced a business card between his fingers and pushed it into the top pocket of my suit with an arrogant grin, that did something to my insides. Either there were fledgling butterflies in there or I'd got a bad case of indigestion.

'Come out for a drink with me. A week on Friday. Here's my card. Text me.'

Chapter Two

Ashwin Laghari,
Financial Director

When I got to the office I'd flipped the card backwards and forwards over my hand. It had been ages since I'd had so much as a sniff of a date. All work and no play made Claire very dull. And I didn't want to be dull. He'd sparked something that had lit a little glow of excitement in what was otherwise a fairly barren landscape. While sitting at my desk, something had made me send a distinctly out-of-character, playful text to Ashwin Laghari, of the sexy long legs and unusual, piercing eyes. He wasn't having things all his own way and besides, on Friday nights I tended to stay late in the office and get as much done as I could before heading home. My reply had been:

Dinner, a week on Saturday. 8pm. The Beech House. Coffee Girl. x

I swallowed as a twinge of nerves flashed in the pit of my stomach. Ashwin Laghari. After a whole day of radio silence, he'd finally responded to my text.

You strike a hard bargain. Saturday it is. See you there.

Despite its brevity, I must have read it dozens of times over the last ten days and now here I was on Saturday afternoon, less than three hours to lift off. I'd kept my eyes peeled for him on my daily walk across the park to the train station but hadn't seen him once. Maybe he didn't live around here. What if he'd been on his way to work after a one-night stand? What if he was a complete womaniser?

And what if he was? I was overdue some fun. I didn't get the impression he was a 'for keeps' sort of guy. Far too full of himself, but there'd been that definite sexual frisson.

Ashwin Laghari. I kept twisting his name around my tongue. I liked the sound of it. His full name had a melodic feel to it. I wondered if he had any middle names and how they'd fit. I'd have to ask him tonight. And then my sensible gene reared its prudent, forthright self.

For goodness' sake, Claire, what is the matter with you? He's a player. You challenged him. He waited a whole day to respond to your text. This is a game. You might have won that round insisting on Saturday instead of Friday but he wants round two. That's all.

But less-sensible me, who seemed to be determined by my hormones, suggested that maybe he had also felt that sexual frisson and was keen to explore it too.

Armed with his name, I'd done a little bit of research. No more than you'd do before meeting a new business colleague. Not full-on stalking. A bit of LinkedIn, a quick trawl of

Facebook, Twitter, and Instagram. Okay, I might have done a search on Google images. Just to remind myself what he looked like, in case after intensively staring at his face for those fifteen minutes I'd forgotten some aspect of his features. He cropped up in all his gorgeousness a couple of times, always in a suit shaking the hand of some important guy. LinkedIn had given me plenty of information. Graduate from Leeds with a first in Mechanical Engineering. Two years with First Direct and then a move to London and stellar promotions ever since and then back north. Clearly, he was a smart cookie.

Why, oh why, had I chosen The Beech House? Intimate, quiet, with perfect ambient lighting. Ideal for a romantic date. I should have selected somewhere swankier, more contemporary and more show off-y where the staff squinted at you as if you were beneath contempt and everything was far too much trouble for them.

The fussy, friendly maître d' greeted me with a smile of pleasure, briefly dousing my shimmering nerves, which had been making themselves felt ever since I raced into my flat from my sister Alice's to get ready. I'd managed to fob her off last Saturday but couldn't avoid it today. An afternoon's hedge trimming had left me a sweaty, bug-infested mess and now the butterflies in my stomach were manically trying to beat their way out. Why was I so damn nervous?

'I've booked a table for two.' I paused, wiping my slightly damp palms on my favourite black trousers.

'The name?' he asked.

Playing it cool, I hadn't responded to the last text when

he'd asked for my name. Ashwin Laghari only knew me as Coffee Girl. I said it, maintaining eye contact with the man as if this was a perfectly acceptable name and there was nothing out of the ordinary with it.

'Certainly, madam.' He didn't bat an eyelid. 'Allow me. The gentleman has already arrived.'

I followed him, weaving through cosy candlelit tables, towards the back of the restaurant, wishing he'd slow down a little. My legs felt a little unsteady and my tongue had already glued itself to the roof of my mouth. This was ridiculous. I'd met and conversed easily with people from all over the world, talked to conference audiences over a thousand strong and presented to chief executives and board directors all the time and never betrayed a flicker of what I was feeling.

Stiffening my spine and tilting my chin, I sucked in a breath and two seconds later I was at the table and the waiter melted away.

Ashwin Laghari was every bit as gorgeous as I remembered and so was the slightly mocking smile. He stood up.

'You came,' he said, his voice deeper and more mellow than I had recalled.

'I did,' I said, sliding onto the chair opposite him.

He suddenly grinned. 'Busy on Friday, were you?'

'No,' I paused for a minute before giving him a catlike smile; he didn't need to know that I'd been at work until nine, 'but I wanted to put you in your place.'

'Why didn't I guess as much?' Those fascinating eyes twinkled at me. 'Am I allowed to know your name?'

'Yes, but I'm not sure it's been worth waiting for. Do you have any middle names, Ashwin Laghari?'

'I'm always Ash to my friends.' His eyes dipped to my mouth. 'Although I like the way you say my name.'

'I like it too,' I said, feeling flirtatious and mysterious but not quite enough to dare to say it again.

'No middle names.'

'Good,' I said. I didn't like the thought of them disturbing the melodic symmetry of his name.

'When you search for Coffee Girl on LinkedIn, it's not that informative.'

'Leeds. First. Mechanical Engineering. Currently at Beechwood Harrington,' I quipped.

'Unfair advantage.'

'Claire Harrison. Manchester. First. Currently at Cunningham, Wilding and Taylor.' I paused and, unable to help myself, gave him a direct, sultry look and lowered my voice to say, 'Now we're equal.'

If only that were true. He was clearly self-possessed and brilliant whereas for the last couple of weeks, no matter how hard I worked, I felt like I was sinking into quicksand. There never seemed to be enough time in the day to do anything.

He smiled back, his voice laden with darkness and said, 'I don't think we're ever going to be equal.' The knowing look did something to my pulse. 'I took the liberty of ordering a bottle of wine.' He gave me another look.

'What, no champagne?' I said as he lifted the bottle of very, very expensive red wine.

'You don't strike me as a champagne girl. That would be too much of a cliché. I chose something deeper, darker, and smoother.'

I raised an eyebrow at this blatant smooth-talking bollocks.

His face creased into a grin. 'And it's a bloody nice wine.

Usually the champagne they have in these places isn't the best. Would you like to try some? I gambled on you drinking red, but if you don't, I can order something else.'

'Lucky punt,' I said, lifting my glass and letting him pour a mouthful for me to try. I lifted the glass, swirled, sniffed, and sipped. 'Nice, very nice.'

'Of course,' he said with a lift of one eyebrow.

God, he was one cocky git but I couldn't help liking his sheer arrogant confidence. Somehow it was reassuring that he was so in command of himself and – I couldn't believe I was thinking it – quite sexy.

We lifted our glasses in a toast. 'Cheers,' I said.

'To ill-advised meetings,' he said.

I stared at the rich ruby colour, suddenly a little shy. That almost sounded like… as if he were taking this seriously. I wasn't expecting this to go anywhere. Gorgeous as he was, I'd pigeon-holed him in the laddish box. For him, this whole date was a challenge. Yes, there'd been sexual chemistry and I suspected he might use it to try and talk me into bed, but he was a work-hard, play-hard city-type. I didn't expect to see him again after tonight and, to be honest, did I even have the time?

'How did your meeting go? With the board and the CEO from London.'

I glanced up at him, surprised he'd remembered. He actually appeared interested. Okay, now that was smooth.

'It went well, thanks.' In fact, it was ancient history. I was already preparing for the next big meeting. 'How about yours?'

'Given that I was wearing a Marks & Spencer suit, very well. Good tip by the way. Thank you. I got my PA to postpone the meeting for half an hour and I was the first customer into the store that morning. Fastest purchase ever, I reckon.'

'I'm impressed… that you followed my advice.'

'I think I might have thought of it myself.'

'Yes,' I paused, 'but you might have resisted out of sheer pig-headedness.' There was another of our direct eye-meets and my lips twitched as he laughed, twinkly-eyed and appreciative.

'Was I that ungrateful? Sorry, I was a bit stressed that morning. Stupid eh? I can barely remember what the meeting was about now.' He leaned forward, lowering his voice as if about to impart a great secret, 'And do you know what?'

I shook my head. He peered covertly around the restaurant before whispering. 'No one noticed it wasn't designer.' Widening his eyes to emphasise the point, he added, still in a whisper, 'I've worn it all week.'

I burst out laughing. 'So you're a convert now?'

'Too right. I've been a mug, spending ridiculous sums of money on suits when no other bugger can tell the damn difference. I even asked Gav what he thought of my new suit. And he thought it was a Hugo Boss.' He grinned at me and I smiled back, our eyes meeting with a flash of warmth. 'What about you?'

'My PA brought in the most hideous shirt in mint green with this huge bow on the front. Remember Mrs Slocombe from *Are You Being Served?*'

Those sexy eyebrows rose. 'Wasn't she the one with the naughty pussy?'

I almost choked on the wine. Although his face was deadpan, his eyes danced with devilment.

Trying to keep it cool, I ignored his words. 'It clashed

horribly with my suit. It almost drowned me as well. I must have looked ridiculous.'

'I can't imagine that.' He eyed my outfit, which was insanely expensive but totally understated. 'I imagine you're always immaculate.' I liked the way his gaze didn't linger on my cleavage. His voice softened and, to my surprise, he said, 'You look lovely.'

He nodded his head towards my soft black jersey top with tiny specks of silver woven into the fabric, which I'd chosen deliberately to hide my gardening wounds. I was covered in scratches from that bloody hedge I'd trimmed for Alice. As a result, it hadn't been my first choice. I'd wanted to wear a sleeveless black vest which I'd initially thought would be far sexier but now I realised from his appreciative expression that this was more subtle. The soft fabric clinging to my skin hinted at what was underneath rather than blatantly displaying everything for show. Maybe I had something to thank Alice for after all.

It was, however, a little warm and without thinking, perhaps because I'd relaxed after his unexpected compliments and sudden seriousness, I pushed back my sleeves and rested my arms on the table.

'What happened to you?' he asked, reaching out to touch my arms. 'Are you okay?' There was genuine concern in his eyes.

I smiled back at him, my voice a little breathless. 'I'm fine. Just a run-in with a hedge.'

'You challenged it to unarmed combat?'

'Yes, I'm a regular garden ninja.'

Despite a soak in the bath, my arms were worse now because I'd had some kind of allergic reaction. Ash reached over the table and touched one of the many welts on my forearm. His barely-there touch sparked a tingle on my skin. I glanced up sharply and his eyes were kind rather than mocking. 'You probably want some Savlon on those.'

I gave my arm a rueful rub and rolled my shoulders. 'Every bit of me seems to be aching.' Why was I telling him that? Oh God, would he think I was sending out invitations to give me an all-over massage?

'Do you do a lot of gardening?'

'No, I've moved recently and the previous owners, Lord love them, thankfully created a very low-maintenance garden. Keeping a basil plant alive is the sum total of my green-fingered accomplishments. These scars came from my sister needing help with her garden.'

'And you can't say no to sisters.'

'Sadly no,' I sighed.

'I get it too. My sister calls on my services a lot. I've no idea why. Do I look like a DIY expert to you?' He held up artistic hands with long, elegant fingers.

It gave me the opportunity to take stock of him, instead of the surreptitious checking out I'd been doing since I arrived. He wore a grey V-neck T-shirt, which fitted rather well, the soft jersey moulding to a broad chest, the dip of the vee revealing a few crisp, dark hairs.

No, he didn't look like a DIY expert; he looked flipping gorgeous. Absolutely edible, and I wanted to peel that T-shirt right off him, touch his golden skin, smooth a hand over that chest and run my fingers across the firm biceps beneath his T-shirt sleeves. I wanted... His mesmerising eyes darkened, the pupils wide.

My breath caught in my throat. The pause in the

conversation stretched out as we stared at each other, the same fizz of sexual tension in the air that I'd sensed the first time we met.

I knew then that I was going to throw all caution to the wind. I was going to sleep with Ashwin Laghari. I was going to revel in touching every inch of his skin, stare into those delicious eyes and enjoy every minute of exploring that hot body.

And he wasn't going to be saying no. His hand was on my forearm again, stroking my wrist, his eyes holding mine.

His smile was gentle rather than triumphant; it felt like the gamesmanship had died. Somehow, both of us had relaxed – and more – into the evening.

I'm not sure how long we'd have enjoyed that sexually-charged silence but it was interrupted by the waiter coming to take our orders. Of course, we hadn't so much as glanced at the menu. Suddenly I really wasn't that hungry and food seemed an obstacle in the way of the evening.

'So you have a sister,' I said.

'And a brother. And my sister seems to think DIY is part of my DNA. She's a brain surgeon, for God's sake. She's licensed to use a scalpel.'

'A surgeon.' I was impressed.

'Of course.' In the candlelight, his skin glowed like warm honey and he smiled. 'My sister's a surgeon. My brother's a barrister.' At this he grinned cheerfully. 'My mum is a real tiger mum. She's white. Dad's a doctor, born here; his dad is Indian, came over from Uganda just before Idi Amin kicked the Asian population out in the seventies. What about you? Brothers, sisters?'

'Just one. Alice. Single mum. I have two nieces.'

'You close?'

I sputtered out a laugh. 'Not especially. Alice prefers a more alternative lifestyle. She doesn't really approve of corporates.'

'She'd hate me.'

I wrinkled my nose and nodded. 'Yeah, probably.'

'Good job you don't give a toss about what she thinks then,' he said with an arrogant laugh.

'Are you always this sure of yourself?' I asked.

'Pretty much. What's the point otherwise?' His eyes met mine, guileless and direct. 'You could spend a lifetime worrying about what others think of you and where would that get you? Would you rather I lie to you and pretend to be modest?'

'No,' I laughed. I rather like his unashamed arrogance. 'So what do you do when you're not spraying coffee over unsuspecting commuters or working?'

'The usual. Gym. See friends. You know… the job's pretty all encompassing.'

Gym. Friends. It didn't sound like much. And if he were like me, I knew the type of friends he meant. People you drank with after work. The others tended to drift away when you cancelled things once too often. I nodded in sympathy. 'Don't I know it.'

'But if you enjoy it then none of that really matters.' Ash's gaze was steady but I caught the question buried in the words.

'Do you ever wonder if it's worth it?' The words came out before I was ready for them and I was halfway to thinking of a way to retract the comment when I realised Ash was considering my words quite carefully.

'Yes.' He rested his chin on his hand. In the clipped,

unencumbered word, I felt a ripple of unease that mirrored my own.

'Succinct.'

'I was trying to think of the best way to put it into words. There's a fear, isn't there? Deep rooted, submerged, but it's there. What if it isn't worth it? What if the hours we put in aren't worth the stress? What's left?'

For a moment we held each other's gazes as if the other was some kind of lifeline, holding fast against the emptiness of the answer. One that neither of us really wanted to visit. What drove us? Was it fear or lack of courage? The moment of honesty shimmered between us and I felt as if we'd taken a step below the surface. We were more alike than we'd realised.

'I don't know,' I admitted. 'It scares me sometimes. Maybe that's why I keep working so hard, to fill the void. Because without work, I'm not sure... I'm not sure what I'd have.'

Or who I was? In the office I was the invincible go-getter, a role model, and the epitome of success. I avoided thinking about life outside of work and luckily there wasn't too much of it because my job was all consuming.

'Which is why there's a lot to be said for job satisfaction,' I said, feeling the need for firmer ground. For a moment I'd strayed into quicksand that had no place in my life. Those sorts of thoughts belonged to dead-of-night insomniac moments, when a person questioned life, the universe, and everything, not just the unremitting pressure of their job. Pressure came with the territory. 'Not everyone has that. Imagine being in a job that you hate.'

'Can't.' He gave a mock shudder which immediately lifted the shadow that had touched our conversation. 'I guess we are both lucky in that way. I love my job.'

'Me too. Although it's been a busy week and I'm absolutely knackered.' I deliberately lightened my tone, signalling that we'd left that line of philosophical enquiry behind but I was aware – and so, I could tell from his steady regard, was he – of that moment of connection between us.

'Do you always get the early train?' Ash didn't comment on my uncharacteristic admission of weakness for which I was fervently grateful. Like me, he probably despised weakness. 'How come I've never seen you before?'

'Because you weren't looking,' I responded with a twisted, cool smile, feeling a little more myself.

He gave me an equally cool look and we were back to being sparring partners again. 'I'd have noticed you... the attitude at the very least. You walk like a power house.'

'That sounds... not attractive.' But I rather liked it all the same. Anything else might have been a cliché.

'With purpose, determination. Like you know exactly where you're going and why. In my book, that's very attractive.'

He said it without the flirtatious smirk and that made the compliment all the sweeter.

'I like a woman who knows herself.'

'That's good then. A lot of men are intimidated by that.'

'You've just had poor taste in men.'

'Did I say they were relationships?'

'You didn't need to.'

'Arrogant, much?'

'Yeah. I reckon I've earned it. And so have you.'

'Arrogant is all right for a man. Women tend to get called big headed, up herself, too big for her boots.'

Ash shrugged. 'There aren't many women where I work.

28

And sadly, I agree. They don't get treated equally, despite all the HR policies that say otherwise.'

'Which is why I have to work five times as hard to prove I'm "suitable for partnership". Hence where we came in. Is it worth it?'

'I guess it will be when you make partner. Is it likely?'

'I bloody hope so. I feel like I'm jumping through enough flaming hoops. That morning... my presentation was supposed to nail it but they want me to complete another project, naturally with impossible deadlines, which of course I will deliver because I always do.' I said it blithely, as if impossible deadlines and leaping over burning skyscrapers were all in a day's work, but actually this latest project was giving me sleepless nights. This time the deadlines really were impossible but I'd never missed a deadline in my life and I wasn't about to start now.

After the meal we finished coffee, followed by flaming sambucas, which prolonged the evening. The sky was deepening to a purple hue when we came out of the restaurant and my nerves kicked in again.

I had a first-date rule: don't sleep with him.

'I'll walk you home.' We'd already identified during dinner that we both lived on the south side of the park. It was a purely practical suggestion. I was not going to sleep with him. 'Are you happy to walk through the park?'

'Yes.' Victoria Park was the jewel in the crown of Churchstone, a proper municipal park with regimented borders bursting with colour in every season, well-lit with traditional iron curlicued lamps that guarded the wide paths like benign sentries.

I gave him a considering appraisal, enjoying taking another look at his body. My libido purred into life and I had to force my hands down by my sides and fight against the sudden urge to smooth my fingers over the jersey fabric covering his chest.

'I bet you could fight off any marauding teenagers. I wouldn't normally walk through there at this time of night.'

'Don't worry, I'll protect you.' To my surprise, he took my hand and squeezed it in an old-fashioned sort of gesture. And he didn't let go. He laced his fingers between mine and we began to walk, hand in hand, towards the park.

Those wretched butterflies had taken flight again and were getting in a right old tizzy at the touch of his warm skin on mine and the way our forearms bumped as we walked. When we entered the cool seclusion of the park, lit by the pools of lamplight, cedar scenting the air with its distinctive pencil-shaving smell, it felt as if there were magic in the air. An almost-full moon painted the trees silver and bathed the shrubs in a soft light. Conscious of our solitude, the slow pace of his footsteps in tandem with mine, and the warm caress of his hand, my mind went into overdrive. What if he invited me back for coffee? I didn't want the evening to end. I'd want to say yes, but everyone knew what that meant. But if I said yes but didn't plan to sleep with him, should I say so at the outset? Then there'd be no confusion. No expectation.

'I haven't decided yet whether I'm going to sleep with you,' I mused out loud. We'd been honest with each other throughout dinner and I wanted it out there, up for discussion.

'I wasn't aware I'd asked you to,' he responded, his voice deep and smooth.

'No, I know, but we're both thinking about it.'

He'd stopped under one of the lamps, the light casting shadows over his face. Amusement danced in his eyes.

'Does that mean you want to?' he asked, with a lift of that eyebrow again. He was a cocky sod.

'Yes, but I'm not sure if it's a good idea or not.' Thank goodness in the monochrome light, he couldn't see my blush because, as forthright as I sounded, I was only being like this because I really did fancy him and since the first day I met him there'd been that innate, if somewhat combative, honesty between us. 'I'm still trying to work out if you're a... womaniser,' I paused to select the word. I also wanted to know whether he habitually slept around. He was certainly good-looking and confident enough to. I bet he had plenty of offers.

Over dinner there'd been no mention of previous relationships and I hadn't wanted to probe. Was it because I didn't want to be disappointed in him? Because I wanted to preserve the mystery about Ashwin Laghari? No one could deny he was gorgeous but he did seem to take it for granted. His arrogance was based on self-confidence and ability rather than vanity.

'What do you think?' he asked without any nuance in his voice. I knew he wanted honesty as much as I did.

'I'd like to think not but... the good-looks fairy certainly spent a lot of time in your department and with the city-boy lifestyle there's a certain reputation.'

He shrugged. 'I don't have time for one relationship let alone more than one. Or were you asking if I'm predilected towards one-night stands?'

'I guess, yes. I was also trying to determine when you last

31

slept with someone? Last night? Last week? Last month? Last year?'

An unexpected stab of jealousy pricked at the thought of him in bed with someone else.

'Ah. You want to know if I sleep around.' His eyes narrowed and a smile danced around his lips. 'Do you?'

'No. I pride myself on this thing called self-respect but...' I gave him a superior look. 'If I want to sleep with someone, I'm not ashamed of it.'

'Good for you. I don't sleep around,' he smirked. 'Not so sure about the self-respect. I'm fussy.' He gave a self-deprecating laugh. 'I'm very choosy about who I sleep with. I don't like going back to strange places. Unknown quantities. I like places to be clean and tidy. And I don't like taking people back to my place.'

'Clean bedsheets,' I quipped. 'No hair in the shower.'

He gave me a sharp glance, as if I were taking the piss. I held up my hands. 'I'm serious. I'm a neat freak and I like things to be clean, especially bed sheets.' I shuddered. 'I shared a flat with a girl at university who didn't wash her sheets for the whole term.'

'That,' said Ash. 'Exactly that.' He shot me an evil grin. 'Sounds like we might be a match.' There was unmistakable challenge in his words. 'And to answer your question. At least six months ago. Can I ask you a question?'

'Over a year ago,' I said. 'I'm choosy too.' There, right back at you.

His lips quirked. 'That wasn't my question.' For about the second time in ten minutes, I blushed scarlet to the very tips of my ears. I wasn't anywhere near as sophisticated in the sexual-relationships department as I wanted to sound. That was the problem when you put everything into your career. Your sex life took the hit. Competent and confident in the boardroom, inexperienced and a bit daunted in the bedroom.

He took a step forward and put both hands on my waist, holding me gently, his eyes roving over my face, suddenly soft. 'I was going to ask if I could kiss you?'

For all his arrogance, Ash completely had me with his softly voiced question. The bottom of my stomach fell away and all those pesky butterflies took flight, a cloud around me, brushing my skin with tingles of excited awareness.

His eyes held mine as I nodded, just the once, too fizzy to utter a word. My heart pitter pattered like a crazy thing in my chest but outside everything seemed to freeze and stand still when his lips touched mine. I hardly dared breathe for fear of spoiling the perfect moment. It was a kiss so perfect, I knew I'd remember this moment in the pooling lamplight. Every second would be burned into my memory banks, sealed into its own little vault. Our noses didn't bump. His teeth didn't knock mine. His mouth wasn't hard, pushing against mine. Featherlight, his lips skimmed in a barely-there kiss. Our skin brushed lightly. I slid my arms around his neck, wanting to touch him, to feel the warmth of his skin under my fingertips.

Then he lifted his head, his eyes meeting mine and he gave me a smile of such sweetness it completely tugged at my heart strings. I lifted my mouth to his and kissed him, feeling the hitch of his breath as my lips skated over his in gentle exploration, savouring the exquisite sensation of skin on skin. With a gentle exhalation, his fingers on my waist tightened and he pulled me closer, chest to chest, deepening the kiss.

After a while, we both pulled apart. I felt a little dazed.

'That was quite a kiss, Coffee Girl.'

'You're quite a kisser, Ashwin Laghari.'

He laughed and squeezed my waist. 'No one ever calls me that, you know, but I rather like it when you do. You make me sound like some sexy magician.'

With those beguiling kisses he definitely had a touch of magic about him.

'Would you like to come back to my place? I promise my sheets are clean.' He held up a hand. 'Not because I was hoping to score tonight… I thought you might be too much of a ballbreaker.'

'Charming. What changed your mind?'

'Because inside, I think we have a lot more in common than either of us would like to admit. And, just for the record, I always do my laundry on Saturday.'

Chapter Three

'Claire, can I have a word? It's urgent. My office in ten.'

My heart sank at Alastair's words. It was five to eight on Monday morning and I'd literally just walked through the door – in fact, almost walked into the door frame I was so tired and my eyesight was a little blurry. *Stay calm, Claire. You got the report done. It's all cool.* I heaved out a sigh, punch drunk with fatigue. I'd pulled an all-nighter to get the damned thing done.

'Morning, Claire. Good weekend?' Karen, the HR director, grinned at me as she ducked her head into my office.

'It was actually.' I grinned back, suddenly boosted by the memory of waking up in Ash's bed on Sunday morning.

'Anything you want to share?'

'Not just now.' I gave her a mischievous smile. 'Maybe over a glass of prosecco, one night.'

'Just let me know when.'

'Might not be this week.' I winced. As she walked off with a cheery wave over her shoulder, I let myself take an indulgent dip into the memories of Saturday night and Sunday morning.

I'd woken late on Sunday. Sadly, the delicious lassitude of my muscles had long since dissipated but thinking about Ash's body moving over mine, the breathless sighs of both of us and the delicious intimacy we'd shared, warmed me as I sat down at my desk. God, he'd been lovely. A considerate, passionate, thoughtful and, I thought with a sudden naughty smile, very inventive lover. That competitive streak in both of us had pushed us to challenge each other well beyond limits that I suspected normally bound us. I almost groaned out loud at the deliciousness of his shuddering uncontrolled orgasm and the sheer feminine satisfaction that I, Claire, had been able to bring a man to this. Not that he'd been without his own power. I'd never had sex like it and was still a little surprised by my own loss of control and the way I'd begged him, gasping, 'please, please, please' over and over again.

Even now I was getting a little hot and bothered at the recollection of the way our bodies had moved together.

I'd woken up on Sunday immediately aware of where I was and smiling at the weight of Ash's arm draped over my back and the sun streaming in through the window. We'd been in far too much haste to bother with things like closing curtains. That smile vanished quickly when I realised the time. I'd felt a little sick when I saw it was half past nine.

'I'm sorry, Ash, I've got to go.' I pulled off the sheets but he tugged me back.

'Not even a good morning kiss,' he teased, pulling me down onto his warm body. He was impossible to resist but eventually I forced myself to sit up. 'I really have to go. I have so much to do. I've got this big report to hand in on Monday and I'm...' My stomach had turned over at just how much I had to do and how much time I'd lost helping my sister yesterday. Alice and her bloody hedge. If it weren't for her, I might have been able to give in to the temptation of slow Sunday-morning sex. I was beginning to recognise the familiar signs of stress creeping through my body.

'Hey, don't look so worried. I get it. My laptop's calling me too.'

'And the boy gets the prize,' I quipped with a grateful smile. He really did understand.

'I'm with you, Claire. I completely understand.'

I kissed him smartly on the nose, wishing like crazy I could kiss that lush mouth and go back for round two. It was possibly my biggest regret for a very long time. I hated having to drag myself away.

At the front door, Ash gave me a long, heated kiss that had us both breathing heavily.

'Who needs exercise? This is definitely pushing up my heart rate,' said Ash, pushing my hair back over my shoulder.

'I wish I could stay.'

'Don't worry.'

He kissed me again and it was another minute before I came up for air. 'I really do have to go.'

'I know.' He bent and teased my lips again. I felt my resolve weakening but fear raised its ugly head. There was a chance I might not get the report done in time.

'I've got to go.' I pulled away and put a good metre between us so I wouldn't be tempted again.

'I'll text you tomorrow. Dinner Friday?'

I grinned at him. 'Or Saturday.'

He raised a cocky eyebrow in response. 'You don't need to

play hard to get now. I've already had you.'

'Or I had you.' I tilted my head with a superior smile and turned and walked away, wishing with every step that I could have stayed.

Even now, on Monday morning, I was still rather pleased with that quip and the accompanying smile carried me all the way to Alastair's office. Just outside, my phone beeped and I paused. Normally I'd have ignored my phone but a slew of distracting texts yesterday had reprogrammed my response to the text alert.

Morning, sexy girl. Hope you slept well. Looking forward to Friday. x

I glanced at Alastair's closed door.

Morning, Ashwin Laghari. Could have sworn we said Saturday. x

Before I could even put my phone back in my pocket, the message came back.

How about we compromise… and do both. xxx

I smiled and, inside my chest, my heart did a funny little bunny hop of happiness.

'There you are, Claire.' Alastair, a man of few words, waved me in. 'The Ashdown Report—'

'Don't worry, it's all done. I just need to get Ros to print off a dozen copies, bind, and distribute them.'

'Ah, that's why I wanted to see you. The client's had a change of heart. They've decided that they'd like to look at a different sector of the construction industry, education rather than retail. I'm afraid we're going to have to start again.'

That would be the royal we, would it?

'And I know education isn't your area of expertise but you're a quick study and we've got all the stats and data on the market.'

Yes *we* did but they weren't at *one's* finger tips. *We* would take some time digging them up.

'Won't take someone like you that long to get up to speed.'

No, not more than a day or so.

'Obviously we'll bill them for your hours to date, so it's not a problem.' His smile was optimistic. 'You know how it is. What the client wants, the client gets.'

I kept a bland smile on my face. *Not a problem? No, not for you mate.* That flaming report had taken hours and hours. I'd worked all last night, finishing at four and waking at six. I'd had two hours of pretty shitty, restless sleep. Linking my fingers, I twisted them together wondering what he might say if I slammed both hands on the desk and told him what he could do with his 'what the client wants' line.

'They want it by the end of the week. Not going to be a problem, is it?'

Of course, it wasn't; it never was, but bloody Alastair was already looking at his computer screen. Dismissed, I turned and walked out, every step weary. I'd only walked a few paces when I realised something odd was happening to me. My throat was doing a strange convulsing thing and I couldn't seem to control the odd hiccoughing in my diaphragm. No! I was not, not, *not* going to cry.

Oh God, I'm going to cry.

Picking up my pace, I darted to the ladies' loo, praying

there were no other eager beavers in this morning. Slamming one of the doors and fumbling with the lock, I dropped onto the loo seat and sank my head in my hands. The Ashdown report had taken over a week to perfect. Pulling a whole new report together by Friday on top of everything else I needed to do this week... shit. The sob bubbled in my throat and I gasped, trying to fight against it. I did not cry at work. Never. I sucked in a deep breath. Held on to it. Breathed out slowly.

Breathe, Claire. Breathe.

Even with the slow, careful breathing, it took a whole ten minutes before I felt as if I could even stand up. It was just extreme tiredness. Two hours of sleep did that to a body. I had this. I could do the report. It would just take a lot of hours.

I finally emerged from the ladies, fifteen long, panicky minutes later and strode to my office, rolling up my metaphorical sleeves as I went. I could do this.

When I finally allowed myself the treat of checking my messages at half past six, hoping there might be a few texts from Ash, my spirits nose-dived when I realised there hadn't been anything since the first ones this morning. I read them again, a little sunshine dancing in my heart. He'd obviously had as busy a day as me. The thought gave me a sense of solidarity. Me and Ash hard at work, both bossing it. We were so similar above and below the surface.

There was a text from my mother.

Hi darling, can we change the time tomorrow? Could you make it 6pm instead of 7.30? See you soon xxx

I closed my eyes. Damn, I'd completely forgotten. Reluctantly, I picked up the phone.

'Hi Mum, it's Claire.'

'Hi, darling. Did you get my text?'

'Yes, that's why I'm ringing. I'm not going to be able—'

'Claire, don't you dare say you're not coming.'

'Mum, I can't. I've just been given—'

'But darling, it's the last time we'll see you before we go.'

'I know, Mum—'

'We'll be gone for four months.'

To be fair, with Mum and Dad's imminent departure on a four-month cruise, tomorrow's date had been reserved for two weeks. It was a measure of my state of mind that I'd forgotten. I normally kept a pretty good handle on my diary.

'Okay, Mum. But let's stick to seven-thirty.' That would allow a couple of additional hours in the office.

'But then it's late for the girls and Alice wants to leave at a reasonable hour because she has a yoga class in the morning.'

Alice had a yoga class! I rubbed at my forehead trying to ease the tightening bands of headache gathering there. *Bully for bloody, bendy Alice.*

'Well, she should have thought about that, earlier. We said seven-thirty two weeks ago.'

'Claire, please,' sighed my mother in her familiar referee voice. 'Your Dad and I really want to see you before we go. And you work far too hard, darling. Take a night off.'

If it weren't for the fact that this really was the only chance I'd see them for four months, I might have stood my ground.

'I'll see you at six, then,' I said with finality and hung up, annoyed at myself for being annoyed at Alice for derailing the evening.

That was her default. Derailing things. At sixteen she announced she was pregnant, on the morning of my first A-level exam. You try concentrating after that bombshell. Conscious that she was missing the best years of her life, my parents became surrogate parents themselves rather than grandparents. A huge mistake, in my opinion. Somehow Alice managed to get pregnant a second time with Ava, just four years after Poppy.

In recent years, my parents had bought her a small terraced house in Churchstone. It was pure chance I'd moved to the same small market town six months ago. The gorgeous perfection of the house more than made up for its proximity to my sister.

Amazingly, on first viewing, it had ticked every box on my extremely detailed – I overhead the estate agent use the word 'demanding' – list and instantly I knew it was my Instagram perfect I've-made-it home. Or rather, it would be when I got round to finding the right workmen to do the renovations and chose some decent furniture. Bizarrely, it had been the one and only time I'd gone with my gut and it had been the biggest purchase of my life.

I winced and woke up my computer. The last thing I had time for right now was daydreaming how my house might look one day. If I didn't get this blasted report done, I could kiss goodbye to a partnership and then buying the house would have been a complete waste of time.

But I did have one thing to do. I picked up my phone, smiling again at Ash's earlier text and sent one back.

I have been known to compromise but don't get used to it. x

Chapter Four

I checked my emails and my palms turned clammy. Twelve already and it was only ten past nine. I studied the busy receptionist and prayed that the doctor was running to time. I was going to be an hour late into work. If the festering wound on my arm from trimming Alice's hedge hadn't started leaking greenish stuff I probably would have cancelled today's appointment.

I typed a couple of quick responses to my emails, although it was like a game of whack-a-mole. No sooner had I answered five, another six had popped up.

With a heavy sigh, out of habit rather than any real hope, I checked my text messages.

Nothing. The familiar lump in my throat rose. Not one text from Ashwin Laghari in over two weeks.

Whatever had happened with him had burned fast and furious and like a firework. It had clearly been a one-time-only deal but it still left this odd, hollow pain in my chest.

I reread, for what must have been the hundred millionth

time, the last text he'd sent. What had made him change his mind?

Hadn't that brief, sizzling connection meant anything to him? I'd shared with him a glimpse of my fears because I'd thought he understood. The rejection hit hard. I'd even cried again at work one day but that had probably had as much to do with realising I was going to miss the Ashdown report deadline. It was the one and only deadline I'd ever missed and it felt like a huge great blot on my career. And the more I worried about it, the more I struggled to meet the next deadline and the one after that. It was as if I was caught upside down in some whirlwind and I couldn't right myself.

'Let's have a look then,' said Dr Boulter with a kind smile.

I rolled up my sleeve to show him the gash – thanks, Alice's hedge – which had not healed properly and had been looking decidedly manky for weeks and this morning had reached a whole new level of manky. Around the wound my skin was red and inflamed and had acquired a furnace-level heat. My whole forearm was now tender to the touch.

'Ouch.' With gentle gloved fingers he prodded my arm and a glistening gob of greenish yellow pus welled up and oozed from the jagged edges. I flinched.

'This is nasty. How long has it been like that?'

'Er… a couple of weeks,' I admitted, shamefaced.

He raised an eyebrow. 'Why haven't you been to see me before now? You've got a nasty infection. This needs antibiotics.'

For some stupid reason, tears filled my eyes and I had to swallow back the lump that had, if I was honest, taken up permanent residence in my throat.

'Claire?'

44

That was the problem when your GP was an old golf buddy of your dad's and had known you from when you were in ankle socks. No, I certainly didn't come to see him about women's things, instead opting for one of the female doctors in the practice, but I did come for minor things like stupid, flipping scratches that refused to heal.

Ashwin Laghari – bugger his gorgeous, indifferent soul – had probably been right about the Savlon but in that glorious immediate-post-date haze I'd completely forgotten about applying antibiotic cream. Yeah, I was holding him personally responsible for my infected arm. The bastard.

'Claire?' Dr Boulter's voice broke into my thoughts. Damn, he was being kind. I didn't want kind. I wanted brusque and curt.

'Claire?' he asked again gently as I struggled to stem the rising flood of tears. Shit, this was embarrassing. But it was no good. They were on a roll, and I knew I'd lost it when the sob burst free.

Suddenly I was in floods of tears and I had no idea why, and he was handing over tissues from the box on his desk. Snuffly and snotty, I grabbed them like a life belt but as fast as I mopped up, a fresh burst of sobs thrust their way out

Finally I was able to stutter, 'Oh God, I'm… I don't know w-what's w-wrong with m-me.'

He gave me a kind but stern look. 'Want to tell me what's going on?'

'It's… nothing. Just… ev-everything. Just a lot on at work. It's quite full-on at the moment.' I found myself taking the step off the cliff. 'I've got this horrible feeling that something bad is going to happen all the time and I didn't get much sleep last night.'

'Last night?'

I pulled a face as I acknowledged the truth. 'Well, actually, I haven't slept properly for weeks. I'm just so tired.' Since missing my deadline, my confidence seemed to have crumbled. My anxiety levels were through the roof and I didn't seem to be able to get them under control. Making the slightest decision at work suddenly had me tied up in knots. It terrified me. I'd always known what to do.

'Are you eating properly?' He eyed my face and I knew he was taking in the dark shadows under my eyes and the gaunt hollows under my cheekbones.

The gallic shrug didn't fool him.

———

Five minutes later, while I was still feeling light-headed from the aftermath of the emotional outburst, he weighed me, took my blood pressure, shone a light in my eyes and asked lots of searching questions, especially about work.

After releasing the cuff on my arm, he sat heavily in his chair and pulled the lid from his fountain pen, holding it poised over a white pad he'd pulled out from the top drawer of his desk.

'I think you're suffering from stress, Claire. Your blood pressure is 180/100.'

I shrugged. 'Everyone gets stressed at work. It's okay, I just need to catch up on some sleep.'

'No, Claire.' Now Dr Boulter was brusque and curt. 'You need to take a complete break.'

I laughed defensively. 'I can't do that. I've got far too much to do.'

He studied me through narrowed eyes and then began writing on the pad. 'I'm going to sign you off from work for a month and give you some medication to reduce your blood pressure.'

'What? No. I'm… I'm not that stressed. I mean, I'm a bit on edge and over-tired.'

He sat back in his chair, lifted his chin and then pointed to the framed certificate on the wall. 'Do you have one of those?'

'No.'

'Exactly, so please extend me the professional courtesy of knowing what I'm talking about. I wouldn't presume to tell you how to do your job.' His serious tones shocked me. I'd never heard him speak like that before.

I stared at him for a moment before finding the words and it was only fear that gave them a voice.

'But a month? That's a long time. I can't be off for a month. Can't I just have the medication for my blood pressure? I'll try to take it a bit easier.'

Didn't he understand that if I took a month off my career could be over? People at my level didn't take time off for stress.

'If I believed you for a minute, I might consider it. This has been a long time coming, Claire. The last time you came to see me, I gave you the benefit of the doubt because you said it had been a particularly busy month. I can't overlook it again. You need to look at your whole lifestyle. Start eating properly. Taking more exercise. And in the short term taking some time away from work.'

'But—'

He held up a hand. 'If I said you had a broken leg and couldn't walk on it for a month, what would you do?'

I stared mutinously at him.

'Your mind needs a rest. The work will be still be there. In fact, you need to talk to your HR people about your workload. You've said yourself that the department is a person down. They need to sort that out.'

Well of course they did, but complaining about such things was below my paygrade. I was the capable, efficient one. People like me did *not* get signed off with stress.

Apparently I was wrong. They did. Starting with immediate effect.

Feeling as if I was having an out of body experience, I left the doctor's surgery and went home via the post office, standing for a full five minutes in front of the post box before I finally committed the toxic sick note to its open mouth so that it could wing its way to the HR department. Then I had to make the embarrassing phone call to my boss, Alastair, during which I had to admit the shameful truth. Me, Claire Harrison, rising star, had been mown down by stress. It was all I could do not to cry down the phone. He was surprisingly sympathetic and actually said he'd been a little worried about me and to take as much time off as I felt I needed since I was a valued member of staff. A small part of me wanted to say, 'so why the bloody hell haven't you done more about recruiting the missing body,' but it wasn't the sort of thing you said to your boss, no matter how understanding he sounded.

And now I was left, swollen eyed and lost, wondering what on earth I was going to do with myself. I couldn't even phone Mum and invite myself into one of her soothing hugs because she was presently bobbing on a large boat probably somewhere in the Atlantic. She and Dad had left Southampton over a week ago.

'Claire?' The voice made me lift my head. I realised I must have looked a right idiot standing in the middle of the street, my mobile in my hand, with a vacant expression on my face. 'Claire? What are you doing?'

My sister peered suspiciously at me. 'Shouldn't you be at work? Greasing the wheels of industry and making sackfuls of money?'

'I've been to the doctor.' Already I felt as if I was skiving.

'Oh God, you're not ill, are you?' She peered at my saggy, red eyes. 'Is it serious?'

And once again, completely against my control, tears flowed like tea from a leaky teapot.

'It's not cancer, is it?'

How like Alice to immediately jump to the worst conclusion.

'No. I've…' I could hardly bring myself to say it. In fact, she was the last person I wanted to admit it to. Our relationship was such that she'd probably say it was karma or something but I didn't have the wherewithal to lie; I felt too battered, as if I'd just been rescued from a shipwreck. All that crying, probably, and so I said it: 'I've been signed off with stress.'

'Oh,' she said with a slight air of disappointment as if to say, *is that all?*. Then her eyes brightened with sudden beady avarice. 'Do you want to go to The Friendly Bean for a coffee?'

Even as listless and drained as I felt, like the last lone piece of spaghetti abandoned in the pan, some small part of my brain thought, *that's odd*. Her response was quite *un-Alice-like* but I allowed myself to be steered down the street and across the road into the park, perhaps because I didn't know what else to do.

The Friendly Bean, though it was situated in the middle of Victoria Park, was the place to go in Churchstone. It was a funky café run by Sascha, a statuesque young woman with wild, thick blonde curls piled up on top of her head, secured by a succession of paisley scarves that changed with the seasons. The old Victorian pavilion was eclectically furnished with a mix of church pews, softened by plump velvet cushions, old-fashioned school desks, stools made from tractor seats which were more comfortable than they appeared, and worn sofas that welcomed you into their lumpy embrace. It was always teeming with customers. This morning was no exception but Alice made a beeline for an empty corner with a battered leather chesterfield armchair and a padded stool, plumping for the armchair and calling over her shoulder, 'Mine's a cappuccino.'

Having a clear purpose stirred me from my fug, with the quick observation that Alice had neatly manoeuvred me into paying. I should have realised that altruism had little to do with her quick invitation.

I handed her the coffee and sat down on the stool next to her, taking a grateful sip of my own Americano. The noise and bustle of The Friendly Bean with its yummy mummies and smattering of people working at laptops made me feel more grounded and a bit more normal, although a headache was digging in, its tight bands of pain circling my skull.

'So. Signed off. Stress. How long for?' Alice's sharp interest was palpable as she studied me, her nose almost quivering like a squirrel's.

I sighed, not quite believing it. Nothing seemed real at the moment. It was as if I were floating through fog. 'A month.' A whole month. What on earth was I going to do with myself? The thought of it was causing me more anxiety than going to work had been doing for the last... longer than a week, I realised, at last facing up to the truth. I'd had this about-to-step-off-a-cliff feeling for the last two... go on then, three months. In my usual overachieving way, I'd been successful at masking it.

'A month. Will they pay you?'

'I guess so.' I hadn't even thought about it. Sick pay wasn't something I'd ever had to consider before.

'Well that's good. You can still enjoy yourself then.'

'Mmm.' I nodded while thinking, *enjoy myself? Doing what?*

'So what are you going to do with yourself?'

Why did she have to ask that? My stomach knotted itself like crazy macramé. What indeed? But I'd only just walked out of the surgery; I think I was still in shock.

'I know.' She straightened as if the thought had just light-bulbed its way into her head, at which point I knew her invitation to coffee had had an agenda.

'You can look after the girls and I can go to India.' Her beam was brilliant, her eyes sparkling with enthusiasm and delight. 'That will give you something to do.'

Funny how Alice managed to make it sound as if she were doing me a huge favour.

'I can, can I?' I raised a sarcastic eyebrow feeling a little more like myself. This was so typical of Alice.

'Yes. It's perfect.'

I stared at her, noting the heightened colour on her cheeks as she clapped her hands together. 'Serendipity. It was meant to happen.'

'And how do you figure that?' Sometimes I did think she was barking mad, although more often than not, she was just manipulative.

'You being signed off at exactly the time I'm supposed to go to India. It's karma. You've got to say yes, Claire. I'll never get this chance again. Jon will let me have all my board and lodgings for free. And it's only for a week, so you'll still have three whole weeks of holiday. And the girls will love it. And I've always, always wanted to go to India. I might have to get you to lend me the money for the flight, though.'

'Whoa, whoa!' I held up my hand. 'Slow down. What are you talking about?'

'India,' she said with exasperation as if I were completely stupid. 'I've been invited to go. I only have to pay for my flights.'

'Alice, you can't just go to India. You need jabs and things.

'Poo, don't be silly. Of course, I can. I'm not you. Don't even think about being a mean, old stiff and making me turn down this amazing opportunity. It's been my dream to go to India forever.'

Translated as, *since she met Jon at Yoga class six months ago.*

'But what about the girls? You can't take them with you. Don't they have school?'

'Of course I'm not taking them. Don't be silly.'

'Well who's going to look after them?'

'You are, of course. It makes perfect sense. It's not as if you've got anything else to do.' She folded her arms and gave me a bright look of triumph. 'You were complaining you never saw them.'

'I think what I actually said was that you don't ask me to

babysit anymore. It was an observation rather than a complaint. Not quite the same thing.'

'Well, here's your chance. You can babysit every night for a week.'

'Gosh, how kind of you. I don't suppose it's occurred to you that I have my own life, thank you very much.'

'Yeah and how's that going right now?' Alice's eyes gleamed maliciously. 'All those friends of yours queuing up to see you, are they?'

I bit my lip and kept my expression bland even though she'd touched a raw nerve. Friends were few and far between. With the unexpected precision of a well-targeted dart, I remembered my conversation with Ashwin Laghari. I'd lost some good friends over the years, sacrificed on the altar of my job. They tend to give up when you repeatedly turn down invitations, but when you're snowed under it doesn't seem to matter. You only realise the loss when it's too late.

'I've got plenty of things to do. A whole house to decorate, actually.' There, that's what I would do. As soon as I'd finished my coffee I'd go and buy some magazines, *Ideal Home* or something. And a *BBC Good Food Magazine*. I'd start cooking, so that I ate properly. And I'd take some of those exercise classes. Get really fit. I'd alternate between Pilates and HIIT classes. Go running every morning. Dave, a colleague, had been badgering me to join the company team to do a charity 5k run. I could use the time to train. Or I might even learn a language.

'Claire, are you listening to me?'

She waved a hand across my face and I realised with a wry smile that I hadn't heard a word.

'Alice, you can't go to India. Not without planning it

53

properly. Why don't you wait until the school holidays when Mum and Dad are back? The girls are used to staying with them.'

'Don't you understand? If I don't go now I'll never be able to go. This is a once-in-a-lifetime opportunity. This place is booked up years in advance. I'd never be able to afford it. Please, Claire. I'm suffocating. I've been with the children night and day for the last ten years. I deserve some time off for good behaviour. They can spend some quality time with their favourite auntie.'

'I'm their only auntie.' My dry sarcasm was wasted on her.

'And they'll be at school most of the time, so you'll have the days to yourself.'

'Alice, I can't have the girls.'

'Why not? Give me one good reason. It's only for a week.'

I opened my mouth, about to tell her all the reasons why, but then it struck me that perhaps I might enjoy getting to know my nieces. After all, it would only be for a week and I had four to fill.

Chapter Five

'Claire, you'll have to sort this out. I just haven't had time.' Alice lugged an overflowing laundry basket down the stairs leaving a trail of broken wicker twigs in her wake. 'It's the girls' uniforms. They'll need them for Monday.'

Somehow, Alice, who was incapable of finding and affording a man to sort her hedge out, had managed to book and pay for a flight to India, get a few injections and pack bulging bin bags of belongings for each of her children.

It was Friday evening, a mere five days since I'd bumped into my sister in the street, and I'd arrived to collect Ava and Poppy as Alice was leaving at crazy o'clock the next morning.

'And what about school? What time do they have to be there? And what time do they finish? Does the school know I'm looking after them? What are their teachers called?' There was so much I didn't know and faced with the bin bags – which were really bothering me; surely Alice had some proper holdalls or something? – and not much else, I felt woefully underprepared. Surely I needed lists of where they needed to be and when, along with names and telephone numbers.

'Don't fuss, Claire. Poppy will be able to tell you everything. And don't let her boss Ava about all the time.'

'I'm hardly fussing.' Looking after two children was a big responsibility. 'I'm just asking for basic information. Like food. What do they like to eat?'

Alice rolled her eyes. 'Food? They're children not some strange species. Fish fingers, spaghetti hoops, chicken nuggets. That sort of thing. Honestly Claire, you need to come down off that pedestal of yours and live in the real world.'

'And you need to stop being so rude. I'm doing you a massive favour here.'

Alice blinked at me. She wasn't used to people standing up to her. My parents went to endless lengths to keep the peace. They always had done. I wasn't so forgiving.

'I'm hoping they like pizza,' I said to thin air. Alice had ducked under the stairs and was scrabbling about looking for something. Ignore and avoid – her usual policy when there were things she didn't want to hear or face.

She emerged with one little girl's shoe. 'You might have to go shopping. Poppy keeps moaning that her toes are at the end… again.'

'I can do that. Anything else?'

'No.'

I followed her into the untidy lounge where my eldest niece, ten-year-old Poppy, had sprawled her lanky length along the sofa and was watching television. She was all arms and legs at the moment, as if they'd grown ahead of the rest of her. Her clothes looked as if they were racing to keep up as well although at least, unlike Ava's, they were clean. Six-year-old Ava had a magnetic ability to attract every sort of dirt known to man and always appeared to have been dragged through the proverbial hedge backwards, forwards, and upside down. A cloud of tangles circled her chubby face, dimples pierced her knees and elbows, and there was a long bloom of orange juice all down her white aertex school shirt.

'Okay, babes. Time to go. Auntie Claire is here.'

Ava began scooping up the collection of toys surrounding her which spilled over her arms as she dropped one as soon as she'd picked up another.

'But Alice, this hasn't finished yet,' said Poppy, not even turning from the television. Clearly now she was ten, she was too cool to give me a hug or call my sister 'Mum'. I could never be sure whether Alice encouraged it or not.

Once upon a time, when she was younger and I babysat more often, we'd been pals.

'Auntie Claire has a television.' Alice paused. 'Oh God, you do, don't you? It wouldn't surprise me if you didn't.'

I gave her a withering look. 'Funnily enough, yes. Flat screen and everything.'

'Well of course you do, Miss Moneybags. Not everyone has the cash to splash.' Her mouth pursed into an angry pout.

Tough. Maybe I shouldn't have dissed her ancient chunky television but every now and then one of her needles hit home and I couldn't help retaliating.

'Does it have cartoons?' asked Ava suddenly glancing up from her toys.

'Er, I think so.'

'You mean DVDs, stupid,' snapped Poppy.

'I'm not stupid.'

'Yes you are.'

57

Ava went over and pulled one of Poppy's plaits with a sharp tug and threw one of her toys at her head. Poppy seized it and hurled it back, hitting Ava square in the face.

Ava immediately began to wail, indignation giving her lungs a certain power.

'Poppy!' snapped Alice rushing over to scoop Ava into her arms. 'It's okay, baby. Poppy Harrison, apologise to your sister this minute.'

I frowned. Hardly fair. Ava had clearly started it, but unfortunately the scenario was horribly familiar.

Poppy pursed her small mouth and glared at her sister. 'Soz', she said with begrudging defiance.

Alice rocked Ava for a minute until the overloud noisy sobs abated. 'Poppy, you're the oldest; you're supposed to be nice to your little sister.'

Old patterns, I thought.

Look after Alice, she's only little. Remember, Alice is the youngest.

'What about the house?' I asked. 'Bills etc. Anything need sorting out?'

Alice shrugged. 'Dad takes care of all that. Everything's on direct debit.'

Dad really did take care of everything. At our farewell dinner he'd taken me aside and asked me to keep an eye on Alice while he and Mum were away with the words, 'Seriously, I'd like to wring the neck of the guy she got in to do the hedge. It cost me £150 and you should see the state of it. She needs a bit of support with that sort of thing. I think they see her coming.'

I absentmindedly rubbed at the scratch on my arm, which

was finally healing thanks to the course of antibiotics. 'Anything else?'

Alice shrugged. 'Don't think so.'

She stood on the doorstep to see us off, both girls waving madly from the car.

'Who wants to make pizza when we get in?' I asked, determined that for the next seven days I was going to be 'fun Auntie Claire' and that they would have such a good time they wouldn't miss their mum too much.

'Me, me!' yelled Ava from the back.

'That sounds cool,' said Poppy with an approving nod as she sat next to me in the front seat.

I nodded back. They were both good kids; there was no reason that this week shouldn't be a breeze. All I had to do was entertain them over the weekend, get them to school each day next week and feed them each evening. My stomach started to knot at the thought of all that that entailed. What if I couldn't do it all? What did I know about children?

Chapter Six

Oh my God, I was dying. Already, Monday morning was a train wreck. I wished I was in the office where I knew exactly what I was doing. Who knew getting two children up, dressed, fed, and ready for school could be such hard work? I was making enough of a hash of my own life at the moment, how did I think I could manage the lives of two little girls as well?

Despite doing several Everest-sized mounds of washing – I think Alice had been saving it all up – I'd missed Poppy's school shirts and she'd thrown a teenager-in-training strop when I'd suggested she wear one of last week's.

'You can't be serious,' she'd yelled. 'That will ruin my life.'

'I hardly think so,' I said, almost laughing at the drama, except it wasn't funny, and I went into the utility room to rummage in the pile. I found a Poppy-sized white short-sleeved shirt with the school logo and gave it a quick shake. It seemed clean enough.

'Look, here you go. This will do and I'll wash the rest today.'

'No,' she wailed.

I closed my eyes and counted to ten. 'Poppy, just for today, please wear this shirt.'

'No! You're being mean and horrid.' She snatched it from my hand. Bright tears shone in her eyes and then she left the kitchen, slamming the door with enough force that all the dishes on the draining board rattled.

'I haven't done my homework,' announced Ava placidly from the kitchen table where she was toying with her toast as Poppy's feet thundered up the stairs.

'I think that, under the circumstances, your teacher won't mind,' I said calmly. *Why hadn't she said anything last night?*

'Do you think?' asked Ava. 'She gets really, really cross.' She began pulling things out of her book bag, endless bits of paper which dragged in the bacon grease on her plate, a couple of reading books, and assorted bits of artwork as there was another almighty crash of a door slamming upstairs. 'Do you like my lantern?' She held up a bedraggled bit of paper Sellotaped together into a tube with long slashes down the side. 'Here,' she produced a yellow exercise book.

'What were you supposed to do?' I looked up at the ceiling wondering whether I should go after Poppy.

'Spellings.'

'Maybe we can practise them on the way to school.'

But she'd already opened the book and with her lip between her teeth had begun copying the list of ten words.

'You need to go and get dressed Ava.' My voice was firm, even though inside I felt a slight sense of panic.

'But...'

61

JULES WAKE

'There isn't time.'

'Pleeease, Auntie Claire.' Her eyes started to brim with tears. 'I'll b-be b-bottom again. I'm always bottom an' Lucy Chambers always gets ten out of ten.'

I winced. The girls had been so good all weekend and quite brave about their mother going away without them. Alice had made it sound as if she was going to have the jolliest adventure and she would bring them back something lovely. I had my doubts about that. The retreat she was going to was in the foothills of the Himalayas and was an hour's domestic flight from Delhi. It looked very beautiful but also very remote.

'Okay, two minutes. Let's have a look.'

Where had I got the foolish notion that getting two children up and ready for school would take only an hour and a half and that we could leave at eight-thirty and be at school in plenty of time?

And now it seemed I couldn't even run and breathe at the same time. I was back from my first school run and attempting a gentle jog. Bent double, I tried to suck in another breath. Definitely dying.

With a wheeze I straightened. This was supposed to be the start of my new keep-fit regime. Unable to help myself – it was a legitimate reason for contacting work – I'd emailed Dave and volunteered to join the 5k team. I might also have asked how things were going in the office.

With disgust I glanced back down the leafy path. I hadn't even run that far.

There was only one thing for it: coffee. And thank God for

62

The Friendly Bean, which was within staggering in distance. Urging my protesting wobbly thighs back into action, I walked to the café, grateful for the emergency fiver tucked into my phone case.

With coffee in hand, too self-conscious and aware of my beet-red face and underarm circles to stay inside, I limped out to the small enclosed area a little way beyond the café. Circled by shrubs and bushes, it had a small paved area with a pair of benches at right angles to each other bookmarked on either end by an abundant flower bed. It was filled with blousy peonies in shades of pale pink and dark rhubarb red, like big pom-poms surrounded by fans of dark green leaves. I stared at them for a moment, struck by the colours. When was the last time I'd actually noticed flowers? Or even had time to sit and look at them. Or to smell them. Everything had been grey for so long. Without thinking, I leaned over to take a deep sniff.

'Gorgeous, aren't they?' said a voice.

Startled, I looked up to see an elderly lady with a fine frizz of soft white hair around her head, like a snowy aura, marching towards me. Something rattled at the back of my brain; she seemed awfully familiar.

She plonked herself down on my bench, almost spilling the coffee I'd put down next to me.

'Lovely morning. You carry on with your communing with nature, dear. Don't mind me.'

Feeling a little caught-on-the-hop, I gave her a weak smile. I didn't normally 'commune with nature' as she'd put it. I probably looked a bit strange. Oh, to be in one of my smart suits like a normal person. I wanted to tell her that actually I had a very responsible job and was a 'someone' in real life. I closed my eyes as if doing so would shut her out and I could ignore her. I didn't want to be that person who was desperate to talk to someone because it might be the only adult conversation I had all day. Maybe I could phone Ros and see how things were in the office. I winced thinking of all the things I should be doing there. The list started to snowball and I had to force myself to open my eyes.

The cheek! I looked into twinkling blue eyes peering at me over the top of… *my* takeaway coffee cup.

'Help yourself, why don't you?' I said, taken aback but trying to gain the upper hand. My withering sarcasm failed to make so much as a dent in her cheery smile.

'Don't mind if I do.' Without a care, she lifted my coffee in toast and took another slurp. 'Oh, that hits the spot. I do adore a good cup of coffee. That's one of the things I do miss.'

For a moment I stared at her, completely thrown by her blithe disregard of my indignation.

'It's not good for me,' she said. 'Bad for the old ticker, apparently. Why is it all the good stuff is so terribly bad for you? I mean, Brussels sprouts, they taste bloody awful and do dreadful things to your digestive system. I remember my Great Uncle Vincent – that man could clear a room… Why aren't they bad for you? Swede, another disgusting, tasteless vegetable; why couldn't that be terribly bad for you instead of chocolate and wine? I do love a good glass of Malbec. And the health police constantly on at you. I keep telling them I'm too old to care but… they insist on serving bloody decaffeinated rubbish. Instant at that. I ask you. I mean, what do you think about decaffeinated anything… a crime against human nature, I think. Stands to reason. God put caffeine in for a good reason. Not that I'm awfully matey with him up there right now. Guess I might decide to become better acquainted when I get closer to shuffling off the old mortal coil. You find that they all become God-botherers when they get older. I call it hedging your bets. Not me. If he doesn't like me the way I am, tough cookies.' She held out the coffee cup. 'Here you go, dear. Don't worry, I drank out of this side and I've got nothing worth mentioning. Not that I can recall anyway.' Her brow furrowed as if she were giving it serious thought.

My lips twitched and much as I wanted to maintain a dignified distance and ignore her unwanted presence, I was intrigued and, to be honest, entertained by her. I rather liked her forthright untarnished views. She said it as she saw it and it was very refreshing.

I could see exactly which side she'd drunk from by the ring of fuchsia-pink lipstick lining the cup, so I took a sip of my coffee from the other side. It must be hell to have to go without coffee.

'I'm Hilda.'

'Claire.'

'So what are you doing here?' She eyed my shoes. 'Running?' She lifted her own feet and regarded her Day-glo trainers with satisfaction.

I laughed. 'That was my intention. I'm a bit out of practice. Today was more about shuffling. I didn't get very far.'

'You'll get better. I've not seen you here before. It's very good for you. Running, that is. A bit every day and you'll soon be up and… running.' With a chortle at her pun, she poked me in the thighs. 'Gets the endorphins going. Do you work in an office?'

I nodded, not wanting to admit that I was on temporary hiatus. It would be too embarrassing explaining why. She might think I was taking the easy way out, time off when there was nothing really wrong with me. I clenched my fists under my thighs. And she'd be right. Dr Boulter had overreacted. I could probably go back next week once I'd caught up on a bit of sleep.

'You don't want to get an office bottom, do you?'

'Sorry?'

'Office bottom, also known as spreading arse. Too much sitting down.'

'Ah, no. I don't.'

'So, a bit further every day and before you know it you'll be running a marathon,' she said with an air of complacency. 'I can tell we're going to get on famously. What did you say your name was again? That's the downside to being old: butterfly brain. By the time you get to my age, it's so full of stuff, I lose things in there.'

I smiled, rather charmed by her description that shied away from forgetfulness.

'I'm Claire.'

'Pleased to meet you Claire and welcome to Command Centre.'

'Command Centre?' This woman veered from sensible and stately to completely whacky in nought to sixty. I wasn't quite sure what to make of her.

'Yes, this is my little spot. I know everything that goes on in this park.' She patted the plump pink peony heads at the end of the bench on which we were sitting as if they were pet dogs, thereby loosening a few drops of rain. 'It's my personal fiefdom, if you like. I've lived around here off and on for sixty years.' She pointed to the rather smart Regency houses that just peeped over the trees to the south of the park. 'I used to live in one of those when my son was small. He used to want to come to the park a lot then. Play on the swings. Feed the ducks. Children,' she sighed, 'they grow up so quickly. One minute they're clinging to your hands, the next minute they're packing you off to a home. Of course, he hasn't been here for years. Do you have children?'

'Er… no.'

'You don't sound very sure.'

'I'm looking after my nieces for a week while their mother is away and I've just taken them to school.'

'Ah, that must be fun. How old are they?'

Mmm, the jury was out on the fun bit. This morning had been a bit of a nightmare. 'Poppy's ten and Ava's six'

'Lovely ages. Shame they have to grow up really. My son's turned into a pompous twerp.'

'How old is he?' I bit back a smile at her weary dismissal.

'Forty-five going on ninety-five.' She shook her head and pursed her walnut-wrinkled mouth. 'Don't ever let anyone dump you in a home. I come here every day, just to get out of that dreary place.

'Where do you live?'

'Dreary place, weren't you listening?' She gave me a mischievous grin. 'Also known as The Sunnyside Memorial Home for the half-dead and totally bewildered. My son insisted. I had a bit of a fall and broke my hip. He was all for putting me in a care home on the south coast. I'm old but I'm not senile.' She gave me a wicked grin. 'So I started running again, just to annoy him.'

'How does that annoy him? I'd have thought he'd be rather proud of you running at your…' my voice petered out.

'Oh Lord girl, don't be shy. At my great age. It's all right, you can say it. With these wrinkles, I'm in no position to be getting coy about how old I am. If I'm still running every day, there's no way he'll get a doctor to say I'm not fit enough to live independently. I run around the park, just one loop, every single day. Rain or shine. And no one's going to stop me.'

'I remember you,' I blurted out. 'Sunshine-yellow tracksuit.' Startler of pigeons. Harbinger of coffee disasters.

'That's my particular favourite. So good of you to notice it. I have a rather lovely emerald green one as well. Which reminds me, I haven't done my stretches and at my age, they're a must.'

She stood up and began doing a series of lunges. I watched in amusement as she bounced around the small area with more enthusiasm than skill.

Finally, jogging on the spot, she waved a hand at me. 'Right, toodle-pip. Same time tomorrow.'

I shrugged. Today's attempt at running had been woeful. Maybe I'd been a bit hasty emailing Dave about the 5k. The treadmill in the gym always seemed so much easier. Maybe I'd get the train into Leeds and visit the gym instead.

With a sniff, she turned and began to jog away down the path to join the main drag through the park.

I watched her retreating figure. At least it had been nice to have some company; she was a character and she'd made me smile quite a few times. In fact, my face felt positively mobile for once instead of having that stretched, clenched-teeth feeling that, now I thought about it, had been around for a lot longer than a few weeks. When was the last time I'd felt anything other than an insidious sense of doom and that everything was about to go wrong?

Chapter Seven

The kitchen looked as if a small tornado had swept through it. Spilled milk on the table, dried cornflakes in the bowls, which had acquired superglue-like properties, and abandoned toast crusts – apparently Ava's hair was curly enough – as well as a pool of sticky orange juice that had been tramped across the floor, down the hall, and there was one tacky footprint on the cream lounge carpet. *Breathe, Claire.* It was okay. I could do this. I'd got the girls to school... and only five minutes late. I didn't dare look at the bedroom where I knew there'd be a pile of abandoned school uniform items. Who knew children could generate so many dirty clothes? Little Ava could attract food, mud, and paint to her clothes, skin, and hair in equal quantities. There were even red paint and orange juice stains on her white ankle socks – although grey would have been a better description; they hadn't been white for a long time.

The mess set all my tidy-senses tingling, bringing with them that familiar on-edge something-bad-was-going-to-happen feeling. As soon as I'd cleaned the juice from the floor by the fridge, I realised that underneath the fridge was filthy. So I pulled that out. Then I attacked the dust behind it. But the sides of the kitchen cupboards beside it were disgusting, so I cleaned off the sheen of grease, only to find that the extractor fan was also covered in a film of the same grease. With each bowl of hot soapy water I filled, I felt like the sorcerer's apprentice. Each time I pulled out or moved something, there was more to do. The tiles behind the cooker were food-stained. The ceiling needed painting. The flooring was marked.

I stopped, realising that my breath was coming in shallow pants. This was ridiculous.

But even though my brain registered the onset of panic, I was still taking the shelves out of the oven to scrub them.

This was crazy. I should be at work, not doing this. Work, where I knew what needed to be done. Knew what I had to do. Where I had a million things to do. There were reports to be written. Data to be analysed. By now a gazillion emails to be responded to.

I also missed the routine of going to work. Getting up at six. Leaving at six forty-five. Wearing a smart suit. Being someone. Being recognised in the office. People there knew who I was: a senior manager. I missed having things to do.

Oh God, I needed something to take my mind off things.

I grabbed the *BBC Good Food Magazine*, almost in desperation. Cooking. That would give me something to do. And I was not going to think of the meeting that I should have been at in Bradford this morning. Who was taking it instead of me? Would they be presenting my work? Would the client know where I was? Surely the company wouldn't tell them I was off with stress. Please no. And would they have found the additional notes I'd made?

I put down the magazine in despair. I looked at my watch as I spotted the cobweb in the corner of the room. Should I phone Ros and tell her where to find the notes? She could email them over. I could almost feel my blood pressure rising just thinking about it all.

'Hi Ros, it's me,' I said at the same time as reaching up the wall with a duster.

'Claire, how are you feeling?'

'I feel fine,' I snapped, immediately irritated and frustrated because I'd spotted another bloody cobweb. 'I'm not ill.'

'No, dear. Now, if you're phoning about work, I'm not to speak to you. If you want me to tell you that TJ got an A in his biology exam, I can do that. And Rissa was in a dance show last week and Ty took a catch in his cricket match.'

'But I just need you to tell the team that I—'

'Claire. You are signed off. I'm telling you, you're not my boss at the moment. So I get to boss you around. And I'm telling you: clear your head. Work will carry on, just fine. I'm going to miss you but you have to give yourself some time.'

'But there's nothing—'

'I'm no doctor but even I could tell you haven't been right these past months.'

'What? That's rubbish.' Even as I said it, I could feel a slight trembling of my hands.

'Claire. You've been running on empty for a long time. Now, make the most of this time. Learn to dance, enjoy the sunshine, and smell the flowers. Do the things you enjoy instead of being cooped up in this stuffy place. It's just a job, honey.'

I reached for the cobweb and noticed my hands really were shaking. Do things I enjoy? What things? I enjoyed work. I wanted to be there.

It had never ever been *just a job*. I was a career woman. On track to make partner.

My stomach lurched with the horror of realisation.

They wouldn't give a partnership to someone who'd been signed off with stress. My career was toast. And my kitchen was a mess. Just look at the state of it. I couldn't even manage to get that straight, so how the hell could I hope to salvage my career?

The panic that, like a malignant shadow, had been dogging me all morning with the frantic cleaning, suddenly engulfed me. My throat closed up and my breath stuttered in my chest.

I put my head down on the kitchen table and wept.

The bout of crying left me feeling worn out and lethargic, too tired to do more than raise my head from the table and glare around at the kitchen with all the half-finished jobs. I was as wobbly as a new-born giraffe and didn't trust my legs to stand up yet.

For the first time, it occurred to me that perhaps Dr Boulter had a point and that I should think about taking better care of myself. I was clearly run-down. I scowled at the tatty kitchen floor which looked no better for my manic scrubbing and the hideous red and orange wallpaper on the 'feature' wall. This was supposed to be my grown-up, Instagram-perfect, I've-made-it home. It was laughable; I couldn't even get my house straight let alone do my job. An epic fail on both counts.

Oh God, I had to sort myself out. Prove to them back at work that I was fine. Dr Boulter might be right about my need to be healthier but he was wrong about the stress. I snatched up the *BBC Good Food Magazine*. In the next three weeks, I was going to cook. Proper nutritious meals. Get myself back on track. Proper exercise, proper meals, just like the doctor had ordered. But would it help?

———————

I didn't know any of the mums in the playground and felt just as self-conscious waiting outside Ava's classroom as I had that morning. Poppy, apparently, was old enough to be released into the wild by herself and was allowed to come and find me. Alice had had to give approval for me to collect the girls and this morning yesterday I'd had to check in with the teacher, Miss Parr – a smiley, fresh-faced girl of at least twelve – whom Ava clearly adored.

Keeping my head down, I focused on my phone to avoid the other mums' speculative looks. Had Alice told them what had happened? I was embarrassed that they might know about my health issues and that I wasn't currently working.

I'd managed to fill the rest of my day by doing some cooking and tidying up the bedroom Ava and Poppy were sharing. Neither were thrilled about having to share the big double bed, and I didn't blame them, but I hadn't got around to furnishing the third or fourth bedrooms since moving from my two-bedroom flat in Headingly. Ava's rumpled side of the bed had looked as if rampaging squirrels had run amok in her sheets overnight, scattering the pile of soft toys she'd insisted she had to bring. Nine in all, each of which had a name and a reason as to why it had to accompany her. And at bedtime, every last one had to be given a goodnight kiss and cuddle before Ava would climb into bed. In contrast, Poppy hopped straight in and opened up her book. She was currently reading something called *Skulduggery Pleasant* with a slightly macabre front cover. On her side of the bed, the covers had been neatly pulled up and her pyjamas were folded on top of the pillow. Ava's PJ bottoms hung from the shade on the bedside light and the top dangled from the bed post at the end of the bed.

After bringing order to Ava's side of the room, I'd been relieved to find that it was nearly three and time to collect the girls and that somehow I'd managed to fill my first non-working day.

When Ava's teacher, Miss Parr, beckoned me over with a stern expression, I immediately began to worry that I'd forgotten something this morning.

She gave me a tight smile. 'It would be really good if you could do some reading with Ava this evening. We do encourage children to read every day, if possible.'

I glanced down at Ava at her side and winced. Ava's hair was an astonishing bird's nest that had long-ago escaped from this morning's plaits. Clearly, I also needed to do better on the hairdressing front. 'And if you could practise spellings with her too, well…' She paused and gave me one of those non smiles that contained a definite touch of admonishment, 'that would really help her.'

'Of course,' I said a little too eagerly, wanting to be the perfect mother-substitute in Alice's absence. Ava's hand snuck into mine and I remembered her tears and her woeful cry that she was always bottom.

It was something I had intended to ask Alice about when

she called but my sister hadn't been in touch at all since she'd left last Friday which made me feel faintly uneasy. I had to remind myself that this was typical Alice. Trying to curb my irritation, I decided to send her a chatty text telling her the girls were great and suggesting that she video-chatted with them this evening.

Surely they had Wi-Fi at the retreat? Even Mum had sent an email from the middle of the ocean. She was thrilled that Alice had managed to get a holiday and I got kudos for being such a good sister.

'Did you bring a snack?' asked Ava as we crossed the playground, Poppy skipping towards us.

'No but you can have something when we get in.'

'But I'm starving,' she wailed. 'Can we get some sweeties from the shop?'

'Why don't you wait until we get home? I've bought some nice grapes and bananas.'

A pout appeared on her face. 'Hello Poppy,' I turned with relief to my elder niece.

'Hello, Auntie Claire. I've got a letter about a school trip. Can I go?'

'I got letters too,' announced Ava, lifting her plump arm and waving her book bag at me.

'Let's get home and then we can look at the letters,' I said with a sudden surge of pleasure at being needed and having something to do. Letters I could do. This was something I could deal with and be efficient-Claire again. The Claire I was at work. 'And who likes spaghetti Bolognese?'

'Me, me,' cried Ava dancing around my feet.

'My favourite,' said Poppy with quieter enthusiasm. 'Did you make it or is it a packet one? You know they're full of trans-fatty acids.' Her small pink mouth pursed in disapproval.

'I made it,' I said. 'Well, the sauce.'

'By yourself?' Ava's saucer-eyed admiration and Poppy's approving nod made me grin at them both. Feeling like a hero was something I could get used. After my ridiculous meltdown earlier, this was balm to my soul. It had been a long time since I'd felt such a sense of achievement. Although, if homemade spaghetti Bolognese brought me superhero status, it showed just how far I'd fallen.

Listening to their happy chatter about their days – what they'd eaten, how brilliant super-speller Lucy Chambers was at maths and how the five-a-day fruit and veg maxim should really be ten-a-day and a host of other nutritional facts that Poppy had absorbed in Science – took us from the playground to the edge of the park. The same park I was striding through not that long ago, feeling like I could take on the world. How quickly things had changed.

'Can I go on the swings? Can I? Can I?' asked Ava, her chubby legs already deviating from the main path that cut through the park to my house towards the enclosed playground area.

'That all right with you, Poppy?' I asked, giving my watch a quick glance. We had plenty of time and nowhere to be. Unlike Ros's kids who had Cubs, ballet, trampolining, and football to be ferried to, Alice's children didn't appear to have any after-school activities.

She looked surprised and shrugged. 'I guess. I've got my book with me.'

I'd noticed that Ava got her own way an awful lot. Alice always deferred to her while poor old Poppy often had to play the sensible older sister. It was a role I remembered well.

We diverted to the small play area which had a couple of swings, a roundabout, a rope walk, and several one-seater rocking animals on large springs for which Ava made a beeline. Poppy chose a swing and before long was flying high, her long spindly legs earnestly propelling her backwards and forwards.

Ava, with her butterfly attention, zig zagged from ride to ride, calling for me to watch, catch, and chat to her before I escorted her to the slide where she directed me from her Nelson's Column position at the top of the steps. Her bossiness with her precise instructions, *no there, not there*, was quite comical, although I caught Poppy rolling her eyes from where she now sat on one of the benches by the fence with a book.

A few minutes later I heard a snuffling noise and when I looked behind me, I saw a scruffy grey and white lurcher loitering by the fence. The next time I glanced over he'd poked his nose through a gap and I watched as Poppy put out a tentative hand to stroke the top of its head. I heard her crooning gently to the dog as it tipped his head to one side as if paying careful attention to her. The dog was just like her: all skinny legs and big brown eyes.

'Look! Doggy! Doggy!' cried Ava leaping from the end of the slide and barrelling over towards Poppy with her sturdy body. 'Doggy!' she screeched even more loudly, climbing on the fence and leaning over, waving her arms like a whirling dervish towards the dog. The dog, which had been quietly making friends with Poppy, immediately began bouncing about, its back legs springing from side to side, barking in a high pitch which was growing ever more hysterical.

'Stop it, Ava,' snapped Poppy. 'You're winding it up.'

'Not,' said Ava as she withdrew, not quite so confident now. The dog jumped up and startled Ava who fell backwards and started to cry.

'Serves you right,' said Poppy crossly.

Ava wailed. The dog barked and Poppy glowered.

I scooped Ava up and sat down on the bench, ignoring the dog. 'What have you done? Where does it hurt?'

'My b-bottom,' sniffed Ava, rubbing at the damaged area, pulling up her skirt and exposing her knickers with gay, exhibitionist disregard. Surreptitiously I tugged the skirt down.

'Ava, you frightened the dog,' I said sternly. 'And I don't think you're hurt, just a bit shocked. I'm sure you'll be fine. See, Poppy's just sitting quietly and letting the dog come to her.'

She gazed up at me, her tears drying instantly at my no-nonsense lack of sympathy.

Now that Ava had calmed down, the dog had quietened too and was pressing up against the fence, sticking its head through the metal bars again. Poppy edged forwards and scratched its head. 'He likes this. You just made him all over excited, Ava. See, he's lovely. Like a hairy carpet.' He certainly seemed to enjoy her attentions and was now sitting on the other side of the fence, his dark eyes watchful, grey tufty ears twitching and lifting as if he were following our conversation.

'Mmm,' I said, wondering whether I should encourage Ava

to approach the dog slowly so she wouldn't be frightened in the future.

'There now, he's calmed down.' Poppy continued to stroke him. 'I wonder where his owners are. He doesn't have a collar on.'

'Maybe he slipped his lead.' I said, looking at the scruffy animal.

'Do you think we ought to take him home with us?'

'No, I'm sure he'll find his – or her – way home,' I said firmly. The last thing I wanted was an extra addition to the household. I wasn't sure what I was doing with two small humans; I certainly wasn't about to throw a dog into the mix.

'Please, Auntie Claire.' Ava had jumped off my lap and was now trying to angle her head through the railings to get closer to the dog. She was so that sort of child that would get stuck. I could see it now and I'd be having to call the fire brigade if she didn't stop.

'Ava, be careful.' I grabbed the collar of her coat and tugged her back. 'We ought to be going home. I thought you were hungry.'

'Yes, but I'm chocolate-biscuit kind of hungry,' she said, her eyes ever hopeful.

'Let's go home and see what we can find.' I gave in, knowing that I had bought a secret bag of bite-sized chocolate treats and a packet of chocolate digestives.

Of course the dog wanted to follow us and bounded around our legs with playful hopefulness.

'Home, boy,' said Poppy with more authority than I'd have given her credit for.

'See, he wants to come home with us,' said Ava tugging on my hand, looking up at me with angelic pleading.

'Well, he's not.' It was all I could do not to smile at her cupid-bow mouth quivering in distress and her mercurial change of heart.

'I think he's probably run away from home because his owners were mean,' she announced.

'It is odd he hasn't got a collar on,' said Poppy, ever thoughtful.

'And it isn't our problem,' I said firmly. 'Just ignore him. Don't pay him any attention and he'll soon get bored.' For some reason, we'd all assigned the dog as male.

Ava gave me a mutinous stare from under the snarled tangle of curls masquerading as a fringe, her bottom lip standing proud. Any second she was going to dig her heels in and refuse to abandon the dog.

'Home,' I said, firmly. 'Biscuits. Chocolate.' As if she were the dog.

'Okay, then,' she said and reluctantly followed me. Poppy eyed me with disapproval but trailed after us, throwing backward glances at the dog, who had now got the message and stood whining, its head down and its tail between its legs. It really, really wasn't my problem but I did wonder for a fleeting second if dogs ate Bolognese sauce. No, I told myself, adorable and needy as he was, I could not add any more into the mix.

'Come on, its owners will probably be searching for him. If we take him home, they won't be able to find him, will they?'

'I spose not,' said Poppy, dragging her feet.

There was plenty of Bolognese sauce; perhaps if I washed the sauce off the mince it would be all right? But then the thought became moot because with a joyful bark, the dog pricked up his ears at the sound of another dog in the distance and ran off.

Ava was already asking what sort of biscuits I had.

'Why don't you have a dog, Auntie Claire?' asked Poppy as I opened the front door, ushering the two of them in and the three of us, the habit already formed, headed towards the kitchen.

'I…' To be honest, I'd never thought about it before. 'Well, I'm out at work all the time and it wouldn't be fair to have a dog if I'm not here. They need company; they get lonely if they're left on their own all day.'

'Oh, yes. Mummy says you have a very important job.' I could hear the weight of disapproval in her words. 'And that you have lots of money.'

'I don't know about lots of money,' I said with a half laugh. How did you measure riches? I certainly didn't have to worry about paying the bills but I wouldn't be buying a Ferrari anytime soon. 'But I do earn enough to buy mini-Crunchies.'

'Crunchies!' squealed Ava. 'My favourite.'

'No, they're not,' said Poppy, her voice full of elder-sister scorn. 'You said it was Caramel last week. You're just a piglet.'

'Am not.' Ava thrust her pink face forward, quivering with indignation. With her riot of pigtail curls, round face, and shrill cry she was rather reminiscent of a sturdy piglet.

'No one will get anything if you carry on bickering,' I said firmly and they both cast baleful looks my way but they did stop. 'You need to be nice to each other.'

'I got a picture for you.' Ava dug through her book bag spilling pieces of paper all over the floor. 'It's for your fridge.' She waved a paint-splodged picture painted on the reverse of a piece of wall paper at me. 'It's a caterpillar. We're doing insects. It's a hungry caterpillar, like me. You can have it. Mummy has lots already. When is she coming home?' Ava's lower lip quivered for real this time.

Surreptitiously I checked my phone, hoping for a text from Alice. Still no word. What was she playing at?

'Hey there, she'll be home soon. On Friday. Why don't we try to Facetime her after tea?'

Ava's face crumpled and her eyes narrowed with suspicion.

'Four more sleeps,' said Poppy patting her sister on the shoulder. 'That's all.'

I gave her a grateful smile, realising that Ava's concept and understanding of time had yet to develop.

'Yes, four more sleeps. Now where shall I put this picture? I don't have any fridge magnets.'

Ava, her attention thankfully diverted, looked around the room wrinkling her nose.

'You need to get some more pictures. It's not very pretty in here.'

'Ava,' hissed Poppy. 'You're being rude. Remember, Mum says sometimes you're not supposed to tell people the truth.'

That sounded so typical of Alice. Why tell the truth when you could get away with the lie? Like telling Dad she'd used his money to pay for a gardener the other day.

Ava gave a disgruntled huff and put her pudgy, little hands on her hips in a housewifely fashion that had me hiding a smile. 'Honestly, how am I supposed to know when to tell the truth and when to tell a lie?'

Poppy shrugged.

'Why don't I put it here?' I said loudly, drawing both girls' attention back to the picture and propping the gaudily splashed painting on the windowsill next to the lone, newly purchased basil plant.

Ava gave a regal nod of acknowledgement and Poppy shot me a brief smile, grateful to be spared further embarrassment from her sister. I poured them both a glass of juice and unearthed the mini-Crunchie bars from my secret hiding place. They looked so good I had to have one too.

While they were busy chomping their chocolate, I scooped up all the folded bits of paper, which turned out to be letters from the school about missing library books, overdue dinner money, a second request for money for a school trip to Harewood Bird Garden and a reminder about parent-teacher consultation appointments.

'Have you got letters too, Poppy?' I asked as the three of us sat at the kitchen table.

She nodded, shamefaced, and handed over a sheaf of more of the same. I quickly sorted them into piles of things I could do something about and things that could wait until Alice got back next week, and ones that were very overdue demands for money. I then sat and wrote a bunch of cheques while the girls drank juice and ate their Crunchies. Then I went through Ava's book bag, which was full of rubbish and one letter dated three weeks earlier asking Alice to make an appointment to discuss Ava's progress. I put that on the pile for Alice, making a mental note to bring it to her attention as soon as she got back.

What I needed was a to-do list. Once I'd started, everything seemed a lot clearer. I could do this.

- *Read with Ava*
- *Spellings with Ava*

'Have you got any homework, Poppy?' I asked, prompted by my list.

'Yes, Maths.' She pulled a face. 'It's hard.'

'Do you want some help with it?'

Her eyes widened. 'Mummy always says it's my homework and I have to do it.'

'Yes, but a little help will make it less hard,' I suggested.

Her sudden beam warmed me. 'That would be awesome, if you could.'

I added it to my list. 'What other things do you need this week? PE kits? Library books? Anything else.'

'PE is on Monday and Friday for me,' said Poppy.

Predictably, Ava didn't have a clue but luckily it was written in her planner.

I added everything to my growing list.

'And it's Stationery Club day on Friday, so I need fifty pence to buy a new ruler.'

'An' me. I need a new pencil sharpener and a pencil and a pen,' added Ava.

By the time it was teatime, I'd put together a comprehensive list and timetable for the rest of the week. When I looked at it, I immediately felt calmer. *See, I could do this.* I just needed to be organised.

Over the next four days, I would work through the list and everything would run like clockwork. We would eat nutritious, homemade meals, the girls would have everything they needed for school, and I would get them there on time every morning. If I could just manage all this, I could show myself that I was getting back on track. Getting back to the smart, efficient, super-employee I once was.

Now, if only Alice would phone.

Chapter Eight

Day three of the school run and... well, I couldn't say I'd completely nailed things on the domestic front but I was getting there. Having dropped the girls off at school, I was heading into Leeds to go the gym and hit the treadmill for some running practice.

It was weird being at the station at this time; I wasn't used to travelling after nine. The emptiness of the platform made me feel slightly paranoid, as if people might be watching me and wondering why I was here at this time. Quickly, I boarded a waiting train which wasn't due to leave for another ten minutes. As I sat there, my mind started ticking. What if someone from work saw me? What would I say to them? It didn't look as if there was anything wrong with me. Would they think I was skiving? Would they pity me?

Just as the train was about to pull out, I grabbed my gym bag and jumped off, my heart beating so hard it felt like a jackhammer against my ribs. My vision went black for a second and I thought I might faint.

In the brisk spring morning, I watched the departing train, my heart racing and my body tense.

This was crazy. What was wrong with me? It was just a train. On Monday it had been the kitchen. Why was I overreacting to things so badly? Feeling self-conscious, I grabbed a coffee from the kiosk and scuttled out of the station. I would get the next train but I'd wait in the park.

As soon as I was through the gates, I picked up my pace and ducked off the main path into the little flower-filled garden with its two benches. Immediately I felt safe, tucked out of sight there, and when I sat down, I sank my head in my hands and concentrated on taking deep breaths, still a little scared by my ridiculous reaction on the train. It had frightened me. Surely, now I wasn't at work I should be feeling better?

'You're here again. And ready to run.'

I opened one eye. Hilda.

I'd been trying mindfulness, the sort of thing that Alice lapped up.

'No, not running but I'm… I'm on my way to… out.' There was still time for me to go into Leeds. There was a spin class at eleven. I could, *would*, go to the gym, maybe after my coffee. Exercise would help. Endorphins. All that stuff. I just needed to get there.

I gave the old lady a weak smile. Today she wore an emerald-green tracksuit and was jogging on the spot with sitcom-style enthusiasm that at any other time might have had me biting my lips to stop a laugh escaping.

'So if you're not running, where are you off to in your black

Lycra with your big bag? A cat-burgling mission? Is your bag full of tools? And a utility belt?' Her face sharpened with interest. 'Do you know how to pick a lock?'

'No.' I managed a laugh; she was outrageous. 'But I sometimes think it would be handy.'

'It is,' said Hilda, her big blue eyes guileless. 'Jolly handy. I'll teach you some time. I used to break into my ex-husband's house all the time. Move things round. Just to mess with him.' She waggled her eyebrows naughtily.

I frowned, wondering if she was telling the truth or not. The woman was a little bit bonkers. 'Unfortunately, much as I'd like to sound far more interesting than I am, I'm going to the gym.' There, I'd said it out loud. It was like visualisation, wasn't it? If I said it, I'd be more likely to get my brain in gear and go.

'Why would you do something like that? How much do you pay for your gym membership?' She tipped her head with bird-like interest, her wispy hair being pulled in all directions by the sharp spring breeze. Her direct approach prompted me to make a direct reply. Hilda's straight talking was hugely refreshing.

'It's subsidised by the company so I only pay £75 per month.'

'If you ran in the park, you could save yourself £900,' she said with lightning acuity. There was nothing wrong with her brain. 'And you could afford to buy large cappuccinos, instead of these silly regular ones.' Nothing wrong with her imagination either. With breath-taking audacity, she picked up my coffee and helped herself, murmuring, 'Oh, that's good.'

I shot her a quick frown and then said, 'You said the other

day you didn't have anything catching. You didn't ask whether I had.'

She grinned back at me with perfectly even-sized pearly whites, which I suspected were dentures.

'Excellent. Please tell me you have one of those sexually transmitted diseases. I do hope so; that would shock the hell out of my doctor.'

An unexpected laugh exploded out of my mouth. 'I almost wish I had.' I held out my hand. 'I need to get a move on if I'm going to make my spinning class.'

She calmly took another long sip of my coffee before handing it back. 'Well, by all that is holy, that is stupid. Why don't you get a bicycle? You can cycle here for free. In the fresh air. You can pick a bike up down the tip for nothing. I've never seen the point of spinning. Ridiculous. Same as running on a treadmill. How you can possibly feel a sense of achievement when you've not really moved anywhere? I don't hold with it at all. You've got all this lovely park right on your doorstep. Where is this gym of yours?'

'It's across the road from where I work in the city centre. I sometimes go before work.'

'You'd be better off running here. And the coffee in the park is far superior to this. I mean, thank God for caffeine, but where did you get it?'

'The train station, and no one's forcing you to drink it.' She was right though; the coffee in The Friendly Bean was infinitely better than this.

'Why don't you go for a little jog now? I'll stay here and keep an eye on your bag... and I'll do you a favour and finish this for you. Then you can treat yourself to a decent one from Sascha at the café when you've earned it.'

While part of me really, really wanted to tell this twinkly-eyed woman to get off my case and leave me alone, there was a much bigger part that insisted it was a lot easier to give in. I was still feeling limp and pathetic, although she had brightened my day. She might be outrageous, but in the words of Douglas Adams, she was mostly harmless. Reluctantly, I got to my feet.

'That's the ticket, dear.'

I smiled at her and set off at a gentle jog.

The minute I was out of sight, I slowed to a walk. I wasn't in a running mood.

Being outside did feel quite good. Far better than being in the gym at the mercy of the disparaging orange digital dashboard that inevitably told you that you were way off your target distance and your pace was pitiful. Above me, the pink and white blossom of horse chestnut trees bloomed and blousy green leaves bounced gently in the light breeze, creating dappled shadows on the path. It was certainly prettier. From the play area on the other side of the trees, I could hear the happy shrieks of toddlers lightly carried on the wind. This wasn't so bad after all. The park had been a deciding factor in buying the house; I should make more of living on its doorstep. When I ambled around the bend out of the shadow of the trees into an open, grassy area filled with beds of bright-faced pansies in purples and yellows, their heads nodding in rippling unison, I spotted another runner in the not-so-far distance. My heart did an unhappy skip of recognition.

It was him. I was sure it was him, although the heavy beard

made me take a second look. Yes, under all that hair, it was definitely him, jogging towards me on the path in baggy grey sweats and a grubby T-shirt, looking as hopelessly unfit and ploddy as I was. Oh God, we were going to pass each other. There was no avoiding it. He hadn't spotted me yet.

A small, embarrassed, resentful flame of anger burst into life. I was going to ignore him. Not even acknowledge him.

How about we compromise… and do both xxx

His last text to me flashed up vividly in my mind. *Yeah, right.* Thanks a lot, Ashwin Laghari, for that one perfect date that had lulled me into thinking there might be something there. For those long exchanges where I thought we were on the same wavelength. For sleeping with me and having perfect, mind-blowing sex that made me think we had something special.

Pretending to be staring into the distance beyond him, I began to run properly, putting in some real effort. I would sail past him looking super fit and professional, as if I ran all the time, and pretend not to notice him.

Unfortunately, my body began to protest almost immediately. My breath screamed in my lungs and my heart thumped uncomfortably hard – although that had as much to do with that bungy-jumping feeling of sick anticipation. Did I want him to see me or not?

Of course I did. Look how smooth and fast my strides were. Look what you missed out on.

Despite my determination to impersonate Mo Farah near the winning post, I very nearly stuttered to a stop because of course I noticed him… but not in a good way. Unruly black hair, a wildman beard, dressed in baggy, unflattering sweats which made his body look a far cry from the slim, toned version with which I'd got up close and personal. As I got closer, I stared with dismay. Closer still and I could see that his skin had a sallow hue instead of the golden tone that had stuck so clearly in my mind.

What the—?

Ashwin Laghari didn't look quite so hot now. We drew level.

Don't look. Don't look.

But I couldn't help myself.

He glanced my way, his eyes doing a quick, indifferent slide and then with a start they came back to my face with a flare of recognition. Those gorgeous amber eyes. Oh flip, they were just as mesmerising as I remembered and a stray butterfly fluttered inconveniently in my stomach with sudden interest. Then his face shut down with blank indifference. He looked down at the floor. *Ouch.* I got the message. He didn't want to know me, which I kind of knew already given that he hadn't bothered to text me even though I'd foolishly sent one completely-against-the-rules desperate text hoping for a response. He ran past. *And bog off to you too*, I thought, itching to turn my head over my shoulder.

Do not look back, Claire. Don't you dare. Don't give him the satisfaction.

Pleased with my self-control, I kept my eyes on the tree-lined horizon and kept running hard, refusing to give him any more headspace.

Instead, I focused on how I was feeling. Now that I'd got into a rhythm, my breathing was easier and my legs had found their own comfortable stride. I was aware of my body working in tandem, muscles, ligaments, bones, and an unfamiliar sense of... was it euphoria? In any case, it felt good. Were those fabled endorphins responsible? It did feel good. I put back my shoulders, feeling my breathing come more easily. *Well done, Hilda!* This was so much nicer than being shouted at in a class full of people on stationary bikes. I was enjoying the pleasant, relaxed feeling rather than jumping with adrenaline and fear of failure because I couldn't keep up with the super-fit, bionic woman female spin-instructor… although I was starting to run out of steam. It was with some relief I spotted The Friendly Coffee Bean.

When I returned – slightly tired, sweaty, and a little triumphant – clutching two coffees, Hilda was waiting on one of the benches and on the other was a familiar figure.

Bugger. Bugger. Bugger.

'Claire. Is that coffee for me?' She reached for it with a big grin on her face. 'How was it? You're glowing. Well done.'

Damn, she had my bag. I could hardly back away now.

'This is Ash,' she said with a wave of her hand. 'He doesn't say much.' If ever a man wanted to be left alone, it was him. Ash slumped further into the bench as if trying to make himself invisible and ducked his head. Ha! As if that sort of tactic was ever going to work with the indefatigable Hilda.

With Hilda patting the bench next to her, I had no choice but to go and sit down.

With a wry smile of resignation, I handed over the coffee cup and plonked myself on the bench, very aware of Ash over on my left but doing my best not to look at him.

'I think we all need some proper introductions,' Hilda announced. 'I'm Hilda Fitzroy-Townsend and this young man has just helped me back here when I got a stitch. Poor chap, I think he thought I was having a heart attack or something.'

'Claire Harrison.' I gave Ash a challenging smirk as if to say, *going to have to acknowledge me now, aren't you?*

'Ashwin Laghari,' came the grudging response, and he shot me a filthy glare.

Bloody cheek! What did he have to be so annoyed about? He was the one that didn't call. He hadn't even had the decency to reply to my text and fob me off with a lazy excuse.

'What a splendid name.' Hilda grinned, completely oblivious to the fizzing animosity virtually setting the air ablaze. 'That sounds like some rich sultan or a wealthy businessman who trades illegal weapons on the black market and has one of those superyachts with all the satellites on them and gun towers. Do you have a yacht?'

Ash glared at her and didn't deign to respond. It was tempting to laugh at his sulky silence but also a little heart breaking. What had happened to the gorgeous, full-of-himself man I'd sat opposite on the train?

'So, Claire, how far did you run?'

I hauled my iPhone out from my trusty pocket to check the health app. I winced in disgust. 'Only 3k. That's rubbish.'

Hilda patted my knee. 'A little bit more every day and you'll be on fire. I run exactly one mile in old money. How about you, Mr Arms Dealer?'

Ash's eyes narrowed but he did dig into his pocket and produced his phone. '2k.' And then to my surprise he asked, 'Which way did you go?'

When I, ultra-politely, talked him through my route – which I did out of courtesy and purely for Hilda's benefit – he shook his head. 'That's probably only two. The phone apps can be unreliable. It often depends on your stride.'

I wrinkled my nose, crestfallen at the information. It gave me the chance to inspect him more closely. His hair had lost its glossy lustre and the long curls were lank and unwashed. Most of his face was hidden behind the scruffy, overgrown beard, a far cry from the neat, well-groomed, designer stubble he had sported before.

Catching me studying him, his dull eyes held mine as a cynical twist touched his mouth. The mouth I'd once kissed. My heart stuttered in my chest. What had happened to flatten him like this? To extinguish that vital spark that had burned so brightly in those fascinating eyes? Where had Ashwin Laghari gone? Where was the gorgeous man who'd kissed me senseless.

The last time I'd seen him there'd been admiration in his eyes. Now, all I could see was bitterness and resignation. And it hurt. More than I could have imagined. Despite trying to forget him after the lack of response to my text, Ashwin Laghari had never really left my thoughts.

Hilda jumped up. 'Well, I expect to see you both here tomorrow. It'll be good for you. Especially *you*.'

I held my breath as she actually poked him in the stomach. I expected him to respond with something like, 'And if I wanted your opinion, rude old lady, I'd ask for it,' but he just sank into himself a little more, if that were possible.

The defeated gesture hit hard. He seemed so lost. I wanted to reach out and give him a hug and tell Hilda to leave him alone but she took a step back, a little frown deepening the wrinkles on her forehead, for once actually cowed. 'Well, I can't hang about here. I've got things to do and places to run.' And in a flash of white, she jogged away her Day-glo trainers, flickering like little rainbows across the path.

I waited a little while until her figure disappeared from view.

I should have been furious with him but there was something about his dejected slump that tugged at me and also a strange feeling of solidarity. He looked a little like I felt inside. Stripped of my job, I'd become a sort of non-person. My job was a part of – most of – who I was. It gave me self-esteem, prestige, and a sense of superiority. Yeah, shoot me for that, but I was good at what I did. Better than most and I liked being the best and I liked being admired. I'd always been *someone* at work.

Ash looked like he'd been stripped of being someone too.

'Are you okay?' I asked, putting out a tentative hand towards him.

He flinched and it made me wonder how long it was since he'd been touched. Although he appeared unkempt, he didn't smell of booze or anything. I withdrew my hand but kept my eyes on him, willing him to respond. Eventually he looked up and I saw a touch of wild confusion in those magnificent eyes. I held his gaze. 'Ashwin?'

He blinked a couple of times, his eyes sharpening for a second as if I'd just come into focus.

'No,' he said in a faraway voice, lifting a hand to rub at his forehead. 'No, I'm not.'

A hand squeezed at my heart. 'Can I do anything to help?' I asked, reaching out to touch him again. He stared down at my hand, my fingertips just grazing his wrist, the touch barely there, and then he lifted his head. His mouth flattened and he rose to his feet in one quick, fluid movement, dislodging my hand. 'Not you, no.' He took a step and then turned around.

Well, stuff you.

All my sympathy evaporated but as he walked away, his shoulders slumped and his gait heavy, I sighed.

He looked like he could use a friend. God only knew, I did too. Hilda had spread more sunshine in my life in the last few mornings than I'd felt for a long time. I pulled out my phone and tapped out a quick text.

Here, if you need a friend. Claire.

Chapter Nine

G od, the first sip of coffee… Caffeine. Heaven.

I slumped on the park bench. What a morning. Thursday, my fourth school run, and the worst yet; I'd left both my nieces in tears at school and had the added humiliation of having to sign the *late book*. Who'd invented that for goodness' sake? Apparently it wasn't enough to admit that children were late. You also had to write a short essay – okay, slight exaggeration there – explaining why they were late and this essay was left out in public for all the world – and the bitchy school-gate mums – to see. I rather admired the woman at the top of the page who'd written in the *Reason for Lateness* column:

> *Because their bastard father, who left us for a younger trollop, let them stay up until silly o'clock playing on the Xbox all weekend and now they're knackered and I'm the patsy who has to play the bad guy to get them out of sodding bed.*

Way to go, Claire. Late and tearful children. Last night had lulled me into a false sense of security. Tea had gone down well – homemade lemon chicken (thank you again, *BBC Good Food Magazine*) had turned me into a cooking hero and earned major brownie points. I'd helped Ava with her spelling and let Poppy watch *Hollyoaks* while Ava had a bath and then I'd put both to bed at a reasonable hour.

But somehow, this morning, all hell had broken loose. I woke at eight instead of seven because my alarm hadn't gone off. That would be because Poppy had unplugged it to charge her kindle because I wouldn't let her have it in her room overnight after I'd caught her reading at midnight the previous night. Ava decided to have a meltdown because I wouldn't let her have boiled eggs for breakfast and when I did make them she refused to eat them because they were hard boiled and the soldiers weren't cut the right way. Then, just as we were leaving the house, Poppy reminded me that Thursday was packed-lunch day.

I'd gone from favourite Auntie Claire to the devil incarnate in the space of twelve hours and I didn't like myself a whole lot either. I'd shouted like a fishwife at both of them. Thank God Alice was coming home tomorrow. I think I'd demonstrated rather effectively why I was not cut out to be a mum. This was far more stressful than being at work.

I miss working.

This lack of purpose was doing my head in. I wanted to talk to adults. Have conversations with real people. Self-loathing made the tears prick at my eyes again.

God, I hate myself. And I hate being so utterly adrift.

My coffee cup was moved and two plump sunshine-yellow legs appeared next to mine. An arm slid around my shoulders and pulled me into a lavender-scented hug. 'There, there, Claire. You cry it all out, dear.'

Held fast in her tight embrace, I did just that until at last, a snotty, snivelling wreck, I lifted my head and peered into Hilda's concerned eyes. She handed me my coffee and placed a pack of travel tissues, which looked like they'd been around the world a time or two, on my lap. Taking the cup, I sucked in a breath before sipping at the coffee, avoiding her worried expression by staring down at her Day-glo trainers.

Offering the cup back to her, I fought my way into the dog-eared pack of tissues and blew my nose with an inelegant elephant-snort before wiping my sticky, tear-stained face.

I sucked in another deep breath, trying to balance my world and pull myself together feeling horribly embarrassed. I never cried – and certainly not on other people – but I seemed to have been doing an awful lot of it recently.

'So why the tears, dear? Do you want to talk about it?'

Talk about it? Not really. No. I didn't share my failures. I kept them to myself and made sure I was better next time. Today I was just having another weak moment.

Hilda's arm was still around me, her fingers rubbing soothing circles across the top of my shoulder. 'Things are never as bad as they seem.' She paused and tilted her head to one side. 'Actually, that's bollocks, isn't it? I always swore after my husband died, the second one, that I would never indulge in platitudes. I think that could be counted as a whopper. In actual fact, things are often far worse than they seem. So, spit it out and let's see if it is.'

She said it in such a cheerful matter-of-fact way that for some reason I felt beholden to answer her, even though it went against my natural instincts.

'I'm looking after my two nieces and… it would appear I'm not very good with children. I thought I was super organised. That I had this nailed. Nutritious meals, clean clothes, clean house.' Compared to Alice, I was flying on all three fronts. But I held myself to higher standards.

'In fact, I'm terrible at it and this morning I made them both cry and they're missing their mother and I can't get hold of her and now I feel like shit because it's not their fault she's gone away. And…' Oh God, I was really going to say it out loud. 'And I've been signed off work with stress. For four weeks. I'm never off work… and I was going for partner and now that might not happen. I mean stress… who gets that? Not partners. And if it weren't for the children, I'm not sure I'd know what to do with myself.' There I'd said it out loud.

I don't know what to do with myself without my job.

Was that really all I had in life?

'Well, the children are both still alive, so that's a plus.' Hilda's cheerful shrug made me laugh in spite of myself.

'Although, I guess there's still plenty of time to kill them off, if you're really not good with children.'

'Thanks for the vote of confidence,' I said, but she had a point. Apart from this morning, they were usually quite happy so I must have been doing something right… and they both seemed to really like my cooking.

'I said no platitudes. Caring for other people's children is always a nightmare. Your own are bad enough.'

'Tell me about it. Trying to get them to school this morning was a disaster. We were half an hour late.'

She leaned back against the bench and crossed her legs. 'Anyone die?'

'No!' I laughed again.

'Well then, that's a start. Was it really that bad?'

As I began to relay the full domestic drama of the morning to her evident enjoyment, I realised I'd got myself into a state about absolutely nothing. Rather than sympathise, she chuckled every so often and when I finished she said, 'Sorry, dear. But that's the most entertaining thing I've heard for a while. Where I live, most people are nearly dead and if they're not they're dead bores. The most excitement we get is if the Siamese cat from the church next door comes into the lounge. Freda Erickson is highly allergic and you should hear her sneeze. Like a whooping donkey, she is. These two girls sound like a real pair of monkeys. Of course, you know they were playing you.'

'Really?'

'You think your sister makes them a boiled egg and soldiers before school? I was a working mum once.' She seemed sad for a moment before adding sharply, 'Children always try it on for other people if they think they can get away it. Can I give you some advice?'

'Feel free but I suspect you're going to give it to me whether I like it or not,' I observed shrewdly.

'You know me so well. Routines. That's what you need with children. Routines. Then they know where they are. And tell them in advance so there are no nasty surprises. We're going to have a bath, then a story, and then it's bedtime. Same in the mornings. Be consistent. None of this new-age fannying-around nonsense, letting children find their own rhythms and set their own timetables. And I don't approve of smacking children, although in my day it was very much the thing.'

'I wouldn't dream of smacking them,' I said.

101

'I should hope not, although I'm surprised you didn't run one of the little devils through with the breadknife.'

I laughed and gave her a startled glance as she patted my hand with her gnarled, veined fingers. 'Show me a mother who has never lost her temper with her children and I show you a big fat fibber or Mother Theresa. But I do think you need to find something to do with your time. You're like me. Work is all encompassing and when it isn't there, it leaves rather a big hole.' Her shrewd look told me she understood exactly how I felt. It was as comforting as her hand patting mine, if not more so. 'I thought retirement would kill me at first; luckily I met George. I shall have a think for you. In the meantime, exercise is very good. Have you run yet?'

'No, too busy feeling sorry for myself,' I admitted with a rueful sigh.

'I find it makes me feel much better, even though the old hips aren't too keen and my bunions like to put in the odd complaint. But it releases an endorphin or two and a bout of gratitude that I've survived another one. To be honest, my little daily jog is the only way I can survive the dullness of each day at Drearyside.' Despite the wicked twinkle in her eyes, there was a very slight droop to her mouth.

With a moment of sudden insight, I realised that Hilda and I, despite the disparity in ages, had more in common than differences. She was as adrift in her own way as I was.

'Would you like to come to lunch on Saturday?' I asked impulsively.

'That's very kind of you. I'd love to,' said Hilda, her mouth curving into a huge smile. 'Do you serve decent coffee?'

I laughed. 'Would you like one this morning?'

'I thought you'd never ask. You go do your run. I'm going

to stay here and do a spot of Tai Chi. You know, a few Snake Pounced On by an Eagle movements and a Kicked up the Arse by a Donkey pose.' She grinned and I wasn't sure if they were real things or not. Knowing her, as I was coming to, I suspected she might have made them up.

'Thanks for the tissues.'

'Anytime, dear,' she said gazing off into the distance as she held her arms aloft, striking the most peculiar pose. I guessed she knew what she was doing.

'I'll do my circuit and bring you coffee.' It was the least I could do when I'd just sobbed all over her for no real reason. Now I'd calmed down, I couldn't quite understand why I'd got myself into such a state. Maybe I wasn't fine… no matter how much I kept telling myself I was.

Cresting the rise of the hill, I tried to convince myself that today I was breathing more easily. I spotted Ash in the distance in the same shapeless grey tracksuit and if I'd had the puff to do it, I would have laughed out loud at the comedy-gold moment of him trying to run with a dog weaving in and out of his legs and wagging its tail as if this was the greatest game ever. It was the same dog I'd seen the other day in the park with the girls. Although, as I grew steadily closer, Ash made the mistake of stopping and addressing the dog in a serious way. I watched as the dog sat down and stared up at Ash as if paying careful attention to every word, occasionally tilting his head to one side. Clearly happy with the lecture he'd delivered, Ash gave the dog a nod goodbye, a 'stay' wag of the finger and jogged away, giving a last glance over his shoulder to check the dog remained seated.

As I approached him, Ash gave me a brief nod of pride as if to say, *champion dog whisperer right here*, and then passed on by. He'd never responded to my text but then, I hadn't really expected him to. It was a puzzle as to why he'd exhibited so much antipathy. I ran a few more steps and then began to laugh to myself because the dog leapt to his feet, trotted past me, and when I looked behind me he was trotting along, following Ash at a safe distance. So much for dog whispering skills. What would Ash say when he realised the dog was still on his tail?

Today, I forced myself to add in an extra loop of one of the paths which circled past the pretty bell-topped bandstand which could have done with some TLC and a small neatly-pruned rose garden, before finally wending my way back to The Friendly Bean. Surely I must be up to 4k by now.

'Back again,' observed Sascha. 'You're a glutton for punishment. Just watching you makes me feel like I'm burning a few calories. You need one of our loyalty cards. You get a free coffee every time you buy six.'

'Well at this rate, it's probably worth doing. I'd like two today.'

'Just moved here?'

'I've been here about six months. On Park Road.'

'Nice,' she said, pouring frothing milk into mine and Hilda's cappuccinos.

'Mmm,' I said noncommittally. The house was nice but could be so much nicer still. That would be my next project. I'd start this weekend as soon as the girls had gone.

'Same time tomorrow?' she asked, handing over the coffees.

'Probably,' I nodded. Routine, Hilda had said. That was what I needed – not just the children, although I only had them for one more morning, but me too. Next week I wouldn't need to do the school run but I would still set my alarm clock and do my circuit of the park. And then I'd start properly on doing up the house.

I picked up the two coffees and headed for Hilda and her bench.

I was greeted with a bark and a bundle of wiry fur jumping up at me, towards the coffees. I held them stiff-armed, up and out of reach, while Ash, with unexpected gallantry, leapt to his feet and put himself between me and the dog.

'Down,' he said firmly in an authoritative voice that gave me a spine-tingling reminder of the old Ash.

'Ash has got a new friend,' announced Hilda blithely, reaching for her coffee.

'So I see.'

Ash shot us both a lacklustre, weary glare, as the lurcher slunk over and sat at his feet, looking up at him with adoration. In that instant, I wanted to shake him, like a snow globe, to wake up his emotions and become that vibrant, exciting man I'd met before. But then maybe he thought the same when he saw me; I wasn't exactly firing on all cylinders these days. But that was all about to change. I was going to make the most of this time before I went back to work. Get as fit and healthy as possible so that when I did go back, I'd be a super-improved version of me.

'He was here the other day at the playground.' I sat down

next to Hilda and watched as the dog tilted one enquiring, lopsided ear at my voice.

'Poor thing's been abandoned. See, he's starving… the way he's sniffing the coffee.' Hilda calmly pulled two pieces of toast wrapped in clingfilm from her pocket.

'I was saving these for later but I think his need is greater, isn't it sunshine?'

The dog was immediately at her feet, one foot pawing the ground with a gentle whine.

'Here you go boy. Only marmalade I'm afraid but better than nothing.' She held out the piece of toast; the dog rose onto its hindlegs and snapped it out of her fingers, before backing away a safe distance. It dropped the toast onto the floor and chased it with desperate hunger around the paving stone before finally manging to hold it down with one paw to gain purchase.

'Do you always come armed with toast?' asked Ash, as the three of us watched the dog slavishly rounding up every last crumb.

'Armed and dangerous, me,' said Hilda with a chuckle, tossing the second piece to the dog, who gave a little yip of pleasure and repeated the same little dance before pinning the toast down and wolfing it down in a couple of mouthfuls.

'The wardens make a fuss if you don't eat breakfast. I wasn't hungry this morning but they only agreed to release me into the wild when I said I'd take my toast with me for my constitutional.'

'Poor chap is starving,' I said as the dog came to sit in front of Hilda, his warm brown eyes full of hope as he gazed up at her.

'Yes, he needs a good meal. Ash, you'll have to take him.'

'Me!' Ash sat up straight, as though he'd been poked with a cattle prod, a familiar golden flash in his eyes which caught me unawares.

Damn. A sudden buzz of attraction shot through me and I swallowed a hefty slug of coffee to chase it away.

'Yes, you. I can't take him back to the home. And Claire's got enough on her plate. The company will do you good.'

'But he's someone else's dog. I can't just take him home. Besides, I don't want a dog.'

Hilda laughed. 'Of course you do.'

Ash frowned but before he could deny it again, she added, 'But like you say, he might just be lost. If we take him to the rescue centre, Melanie there will check him over. Scan him to see if he has a chip.'

'*We?*' Those eyes flashed again and I crossed my legs. *Nothing to see here*, I told my libido firmly.

'You have got a car, haven't you?'

'Yes.'

'Well then. Just look at him. He's your dog.'

I bit back a smile because it was true. The dog, it appeared, had taken ownership of Ash. Having given up on the possibility of more toast, he had sidled up to Ash's leg and was leaning so hard against it that if Ash moved his leg the dog would topple right over.

And just out of sight, Ash's hand was surreptitiously rubbing the dog's chest.

'You take the dog home, feed him, and pick me up at Sunnyside in an hour and a half, and we'll go to the rescue place,' said Hilda. 'Claire, do you want to come too?'

'She can't,' said Ash. 'I've got a Porsche. Not much room in the back, not with a dog as well.'

'A Porsche? Oh, well. Claire looks quite bendy; I'm sure she can squeeze in the back.'

'I'm sure she's got better things to be doing.' Bitterness ground into the lines around his mouth.

'No, she hasn't. Claire's been signed off with stress for the rest of the month.'

Hilda's chatty confidence made me blush a brilliant scarlet. I could have killed her. It was the last thing I wanted Ash to know. I waited for some sarcastic response and when it didn't come, I dared to glance his way. He studied me with an impassive expression that was totally unreadable.

'She needs something to do, don't you, dear?'

Chapter Ten

Being in the back of a Porsche 911 with a hairy dog breathing down my neck did not rank high on my needing-something-to-do list. Clambering in had been an exercise in contortion to start with, especially as the dog was already taking up most of the miniscule back seat. As soon as I'd nestled my bum into the soft cream leather seat, the dog began to fidget; one minute he was sprawled on my lap, the next leaning against me, his wet nose on my neck and a second later he was trying to climb over the gear stick to the front seat.

'Sit,' said Ash, gruff and deep, after the dog's third attempt to scramble into the front. 'Can you at least try and hold him?' he snapped.

'Yeah, right,' I said, wrapping both arms around him and hauling the dog back. Without warning, he flopped onto me, knocking me sideways, snuggled in, and laid his head on my lap, gazing up with those quizzical, warm brown eyes. 'Stupid dog,' I whispered, as I stroked the baby punk-rocker Mohican on his head, my fingers working into the soft fur around his floppy ears. I felt the reassuring beat of his heart, slow and steady against my leg.

'He really likes you, Claire.' Hilda's head bobbed around the head rest.

'No,' I said.

She pretended innocence and turned back to Ash, who was programming the sat nav.

'You won't need that,' she said. 'I'll direct you. You need to head down Church Road and then at the bottom take a left out towards Hookleigh. The rescue place is in Lower Hookleigh.'

'How do you know about it?' I asked.

'The rescue centre sometimes brings dogs to the old folks' home to cheer us up. I have to say, it does wonders for some of the old dears. Proper perks them up, it does.'

It amused me, the way she refused to identify herself with the other residents.

With a throaty roar, the engine burst into life and with my hand on the dog's head, stroking his soft ears, I leaned back and tried to get as comfortable as I could while squished in with my knees almost touching my chin.

Behind the wheel, Ash had regained some of that old Ashwin Laghari confidence and drove with flashy style, handling the car with obvious skill – not that I appreciated it that much from the position I was in, wedged up against the back of his seat.

'Hilda,' Ash's voice cut in. 'The signpost says Hookleigh is to the right.'

'Oh, yes, sorry dear. I never was very good at left and right. Caused the occasional problem when I was on surveillance duties in MI6.'

Ash caught my eye in the mirror and raised an eyebrow but

neither of us said anything. At that moment, the dog let out an enormous fart.

'Dear me,' said Hilda. 'I've been saying for ages that marmalade wasn't any good for us. No wonder all the old fellas are trumping left, right, and centre. I'll have to have a word with the management.'

'Thanks, dog,' I said trying to hold my breath as Ash wound down the windows.

Ash chuckled but when I met his eyes again in the mirror, they suddenly went serious and held mine long enough to make my heart do a funny flip in my chest. He looked as if he were trying to figure something out about me and I had to turn away. He'd had his chance; he wasn't getting another one.

Melanie at the rescue centre bounded over to us with button-bright eyes and the smiliest face I'd ever seen. In her grey overalls and bright red wellies, she could have doubled as a member of some futuristic militia. Without bothering to address any of us, she immediately dropped to her knees in front of the dog.

'Aren't you a gorgeous lad, then?' she said in a broad Yorkshire accent as she held out her hand and ruffled the fur around his neck. The dog sniffed and whined, poking his nose at her hand. 'And hungry. He can smell food on me.'

'I've just fed him a couple of cooked organic chicken fillets,' protested Ash.

'If he hasn't eaten for a few days, you need to go slowly.' Melanie rubbed his ears and I swear the dog let out a sigh of contentment. 'Where's he come from?'

'We found him in the park,' said Hilda. 'He's been there a couple of days we think.'

'Hmm, no collar and if he's had a bath or been groomed in the last month, I'm a flaming Christmas tree fairy… which,' she brushed a hand over her lumpy overalls, 'I'm clearly not.' She lifted the pads of his feet to examine them, shaking her wiry deep-auburn curls. 'Abandoned, I'm guessing. Bloody folk, don't deserve to have dogs. How hard is it? Feed 'em, walk 'em, love 'em. Piece of piss, you'd o' thought.'

She hauled a small handheld device from one of her deep, utilitarian pockets, very like the scanners you get in supermarkets. 'I can check him for a chip but I'm not holding out much hope.'

She ran the scanner over the dog's neck, shoulders and upper bag. 'Thought as much. People who are likely to abandon a dog rather than try to rehome it aren't going to go to the trouble and expense of getting it chipped.'

Rising to her feet, she put her hands on her hips and surveyed the three of us with a shake of her head. 'I can't take him, I'm afraid. We're full as full can be. And I'm struggling to feed this lot as it is.' She waved her hand towards a row of stone buildings from which emanated a range of barks and yips.

'There's three of you.' Now her smiley face had morphed into that of a stern slightly disapproving head mistress.

Ash and I both shifted our feet like a pair of naughty school children.

'I'd have him like a shot but they're not that keen on pets at Drearyside, you know that, Melanie,' said Hilda, smugness radiating in her voice as she beamed at Ash and me.

'Yeah, real shame. They'd do some of those inmates the

power of good. That Elsie Goodman actually smiled when I brought the little black and white terrier in three weeks back. Miserable old crow hasn't cracked her face in years.'

'That one was born like that.' Hilda's slightly plummy voice had suddenly adopted a distinct touch of Yorkshire. 'I hear she had a fearsome reputation when she ran the haberdasher's in the High Street.'

'I remember it well. Me mam used to send our dad to buy her wool because she was so flaming scared of her.'

'And look what one little dog can do. They bring so much joy.' Hilda levelled another of her overbright smiles our way. Conniving old bat.

'Aye. What about you?' She turned her eyes on Ash. The dog was leaning against his leg.

'I don't want a dog,' said Ash. 'I'm just the taxi driver.'

Melanie raised a supercilious eyebrow. 'With a vehicle like that you can afford to feed him.'

'Happy to make a donation,' said Ash with the hopeful look of someone who'd just seen a way to slip the leash.

'Happy to take one but I can't magic up another run.' Her eyes narrowed with the cunning of a fox. 'If you can house him temporarily, I might be able to see what I can do.'

Before Ash could say anything, Hilda jumped right in. 'You could do that. You said you were between jobs, so it'll be perfect. And he really likes you. And I can dog-sit if you have to go out for any length of time. Besides, you need a dog more than Claire.'

At that, Ash and I exchanged startled looks.

'That's sorted then.' Mel beamed as Ash realised events had escaped him and started to splutter objections but she talked right over them. 'I can sell you some dog food, a collar and a lead, and a dog bed, if you want one.'

'Done,' said Hilda, turning back to Ash and patting his shoulder. 'That's helpful, isn't it? We don't have to go shopping.' She followed Mel who bustled away to an office building on the other side of the flagstone courtyard.

Ash frowned and then lifted his head my way. 'How did that just happen?'

I lifted my shoulders trying to hide a smile, relieved that I'd escaped the Hilda treatment.

'I'm not sure.'

I was dying to ask what 'between jobs' meant. Gardening leave? Annual leave? What had reduced the arrogant, super-confident Ashwin Laghari to the sullen, bitter Ash in his grubby grey sweats. Although, as I glanced down at what had quickly become my uniform of leggings, T-shirt and navy sweatshirt with a big Superman S emblazoned on the front, I wasn't much better. Funnily enough though, I didn't miss my little suits with their neat lapels and nipped in waists half as much as I'd thought I would.

Chapter Eleven

F our o'clock in the morning phone calls never bode well and, as I ran down the chilly wooden stairs, my brain quickly jumped to a million conclusions. My parents.

Oh God, please let my parents be all right.

Fear clenched at my heart as I grabbed the receiver.

'Why don't you answer your mobile?'

Alice's petulant voice came down the line, tinny and aggrieved.

'What?' Bleary-eyed and forcefully ejected from sleep, my brain hadn't quite caught up with my feet.

'Your mobile. You didn't answer.'

'I left it downstairs,' I finally managed to muster the words. 'How are you? Have you had a great time? What time does your flight leave?' I assumed she was just about to board the aeroplane. 'The girls are very excited about coming to pick you up.' They'd missed her so much. It would be just like that *Love Actually* sequence that never failed to make me cry, the one with the people being met by their loved ones at the airport.

We were planning to make a hasty exit from school, drive to Manchester and meet her flight which was due to land at five-thirty.

'Thing is Claire, I've... erm... well there's been a bit of... I missed the internal flight. There's been a landslide.'

'*What?*' Missing a flight was one of my worst nightmares. 'Oh my God. Are you okay?'

'Calm down, Claire. I knew you'd be like this. You really do need get your chakras realigned, you know.'

'But you missed your flight. What are you going to do?' My voice pitched with the anxiety that my sister should have been feeling.

'Well there's not a lot I can do but it's all fine. It is what it is.' Her businesslike tone was suddenly replaced by a far dreamier one. 'Oh God, Claire, you should see it. It's so beautiful here. I've never felt so much in touch with my life-force. The resort is just amazing, you know, and the people and... I love India. It's so spiritual; I feel like me again. Cleansed and whole. I can breathe again. Like I've been in an iron lung or something for most of my life, you know, and now I'm free. Released like a butterfly from a cocoon to taste the nectar of life. I'm all gossamer wings and floating free. It's the most amazing feeling.'

'The girls are going to be gutted,' I said, swallowing a lump in my throat. Ava would be devastated, with lots of tears and drama but far worse, Poppy would be stoic. I could picture her fine-boned, impassive little face. Poppy did stoicism a little too well. 'So when's the next flight?'

There was a too long pause.

'The thing is... well, not until... next Sunday.'

'Next Sunday? Not this Sunday?'

'Yeah, well, like I said, the landslide...'

'So are you stranded there?'

'Yes,' she seized on my words with undue relief. 'But it's okay. It's only another week. I think I'll be back next Sunday. Can't guarantee it but I'll call you. Besides, with school and their friends, the girls aren't going to miss me. And this really has been a life-changing trip. I'll be able to give them so much more as a person when I get back.'

'Can you really not get back any sooner?' I asked, my mind racing through the practicalities. 'You've got parents' evening and stuff next week.'

'Claire, you can manage all that for me standing on your head. Besides, it's always the same old lecture about not doing homework or reading with Ava.'

'But—'

'Claire, chill. The girls will be fine with you.'

Would they? I could do the practical stuff but... they needed their mum, and even I knew I was a pretty poor substitute.

'So have you got a flight? Can you give me the flight number? What time should I pick you up?'

'I'm not actually booked on one yet... Communication here is... quite difficult.'

And yet our mobile call was completely crackle free.

'But it will be Sunday.'

'Sunday, or possibly Monday.'

'Alice!'

'I can't help it. I don't know. I can't magic up a plane ticket. But most likely Sunday.'

'But you must have some idea.'

'As soon as I do I'll let you know.'

'But what am I supposed to tell the girls? Will you Facetime them this evening? Have you got Wi-Fi?'

'I'll try.'

'No, Alice. You *must*. They miss you.'

'Tell them Mummy loves them and she'll be home as soon as she can.'

I groaned. That kind of vagueness wasn't fair to them.

'Oh Claire, live a little. There's so much more to life. It's so beautiful here. I feel so alive. No clocks to watch, nowhere to be, just spiritual cleanliness. It's amazing. Don't worry, the girls will be fine and it will do you good to connect with them. No offence, but what else are you going to do until you go back to work?'

———

Sleep eluded me after that and I spent the rest of the early hours racking my brains as to how I was going to break the news to the girls and how I might make it up to them this weekend. Disney movies at the cinema were in short supply at the moment.

Predictably, Ava cried big, noisy sobs on my lap in the kitchen until I made her a bacon sandwich for breakfast and Poppy just nodded, her face tightening with a terse frown. She didn't say anything and as soon as she'd eaten her toast, she disappeared upstairs.

'Come on, Ava. Let's sort your hair out.' As usual, it looked like a bird's nest that a couple of noisy crows had fought over. 'You go up and find the brush and bobbles. I'll be up in a minute. I'll just wash up quickly.'

I'd only just filled the washing up bowl with hot soapy

suds when an outraged scream came from upstairs. And yes, I bloody left the tap running as I hared off into the hall and sprinted up the stairs to the girls' bedroom.

Sending a quick narrow-eyed squint of suspicion at Poppy, who stood just inside the door with a far too innocent expression framing her face, I hurried into the bedroom to find Ava wailing and, like a whirling dervish, clutching an armful of toys and pawing through a mound of clothes on her side of the bed.

'What's going on?' I asked.

Ava's face crumpled and she started to sob. 'P-Poppy's being mean. She did it.'

I turned to see Poppy standing ramrod straight, her hands stiff by her sides.

'Did you do this?' I asked pointing at the pile of clothes.

She lifted one shoulder in defiant lethargy. 'I'm fed up with her mess. She always leaves clothes and toys everywhere. I just tidied them up for her.'

Count to ten, Claire. Count to ten. 'You mean, you dumped them on her side of the bed.' Points for sounding calm and in control, I told myself; in my dressing-gown pockets, my fingers were clenched into tight little fists. This counted as stress and I was supposed to be avoiding it. I could feel my blood pressure rising.

'Serves her right.' Poppy's mouth crushed itself into a mutinous scowl.

This was just a reaction to Alice not coming home. It wasn't their fault. I chewed at my lip and assessed the inadequate room. They were going to have to share for another week and I could relate to Poppy's frustration; Ava's cheerful disregard for shelves, cupboards, and wardrobes drove me mad too.

'Poppy, you need to help Ava tidy up her bed. Ava, stop making a fuss. You need to put all your clothes away properly.' I raised a finger as both of them began to protest and said in my best scary-Auntie, second-cousin-to-Darth-Vader, voice which seemed to hold a measure of authority, 'And I don't want to hear another word from either of you. We're leaving for school in twenty minutes.' I gave them a bland, I've-got-this-taped, Mary Poppins, serene smile while inside my heart was thumping uncomfortably but it was rather satisfying to see them both jump to it. For once, I almost felt like I knew what I was doing with them. *Thank you, Hilda.* Her words of wisdom had helped; we had a good routine, and after living with them for a whole week, I now had a much better understanding of what made each of them tick.

———

Later that morning, Hilda bounced up to the bench as I was recovering from my longest run yet – according to my phone I'd notched up 4k today, and despite Ash's claims that it was probably wrong, I was taking it. Buoyed up by my success with the girls this morning – not only did we make it to school on time but I also remembered their PE kits – I'd pushed myself to do an additional loop of the park and it had felt good. I was starting to get addicted to the endorphins that running was definitely releasing.

'Morning,' she chirruped and before I could swipe it out of reach, she lunged for my coffee.

Feeling pleasantly weary, I grinned when she pulled a face. 'Ugh, where's my cappuccino?'

'One, it's not *your* cappuccino and two, it serves you right.'

'Polygamous coffee drinking is all wrong.'

'Says who? I needed the espresso this morning. I've been up half the night.'

'Me, of course,' said Hilda, calmly digging out a couple of sachets of sugar from her pocket and dumping them in my double espresso before I could stop her.

'What did you do that for?'

'It's the only way I can drink black coffee,' she replied, as if this was entirely reasonable and she'd not just poisoned my drink.

'You might as well have it now,' I muttered sulkily.

'I will, thank you. So why black this morning?'

'My bloody sister rang at ridiculous o'clock this morning.'

'Oh dear, is her flight delayed?'

'You could say that.' I sighed heavily. 'By a week.'

'Good Lord, where's she gone? Mars?'

'No, India. The good news is that she's found herself; the bad news is that there's been a landslide and she can't get to the airport.'

'Convenient,' said Hilda. 'And she discovered this today.'

'Apparently so.' She put voice to my own sceptical thoughts. 'And my nieces are upset of course.' And I was furious that Alice hadn't been more proactive about speaking to them. 'We had tears this morning.' I was going to phone if she didn't Facetime later and force her to speak to the girls.

'Understandable. But they're young; you just need to take their minds off things. Cake always helps.'

'It would if I could bake.'

'Well, I can help with that. I'm a whizz in the kitchen. Dear Mary – Mary Berry, you know – always said I had the lightest touch with a sponge. I miss baking. I don't get the chance these days and I'm not allowed anywhere near the kitchen at Drearyside, not since I got peckish in the middle of the night and nipped into the kitchen to make some popcorn. I set off the smoke alarms. You'd have thought they might have been quite grateful that they got the chance to test them thoroughly when it was a false alarm. But if they will make them so sensitive, what do they expect?'

I winced, visions of dozens of winceyette-clad pensioners clutching hot water bottles in some car park filling my head. Evacuating an old people's home in the middle of the night must have been a nightmare.

'So what sort of cake do you think they'd like?'

'I think it's going to take more than cake. They're both a bit upset and another week of sharing a room and a double bed isn't going to help. Ava's a fidget and really messy while Poppy is neat and tidy even in her sleep.'

'And they have to share a room, do they?'

I wrinkled my nose. 'It's the only room with an extra bed in. I moved in a while back but just haven't got around to furnishing the other bedrooms.' Which was ridiculous. What had stopped me? Work, as usual.

Now I had a reason to get on and do it. Not for me, but for the girls.

'Actually… sorry, Hilda, do you mind if we take a rain check tomorrow. I'm going to take Poppy and Ava to Ikea, buy them some furniture, and they can have a bedroom each. They can choose their own bedrooms. That might cheer them up a bit.'

Hilda sat up straighter. 'What an excellent idea. I've heard so much about Ikea. I'll come too.'

I stared at her for a minute. With her and the girls in the car there wouldn't be any room for furniture. I needed to hire a van if I was thinking of kitting out two bedrooms with beds and furniture... in which case there would be space in my car to take her with us. 'Okay. We can go and select everything in the morning and hire a man with a van to pick it up at lunchtime and take it back to the house.'

'That's easy. My neighbour Dottie, her son Vin, is the man with the van.' She pulled out her phone and before I had even thought about opening my mouth to protest she started speaking. 'Dottie, Hilda. HILDA,' she shouted, muttering an aside to me, 'Daft old bat's not got her hearing aid in. Dottie. It's Hilda. Yes, Hilda. Thank goodness for that. Yes, I'm fine. Just out for my morning constitutional.' She rolled her eyes and put her hand over her phone as if it were a landline telephone, which amused me because she clearly had no idea how a mobile worked. 'Wants me to pick up some condoms for her. Yes Dottie. I'll do that. Thin Feel. Got it. Not the Intense ones. Now what's Vin up to tomorrow? Can you give me his number?' Hilda opened the flap of the ever-present silver lamé messenger bag and dug around before offering me a pen and a tiny notebook. 'Zero, seven...' She reeled off the numbers and I dutifully wrote them down. 'Thanks Dottie. See you soon.' Without even pausing to draw breath, she took the notebook from me and dialled the number.

'Vin, Hilda here. I need you tomorrow.' She mouthed, 'Twelve-thirty?'

I nodded.

'Can you meet me at Ikea in Leeds? Twelve-thirty tomorrow. And mates' rates.'

I heard the rich laugh down the phone telling Hilda she was a 'right one'.

And just like that, it was all organised, Hilda preening like a sunshine-yellow peacock. 'That's all sorted. I've always wanted to go to Ikea and see what all the fuss is about.'

'Are you sure?' A morning in Ikea was a lot of people's idea of hell.

'It's the best offer I'm going to get. It's that or leathery bacon and Arthur Sanditon reading out this week's obituaries from the Times.'

I worked out the timing in my head. 'We can have lunch there. Would you like me to pick you up?' Hilda wasn't keen on me coming to the old people's home, so we arranged to meet on a nearby corner. Her reason being that every Tom, Dick, and Herbert in the home would want her to get a 'bit o' shopping' for them.

'Hopefully the place will be crawling with handsome Swedes. Now, have you seen Ash this morning? I've had the most brilliant idea.'

I sat there with my mouth doing the goldfish thing because sometimes it was just impossible to keep up with the hairpin bends and racing turns of her conversation.

Finally, I caught up. 'Yes, he was running with the dog but heading towards the other side of the park when I was coming this way.' He had even given me a perfunctory nod.

'Excellent, he'll be here soon.'

It struck me that in just one week, the three of us had fallen into a pattern of meeting here, even though Ash clearly eschewed company and pretended that his being here at the same time each day was completely coincidental.

'So what's this brilliant idea?' I asked, a touch nervous, well aware that I'd only just missed being saddled with a dog by the skin of my teeth.

Hilda's shark-like smile only added to my nerves.

'Don't you think it's brilliant?' Hilda sat back on our bench fifteen minutes later and clasped her hands over her heart. Opposite, on his own bench, Ash shuffled as uncomfortably as me.

'Come on people, where's the enthusiasm? It's not as if either of you have got anything better to do.'

When she put it like that she had a point, if a somewhat blunt one.

'It's… it's an idea, Hilda,' I said, 'but… well, we don't know if anyone else would be interested.'

'Of course, they will. Remember the bible. About Noah's Ark. Build it and they will come. Remember.'

'I think that was a Kevin Costner film actually,' said Ash. 'I'm not sure there's much call for a baseball field in Churchstone.'

'You know what I mean, young man.' Hilda was suddenly at her Maggie Smith Dowager Countess finest. 'It would be a wonderful thing for Churchstone. I've been doing some research on the interweb. There are these parkruns all over the country. Hundreds of them. I don't see why we couldn't have one here. The nearest one is in Harrogate and that's a forty-minute drive away. I can see it now. A real community event. Bring everyone, like you two, together.'

Ash and I exchanged indignant looks but Hilda ploughed on, oblivious. 'And it's not as if the park is used as much as it should be. It would encourage people to come here. And it would make people exercise a lot more. You could run with... the dog.'

'Bill,' said Ash.

'Bill?' Hilda was back to maiden aunt again.

'He looks like a Bill,' said Ash, standing his ground before adding with a supercilious sneer, 'And no one else wanted responsibility so I feel I'm entitled to name him.'

Hilda suddenly looked very smug. 'Very good. Now, what do you say?'

It sounded a completely mad idea to me. Who would want to come and run around the park? The three of us were hardly serious runners but with Hilda's bird-bright eyes focused with such expectancy on me, I said, 'I don't suppose it could do any harm to make a few enquiries.' And enquiries would probably kill the idea stone dead; the council were bound to object.

'Hilda, have you ever done a parkrun?' asked Ash. 'Have you any idea what's involved?'

'No.' She sniffed at her regal finest. 'But there was a man on Radio 4 and he said jolly good things about them. I think it's just what this park needs. Everyone knows more people need to exercise. Running can help prevent heart disease, cardiovascular problems and strokes. And look at you. Slimming down already.'

Ash's mouth twitched but he turned to me without acknowledging her comment. 'What about you? Have you done one?'

'No and I've not been tempted before. Although there's a guy at work'—Dave, who'd set up the charity team—'and he does the one in Hyde Park in Leeds. But he's a proper runner. Runs to work every day. Five miles. Has an extensive wardrobe of Lycra and does marathons in places like Athens and Boston for his holidays. They do not sound like fun holidays to me.' I shuddered.

As far as I was concerned, I was not a proper runner. Jogging around the park each day on my own was a means to an end, to make me fitter and healthier, so that I'd be stronger when I got back to work, and signing up for Dave's team had been my attempt at keeping a channel open with work. Despite that, I was starting to enjoy my daily run; it gave my day a format and was good thinking time. Just this morning I'd been planning the colours for the kitchen. I fancied something really sophisticated and stylish. Dark and pale grey walls and black slate floors. Why hadn't I been able to focus on this sort of thing before? I knew the answer straight away. I'd let work take up far too much headspace.

'Claire.' Hilda was waving a hand in front of my face.

'Sorry, I was thinking.'

'You see,' crowed Hilda to Ash. 'Claire thinks it's a good idea.'

'Why don't we have a think about it over the weekend and talk next week?' suggested Ash.

I shot him a grateful smile and he gave me shy smile over the top of Hilda's cloud of white hair.

'Excellent,' said Hilda. 'We'll reconvene on Monday.'

Chapter Twelve

'I want a princess bed like this.' Ava grabbed a fistful of the diaphanous fabric swathed around the head of the little wooden bed. 'It's so pretty. And please, please, please can I have some fairy lights too and the pink elephant. I'll be ever so good.'

I laughed at the sight of her hopeful parted lips which had fallen into an 'O' of wonderment as she gazed at the room set in Ikea, which had overdosed on pink and white and pretty things. The centre piece, a white-framed bed, was curtained by gauzy drapes and dressed with a bubble-gum pink duvet set and a pile of cushions and soft toys. Even the more reserved Poppy was touching the fairy lights and chains of pink and mauve butterflies with a tentative hand.

'It's a bit babyish,' said Poppy dubiously. Ava's eyes widened with hurt indignation, but before the pet lip began to protrude, Hilda said, 'But perfect for a princess though,' a sage twinkle in her eye as she dropped a quick curtesy. 'I can see you sleeping in this bed, Princess Ava.' Then she added to

Poppy, 'But I can see that a young lady like you will want something more sophisticated.'

I grinned gratefully at her diplomacy.

Despite Poppy's disparagement, with a change of duvet and colour scheme, this bed and furniture would move with the times. As far as Ava was concerned, the net above the bed and the fairy lights were the clinchers, so they were added to the list of things we had to hunt down in the marketplace part of the store.

Poppy was less easy to please. Her eyes kept straying to the price tags of everything and she didn't seem to want to commit whole heartedly to anything. Luckily, Ava was being entertained by Hilda and they were busy conducting a thorough inspection of all the available styles of fairy lights in the different room sets and discussing their merits in great detail.

'What about this one?' I asked for the fifth time putting my hand on the end of a more grown-up, simple pine bed.

'Yes, that's fine.'

I was about to write down the code for the bed when something stopped me. I didn't want it to be just fine. I wanted Poppy to love her new bedroom and everything in it. Alice might not care about material things and sometimes I felt she revelled in her altruistic saintliness – it was all very commendable – but she didn't half go on about it as if she were saving the planet single handed. But at this age, sometimes things mattered and rubbed away like a deep burr. One memory that had always stuck with me, from probably when I was about Poppy's age, was how I'd hankered for a particular duvet cover and been so disappointed when my mum had chosen a different one, a sensible plain one in navy blue. Alice had thrown a major tantrum and had been allowed to have a Little Mermaid set instead, that two weeks later she had hated.

Poppy liked things to be just so. I could relate to that. She reminded me of myself at the same age.

No, fine would not do.

Turning away from the pine bed, I started another circuit of the area, this time not saying anything, just watching Poppy. She didn't give much away but when I saw her hand rest on an old-fashioned white metal-framed bed, I knew that was the bed she wanted. A cross between an old nursery bed and a pretty day bed, it was feminine but also grown-up and immediately I knew it would suit her perfectly.

'I think that one's very nice,' I said.

'It is but… it's quite expensive. I don't want you to spend a lot of money. It's only for a week.'

'Yes, but I need to put furniture in those bedrooms and I haven't been able to choose any before. It's lovely that you're helping me. And wouldn't it be nice to know you have your own room somewhere else? You and Ava could come and stay if Mummy's going out or something.'

Suddenly I hoped that Alice would let me babysit more often and that perhaps the girls could come and stay occasionally, either together or individually. Poppy needed some space of her own instead of always being the older sister. I'd really enjoyed getting to know my nieces a little better over the last few days. Two distinct personalities had emerged, real people in their own right, instead of being someone else's children. *My* nieces. I felt a tiny butterfly flutter in my chest at the thought. They were mine now.

'I'd like that,' she said shyly. 'Are you sure this isn't too much money?' She bit her lip, worry gnawing lines into her brow. 'I do like this one.'

'I promise it's not too much money, if that's the one you'd like.'

'I'd love it, Auntie Claire,' she breathed, the dreamy smile on her face making my heart do a funny little forward-roll.

By the time we came out of the marketplace, we'd had to commandeer a second trolley and both were like teetering, rainbow-coloured leaning Towers of Pisa of stuff. Colourful patterned cushions topped rugs, duvets, bedding sets, pillows and three sets of brightly coloured towels, dusky pink for Ava, pale blue for Poppy and lime green for Hilda. There were also scented candles, bedside lamps, and four boxes of fairy lights – after Poppy had succumbed and so had I, Hilda decided that she wanted a set too. Hilda had also decided to buy herself a five-foot palm tree and a magnifying mirror to help her pluck the grey hairs from her lady beard. The man next to her when she'd announced this had looked as if he'd swallowed his tongue.

Getting that lot through the checkout was a logistical nightmare and I was very grateful that Hilda supervised Ava, leaving the far more helpful and sensible Poppy to assist me. Thank goodness Hilda had come too; I'd never have managed. And it would never have occurred to me to ask anyone to come along and help, which now seemed rather silly.

'Looks like you've got your hands full here,' drawled a languid voice and I glanced up to see Ash, with a cup of tea in each hand, standing in the doorway.

'Let me guess, Hilda sent for you,' I said with a sigh, gazing around at the pieces and screws that I'd organised in preparation for building Ava's chest of drawers. Poppy and I had managed to construct two drawers so far, Ava's bed was now complete, and we'd had the unmatched joy of ripping the plastic off the mattress and watching it unfurl and bounce into shape like an unruly caterpillar.

'Thought you needed some help.'

I sighed. There was no point denying it. I still had a chest of drawers, a wardrobe, and a bed to build. 'Well, it's very kind of you. I know how much you love DIY.'

As soon as the words popped out of my head, I wanted to haul them back in again. It was tacit acknowledgement that we'd met before, something we'd so far avoided.

He frowned for a second, as if trying to work it out and then with a flash of recognition he nodded.

'This is Poppy, my extremely able assistant.'

'Hi Poppy.' He smiled and handed over the mug of tea to me. 'Hilda says there's a glass of squash for you and,' he sniffed the air at the smells of baking wafting up from the kitchen, 'she needs people to lick out the bowl apparently.'

Poppy jumped to her feet and glanced at me.

'Go, go, go but if there's cake, save me some.'

'Cake!' Her eyes widened and she rushed off, her feet clattering down the bare floorboards of the stairs.

Ash gave me a cool look. 'You didn't mention children.'

My smile was humourless, although I took more than a little satisfaction in wrong footing him. 'That's because they're my nieces. I'm caring for them while my sister is away.'

'Oh. Sorry.'

I shrugged and took a reviving sip of tea, as much to avoid

looking at him as anything else. Did he feel as awkward as I did? It felt odd, the two of us in this room, in my house, with an ocean of unsaid things between us.

'How long have you lived here?' he asked, staring around at the bare room.

'Only six months. I had an apartment in Leeds before but it...' I was about to stray into the personal and admit weakness, not something I wanted to do in front of him. My plan had always been to turn this house into an Instagram-worthy dream home but I'd just never had the time before. Not that two children's bedrooms furnished with Ikea bits had been part of my grand plan. I'd intended them to be guest rooms, although now it struck me, who the hell had I thought would be coming to stay? I hadn't had friends over in I don't know how long.

He lifted one of his eyebrows but didn't say anything. The half-finished sentence hung in the air and, now, not finishing it felt like a weakness.

I knelt on the floor, hiding my face behind a curtain of hair and gathered the pieces to make up drawer number three. 'My flat never really felt like home.' More of a stepping stone, a handy bolt-hole for the time between work. The move to this house was supposed to have been the next part of my life. The part where things happened, where I became a partner, and threw dinner parties for other successful people and they stayed over, where my parents came for lunch and cooed over how lovely I'd made everything and my dad congratulated me on what a good investment I'd made, but it had just been more of the same, only in slightly nicer surroundings.

'And this does?' he looked at the plain walls and the ceiling with its unadorned central light bulb.

I glowered at him and crawled across the floor to one of the big blue bags and began to rummage through it.

'Here, make yourself useful.' I tossed the pink lamp shade at him, aiming for his head.

Of course, he caught it easily, stretching up and plucking it out of the air, his T-shirt coming loose from his waistband. The quick glimpse of golden skin and dark hairs heading downwards made my mouth go dry and my stomach muscles tighten.

He raised that cocky bloody eyebrow again, a smile on his lips as if he knew exactly what my pathetic, hard-done-by libido was feeling. It irritated the hell out of me.

'And when you've done that, you can help build this.' I indicated the neat pile of wooden pieces laid out in readiness.

'Very organised. I thought you'd be that type. I bet you've read the instructions too.'

'Of course.' *God, I sound prim and buttoned up.* But around him it was the best way to be. I'd played sexy siren once and where had that got me? A big fat nowhere.

'Well then, we should have this done in no time at all.'

We worked surprisingly well as team, perhaps because both of us were concentrating hard on not touching each other and not saying anything the least bit personal; even my long-married parents bickered like crazy over a DIY project. Ash didn't seem to need the instructions, or if he did, it only took one brief perusal and he was able to work out with unerring ease exactly what should go where. It reminded me of his mechanical engineering degree.

The chest of drawers was coming together nicely until I got one of the drawers stuck on a runner and no matter how I tried I just couldn't quite get the angle right.

'Need a hand?'

Without thinking I looked up and the sight of those long-fingered, artistic hands caused a sudden flashback. I immediately blushed. His eyes regarded me steadily and for a moment I stared back. I saw his mouth tighten and I turned away, too embarrassed by his rejection to acknowledge that night and what had happened between us.

'No, it's fine,' I said matter-of-factly.

'No, it's not. Look the screw is sticking out, impinging on the drawer.' He started forward with a screwdriver.

I glared at him and snatched up my own screwdriver. 'It's fine, I can do it.'

His face softened. 'You don't like asking for help, do you?'

'Do you want to make a start on the next set of drawers?' I said, deliberately ignoring him. I didn't *need* his help. Although it had speeded things up considerably.

By the time Hilda called up the stairs, inviting us down for a break and homemade scones, we'd finished the chest of drawers and had started on Poppy's bed in the other room.

'Look, look, Auntie Claire. Look what we made.' Ava was dancing around the kitchen, her hair its usual tangled mess and her rumpled clothes dusted in white, grinning with delight as she pointed to the big, fat golden scones piled on a plate in the middle of the table.

'They look delicious.' I turned to Hilda. 'I'm very impressed. And you made a cake.'

I turned to the dark chocolate sponge cooling on a rack on the side.

'It wasn't easy. You're worse than Mother Hubbard and you need a tablecloth and some nice napkins. I'm going to take you to Dunelm Mill on Monday.'

'Yes, Hilda.' I gave her a penitent smile. Bless her, she had done her best with my bare cupboards. The table was laid with kitchen-towel serviettes and dinner plates because I didn't have such a thing as tea plates. I rarely entertained and when I did it was usually a shared takeaway with friends, most of whom, I reflected, were people I worked with. Karen, the HR Director at work, was possibly the closest thing I had to a friend. There weren't many women at my level at work and the women I met at networking events were usually as busy as I was. The occasional coffee rarely developed into any kind of friendship. Mary, Ellie and Jenna had been my housemates at uni; we'd had a blast living together in third year but once we'd started work, it had changed, especially as I'd moved north. Seeing them wasted – as I'd thought of it then – a whole weekend when I had so much to do at work. To be fair, Jenna had hung on the longest, even coming to see me a couple of times in Leeds, but when I couldn't make her wedding, she'd given up too. I didn't really blame her. Looking back, I realised I'd been a pretty crap friend. More than crap. How would I feel if someone said their job was more important than me? I felt a touch of shame. Poor Jenna, she definitely deserved better. I ought to send her a card, ask how she was doing.

'You can have the king's chair,' Ava said to Ash, pointing to my desk chair, which had been dragged from my little office room because I only had four chairs.

'Thank you.' Amusement danced on his face.

'Because you've got long hair and kings have long hair,' observed Ava, paying his dark curls close attention. 'You should get Auntie Claire to do plaits for you. She's getting quite good now.'

'I'll bear that in mind, next time I need some plaits.' Ash's grave nod towards the little girl, along with the quick smile he shot me warmed something inside me. Of course he was good with kids too. Just crap at texting, it seemed.

'Now, tea or coffee? I'd recommend tea because Claire only has instant rubbish.'

'I never have time to make proper coffee,' I protested.

'Hmph,' snorted Hilda. 'But at least she does have Yorkshire Tea. Even if I can't find hide nor hair of a teapot.'

'I'll have tea.' Ash wasn't doing a very good job of hiding his smirk. I don't know what he found so funny. How come he was suddenly so available when previously he'd managed to disappear from my life with magician-like ease?

———

The scones, when we all sat down, were delicious and with all the melted butter dripping down our fingers, additional pieces of kitchen towel were required.

'Yummy.' Ava beamed at Hilda.

'You'll have to give Auntie Claire the recipe,' said Poppy. 'They're really good.'

'Well they're so easy, a grown-up girl like you can make them by yourself. You practically made these and you have a lovely light touch. I'll give you the recipe, Poppy.' Hilda's eyes twinkled at Poppy, who beamed back, straightening with pride.

'I can make them for Mummy. And teach her how. She's not... she doesn't like cooking.'

'I'm growed up too,' said Ava, waving a crumbling scone about and scattering crumbs everywhere.

'You are but you mustn't touch the oven without Mummy

or Claire being with you. Next time I shall make you some homemade sausage rolls with my special flaky pastry.'

Next time. I hid my wince. Delicious as the scones were and as tantalising as the cake smelled, a washing-up fairy-godmother would have been quite welcome too. A cooking whirlwind had whipped through the kitchen leaving a sink full of dirty bowls, pools of congealing egg, and a fine dusting of flour all over the floor. I thought I was doing quite well adapting to the children's mess, but having Hilda about was really stretching my neat-freak tendencies thin.

I looked around. Everyone was happy – even Ash had a contemplative smile on his face as he leaned out of range of Ava's crumb storm. With the smell of cake and scones and a circle of people at my table, my kitchen felt positively cosy, and for some stupid unfathomable reason tears pricked at my eyes. It felt like a home. Hilda caught my eye with a warm, knowing smile before turning to answer another one of Ava's busy, random questions. I could get used to having a house full of people. I liked the warm glow it left around my heart. Today I'd been so busy that all those lurking, unwelcome feelings of inadequacy, anxiety, and failure had been firmly displaced.

I checked my watch. It was five o'clock. Still enough time to make the girls' bedrooms their own. With sudden determination, I stood up. Those rooms would be ready by bedtime. It was time this house was turned into a home.

'Are you guys okay for time?' I asked Hilda and Ash.

Ash didn't respond, just shrugged his shoulders, and in that second I knew as well as he did that he had nothing better to do with his Saturday night.

'I've got all the time in the world for these two cuties,' announced Hilda, putting an arm each around Poppy and Ava.

She was perfect grandmother-material and I wondered if she had any grandchildren of her own; she'd only ever mentioned her son and that was in passing.

'Okay, how about we do another couple of hours and then as a thank you for your help, I'll order in takeaway pizza for dinner?' There were a couple of flyers on top of the fridge that had come through the letterbox earlier in the week which I'd kept, never thinking I'd actually get around to using them.

'Yes,' said Ava with predictable enthusiasm. 'I love pizza.'

'I don't think I've ever had takeaway pizza.' Hilda clapped her hands together. 'A new adventure for me.'

'I'll need to get back for the dog unless you wouldn't mind me bringing him here. Poor bugger would enjoy the change of company.'

'Dog!' Poppy's ears pricked up.

I laughed. 'Remember the dog from the park, and I told you—'

'Hairy carpet dog?' Poppy's mouth twitched. Oh, she remembered all right. I'd told her that Hilda had bullied a man in the park into keeping him. She nodded and her eyes shone with pleasure when I said to Ash, 'Of course you can bring Bill.'

'Bill? That's what he's called?' Poppy tilted her head to one side, her eyes narrowing with sharp assessment. 'Why did you call him that?'

Ash lifted his shoulders. 'He seemed like a Bill to me. No nonsense. Ordinary, good bloke. He seemed like a bloke-ish sort of dog. Although I completely agree with you, he does resemble a hairy carpet, but it would be a bit of a mouthful, I think.'

Poppy bestowed one of her rare smiles on him. 'Yes. He is bloke-ish. Bill. That's just right for him.'

'I thought so.' Ash nodded at her and he shared one of his rare smiles with her. I had to turn away; he was a lot kinder than I would ever have imagined.

'Well, that's all sorted,' I said briskly. 'You go and collect the dog when we've ordered the pizzas.' I put the flyers on the table. 'Hilda, why don't you, Poppy, and Ava choose what you fancy. Ash, do you have any preferences?'

'As long as there's no tuna or pineapple on mine, I'm good.'

'Me too,' I said. 'They just aren't pizza.'

'We're agreed on something?' Ash raised that flaming eyebrow again.

'It would appear so.' I shot him a cool smile and then turned to Team Hilda. 'If you guys can decide on pizzas then, if you don't mind, Hilda, if you could be in charge of making up beds, putting on duvet covers and titivating, that would be great.'

'I'm a marvellous titivater,' said Hilda. 'When we had the antiques business I once helped Dame Judi buy a couple of Tiffany lamps for her house in London. And, of course, dear Diana was always asking for our best pieces for Kensington Palace, although you'd have thought the place would be chock-full of fabulous things already. Now girls, let's go and work some magic.'

She flounced ahead of me. In today's tracksuit of orange with two narrow stripes down each leg, she looked like a cross between a hockey mistress and a tangerine. Scooping up Poppy and Ava with her, she trotted up the stairs, leaving Ash and me staring bemusedly after her.

There were a lot of giggles and bumps coming from the room next door and every now and then Poppy would appear to rummage in the blue bags to retrieve another item. When I stopped for a quick loo break, the blue towels had been neatly arranged on the rail in the bathroom, the new toothbrush holder had replaced the old pint glass I'd used before and the handwash had been transferred into the pretty dark blue glass dispenser I'd picked up on a sudden whim.

'That's it,' said Ash, patting the top of the final chest of drawers, an hour and a half and two wardrobes later. Practice had made us much quicker. 'Where do you want it?'

'Next to the bed for the time being. I can put her bedside lamp on it. I'll get some more furniture in here later, but this was all I could carry today and even that was a performance.'

'Are we done?'

'On furniture building yes. I never want to see another Allen key again.'

'Me neither, although it's pretty good in here. I'll go and get Bill.'

'Have you finished?' Ava ran into the room, skipping through the abandoned cardboard, plastic, and polystyrene. I'd heard the three of them go downstairs a while ago, although Hilda had slipped back up to make up Poppy's bed. They'd been in charge of pizza ordering and I was hoping that Hilda had kept a rein on things. If left to her own devices, Ava would have ordered one of everything on the menu.

'Come see my room. Come see.'

Ash gathered up the rubbish and went downstairs while I

went into the room and immediately began to smile. 'Well doesn't this look fabulous.' It was a proper little girl's room.

'Fab-u-lous,' said Ava, running over to switch on the string of fairy lights interwoven in and around the wooden struts of her headboard. 'And see,' she turned the little bedside light off and on a couple of times.

I slid open a drawer, amazed to see that Hilda had done sterling work and had transferred Ava's clothes – although I couldn't imagine they'd stay this neat and tidy for very long.

'And all my babies like the new bed. Hilda says they like staying at the bottom better; they feel more settled because they can't fall off.' I'd thank Hilda for that later, I thought as I spotted Ava's soft toys had been retrieved and had been arranged at the end of the bed. That would make bedtimes a lot more manageable.

'Do you like it?' I asked.

'I lova, lova, lova it.' And she threw her arms around my waist. 'Thank you, Auntie Claire.'

'That's all right. I'm glad you like it so much.' I crouched down and gave her a squeeze; she smelled of cake and baking and I buried my nose in her fine curls, surprised by the sudden surge of protectiveness tightening my chest. I wanted to squidge her to me, hold her fast and not let go. For the second time that day, it occurred to me, *I could get used to this.*

Chapter Thirteen

'Well, that was very nice.' Hilda patted the roll of her tummy contained in the orange tracksuit like a neon sausage. 'A rare treat. And this is very nice wine. I do like a Malbec.'

I picked up my glass and toasted her and Ash, the girls having abandoned the table for *Dr Who* on the TV in the other room and insisted on taking Bill with them, who seemed to be lapping up the attention as well as Ava's greasy fingers. 'Thank you so much for all your help today. There's no way I could have done any of it without you. I really appreciate it.' I paused and gave a self-deprecating laugh. 'I'm not normally very good at asking for help.'

Ash rolled his eyes. 'Tell me about it.'

'Don't fret, dear, it's been our pleasure.' She gave Ash a reproving stare. 'I can't remember the last time I had so much fun. Those girls are a delight. I'd forgotten what it's like to be in a family home.'

'Noisy and chaotic,' I said, although to be honest today had been a lot of fun. Even Ash had chanced his arm and risked a few smiles; he may well have used up his quota.

'It's wonderful. Makes me feel alive again.' She rested her hand on her chin with a happy smile and with her other hand reached over and patted mine. There was a sharp contrast between my pale, smooth skin and hers, paper thin, stretched over a tracery of thick blue-green veins. It was difficult to tell how old Hilda was; you certainly wouldn't guess from the green sparkly gel nails she sported, but looking at her hands I wondered if she might be a lot older than she appeared.

I sneaked a peek at Ash; he wasn't smiling, but then again he wasn't frowning.

'More wine?'

'Yes, dear, that would be lovely and then when we've cleared these plates we can get down to business. Ash, would you mind stacking the dishwasher?'

I refilled our glasses and by the time I sat back down at the table, Hilda had cleared the decks, wiped the surfaces and produced a foolscap lined pad and a handful of pencils.

'I thought we could have a planning meeting.'

Ash's blank expression must have mirrored mine at first before we exchanged bemused frowns.

'What, dear Hilda, are we planning?' Ash's regal tone of long suffering had me pinching my lips together.

'Our parkrun, of course. Don't say you'd forgotten.'

Again, Ash and I exchanged a quick glance and he rolled his eyes.

Hilda sighed. 'And stop doing that, the pair of you.' She leaned over and clipped Ash behind the ear. 'I am neither dotty nor senile. It's a perfectly good idea and it will do both of you the world of good to get involved and do something. And after today, I'm even more convinced we're the people to do it.

'Claire, you're super organised; I can tell from the way you approached the shopping and how you lined up and arranged all the screws before you started building the furniture. Ash, you're clearly a completer-finisher. Given a task, you keep going and you get the job done. And I'm the ideas person. Together we make a perfect team. Churchstone needs a parkrun. I thought someone could talk to Sascha in the coffee place; I'm sure she'll think it's a good idea as we'll be encouraging more people to use the park.'

'Well, she'll certainly sell more coffee that way,' observed Ash dryly.

Hilda turned her head and lifted her chin, giving him a steely glare. He held his hands up in surrender.

'Claire?'

'I... well...' But actually, the idea was starting to sink in. Why not? She was right. Decorating the house wasn't going to take up all my time and I rather liked the idea of a brand-new challenge. Something I'd never done before. And it might be quite nice, when I was back at work, to have something outside the office to focus on. 'Like I said before, it can't hurt to find out what's involved.'

'Ash? You need something to occupy yourself.'

'Thank you, Hilda. But I don't need you interfering in my life.'

'Yes, you do.' She folded her arms with implacable certainty and I had to hide my face.

Ash rolled his eyes again. 'I'll help in the short term but as soon as...' He shrugged and Hilda nodded.

'Fine. Now, I think the first job is to do a parkrun and ask some questions.'

'I've got a better idea,' said Ash. 'I mentioned the parkrun idea to my brother and it turns out I have a cousin – no surprise really; I have dozens – anyway, Darren is very involved. Apparently he's a run director with the parkrun down in Tring. I spoke to him. We could go and do the run there.'

'Run director?' That sounded organised.

'Yeah, they're the person on the day who's in charge of the set up and running the show. They have overall responsibility for setting up the course and briefing all the volunteers like the marshals and timekeepers. Basically, operations manager for the run on the ground.'

Hilda clapped her hands and applauded him. 'You have been doing your homework.'

I'd envisioned an assortment of runners doing their own thing and trying to corral them into doing things properly. This sounded like proper organisation was involved. Suddenly I was much more interested. I missed the detailed planning and knowing exactly where I was at work. Being involved in the organisation of something was much more up my street.

'This is perfect. You should go and see him. Do the run and ask lots of questions,' said Hilda rubbing her hands. 'Where is Tring?'

'Hertfordshire. North of London. But the Porsche could do with a good run. Let me call him.' Ash jumped to his feet and went out into the garden. We watched as he walked up and down, ducking under the clothes airer, with his phone clamped to his ear.

'See. He already looks animated. Good-looking boy, too.'

146

I could tell her bird-bright eyes were focused on me and I deliberately kept mine on Ash's moving figure rather than meet them. While he might have improved physically, there was still that brittle veneer of bitterness that gave his words a bite every now and then, as well as the lost, distant air that made him retreat just when you thought the sun had broken through. What had happened to him to make him so different to how he had been before?

'Right, that's sorted.' He came back in, bringing the chill of the evening with him. 'My cousin has invited us to go down this Friday and do the parkrun on Saturday morning. A fact-finding trip.'

'Excellent, Claire. You'll have to go with him.'

'Me! I can't go!' Not with Ash. Not on my own. Not in a car with him. 'I've got the girls. My sister won't be back until Sunday.' And even that wasn't certain.

'I'll stay here with them,' said Hilda. 'I can't run 5k anyway. But it will be good training for both of you and it doesn't need three of us.'

'I can't leave the girls with you.'

'Why not? I'm perfectly compos mentis. They'll be safe.'

'I didn't mean that, Hilda. I meant, it's too much of an imposition.' I might not have known her for very long but I knew that my nieces couldn't be in safer hands.

'Imposition. Supposition. I offered. Besides, it will be fun. We can have movie night and I can bake cookies. And it'll be a night away from Drearyside. Freedom.'

Ash and Hilda looked at me, Ash with that bloody irritating lift of his eyebrow. First chance I got, I'd shave the bugger off – the thought of which made my lips twitch. Ash's eyes narrowed in suspicion but I just lifted my chin.

'Thank you for my room, Auntie Claire.' Tucked up in bed against the blue and white pillows with her thin arms and narrow face, holding her kindle like a prayer book, Poppy looked like a model for a saintly Victorian headstone.

'That's okay. I'm glad you like it. Both rooms have turned out really well.'

'Now you have to do the rest of the house.' There was a slight smile playing around her lips.

'What's wrong with my house?' I asked with mock indignation, knowing that my own bedroom seemed quite barren in comparison. One pitiful set of fairy lights did not transform four walls, a bed, a wardrobe, and a mirror into a boudoir.

'Nothing… except, it's a bit lonely in places, as if no one really lives here.'

Lonely was an interesting word, as if she'd ascribed the house a personality of its own. There was a lot going on in that young head.

'I'm afraid I just never got around to doing much to it. I never… I guess I never had much time.' Before the words had left my mouth, I knew they weren't true. Time, I had in spades, I just hadn't allocated it very well. Virtually all of it had been apportioned for my job and now I didn't have that excuse.

'Hilda will help you. She has lots of ideas.'

'She also wears orange tracksuits,' I pointed out with a pretend shudder. 'And buys lime-green towels.'

Poppy laughed. 'But she is very kind and she's really good at cooking. I never made a cake before. It was amazing. She let us do everything.'

'Never made a cake before?' I echoed. 'Not even with Nanny?'

Although, come to think of it, my mum wasn't much of a baker; she was a brilliant cook and presided over her kitchen, which was her pride and joy, like a dictatorial chef. She didn't make cakes, but she was a great one for going to M&S to buy really nice treats even when you were thirty-three and quarter.

'No, when we go to Nanny and Grandad's we usually do stuff. She takes us shopping for clothes and things or Grandad takes us to the cinema.' Poppy giggled. 'He really likes Pixar films. Have you seen *Onward*? Grandad took me and Ava three times.'

'Grandad always took me and your mum to the movies.' I smiled at the memory. 'I haven't been for ages. Perhaps we'll go tomorrow, if there's anything on.'

'Cool.'

'Would you mind if Hilda babysits next week? Have I told you about her parkrun idea?'

I explained what little I knew about the concept and that I was going on an investigative mission with Ash.

'Is he your boyfriend?'

'Ash? God no!' I said. 'I don't even know him. Well, only through Hilda.' I swallowed the lie painfully.

'Why don't you have a boyfriend? You're quite pretty, even without make-up. Is it because you don't want any children?'

I stared at her, a cold fist enclosing my heart. 'I never said that.'

'Alice'—it wasn't the first time she'd referred to her mother by name—'said it's because you're married to your job, which I don't understand because how can you marry something that isn't a person? I don't think you can even marry your dog, can you?' Her nose scrunched up rather adorably and I leaned over and kissed it with a smile, even though inside it hurt.

'It's an expression.' I scratched my chin. 'It means that your job comes first all the time. But I would like children one day… I just haven't met a nice man yet.' That was the child-friendly version of the truth. 'And no, you can't marry your dog.'

'Bill's lovely. If he were mine I'd still call him Hairy Carpet Dog. Do you think he can come again?'

'Hmm, Ash is only looking after him for the time being. A bit like I'm looking after you. It's just temporary.'

'Will he go back to his mummy then?'

'He'll have a new mum and dad, I think.' Worry etched tiny frown lines between her fine eyebrows. 'But the people at the rescue centre won't let him go anywhere he isn't loved.'

She sighed. 'That's good. I'd like a dog. Ava wants a puppy but I wouldn't mind a dog like Bill that needs a new home.' With a sudden wriggle, her head shot up and there was a light bulb gleam in her eyes 'Maybe we could have him… I mean, *you*. But me and Ava could come at weekends to see him. Then you wouldn't be on your own when we go home.'

I laughed. 'That would be lovely, except when I go back to work Bill would be on his own all day and then he would be lonely.'

When her face fell, a touch of guilt nagged at me for dousing her hopes. 'Sorry, sweetie. Maybe Bill can come for a sleepover when Ash and I go next Friday?'

'Awesome,' she breathed.

'And now it really is bedtime. Don't read for too long.' I ruffled the top of her head and dropped a quick kiss. 'Night, Poppy.'

'Night, Auntie Claire. And thank you for an ace day.'

I could kill Alice for being so careless with her daughters' love. She hadn't spoken to them for over a week now. Why hadn't she called this evening?

Poppy was such a good kid. In some ways, a lot easier than her sister, whose mercurial moods careered between high and low and needed careful management. Ava was the spoiled baby of the family – a little too much like Alice in many ways. I carried the warmth of Poppy's brilliant smile all the way down the stairs with me and when I got to the bottom, I suddenly found myself looking forward to the week ahead.

Chapter Fourteen

'Will you stop fussing?' Hilda rolled her eyes at me as she nursed a cup of coffee from the brand-new Nespresso coffee machine where she sat at my kitchen table which was now covered in a cheerful oil-cloth decorated with chirpy chickens. I was tapping my pencil against my pad.

'Sorry. It just feels like I'm abdicating my responsibilities by leaving the girls when I'm supposed to be in charge of them.' Especially as I still couldn't get hold of Alice. It was now Tuesday and I hadn't heard a peep out of her. I'd even sent a long email to my parents in desperation, asking them to call her and tell her to ring her daughters.

The planned trip to Tring was just one of the things to arrange on my lengthy list. I was sceptical we'd make it happen or that there would be any real interest but when I'd researched the parkrun website, I'd been staggered by just how big and successful the whole thing was. The more I read, the more impressed I was. There were over one thousand events in twenty-two countries and six million registered runners. My first job was to get permission to use the park, which was already proving tricky but I was prepared to give it a go. That might have been down to post-shopping euphoria this morning.

Honestly, Hilda was costing me a fortune, although my kitchen was much homelier with an initial colour scheme that was nothing like the stylish, sophistication I'd daydreamed of. Following a trip to Dunelm Mill on the outskirts of the town, I was now the owner of a new set of chunky Emma Bridgewater-style china, including a tea pot, utensil pot and a butter dish and six new painted wooden chairs in a soft sage-green which co-ordinated with the chickens on the table cloth. On the seats were padded chair cushions with more chickens and tucked away in the cupboards were various essential baking items including a new electric whisk, bun trays, cookie cutters, and cake tins.

Soft warming colours plus cute poultry wasn't quite the style I'd envisioned for myself but I'd had a change of heart and realised that cosy was so much more inviting and would be much cheerier to live with. The house was turning into a place in which I wanted to spend time, instead of a place to sleep between office hours. The realisation brought an unwelcome nudge of shame. How had I managed to let my life outside work matter so little?

'I've had my own child and four husbands for goodness' sake.' Hilda's words broke my reverie and I turned back to her. 'You can trust me with Ava and Poppy. We're going to have so much fun.'

Maybe it was the fun part that worried me.

'Four?' I sipped my coffee and sighed as the rich flavour hit my tongue. Why had I waited so long to get myself a decent coffee machine?

'Yes, although Frank – he was number three – wasn't official; we never married but everyone thought we were, until his wife turned up at the funeral. Was a surprise to me too.' Her greying eyebrows beetled up to her hairline in exaggerated horror. 'Had one hell of a battle proving that the house was mine. She wanted half. Cheeky madam. I very nearly deeded the house to my son so she couldn't get her mitts on it. Glad I didn't now. He'd have sold it and put me in a home years ago. I'd have died of boredom long before now.'

'How old is your son?' I asked, curiosity getting the better of me. She never talked about him.

'He's nearly forty-six. I had him quite late. Now, husband number two, he was interesting.' She grinned like a mischievous imp. 'Not as handsome as my first but a lot more fun. Actually, quite naughty as it turned out. He ran an antiques business but I heard, a few years after he died, mind, that he'd had a thriving side-line in forgery. Good job I sold the Monet before that came out.'

I blinked but she blithely carried on, so I guessed she was joking.

'I got it in the divorce settlement. This really is very good coffee.' She rose and began putting a fresh capsule in the machine.

'I thought you weren't supposed to have coffee. I don't want to be responsible for making you ill.'

'Oh, pish. Do I look unwell? They do fuss so at the old people's home. Why do you think I spend so much time in the park?' She patted her hair. 'Although, I ought to go to the hairdresser's before I pick the girls up from school on Friday. I don't want anyone thinking you've left them with some batty old lady.'

I laughed. 'It's going to take more than a set and blow dry to convince anyone.'

'You're probably right, dear.' Her smile was placid. 'I'll wear my best tracksuit. The white one with the red go-faster stripes down the side.'

'I don't think I've seen that one.'

'No, probably not. I save it for special occasions.'

I bit my lips trying to suppress a giggle as my mind goggled at what sort of special occasion merited an Adidas-style tracksuit.

'Are you sure you don't mind?' Ash and I were heading off mid-morning on Friday – his idea – to beat the worst of the traffic. It made sense but it meant spending more time with him, which had given me a few sleepless hours last night as I'd be leaving the girls with Hilda for a whole twenty-four hours. We were unlikely to get back before mid-afternoon on the Saturday. That was a lot of time to spend with someone you'd once slept with when the two of you were pretending it had never happened. The bloody sod owed me an explanation.

'We're going to have a lovely time. Lots of baking. Now, how are you getting on with the council and whether we can use the park?'

'Going round in circles,' I groaned. 'It's nuts. I spent yesterday on the phone. You can't actually speak to a real live person. All you get is press one for this and two for that, which is fine but none of them fit what I want and then the flipping thing goes dead. And I've tried online and sent various emails and no one has got back to me yet.' Now that I had identified specific tasks, I was focused on achieving those rather than worrying about whether the whole project was actually viable. At least I could show Hilda I was doing something even if I wasn't convinced it would ever come to anything.

'Typical. And that's what we pay our taxes for. What else have you done?'

'I've been on the parkrun website and found out a bit more. There are local ambassadors who can help, but until we get permission to use the park, we can't do anything. It's all a bit chicken-and-egg. And we're going to need lots of volunteers.'

'That won't be a problem,' said Hilda complacently.

I wasn't so sure about that. 'I don't even know where to start.'

'Why don't you go and see Sascha in The Friendly Bean?' Hilda had a Machiavellian glint in her eye. 'Just think of all the extra custom a parkrun would bring her.'

Hmm, twenty people and a dog, I thought, but I had to admit it was a good idea.

'Okay, perhaps I can ask her to put a poster up. Invite people to a meeting. Find out what sort of interest there might be.'

'She's a sound young woman. There was some scandal about her a while back but I don't listen to that sort of tittle tattle. Honestly, the old dears at Sunnyside have nothing better to do. Gets right on my tits it does.'

'Hilda!' I laughed.

'Claire. I can say far worse, you mark my words. And you should hear the Queen. When we used to dog-sit the corgis when she went away – that was my first husband and I; he was very well connected you know – we always had tea with her. She can swear like a dozen troopers.'

'Really?' I was beginning to think that some of Hilda's

more colourful anecdotes might be grossly fabricated, or at the least somewhat over-embellished.

'Shame I can't come with you to see Sascha but I need to show my face at Sunnyside, make sure they know I'm still alive or they'll be ringing my son and that's the last thing I want.' With that, she picked up her silver lamé messenger bag and disappeared out of the kitchen with her usual cheery, 'Toodle-pip.'

I sat at the kitchen table feeling silence settle on the house and that sense of shame came nudging its way back. I'd neglected so many parts of my life, but Hilda bulldozing her way in had brought sunshine into so many of the dark corners. Even now, thinking about her and all her husbands brought a wry smile to my face. She wouldn't have let Ash get away with ignoring her; she'd have taken the proverbial bull by the horns and given it a damn good shake. I straightened my shoulders and lifted my chin. Which was exactly what he deserved.

Birds were singing their little hearts out as I walked across the park, passing beds filled with tightly packed flowers of pink and white. Spring was definitely running into summer and the sycamore trees shading this part of the path were vibrant with dark green leaves. I slipped off my cardigan to feel the sun on my skin and slowed my pace to enjoy a rare sense of peace.

I'd always lived life at a hundred miles an hour, taking on as much as I could and trying to make sure everything was perfect, which invariably meant I was always running late or trying to catch up with myself. It suddenly struck me, why did I set myself so many goals all the time? And why was I always desperate to be the best I could be? Was it because Alice had been such a trial to my parents so I would always make sure I was never a problem, especially after she got pregnant, when they had enough to worry about? No, even before then I'd learned to be self-sufficient, and because I was academically able I was left to get on with things. But I'd still wanted their attention; I guess that was where my over-achieving and determination to do well had come in.

It had become a self-fulfilling cycle and now an ingrained habit. *No wonder I'd become so stressed.* There, I'd finally admitted it. In the last week, that feeling of being on the cliff edge of catastrophe had finally dissipated. Now, as I walked slowly in the sunshine, I realised that I *had* been stressed. Ridiculously so.

The realisation was like letting all the air out of a balloon. I didn't need to be anywhere by any particular time. The knowledge was hugely liberating. Time was my own to command.

There was absolutely no hurry to get to The Friendly Bean, so I sat down on one of the park benches, taking a minute to sit back and close my eyes, enjoying the sun's warmth on my face and my bare arms. I'd actually put on a dress for this meeting because I found the brusque, businesslike Sascha a little intimidating, which was ridiculous really because at work I was used to dealing with far more high-powered people. It was symptomatic of how much self-confidence I'd lost since I'd been officially told that I wasn't capable of doing my job. I bloody hated that stress diagnosis. It had robbed me of so much. Maybe it was time I started fighting back.

After five minutes, I got to my feet. At the worst, Sascha could say no. But she could also say yes. Hilda's upbeat, can-do attitude with her refusal to consider any of the obstacles I kept raising, had definitely rubbed off on me this morning. Feeling more positive than I had for a very long time, I headed for the café.

When I pushed open the door of The Friendly Bean, there were only a couple of people in there and Sascha's scarf was a vivid rainbow of blues, violets, pinks, and fresh greens, reflecting the colours bursting to life out in the park.

'Hi,' I said.

'Not running today, then,' Sascha nodded towards my outfit.

'No...' I grinned at her. 'Wanted to appear more professional. Have you got a few minutes?'

At this, her sculpted pierced brow rose. 'Are you hoping for a job?'

'No,' I said firmly. 'I want to run an idea by you... to do with the park.'

'Sure. Coffee?'

'Cappuccino, please.'

With experienced barista expertise she whistled up two coffees and as she poured the frothed milk in them she nodded towards the purse in my hand with a shake of her head. 'On the house.'

We sat in the same corner I'd sat in with Alice weeks ago and like a curtain being pulled back, it made me think how much things had changed in that short space of time. The world seemed clearer and brighter and I'd lost that lethargic fug and sensation of dragging my limbs into action. I think it had a lot to do with the running. It gave me a sense of purpose each morning and a goal to strive for. I could almost run a whole 4k now without stopping.

'You okay?' asked the other woman.

'Yeah, yeah, fine.'

'So, what do you want to ask me? If it's about installing outside heaters, it's a no. And if you're trying to sell me environmentally-friendly coffee cups, I'm already on the case. I'm quite happy with my coffee supplier and my sister makes all my cakes. Anything else you've got, I'll listen to.'

'Accountancy services?' I offered laughing.

'My dad.'

'Good because I'm not trying to sell you anything.'

'Thank fuck for that, because I needed a break and you gave me a good excuse to get off my feet. I didn't want to have to cut it short. So, what do you want?'

'A group of us'—that sounded a heck of a lot better than me, an old woman, one man and his dog—'are thinking about setting up a parkrun here, in the park obviously, and I wanted to know if you would help us publicise it by putting up a poster… and I wondered if you might consider letting us use the café to hold a meeting. We need to gather together local volunteers and find out if people would be interested.'

'A parkrun?' Her features sharpened. 'Like the one in Harrogate? My sister's boyfriend goes over every Saturday, rain or shine.'

'Does he?' I said. 'That's a bit of a hike.'

'Bloody loves it, he does. Says it's quite a thing. About five hundred people every Saturday.'

'Really? That many? Wow.' I sat there trying to get my head around the figure. Five hundred people was a lot. 'We're certainly not expecting that many here.'

'Why not? Harrogate's a good forty minutes away. Plenty of folk round here might prefer to run local. And from what

I've heard from Steve, they like to mix it up, visit other parkruns. Tourists, they call themselves.'

'I've no idea what sort of interest there'll be around here.'

'I think you might be surprised.'

'Well, before we even get it off the ground, we need to find out what the interest is and whether we can round up enough people who are willing to help. But first of all, I need to find out if the council will let us use the park and I'm going round in circles. I don't suppose you've got any idea who I might contact at the council?'

Sascha gave a quick dry bark of a laugh. 'Yes. Neil Blenkinsop… yes, that's his name and yes, he's a bit of drip, but a nice enough bloke. Doesn't give me any bother. He's Director of Parks and Leisure.' She dug out a battered leather address book from her pocket and thumbed through the pages. 'Here you go.'

I tapped the number straight into my phone. She eyed it with derision, I noticed.

'So would you put a poster up?'

"Course. No problem. And I'll open up one evening for you to hold a meeting. I might even lay out refreshments.' She grinned.

'Would you?' I stared at her with surprise. 'That's very kind of you.'

'Kind? You think? Where are all those runners going to come for a nice energy-reviving brownie and hot drink after their run? I think I'll call it the Saturday Morning Parkrun Special.'

'There's no guarantee we'll get it off the ground,' I warned, not wanting her to get too carried away.

'Well, you won't if you don't try. Everyone said I'd not

make a go of this when I first started and now look. Now, when are you thinking about holding this meeting?'

'Er… I'm… well…' That involved making proper plans. 'I need to find out if we can use the park first.'

'Phone him now.'

'And I have to have it in writing.'

'Phone him. Isn't that why people carry those things around with them?' She dipped her head with disdain towards my mobile.

'I guess.' I shrugged, realising that I was going to have to make the call there and then.

It was answered on the second ring.

'Neil Blenkinsop.'

'Hi, Mr Blenkinsop, I wonder if you can help me. Sascha at The Friendly Bean has given me your number.'

'Oh,' he said and I got a quick impression of apprehension and resignation. 'How can I help?' he asked in a dry voice.

'Well, we're interested in setting up a parkrun and I wondered how we would go about applying for permission to hold it in Victoria Park.'

'A parkrun? In Victoria Park? In Churchstone?'

'Yes,' I said, trying to inject enthusiastic encouragement in response to his flat tone.

'A 5k run?'

'Yes,' I said.

'Hmm, that's very interesting.' There was a long pause during which my heart began to sink; maybe I should have done this face to face; maybe I should have prepared a bit more of a pitch. 'When would you want to do it?'

'Well, it would be a weekly event. Every Saturday morning.'

'Have you spoken to the Churchstone Harriers?' The abrupt change of subject and his sharpened voice startled me.

'Er, no. I don't know them.'

'Local running club. They go out on Wednesday nights. You should give Charles Engwell a call. He's the chairman. He'll help you. They have a Facebook page. Can you email me a proposal, as soon as?'

'Yes,' I said, casting widening eyes towards Sascha, surprised by this decisiveness.

'There's a town council meeting next Tuesday. Seven o'clock. I can put it on the agenda... but if you contact the harriers and other local runners they could come to the meeting and support the proposal.'

'You... mean you support the idea?'

There was a loud huff on the other end of the line. 'Victoria Park is one of the jewels in the crown of the Dower Dale district council but is currently underutilised. We have one of the most beautiful bandstands in all the country and I can't remember the last time a brass band set foot in it. It's a tragedy. I think most of the footfall in the park, apart from a few dog walkers, are customers of Sascha Comely's establishment. All the children prefer to go to the indoor adventure place while their parents drink in the pub. The council has been assessing various initiatives to encourage people to exercise more; I think this would kill several ducks with one well-placed stone.'

By the time I'd put down my phone, I was feeling quite swept away by his businesslike enthusiasm.

'Well, that was helpful.'

'Blimey O'Riley. You've just discovered what turns Neil Blenkinsop on. Never heard him so popping before.'

'That's popping?'

'Positively for him. Dry old stick normally. Although, come to think of it, I think I read in the parish magazine that he did the Great North Run last year, so I'm guessing you ticked one of his boxes.'

I suddenly realised that in all probability, I'd just cleared the biggest hurdle and that the parkrun might just happen.

Chapter Fifteen

'Have a lovely time,' said Hilda, sticking her head in through the window. Bill promptly tried to do the same, his nose just cresting the top of the wound-down glass, both paws resting on the door. 'Are you sure you've got everything?'

That comment was a bit rich given she'd arrived after lunch with a solitary carrier bag perched on her lap when Ash had picked her up from the home. It had looked as if she'd brought nothing more than a toothbrush with her.

'We're not going on holiday,' I pointed out, already regretting signing up for this trip. What on earth was I going to talk to Ash about for three and half hours, when I had only one burning question and it was the one I refused to ask?

'A change of scene is as good as a rest. It will do both of you good to get away for a night. Who knows, you might even find you like each other after all.'

'Thanks, Hilda,' I said, glowering at her as she beamed at me, all sparkly and winsome as if she were our personal matchmaking fairy-godmother. If only she knew what had happened with him before. I bet she wouldn't be quite so keen to treat him like her favourite grandson.

I heard Ash growl under his breath. Normal service had resumed. Although why he disliked me so much when once upon a time he'd given off such different vibes, I had no idea.

The first ten minutes passed in silence and he shot me a couple of apprehensive glances. As well he might. I was still mentally rehearsing and in no hurry. After all, we had three hours to kill

'Warm enough?' asked Ash, fiddling with the heater. 'You can turn on the heated seat if you get cold.'

'No, I'm fine.' I adjusted my sunglasses; it was another bright spring morning. 'The idea of toying with him, like a cat with a mouse, rather appealed. Let him stew a while.

We lapsed into silence which lasted until we hit the A1M. It was no good; I couldn't sit on it.

'So, Ashwin Laghari, what happened?'

He sighed and shot me a wary glance. 'I owe you an apology.'

'What, and you've only just realised that now?' I snapped, pissed off at his attitude. 'You owe me a hell of a lot more than that. One minute it's all fun frolics and flirty texts. The next a resounding silence. Classy.'

He winced, his hands gripping the steering wheel. 'You're right. It wasn't. I'm sorry. You didn't deserve that.'

'Are you always that much of a bastard?' I enjoyed tossing the words at him, finally releasing the pent-up frustration and anger from the weeks during which I'd checked my texts and agonised over why he had gone quiet on me while cursing over what a fool I'd made of myself.

His jaw clenched.

Good. Before he could say anything, I carried on. 'I'll give you one thing; you're one hell of an actor.' I couldn't bring myself to admit that I'd believed there was a real spark between us. 'Took me right in. Is that a regular thing you do? Or do you keep it for chance encounters on the train?'

His eyes stayed glued to the road ahead but I could see him swallowing.

'Would you believe me if I said it wasn't an act? That night was—'

'Whatever it was, you had a very short memory.'

'I lost my job.' The quiet admission stopped me in my tracks. 'On the Monday. It was totally out of the blue.'

'And what? It robbed you of your ability to text or pick up the phone? You could have at least said something had come up. It still would have been crap but not half as crap as just not bothering.'

I studied his grim profile, the locked jaw, and the steady gaze at the road ahead. I'd wondered why he wasn't working but had assumed he was between jobs, on gardening leave – the usual run of events with high flyers – and like me had just temporarily lost his sense of purpose. Now I'd voiced some of my anger, I felt a touch of sympathy.

'You're right but it…' There was another long pause. 'How did you feel when you were signed off with stress?'

'What?'

'How did you feel? What went wrong?'

'I'm not ashamed of it,' I snapped, feeling wrong-footed. This was supposed to be about him. I kept my eyes fixed on one of the blue motorway signs announcing the next junction.

'Yes, you are.'

He was right. I was deeply ashamed. Everyone at work must know by now. I probably wouldn't be able to get a job anywhere else and at work they'd be constantly watching me. Could I be trusted with important work and decisions in the future? Would I crack again? Would everyone be watching for signs of weakness? I wouldn't be the golden girl any more. The person people went to for a second opinion, the one they deferred to in strategy and planning meetings. Would anyone respect me anymore? I'd lost who I was – cool, calm-under-pressure Claire. There was no chance of making partner now if I couldn't handle a bit of extra work.

'People like me aren't supposed to get stress.'

'I know,' said Ash quietly and I shot him a startled but appreciative glance. I preferred honesty to platitudes. 'But you did… because you're human. It's the body's way of saying, *stop, slow down*. Yes, everyone will know at work. You can't escape that, but you can own it, be honest about it, accept it, and work out how you'll do things differently from now on. People will respect that far more than if you try and pretend it didn't happen or treat it like it's a big secret. And isn't that how you normally conduct yourself at work? Successful managers don't shy away from difficult decisions; they own up to mistakes and put them right; they tackle difficult issues; they're honest with their colleagues. That's how you earn respect. Don't hide from this Claire, learn from it.'

'I never thought it would happen to me,' I said quietly, but gosh, he was right. What he'd said was exactly what I would have advised to someone else in the same position when I was being clear sighted and thinking straight… and I hated hearing it from him of all people.

'At least you've not been fired.'

'What happened?' I asked.

'I was sacked. Although they called it redundancy.' His voice was bitter. 'And now I can't get another job. No one wants someone who's been sacked.'

'Redundancy is very different from being sacked,' I pointed out, still annoyed that he'd made me talk about my stress. 'Haven't you been offered outplacement services? Most decent companies provide them as part of the redundancy package.'

'Unfortunately, it turned out I didn't work for a decent company, which is why I was "made redundant".' With one hand he signified the speech marks around the words. 'Turns out, doing the right thing is the wrong thing.'

'You're talking in riddles. What did you do?' Irritated, I shifted in my seat, crossing my legs in the footwell.

He let out a mirthless laugh. 'You really want to know?'

'Yes.'

'There was a case going through the courts. A colleague of mine, Marine Barnier. She took the company to tribunal over unequal pay. She was paid £30k less than other colleagues who were all men. I was one of them. Her bonuses were also a fraction of ours.'

'Ouch. That's terrible and it shouldn't be allowed to happen.'

'Yeah. I liked her. Smart, tough cookie who deserved better. I said I'd back her when she said she was going to HR. I thought it would be a quick, easy win. Never dreamed it would go to tribunal. Even though they didn't have a leg to stand on, the company dug its heels in. Wouldn't play ball, so she had to go the whole hog.' He paused and pulled a face. 'I was called as a witness. All I had to do was describe the job I did. Which I did, under oath. I would have done it either way but I should have realised it was career suicide. My own dumb arrogance. I thought I was a valuable asset. Clearly not.'

'But the company can't get rid of you because of that.'

'Technically, legally, morally, no… but the day after Marine won the case, there was a reorganisation. Next day, I was made redundant.'

'But they can't do that. They have to give you notice that your job is at risk and go through due process. There are procedures and policies that they have to follow.'

'Not if you want a decent pay off and a reference. Basically, if I accepted the terms – a massive bribe, if you will – I had to walk that day.'

'That's so shitty.' Although it still didn't excuse him not texting.

'Super shitty as they also put the word out. Everyone knows everyone. I worked there twelve years. Not one arse contacted me. They were all too scared of it being catching. And it's all about contacts.' With a quick turn of the steering wheel, he pulled out into the fast lane to overtake, the sudden rush of acceleration pinning me back into my seat. 'I've applied for dozens of jobs. Most of the time I don't even get a response, let alone an interview. I've contacted a score of people on LinkedIn and guess what, I'm suddenly a social pariah.'

'That's crap,' I said, horrified. 'Surely something will come up.' But that was a hopeless platitude. What did I know? I'd not been out in the job market for years. How would I feel? It was bad enough being signed off at the moment. I might be unemployable myself.

'Easy for you to say that.'

'I'm sorry…' I flicked a glance at the overgrown beard and

long hair. And then I really was sorry because I understood exactly how he felt.

'How are you feeling?' I paused, tentative because I knew that if it hadn't been for the cut on my arm, I'd have had to be dragged to the doctors. 'Perhaps… you ought to see a doctor.'

The sudden tightening of his eyes told me everything.

'I can't see how that will help unless they're doubling as recruitment consultants these days?' he asked with a low buzz of menace in his voice. Menace was good. Emotion was good. I'd got a bit too used to him being a lifeless husk. Maybe he needed goading to actually feel something.

I risked being burned. 'Well maybe you are… a bit down. I didn't realise how on edge I was until I went to see a doctor.' And in that moment I realised that it had been a relief to be told there was something wrong with me, that I wasn't going quietly mad in my own head.

'No shit, Sherlock. Of course I'm down. I lost my job. But a doctor isn't going to fix that.'

'Maybe it's worth talking to one, though. What about your sister? Maybe she could help.'

'What, get me a job as a hospital porter? Now there's an idea.'

'It's called being practical and trying to provide a solution. But it's fine; you carry on feeling sorry for yourself instead.'

For a moment, I thought maybe I'd gone too far but then he spat out a humourless laugh.

'We're a right pair. They could probably name some trendy jeans brand after us, Stressed and Depressed. And yes, before you jump on it, I was depressed. I'm starting to feel better now. The running helps. And bloody Hilda poking me in the stomach. I was determined to sort myself out then.

Probably the six cans of lager I was drinking every night didn't help.'

I smiled. 'She can be rather direct.'

'Bloody rude, you mean, but it's very entertaining. I am sorry I never texted. It was nothing to do with the date and everything to do with me feeling sorry for myself. I treated you badly and I do regret it.' He shot me a small, sad smile.

And where did that leave us now, I wondered. Still very much in the wrong place and time.

'And ironically, you're the last person to deserve it. You're the only person who's asked how I'm feeling since I was made redundant.'

'I can't be. What about friends and family?'

I saw him wrinkle his nose. 'I haven't actually told my family. Remember, high achievers all round. I was already the loser because I don't have a "proper" profession. Luckily my folks are away in India for a few months. My sister works such long hours that I get away with the odd text and my brother is far too busy and important to bother with me.'

'Friends?'

'Funny, they tend to melt away when you can't afford to dish out for overpriced continental lager. Splashing the cash loses its appeal when you don't know if you'll still be able to pay your mortgage in a year's time. I got a good pay off... but with jobs not forthcoming, I realised I needed to be careful and that they weren't such great mates after all.'

I rubbed a finger back and forth along the line of my eyebrow. I could relate to that.

Was it any easier if friendships died slowly through neglect or overnight when the rug was pulled out?

'At least we've got Hilda,' I said.

'Pitiful isn't it, two thirty-somethings reliant on a septuagenarian.'

Ash tossed his hair, making me smile. I really did prefer his longer hair and the way it softened the sharp angles of his face.

'Or something to be celebrated.' Hilda had certainly brought some fun and light into my life in the last week. 'Saturday was fun. Better than eating pizza on your own. Who says friends have to be of the same generation?'

Ash didn't say anything for a second or two, giving the impression he was carefully weighing up what I'd said.

'But would we have given her the time of day in the park if we were our previous busy, fulfilled, career-driven high-flying selves?' He took his eyes off the road to dart a sharp glance at me.

'That doesn't make either of us sound particularly nice, does it?'

'No, it doesn't. And there are thousands of lonely old people out there. Not even old, in some cases. Just lonely.'

Both of us lapsed into thought. He was right. Despite work, I'd been lonely for a long time. Moving to Churchstone, I realised, had been a subconscious effort to do something about it, even if it had been totally unrealistic. You had to put some effort in to make and keep friends. Not having a job or going to work certainly brought the flaws in one's life into sharp relief.

Is he as lonely as I am?

'I've been worrying about recruiting volunteers to help with the parkrun, but maybe that's an angle we can tap into. Invite people to get involved. They don't have to run; they can be marshals and all sorts of other things. We're going to need quite a few people and a hardcore, committed team if we're going to sustain it.'

'Sounds like you've been reading up.'

'Hilda has. She's the original silver surfer. Keeps sending me links. Yesterday it was to a blog post entitled, *How to Start a Park Run*. It was quite helpful. Did I tell you I spoke to the council guy?'

I relayed my conversation with Neil Blenkinsop.

'And the Harriers chap is really interested and keen to meet up as soon as possible. Sascha at The Friendly Bean has said we can use the café as our headquarters, if we like.'

'You've made good progress in a week.'

'Hmm, I seem to have been caught up in Hilda's tidal wave. And…' I shrugged, I was enjoying getting involved in something. Once the girls had gone, life was going to be very quiet. I'd got used to them filling a hole in my big, empty house. To my sudden disquiet I realised I wasn't looking forward to them going home at all. I was going to miss them.

Chapter Sixteen

T ring was a pretty place nestled high up on the Chilterns, although at that point we were yet to appreciate just how high up on the Chilterns it was. Darren's house was an end-of-terrace tucked away in one of the narrow streets in the conservation area.

'Hey man,' he greeted Ash at the door. 'What's this?' He tugged at Ash's beard. 'Hipster.'

I kept my laugh to myself; a Hipster channelling Grizzly Adams, perhaps.

'Daz, man.' They clasped hands in typical manly fashion before clapping each other on the back. 'This is Claire.'

'Hi, welcome. Come on in.' He had the lean, lanky build of a runner with pale skin and a rash of freckles running across almost skeletal cheekbones but he also a broad, open smile as he ushered us into the house with friendly ease. The difference between the two cousins was marked. Darren was as open and approachable as Ash was closed off and self-sufficient.

We stepped immediately from the threshold into an open-plan living room and kitchen. It was surprisingly bright and modern with polished wooden floors, the sort of bachelor-sized TV screen you'd expect, a pair of Scandi retro-style two-seater sofas and a breakfast bar with three stools which created a divide between the modern, glossy burgundy kitchen cabinets. On a table tucked under the stairs was an open laptop and the sort of detritus signifying someone working from home.

'I've got a few things to finish up and then I'll be right with you. Tea? Coffee?' he asked over his shoulder as he skirted the breakfast bar. 'And I thought we'd go to the pub for dinner. It's just around the corner; they do good food and great beer.' He grinned. 'Although I stick to one pint on a Friday night these days.'

'Bloody hell. Whatever happened?'

'Parkrun, mate. It's hard enough without six pints sloshing around in your belly. Why don't you take your bags up while I put the kettle on? You're at the top of the stairs on the right. You can't get lost. Oh, and when you use the loo, you have to take the lid off the cistern to fiddle with the ballcock; it's not working properly.'

Ash rolled his eyes and muttered something uncomplimentary about his cousin.

After putting in our respective drinks orders, I carefully avoided looking at Ash as we picked up our bags and went up the staircase leading from the lounge.

There was no missing the layout upstairs. One bathroom and two bedrooms.

Ash pushed open the door to a bedroom into which a double bed had just about been squeezed. A small double bed at that. One side was tucked into the wall under a window, while the other boasted a cardboard box with an Anglepoise light on it. Safe to say, Darren didn't entertain that often.

We both stared at the bed.

'Romcom moment,' said Ash. 'Looks like I'll be sleeping on the sofa.'

Closing my eyes, I sighed. 'Did you see the size of them? For goodness' sake, we're grown adults. It's hardly going to kill us sharing a bed.' I was not going to be the one to point out that we'd done it before. 'And don't you dare do the eyebrow thing.'

'What eyebrow thing?'

'The one where you're all cocky and superior. If you want to sleep on the sofa, be my guest. If you want to sleep here, I'm not some Victorian miss who's going to have the vapours. Sharing the bed is practical.'

'It is... and it's not as if we haven't done it before.' Sure enough, that flipping eyebrow cocked.

'You just had to bring it up, didn't you?' I shot him a withering glare. Annoyingly, he just grinned at me.

'Just checking you hadn't forgotten. Sure you can keep your hands off me?'

'Forgotten?' I tried to be cool while inside I was heating up at the very memory of what he could do with a well-placed kiss. 'Forgotten what?'

He grinned. 'Need a reminder?'

'No, thank you,' I said primly. 'Once was quite enough and that beard is a contraceptive in its own right. No one is going to get close enough to kiss you with that thing.'

He ducked his head but not before I saw the sudden tightening of his face and I wished I could take the words back. I'd meant them to be funny but I'd clearly struck a nerve.

The cocky attitude dropped and he scowled at me.

I felt a little ashamed of myself, especially now I realised that the loss of his job had affected him the same way as me being diagnosed with stress had affected me. The beard was as much a symbol of neglect as it was a lack of self-worth, and having listened to him in the car, I should have had a lot more sympathy.

'Sorry, that wasn't a very nice thing to say.' He turned away and I gripped his arm. 'Ash, I'm sorry. The beard bugs me. You're a good-looking guy; you shouldn't hide behind it. You've got nothing to be ashamed of.'

'Thank you, Miss Harrison. Is this amateur-psychology half-hour?'

'Why do you push people away all the time? I'm trying to be nice.'

He pushed a hand through his unruly hair but didn't meet my steady gaze 'Sorry. Which side do you want?'

'I'll take the right-hand side.' I didn't want to be squashed up against the wall.

'Right.'

It was as much of a peace offering as I was going to get.

He wheeled round and went into the bathroom and when I went out into the tiny hallway, I saw he had taken the lid of the cistern off and was fiddling with the inside workings.

He glanced up. 'Could you go and ask Darren for a tool box?'

'Sure. Can you fix it?'

'Just needs a small adjustment. He's an idiot.'

'Shall I tell him that?'

I returned a minute later with a tatty Sainsbury's carrier bag which held a pitiful collection of assorted screwdrivers, two hammers, a pair of pliers and a spanner and handed it over with a rueful grimace.

'That's it?'

'Don't shoot the messenger.' I held up my hands and he pursed his mouth, removing a screwdriver. I've no idea what he was doing but for some reason I stayed to watch as his hands deftly worked and within ten minutes he sat back on his heels.

'That should do the trick.'

'You've fixed it?' Admiration bubbled beneath the surface of my words.

'It's not rocket science.'

'No, it's plumbing and I always leave it to the experts.'

In our house we'd always had to call in a man-who-can. My Dad's DIY skills stopped at painting and decorating and even then my mother complained about the wonky wallpaper in the spare bedroom.

He shrugged and closed the cistern lid. 'Darren needs a decent set of tools. Could do with a new washer in there but I've cleaned the limescale off the old one; it'll do for the time being.'

I couldn't help being impressed and remembered how brilliant he'd been at assembling the girls' new furniture last weekend. 'Have you always been good with your hands?' As soon as I said it and he smiled slyly, I knew I'd made a tactical error. Talk about a Freudian slip; I'd walked right into that one.

'Why don't *you* tell *me*?' He shot me that challenging stare I remembered so well from when we'd first met and a certain part of my anatomy flooded with heat. Oh, he was good with his hands all right and he bloody knew it. Despite the blush burning my cheeks, a small part of me couldn't help thinking it was good to see that the old Ash was still in there.

Darren did something in computer programming, which was far too boring to talk about he said, when I politely asked what he did as we sat down in the pub with our first and only drinks of the night.

'Like me then,' I said, sipping at a very nice rhubarb and ginger gin and tonic. 'I work for an accountancy firm.'

'Do you earn pots of money, like moneybags Laghari here? Still driving the Porsche?'

'Yes, and just as well with the parking around here. Managed to squeeze it in between a couple of Chelsea tractors.'

'Yeah, it's a nightmare but we're within walking distance of the town and the run in the morning. Although, I'm tempted to move north. You get so much more for your money. Do you live in Churchstone as well?' he asked me.

'Yes.'

'You ought to consider it, seriously,' said Ash. 'You could fit your place into Claire's twice over. She's got a lovely house. Double-fronted terrace. Old York stone, little front garden. It's cute but not small. And it's right on the edge of the park.'

I looked at him in surprise. It was the most complimentary thing he'd said in recent weeks.

'The park where you want to do the run?'

'Yes, that's right,' I replied, reeling from Ash saying a nice thing instead of being his usual cynical self.

'So what do you want to know?'

And for the rest of the evening we picked his brains about

how it all worked, my disquiet growing all the while. There was so much more to it than I'd ever imagined and also a huge amount about the technology involved. That bit had definitely passed me by .

'Oh yes,' said Darren with a gleeful smile. 'You're going to need a minimum of three thousand pounds to get started.'

Ash, mid-drink, spluttered and I put my drink down with a bump.

'Three grand?' he repeated.

'Yeah. There are a lot of upfront costs to consider. And all the kit you're going to need. Folding tables. Scanners. High-vis vests. Walkie-talkies. Cones. Signage. There's quite a list. But I think the parkrun people help you a lot with what you need and they can point you in the direction of grants and stuff.'

There was so much more to think about than any of us had even considered and I was beginning to wonder if we hadn't perhaps been a bit ambitious, chivvied along by Hilda.

'Have either of you registered?'

'No.' We exchanged nonplussed expressions.

'Do we need to?'

'You don't have to,' explained Darren. 'You're just listed as an unknown on the results sheet. But if you do, you get a bar code, which you have scanned at the end of the run. Then, a couple of hours after the run, you receive an email which tells you what your time was, how many people ran, what your age-graded score was. Look that one up. And a whole load of other stuff including what your PB was.'

'PB?'

'Personal best. I can print them off for you back at the house, if you like.'

He'd brought his laptop along and logged in to his parkrun

account to bring up the detailed page of all his results over the last two years and a whole load of stats and information about the event itself. I began to tune out; this stuff didn't interest me, but at the same moment, Ash leaned in. It was the most animated I'd seen him and he began to ask lots of questions about how the technology worked and what information was recorded. I was more interested in the practicalities of what was required to make an event happen. Did Hilda have any idea at all about what we were about to attempt? Suddenly I realised that I felt a decided prickle of interest. Until now, I'd been going through the motions, without really believing that it would ever actually happen... but what if we did pull it off? What if we did make the Churchstone parkrun happen? How great an achievement would that be?

Sharing a bed with someone was no big deal. No big deal at all. Except when it came to it and that awkward shuffling about who would use the bathroom first, ergo who would get into bed first. Thankfully, I'd brought sensible PJs, although the cami top revealed a bit more cleavage of my very average-sized boobs than I'd normally display in public.

I took first dibs on the bathroom, changing in there and cleaning my teeth. When I got back to the bedroom, clutching my toilet bag and towel to my chest, Ash departed without a word. I heaved a silent sigh, switched the lamp on and the main light off and hopped into bed, pulling the duvet up to my chin. For good measure, I tugged the pillow as far to my side of the bed as possible without it falling off and lay there waiting for Ash to return. There was absolutely no reason for the apprehension that danced on the very edge of my nerves – *no Claire, of course not* – as I strained to hear the noises in the bathroom and the signal that he was coming back.

The door squeaked and the floorboards creaked and I heard the door to our room close. I opened my eyes and gulped – a proper cartoon almost-swallow-my-tongue gulp at the sight of a half-naked Ashwin Laghari. My memories had not let me down. He stood there in his boxers, calmly arranging his clothes on the chair tucked in next to the wardrobe on the opposite wall, the muscles of his back rippling as he moved.

As he started to turn, I blinked my eyes shut quickly but temptation proved too much; as soon as I felt the bed dip at the bottom, I opened them again. He knelt on the end of the bed and I got a perfect view of his golden-skinned chest and the dark hair dusting his pecs. Our eyes met and he paused and stared at me. The silence of the room buzzed between us and all my hormones surged up in a tsunami of desire which must have been written all over my face but I couldn't tear my eyes away from his. His movements had pulled down the duvet and I was aware of my exposed skin and my tingling nipples that hardened into come-get-me points.

'If you keep looking at me like that, beard or no beard, I will kiss you.'

And for the life of me, I couldn't think of a single reason why he shouldn't.

'Claire,' he warned, in a low voice that sent a tremor of excitement coursing through me.

I swallowed. What the hell was I thinking?

He moved another pace forward and I stared at him, at those eyes that looked back at me with dark intent. I sucked in a breath, which sounded loud in the quiet, semi-lit room, which was filled with shadows. Unable to tear my gaze away I studied his lips. My pulse flickered and danced with the anticipation of what the much-maligned beard would feel like.

Another pace. A pause. His hands drew level with my waist, one on either side. I swallowed again. Another pace. His knees were placed on either side of mine. His eyes bored into mine. The silence between us was fierce and powerful, almost throbbing in the night air. Another pace and his face was inches away, his body straddling mine. I swallowed. There was a whisper of a smile as his lips curved in response. But he didn't make the final move, just stayed there hovering above me. I knew I had to breach that final space; it was part of the challenge. There would always be a challenge with Ash and that was why I'd liked him so much the first time we'd met.

I let a smile play across my lips and tilted my head back slightly. The challenge was what had been missing between both of us. The spark in each of us had been extinguished, in him just as much as me. And now I felt it roar back into life and I smiled again as I lifted my head and kissed his mouth. With a whisper of a sigh, his body sank onto mine, simultaneously soft and hard, adjusting to my shape as one hand scooped around my waist and the other around my shoulder, his lips moulding to mine as if they were coming home.

It was a leisurely, all-the-time-in-the-world kiss, as our mouths explored, tasted, touched, and tested. My body sang with delight and desire, boneless and weightless. Ash's mouth was soft and hard, teasing and tentative, the bristles gentler than I'd expected, and inside I felt everything soften and melt out of focus.

The soft rap on the door had us scrambling apart and Ash

scooting under the bedclothes to lie on his side in order to hide the erection tenting the sheets.

'Yes,' I said in strained voice.

Darren's head popped around the door.

'Sorry guys, just found out, I'm going to need to leave earlier than you; I've had a text asking me to help set up in the morning.' He proceeded to give us detailed directions, with an additional lengthy explanation as to why we might see people going a different way, as there were a couple of routes to access Tring Park where the run was held. By the time he'd finished, my body had cooled and common sense had set in.

When he pulled the door closed behind him, coward that I was, I leaned over and switched off the light.

'Saved by the bell,' drawled Ash in the dark.

'Probably for the best,' I whispered.

'I'm sure you're right,' he said and turned over so his back was to me. I did the same, although my heart thudded unnecessarily. The kiss had caught me off guard. That sexual chemistry between us still fizzed bright and fierce but I didn't want to get burned. Once Ash got a job again, he'd be his old cocky self and he'd leave me for dust, especially now he realised I wasn't the super-high-flier he'd once thought. I was damaged goods whereas I was sure just as soon as he got another job he'd bounce back and wouldn't want to know me. We were both in the wrong place at the moment.

Sleeping with him, no matter how much I wanted to, wasn't the answer.

Chapter Seventeen

We followed the other runners along the street, up a skinny path sandwiched between a wall and a fence, and up the steps to a bridge which crossed a dual carriageway that left me breathless before we hit the park. It had belonged to the mansion house in the town and had been landscaped in eighteenth-century style with an avenue of trees leading off to the right but the runners all peeled off to the left and as we came to the crest of the hill below us we could see quite a crowd.

'Wow, I wasn't expecting this many people,' I said. They were the first proper words apart from monosyllables that I'd spoken since last night. This morning, when I woke up, I had been thankful to find the bed empty. Darren had printed off our bar codes and they were downstairs next to mugs with tea and coffee laid out on the breakfast bar for us.

'I think Darren said about two to three hundred do it.'

I turned to him. 'Where are we going to get three grand for the set-up costs from?'

He shrugged. 'No idea.'

'I think this is a bigger undertaking than Hilda realises.'

'You're not kidding. But I guess that's why we came. To find out more.'

I stared down at the circus in the dip of the two hills where lots of people were already milling about. There was a gazebo. Tables. A finishing funnel staked out with poles and white tape. A big tarpaulin spread out where people were leaving coats, jackets, and bags. And a few official-looking people in fluorescent vests. 'This is much more than I'd imagined. It's so much bigger.'

'Yup. I think Hilda envisions a dozen people trotting around the park. She doesn't know what's really involved.'

'We can break it to her gently when we get back.'

As we approached, we spotted a sign: *First Timers and Visitors*. This made me slightly nervous. Now, faced with the prospect of running 5k with a lot of very professional runners who were all limbering up and doing proper stretching, I wondered if I'd bitten off more than I could chew. Someone had to come last, I guessed.

Ash tossed his sweatshirt on the tarpaulin and I added mine, stepping back onto the toes of another woman.

'I'm so sorry,' I said. The woman was shorter than me and didn't have what you would call a runner's physique. She looked as if she was in her fifties.

'No worries, love. Gorgeous morning isn't it, although the wind is going to catch us right when we come out on the home straight.'

'Erm… yes. I've not done it before.'

'Have you not? Well, you're in for a treat.' She laughed. 'Once you've got up the hill.'

I nodded. 'I've not actually done a parkrun before.'

'Well, welcome. I hope it won't be your last. I started a year ago and I've never looked back. Sets you up for the day and everyone's so friendly.'

'I'm a bit worried about coming last,' I confided.

'If I can do it, anyone can,' she said. 'Seriously, I've never run before in my life but a friend dragged me. Said I could walk it. Which I did, and then I thought I'd have a go at running a bit and walking a bit. And then I decided by my fifty-fifth birthday I'd run the whole course. And I did it and now it's part of my weekend routine. I come most Saturdays with a couple of friends that I met here and we go for coffee afterwards. Everyone meets up at the Akeman in town.'

'Right,' I said.

'Don't worry, you'll be fine.'

When I turned round, Ash was in conversation with a couple of men – well, one teenager and his dad. I wandered over.

'Claire, this is Dave and his son, Patrick. They do the run every week.'

'When Pat's not had a skinful down the pub the night before,' laughed Dave.

'That's a nice thing to do together.'

Patrick grinned. 'Yeah, especially as I beat the old man every time.'

'Young legs,' said Dave, nudging him, and his son nudged him back and a second later they were barging each other with laddish humour.

There were quite a few youngsters – some younger than Poppy. It hadn't occurred to me that there would be children here – or dogs, for that matter. There were quite a few, all on leads, I was interested to see.

'Have we got any first timers or visitors?' yelled a woman on the slight incline behind me, ringing a bell.

Ash and I plodded over to the placard, and I was relieved to see there were at least fifteen other people.

'Welcome to Tring. This is an out and back course, so you need to keep to the left.' Holding up a map she explained the route, which I found impossible to visualise, but she added the reassuring information, 'We go out and then at the top, you come back the same way. There are marshals along the course; you can't get lost.'

She talked about a couple of other things which were common sense and then finished with, 'And we all meet afterwards for coffee in the local bar. The start line is just over the hill there and the finish line is here, as you can see. Any questions?'

Everyone did that stare-down-at-their-feet thing, not wanting to appear stupid. I was impressed by the thoroughness of the little speech and that, like everyone else, this lady with the very loud voice was a volunteer. It looked from her clothes like she'd be running too.

Runners were still arriving – families, groups of friends, couples, and single people. There was a real mix of shapes and sizes and ages. It wasn't what I was expecting at all.

Then we were called to the start. Here there was another talk as a tall, thin man, well padded-up for the brisk wind that whistled through the little valley we stood in, spoke through a loud-hailer to the crowd swelling before him.

'Any first timers?' A few of us put up our hands and the

lady in front of me turned around and gave me a thumbs up mouthing, 'good luck'.

'Any visitors?'

A hand went up. 'Where are you from?'

'Delamere Forest.'

'Anyone from further afield?'

I knew from Darren that people quite often ran other courses for fun and some even collected them like Munro baggers, the people who climbed the highest peaks in Scotland.

And then there were milestoners. A man in the crowd to my left had completed fifty parkruns and it was then I noticed a couple of red T-shirts with '50' on the back. Another man had volunteered twenty-five times. For each announcement there was a round of applause.

And then, at last, with lots of people setting their Fitbits or smart watches, we were given the off. Everyone surged forward up the hill. My pulse leapt and I was running in the crowd. Ash had already been swallowed up – not that I'd planned on running with him. I think we'd both resolved to ditch each other as soon as we could after last night's debacle.

I'd lain awake for ages beating myself up for being so stupid and letting my hormones do the thinking. They were about as fit to take charge as a toddler in a sweetshop. A man jostled my elbow and I slowed my pace. I needed to concentrate a little as it was quite busy.

We funnelled through a gate onto a tree-lined path that turned sharply right. The crowd had already thinned and up ahead of me I could see a moving sea of runners in a rainbow of coloured tops. And when I said up, it really was up; the route ahead on the soft, mulchy surface was straight up a hill and already my calves were burning.

Blimey, this is hard work.

I was relieved to see that quite a few people around me were already walking and when I glanced over my shoulder, it was even more reassuring to see that I was nowhere near last. Panting hard, with my thighs joining in the protest, I gave in and slowed to a walk. This was too much like hard work. I fell into step next to a small woman who was pumping her arms and walking quickly. She gave me a smile. 'We'll feel better at the end.'

I nodded. She was kidding, right?

And then I heard strains of Bruce Springsteen, which got louder as we approached the crest of the hill. At the top was a very smiley marshal standing beside an obelisk with a boom box perched on the white stone, making encouraging comments and directing us left up another hill. The brief burst of music seemed to recharge the batteries and quite a few of the walkers began to run again. It did seem a lot less steep, so I forced my aching legs into action. This was supposed to be fun. But they said when you got to the top you turned around and came back, so maybe we were near the halfway point.

At the top of this section there was a folly – a Palladian summer house – where the course turned a sharp right again up another flaming hill. I managed a few steps and then lapsed into a walk but I wasn't alone, not by a long way.

'Killer, isn't it?' remarked a man as I drew alongside him. He was panting just as heavily as I was and he wore a '50' T-shirt.

'But you've done loads,' I wheezed, pointing to his top.

'Never gets any easier. I'm better on the down. Once you get up to the top of this it's flatter.'

'Promise?' I hauled in another breath, wondering why the heck I was doing this.

He just huffed in response and began to jog again with a wave of his hand.

At least if we got a run set up at Victoria Park it would be a hell of a lot easier, although there was one steep hill at the far east side. We'd be avoiding that section of the park if I had anything to do with it.

Towards the crest of the hill, the incline softened and I began to run again, pleased to see the path stretching away through the leafy green trees, flat and wide. Phew, I'd made it to the top. Now it was much easier and I could take in my surroundings. Through the trees, I could see last autumn's leaf cover, and the fallen branches from winter storms, with dark green velvety moss growing on the trunks. Up here we were in the lee of the wind and it was much more sheltered.

Then there was a break in the trees affording the most wonderful view of the park spread below with the town beyond and even further in the distance a wide flat plain.

A flash of euphoria ripped through the heavy breathing and aching limbs. I felt glad to be alive.

I can do this.

With a burst of energy, I upped my pace, feeling my legs respond and realising my breathing was easier. I was actually enjoying this. Up ahead, I saw a lone figure sprinting towards to me. What was he doing? And then further behind him was another man.

Then I realised they were the front runners… on their way back. Sprinting? I could barely muster a jog and these guys were going for it. The turning point must be quite close.

It wasn't.

The number of runners coming past started to increase. These were the serious runners, with serious faces and a serious pace. But what struck me was the camaraderie, the cheers of, 'Go John', 'Well done Marie, you can do it' that I heard. There were lots of travelling high fives, encouraging taut grins, and one man even made a love heart with his hands and blew kisses as he passed a woman ahead of me. Unaccountably cheered by this, I laboured up the final mountain climb, determinedly forcing one foot in front of the other at a pace that Hilda could probably outwalk. *Just keep swimming*, I told myself, hearing Dory's voice from the Pixar movies in my head. *Just keep swimming.*

And there it was, the mythical nirvana, the turn. It was manned by a particularly jolly marshal who, despite it being summer, wore a big woolly hat and several layers. He gave me and another woman on my heels a two-handed thumbs up. 'Nearly there, ladies. You've got this. Downhill all the way from here.'

'Thanks, marshal,' panted the other woman, giving him a limp-wristed wave. All I could muster was a bit of a nod. Even so, now I knew exactly what was in store for the rest of the run, I was able to relax a little. I wasn't running into the unknown anymore. There was something very reassuring about knowing that it was downhill all the way. My legs felt less heavy and at last I seemed to have got to the point where my breathing was even; although it was still rasping out with harsh exhalations, I didn't have to suck in desperate burning lungfuls of air.

The runners had thinned out and were now strung out unevenly along the path; I was completely on my own, following a woman a little way ahead and in front of her a small group of about five. All I could hear was the pad-pad of my feet, crunching into the gravelly path and the coo-coo of a couple of wood pigeons hidden in the trees somewhere close by.

My body felt looser; the earlier tension in my shoulders that had pinched hard at the tight muscles had dissipated. There was something about being out in the fresh air, the open countryside around you, with your heart pumping and your muscles, tendons, and bones working in perfect harmony, all doing what they were designed to do. I felt alive and buzzy with the awareness of my body working away. I felt at peace with myself.

Running free felt so much better than being on a treadmill. It didn't matter if I came last; no one was going to say that I'd failed. No one was going to judge me – not even me. The thought was immensely liberating.

I always put so much pressure on myself to be everything to everyone. Self-sufficiency had become a self-fulfilling prophecy. Being capable, being the best meant people had left me to get on with it. I'd isolated myself. I never asked for help. It had to be forced upon me, like Hilda phoning Ash to help with the furniture. I'd never have admitted I couldn't do it on my own.

It was the same at work. I'd backed myself into a corner. No one ever offered aid because they assumed I wouldn't accept it or even that I didn't need it. I never said no to projects or tasks because I didn't want it to seem as if I couldn't hack the challenge. When I'd first started, there'd been the thrill of helping small companies with business problems, dealing with real people and making a difference to their lives. Because I was good, I kept being given the bigger and bigger jobs, the bigger, faceless companies where the employees would have no idea of my impact on them. I'd become so focused on that steady treadmill, never lifting my head to take a good look around, that I'd lost sight of what I really liked about my work. For the first time, it occurred to me that I could get off the treadmill and run free.

Thinking about that spurred me on and, somehow, I'd caught up with the woman ahead of me and now tried to keep pace with her. She stretched out a little in response, pushing the pace, but I kept up with her stride for stride. I could see she was older than me and was panting just as hard as I was.

'You okay?' she asked with a face which I knew was as red and shiny as mine.

'Yes… first… time,' I puffed.

'It gets easier. I… started… a year ago,' she said between breaths. 'Complete convert now. Just ran in the gym. Something about all this…' She waved a hand to the surrounding woodland. 'We're all mad.'

I nodded, trying to conserve some energy as we ran along the flat path along the top of the ridge, going back past the opening in the trees where the stunning view unfolded. The early morning mist had cleared and now the scene showed just how high we'd climbed. The view from up here was amazing and it filled me with a quiet sense of joy, one I hadn't felt for a long time. I'd been too focused on that damned treadmill.

'Makes me feel glad to be alive when I see that,' she said. 'Every time.'

I knew what she meant

The path sloped upwards with a very small incline and I began to slow, the temptation to walk building.

'Come on,' urged the woman. 'You can do it. The worst is over.'

'Promise?' I panted and she laughed – or a close approximation to it.

We ran side by side, our harsh breaths punctuating the morning air and whenever I started to slow, she slowed with me, keeping me going. Then, mercifully, we crested the hill and hit the steep descent. It was heaven, running free down there, letting my legs carry me, my arms flapping loosely by my sides.

'Told you it would get easier.'

'Thank God,' I replied. We zigzagged down the hill, coming back to the obelisk and a crossroad of four paths. The same cheery marshal now had Elvis's 'Jailhouse Rock' pumping out. Like the men at the airports who directed planes into their spots, he gave us a two-handed wave towards the path on the right.

Not far now, I told myself. 'Don't let me hold you back,' I wheezed to my kind companion.

'It's fine. I'm not aiming for a PB or anything. I'm always grateful just to get around.'

I let the words sink in for a minute.

'Can I… ask… why you… do it?'

'Sure,' she gave me a quizzical look and I hastily reassured her.

'I'm here… some friends and I… want to set up a parkrun'—my chest was heaving with the effort. Running, talking, and breathing at the same time was hard work—'in our local area. Fact-finding mission.'

'Ah. That's brilliant. Good luck. It's transformed my life.' She waggled one of her hands in front of her, sporting a tasteful solitaire engagement ring. 'I met my partner here.'

'Really?' Hilda would love that.

'Yes. I'd been divorced for nine years. Never thought I'd meet anyone again.' She laughed wheezily. 'Thought I was destined to be a crazy cat-lady.' We ran a few strides before she picked up the story again. 'My neighbour begged me to come and help marshal one weekend because they were short of volunteers. I came up… saw that there were plenty of women just like me here. Not stick-thin runnery types.' She flashed me a grin. 'So I decided to have a go. Never run in my life. Nearly killed me the first couple of times.' With a laugh she swerved to avoid a branch on the path, 'But… it got me out of the house. I was last the first couple of weeks.'

I pulled a sympathetic face.

She waved a hand. 'Someone has to be. Everyone was so friendly. Nice about it. Even though I was a complete duffer.' She ran a few more paces, clearly trying to conserve her oxygen levels. 'I came back the next week. Then the next.' There was another pause before, with a proud beam, she added, 'I've done seventy now.'

'That's… amazing.' I gasped between breaths.

'Over the weeks I got chatting to a couple of people. A woman invited me to go to the coffee place afterwards. I met Phil. Chatted to him every week for months.' Her smile was rueful. 'He's a slow burner. Eventually he invited me out for dinner. The rest is history.'

'Wow,' I huffed, 'that's a lovely story.'

''Tis for me,' she grinned.

I realised that as she'd been talking we'd unconsciously began to run faster and we were fairly pelting down the hill.

At the bottom, we burst out of the trees head-on into the wind.

'Not far now.'

The finish line was just over the next hill and with that in mind, I forced myself to dig deep and run as hard as I could up the short, steep slope following the other woman. A competitive gene had kicked in and I was determined to keep going.

Up over the hill we went and then it was there, a hundred metres ahead.

'Come on!' yelled my companion, plunging down the hill like a kamikaze pilot. 'Sprint finish.'

I went flying after her, trying as hard as I could to catch her. The finish line loomed closer. I pushed my body harder, my lungs bursting. Then just before the finish, the woman slowed and turned. 'We go over together.'

And, in an extraordinarily generous gesture, we crossed the line at exactly the same time.

And that was the moment I fell in love with the parkrun. The moment when I decided that we would find the three thousand pounds. We would set something up that would encourage people like this lady to come out and take part, something that would give people like the lovely guy with the boom box a job to do every Saturday. We would set something up that would make Ash and me proud of what we'd achieved. We were going to set up the Churchstone parkrun.

Chapter Eighteen

Ash stared at me, his eyes narrowing as he unlocked the car doors. The beep sounded loud in the quiet street.

'What?' I asked, as I slid heavily into the bucket seat after he loaded our bags into the space under the bonnet. My stomach was full after a rather yummy breakfast dished up by Darren – avocado and poached eggs on sourdough toast along with slices of crispy bacon. After the parkrun, I felt I'd earned every single delicious mouthful.

'You're back.'

'Back?' I frowned as I tugged at the seat belt.

His face was hidden from me as he leaned over the steering wheel but then he tossed back his hair and a shot me an almost accusing glare. 'You're all sparkly eyed again.'

'Am I supposed to apologise for that?' I had absolutely no idea what he was talking about.

'That first time I met you, even though you were being a complete ballbreaker—'

'I was not. You were being an arse. You backed...' I realised how ridiculous this was and shut up. He raised that eyebrow and I folded my arms. And then I burst out laughing. 'You make me so mad sometimes, Ash.'

'Is that all?'

'Stop flirting; it doesn't suit you.' Despite my words, I couldn't help my mouth twitching. 'You were saying…?'

'It's like the life-force is back. When I first met you… that's what I noticed. Your eyes sort of sparkled all the time you talked. You were so full of energy.'

I rolled my eyes but actually, I knew what he meant. This morning had been like walking through a wall and coming out into brilliant sunshine. It was only now that I felt normal that I realised how long I'd been functioning in fog.

'Endorphins,' I said, stretching my arms out in front of me, wriggling my fingers. Every bit of me felt alive and buzzing with awareness. 'Did you know that the Tring parkrun is the seventeenth hardest in the country?'

'No. Bloody hell. It was tough though.'

'Well, it was your idea.'

'Should have gone to Harrogate.'

'Yeah but we wouldn't have learned as much. Andy, the guy who set up this run, was really helpful and so was today's run director, Katie.' We'd spent a little while in The Akeman, the local bar-restaurant where many of the runners congregated after the run. We'd picked a few people's brains and met some inspiring people, including Luciana, a complete non-runner who'd lost an astonishing twelve stone, and Elaine who ran with her ten and twelve-year-old daughters every Saturday, and the volunteers who rocked up week in and week out to share the wonderful sense of community. It was truly inspiring. 'I'm so glad we came.' I buzzed with a sense of achievement and also excitement.

'So you really want to go for it?'

'Absolutely.' I turned to him. 'You?'

'I guess. It was… can I say fun? Knackering… but there was a real sense of community there.'

'Everyone was so friendly. And so supportive. I felt like…' I hesitated, wondering if it sounded a bit stupid. 'I felt like I was part of something. Like I belonged… even though I'm not a proper runner.'

'Define "proper runner".'

'Those people that came haring past me when I was still panting my way up the hill like a physically challenged hippo.'

Ash laughed, loud and strong, and it made me realise I hadn't heard him laugh properly since our date. 'If it makes you feel better, a couple of them are former Olympians.'

'That makes me feel almost super human.' I sat up straight in the car with a surge of pride. 'I did the same course as an Olympian.'

'And there were plenty of people who didn't look anything like "proper runners". I was surprised by how many kids were there.'

I sighed a happy sigh. 'It was amazing, and we're going to make it happen at home.'

'Oh God, Hilda's created a monster.'

I rubbed my hands together. 'Too right. In fact, I'm going to put together a list of all the things we need to do. Nothing's going to stop us now.'

'When you look like that, I believe you.' He nodded his head and I knew he was referring to my eyes again. A foolish tingle of happiness danced in my chest. *Very* foolish. Falling for Ash a second time would be a huge mistake.

'Mind if I make a call?' I asked as we drove further north. I could almost feel Ash's sense of gloom returning. It was as if our trip had been a brief holiday. We'd talked initially about the parkrun but the minute we hit the M1, the atmosphere in the car felt as if the barometer pressure had dropped. Even his posture had changed as he slumped into his seat.

'No, go ahead.'

I listened to the overseas dial tone before Alice's cheery voice invited me to leave a message.

'Hi Alice, it's Claire. Just calling to find out if you've got a flight tomorrow and what time you want me to pick you up. The girls are really excited about seeing you. Can you give me a call or text me?'

I hung up.

'Still no word?'

'Par for the course for Alice. She's not big on responsibility.' Even so, it was stretching things.

'And you are.' It was an observation rather than a question.

I shrugged. 'One of us had to be. If we'd both been like her, my parents would have had nervous breakdowns. As it was, my mother came close.'

'Family dynamics – always fun. I think I must be the Alice of our family. The loser.'

'Bollocks, Ash. That's rubbish and you know it.'

His knuckles tightened on the steering wheel.

'Until recently, you were flying. You've hit a bump in the

road. It's derailed you, that's all. We both know that. I think we agree there's no point in platitudes. And it's shit. Not working, not having a purpose. I get it.'

He shot me a reluctant smile, as if grateful for my honesty.

'And I know it's all right for me because I have a job to go back to but you will get another job eventually.'

'You think? I've had so many doors shut in my face. What do I have to do?'

'I was thinking…'

Ash shot me a glare that basically said he didn't want to hear it. It was a challenge in itself.

'Have you thought laterally? You said you were a social pariah in your sector. How about trying a different one?'

There was no answer but he hadn't told me to shut up.

'Your degree. It was in mechanical engineering. Could you transfer into that field but in the financial area? Like finance director or something.'

He kept his eyes trained on the road which meant I'd struck a chord, otherwise he'd have just glared at me.

'It's an idea,' I said, determined to make him think about it.

'Noted,' he said and using the controls on his steering wheel, he turned up the radio.

'You're welcome.' Yeah, I had to have the last word because, after all, this was Ashwin Laghari and I was never going to stop challenging him. If he had half a brain, he'd know I was right.

———————

After a near sleepless night, I slept for most of the rest of the journey and woke up about ten miles from Churchstone, leaving behind a very nice, faintly erotic dream which had involved Ash's naked torso and a lot of kissing.

'You talk in your sleep,' said Ash.

'Do I?' I feigned disinterest although I could feel the furious blush on my face.

'It's okay,' Ash flashed me a sardonic grin, 'you didn't say anything intelligible. Just a lot of mumbling.'

Phew.

'Or it might have been moaning.'

The furious blush turned molten. 'Glad to have entertained you,' I snapped, resting one cheek on the welcome cool of the passenger window.

'You— Oh shit.' He stared into the rearview mirror.

Instinctively I turned and looked over my shoulder out of the rear window. A blue flashing light was following us.

He pulled over into a rather handily placed layby which had probably been the intention of the police car behind us.

'What speed were you doing?' I asked.

'Below the limit. I'm careful, especially in this. Well, I am now. I did a speed awareness course.'

Two police officers, one very tall young man and one short, plump older woman got out of the car. Both had ambivalent expressions on their faces, neither friendly nor hostile. The woman approached Ash's door, the young man behind her.

Ash wound down his window.

'Is this your vehicle sir?'

'Yes.'

'Can I see your driving licence?'

Ash wriggled his wallet out of his back pocket and wordlessly handed the licence to the officer.

'Do you have your insurance documents?'

'No, I don't keep them in the car.'

'MOT certificate?'

'No.'

I'd have been bending over backwards to appear a helpful, eager-beaver, law-abiding citizen. What was with the surly one-word answers? My heart was racing; I couldn't help it. This was exactly the kind of thing I always tried to avoid.

This was the sort of behaviour that got you hauled out of the car and clapped in handcuffs. Not that I knew, never ever having been stopped by the police before. I wondered if Ash had been previously.

'Would you mind telling me where you're going and where you've been?'

Ash shrugged. 'No, we're on our way to Churchstone from Hertfordshire.'

'Churchstone?' The police officer turned to her male colleague.

'I… we live there.'

'Are you acquainted with a Mrs Hilda Fitzroy-Townsend?'

Ash and I glanced at each other and I caught my breath in sudden panic. *The girls.*

'Is she all right?' I blurted out. 'Has something happened to her?' I began to scrabble in my bag for my phone. I'd texted her to tell her we were on our way when we left at twelve.

'Please leave your hands where we can see them.' The woman's voice rapped out with loud authority and I dropped my bag and held up my hands.

'I was just checking to see if I'd had a message from her.'

'You know Mrs Fitzroy-Townsend?'

'Yes.' I nodded.

'Do you know where she is?'

I lifted my head, worried now, and there was a hardness in the other woman's expression.

'Well, I know where she should be,' I said. 'Do you want me to ring her?'

The two police officers exchanged identical bland expressions with each other.

'We would like to see Mrs Fitzroy-Townsend for ourselves. There are concerns for her safety.'

'Do you think she's had an accident?' I asked.

Now the police were decidedly iron-faced.

'When was the last time you saw Mrs Fitzroy-Townsend?'

'Friday morning.' Ash nodded in confirmation.

'And you've not seen her since then?'

'Well, no. We've been away. She's looking after my nieces. But she was there this morning because she texted me about eight to say everything was all fine.'

The policeman frowned and checked his notebook. 'So you have had contact with Mrs Fitzroy-Townsend this morning?'

'Yes.'

'And where was she this morning?'

'At my house.'

'Which is where?'

I reeled off the address. 'We're just on our way back there.'

'We would like to see Mrs Fitzroy-Townsend. As I said, there are concerns for her safety.'

'So there hasn't been an accident?' This was all very confusing.

'Not that we're aware of. We'd just like to ascertain her whereabouts.'

I frowned. 'Well, in that case, I'm sure she's absolutely fine. I can call her if you'd like.'

'We do need to speak to her. Check that'—she gave me a stern look—'she's there of her own volition.'

'Sorry?' I frowned trying to compute the implications. 'You think I've kidnapped her?'

'We're just trying to confirm her whereabouts. Her family are very worried about her.'

'But didn't they try to ring her?'

'She's not been responding to texts, phone calls, or voicemails. Mrs Fitzroy-Townsend was reported missing yesterday morning and was last seen getting into this vehicle.'

I was confused and worried. The only thing for it was to sign up for a police escort home so we could get to the bottom of things.

Chapter Nineteen

The house was quiet when I opened the front door but there was a lovely smell of baking which boded well.

'Hello, Hilda. We're back,' I called, feeling rather self-conscious in front of the two police officers who were virtually breathing down my neck.

I walked down the black and white tiled hallway towards the back of the house and the kitchen-diner.

'Auntie Claire, Auntie Claire!' Ava darted forward and flung her arms around my hips as if I'd returned from a lengthy transatlantic sea-voyage rather than an overnight trip down the M1. Behind her, Poppy, in an outsized apron, and Hilda with one of my new table cloths tucked in her sweatshirt like a bib, were in the middle of spooning cake mixture into little flowered bun cases.

'We're making butterfly cakes and we made flapjacks and cookies.'

Hilda glanced over her shoulder at us, 'You've made

excellent time… Ah, good afternoon.' She gave the police officers a regal nod. 'We have company.'

'Mrs Fitzroy-Townsend?' asked the policeman.

'Yes. How do you do?' said Hilda turning around and brushing her hands on the tablecloth. 'Can I offer you and the WPC a cup of tea? I'm sure Claire and Ash will want one after their long drive. How was the trip?'

'That would be…' He looked back at his colleague a little uncertainly. 'Perhaps we could speak privately with you in another room?'

'Why would you want to do that? I have nothing to hide from my friends.'

'It would be better,' pressed the WPC, her mouth tightening.

'Better for whom? Claire and Ash are friends. Now what seems to be the problem?'

'Perhaps we can take a seat?'

'Poppy, would you carry on dear, while I handle this? Tiresome, I know,' her wrinkled mouth pursed in walnut crinkles of annoyance and the look she gave the police officers was frigid, her blue eyes positively glacial. 'Ava, if you follow Poppy's instructions to the letter, you may help her. Claire, would you mind if we went into the front room?'

I shook my head and watched as Hilda marched out of the kitchen like Boudicca leading her troops.

A beat later she called. 'You too, Claire and Ash.'

We shared a bemused frown and followed into the sitting room at the front of the house.

'Now, what is all this nonsense about?' said Hilda, sitting in one of the armchairs with her legs crossed, folded her arms

'They seem to think we've kidnapped you,' I said calmly in

an   isn't-that-the-most-ridiculous-thing-you've-ever-heard voice.

The WPC sighed and cut across me.

'Mrs Fitzroy-Townsend, your family is concerned about your welfare and wellbeing because they weren't aware of your whereabouts and were unable to contact you. They filed a missing persons report.'

'How bothersome of him. You mean my son, of course,' said Hilda with a weary sigh. 'As you can see,' she indicated with a body scan hand gesture, 'I'm perfectly safe and well and staying here with my young friends.'

'Perhaps, madam,' said the WPC, 'you might like to get in touch with your family and reassure them.'

'Yes, yes, yes. I suppose it was Farquhar, fussing as usual.'

I tried to hide a snigger behind my hand. No one, surely, called their son *Farquhar*.

Hilda grinned and lifted her shoulders in an apologetic shrug. 'It was before Shrek came out. Although, the prince is actually called Farquaad.'

Now I really did laugh and I could see Ash pinching his lips together.

'I think pregnancy addled my brains but his father insisted. And it's a family name; I believe it was one of the fourth duke's names, although I suppose in the sixteenth century it was quite acceptable. I bet it was him, wasn't it? Always was a fusspot.'

'I believe it was a Mr Farquhar Fitzroy who raised the alarm, after the manager at Sunnyside Memorial Home said that you'd been missing overnight.'

'Stupid, stupid boy. And that damn fool manager. I'm a

grown woman and if I want to go away for the night I do not have to inform that pipsqueak.'

'Do you have a mobile phone?'

Hilda gave him a withering frown and I didn't blame her; there was definitely a patronising tone to his words.

'Young man, I have a mobile phone and I am also of sound mind. I was rounding up Russian spies and enemies of the state during the Cold War before your parents were even born. If I decide to go away for a night or two, it is of no concern to anyone but myself.' There was a silence before she added with a decided note of dismissal, 'It's a great shame you've been brought out on a wild goose chase. Please inform my son that I am quite well.' She stood up.

'Perhaps you would like to ring him yourself, to set his mind at rest.'

'Perhaps I wouldn't,' said Hilda with a regal tilt to her head. 'Now, if there's nothing more, I have cakes to bake with my young friends.' With that, she swept out of the room and headed off towards the kitchen.

'Right, well,' said the police officer, a little put-out.

The WPC's eyes twinkled and she gave me a wry smile. 'Quite a character.'

'She is. I'm sorry you've been put to the trouble of having to come here. We had no idea.' Of course, Hilda's overnight carrier bag made perfect sense now. I'd wondered why she'd brought so little. She'd deliberately not told anyone at the home she was going away. Hoisted by her own petard, I thought. Karma was a bitch.

'Well, we'll be off. If you could encourage her to phone her son, it would be a good idea.'

'I'll do my best,' I said, not holding out any confidence in my chance of success.

'In the meantime, we'll let him know she's safe and sound.'

Of course, Hilda, presiding over butterfly buns and tea and squash with the girls, wasn't the least bit penitent.

'Honestly, what a fuss. I am perfectly entitled to go off on holiday without having to inform anyone. I've a good mind to give the manager of the home a good talking to.'

'They're just concerned for your welfare,' I said gently.

'Poppycock,' she grinned. 'I bet Farquhar was worried I'd gone off and got married again. He was mightily pissed off when I married my fourth husband, George. We got married in Vegas in the Elvis chapel. It was a hoot. I posted pictures on Facebook and Farquhar was livid. He was worried George was marrying me for my money, which of course he was, but as he didn't have long to live, it wasn't as if he was going to get through an awful lot of it. Sadly, he only lasted another couple of months but we had a ball. If you ever get the chance, I highly recommend driving a Harley down Route 101 all the way to Baja. Fabulous.' She then proceeded to tell Poppy and Ava about riding a motorbike and being stopped by a state trooper who wanted to arrest her, which Poppy and Ava listened to round-eyed.

Ash caught my eye, his expression sceptical – Hilda always seemed to have a wealth of interesting stories – and we shared a quick conspiratorial smile.

'So what news?' asked Hilda, after tea and cake had been consumed.

'It's a goer,' I said, sitting up straighter and trying to contain my sudden bounce. 'Although someone might have warned us it's all up hill – talk about hard work. We've almost got permission from the council but there's just the small matter of raising three grand to buy all the equipment.'

'Equipment? echoed Hilda and I explained just what was required and what we'd seen that morning.

'Gosh, it's quite a bit more of an undertaking than I thought it would be. It's a good job you're on the case, Claire. What's the plan for this week?'

I outlined the agenda for the next couple of days, feeling a bit more like me again, using the list I'd made in the car on the way back, which included researching all possible grant providers and local sponsors who might help us raise the cash.

'Tomorrow morning, the girls and I are going to design some leaflets inviting potential volunteers to The Friendly Bean.' I had a small scanner and laser printer that would make light work of the job and it would give the girls something to do before we went to the airport. 'We need to recruit a team of at least twenty people. This week I'll get them printed up and then we'll start distributing to the houses around the park, community notice boards, Facebook, and so on; the running club are going to put some up on their side of town. We also need to come up with some fundraising ideas as three grand is no small feat. Apparently, there are grants and things we can apply for.'

'Which all take time,' Ash added with a downward twist to his lips.

'Excellent,' said Hilda, completely ignoring his pessimistic addendum. 'And when does Alice get back?' Both Poppy and Ava's heads popped up.

My smile was overbright. 'Tomorrow, but I'm still waiting to hear from her what time the plane lands.' My careful glance at my watch didn't escape Hilda's keen-eyed gaze. She gave me a discreet nod, acknowledging my unspoken anxiety.

Alice was a lot more laid back than me. I had to stop worrying. She'd phone at the last minute, probably when she was about to board the plane. In which case, she should be texting or calling very soon.

'I don't want to go home, Auntie Claire. I want to stay here. In my nice new bedroom. There's much more room for my babies.'

'Don't be silly,' snapped Poppy. 'Auntie Claire has to go back to her big job one day.'

'I'm going to miss the two of you,' said Hilda. 'Who's going to help me bake cakes?' There was a slight quiver to her lipstick-stained lips.

Ash looked mournful. 'I'm going to miss the cakes.'

And, oh heck, I was going to miss the girls. When had that happened? It had snuck up on me that somehow having them around had become normal. I'd got used to the noise and busyness of the house – the messy kitchen, the cluttered bathroom and the abandoned book bags in the hallway. Despite all that, this place had turned into a home. Real people lived here and it showed. My house felt like a proper home and that made me feel good inside. I was going to miss everyone, even Ash.

'Perhaps we can have a regular bake-off date,' I suggested. 'I'm sure Mummy won't mind. You could invite her too.' As I said it, I wondered what Hilda and Alice would make of each other. Though both were mavericks in their own way, something told me that they wouldn't be friends.

'In the meantime, when are you going to decorate this room? You've been perusing all those glossy magazines but have you made up your mind what you're going to do yet?' asked Hilda.

I grinned at her. 'Actually, I think I have.' My dreams of dark grey walls and black slate floors had been replaced with something entirely different.

'Excellent. One of the women in the home has a son who does kitchens. She's always showing me pictures. He's actually quite good. Would you like me to get him to pop round? Give you a quote? See what he could do for you?'

'Er… well.' Four expectant faces peered at me and Poppy pointed at the sad wallpaper. 'Yes, but I want it done as soon as possible. This week if he can.' I knew that was a tall order with tradespeople but now I'd made up my mind, I wanted to put the plans in place.

I was due to see Dr Boulter at the end of the week but there was no way he was going to sign me off for any longer. I felt better than I had in a long time.

Hilda was already on her phone texting with teenage-like speed.

Chapter Twenty

When I opened the door on Monday evening, Bill suddenly at my heels like a faithful knight determined to protect my honour, I found a stranger on the doorstep pacing back and forth.

'Claire Harrison?'

At the man's suspicious, angry tone, Bill stepped in front of me, his tufty fur brushing against my hand. I patted his head in quick reassurance as my heart clenched.

'Alice?'

I still hadn't heard from her. I'd tried calling and texting her mobile to no avail all day yesterday and most of this morning. It rang and rang but she didn't answer which puzzled me because if she was on a flight, it would have been switched off... which meant she wasn't in transit yet. So where was she and why wasn't she picking up?

'You're Alice? I want to speak to Claire Harrison. Is she here?'

'No. Yes. I am.'

'What?'

'I'm Claire Harrison. I thought you were... never mind.' I thought he'd been here to deliver bad news.

Bill relaxed against my legs but stayed put. Feeling my heartbeat returning to normal, I peered into small, sharp eyes set in an angry pink face.

'Can I help you?' I asked.

'I expect you know why I'm here.' The voice was querulous but the words were clearly enunciated with a definite public-school clip; his pompous assumption amused rather than intimidated me. As a lifelong fan of *Pride and Prejudice*, he immediately put me in mind of Lady Catherine de Bourgh. It prompted mischief – a hangover from wanting to be Elizabeth Bennet and spending too much time with Hilda who had been so infuriated by the police visit that she'd availed herself of the spare room for a second night just to spite the manager of the home.

'I'm sorry, you have me at a disadvantage.' I stood squarely in the doorway, seeing that he expected to be invited in. Bill sat down next to me but his ears were up and alert, his nose quivering.

'I am Farquhar Fitzroy.'

'Oh,' I said, an air of curious amusement in my voice. Hilda's son? That was unexpected.

'You know why I am here. I am fully conversant with your ploys.' Oh yes, definitely Lady Catherine.

'Well, that's excellent.' I paused, holding on to the door, before giving him an unconcerned smile. 'And what would those be?'

'I know what you're up to.'

'You do?' *Elizabeth, eat your heart out.*

'Miss Harrison. Can we be frank?' I almost laughed out loud.

'Please, be my guest, because I haven't the foggiest idea why you're here or what you want.'

'I'm concerned about the amount of nights my mother is spending under your roof. It really isn't on. And this sudden request for money to be released from her investments...?'

The first part of his speech elicited some sympathy but the final sentence had my hackles rising like a German Shepherd faced with a burglar.

Before I had chance to respond to the insult, Hilda's ringing voice came from the other end of the hall. 'Oh, for goodness' sake, Farky. What are you doing here?' A wealth of exasperation and weariness filled Hilda's words. 'And it's a paltry three thousand pounds.'

'Don't call me that ridiculous name, Mother,' he snapped. 'What are you doing here?'

'I'm sorry, Claire,' she said with a huff of irritation. 'You're going to have to invite him in. He won't go away. He's a pest.'

'I'm not... I'm...' For a moment he floundered, his colour rising, before he gritted his teeth. It was like watching an angry cartoon character regaining control. 'I need to talk to Miss Harrison.' I almost, I say *almost*, felt sorry for him.

'Oh Farky. I don't know why you're doing this but you're making a complete fool of yourself. Claire is my friend; I'm in no danger from her.'

'I think I'm better placed to judge that, Mother.'

'You think a lot of strange things, dear.'

Shaking her head, she wandered back through the house towards the kitchen as I stared after her. 'Would you like to come in?'

'What I'd like is to talk to you in private. However, my mother is determined to show us all up, so, by all means, proceed.'

I led him to the kitchen where Hilda had resumed her seat, picked up her coffee, and was holding up several paint charts. She had arrived with them, Ash in tow, just after I'd picked the girls up from school, ostensibly to have a parkrun meeting. Her words.

'Mother, are you drinking coffee?'

Hilda peered into her cup, a china one she'd insisted I buy and which she then commandeered for her personal use. 'Gosh, so I am. Cappuccino. Jolly nice it is too.'

'What has the doctor said about drinking coffee?'

'Make up your mind, dear. I'm either senile and unable to manage on my own, and therefore how can I possibly be expected to remember anything, or else I'm a grown woman in charge of my own affairs who is perfectly capable of making judgements as to whether the pleasure of drinking coffee outweighs my possible earlier demise.'

I hadn't imagined Farquhar could turn any redder. I was wrong.

It was a second or so before he had collected himself.

'Mother, you are impossible.'

'So you've told me, umpteen times, which begs the question why do you keep trying to make me less impossible?'

In sheer frustration, her son turned to me. 'Miss Harrison. I'm concerned about my mother's wellbeing and I fear she is being taken advantage of.'

'That's very commendable but I'm not—'

'It has come to my attention that you are... you are exerting undue influence over—'

Ash spat his coffee out all over the table and colour charts. Farquhar shot him a quelling look.

'My mother is vulnerable and you seem to have befriended her. It seems rather odd. A young woman befriending an elderly woman. And now this request for money.'

'Actually, Hilda befriended me. And she's become a very good friend indeed. Don't judge people by your own standards. Your mother is of sound mind and in extremely good health,' I thought of her jogging round the park every day and crossed my fingers under the table; I hoped she was. 'She is hardly the sort of person to be unduly influenced, as you put it.'

'Well said, Claire.' She leaned forward. 'Now, Farquhar, I moved into the residence to make you happy. If I choose to spend time elsewhere, that is none of your business.'

'I think it should be my business when I don't know where you are or who you're with. You're a very wealthy, elderly woman and vulnerable to being targeted by less scrupulous people.'

'If you're worried about your inheritance, I really wouldn't. I plan to burn my way through it.'

'No, Mother, I'm worried that you might be associating with people who don't necessarily have your best interests at heart. People who might want to take advantage.'

'Oh, you're not still going on about George, are you? I gave him permission to sell that ring. It was hideous.' Hilda tossed her head but I didn't miss the deepening of the lines around her mouth. 'I didn't want it anyway and would never have missed it.'

Farquhar didn't say anything but his pinky finger tapped on the table.

'Is that the only reason you're here?' she asked, her colour heightened. 'To check up on me?'

'No, Mother. I was concerned about you.'

'Well, as you can see, I'm perfectly fine, which you can tell your little spy at the home. Now, I suggest you trot back to your chambers and do whatever you do and leave me in peace.'

'Mother, you're impossible.' His poor face flushed even redder.

'Do you know Audrey Hepburn said it was actually "I'm possible", which I prefer.' Hilda lifted her chin with imperious disregard but I could see her hands shaking. 'Farquhar, seriously. *Enough*. I am not in any danger and I've had quite enough of this conversation. I'd like you to leave.' Her final words were suspiciously strained.

'You're upsetting your mother. I think it's time you left,' said Ash, rising to his feet and taking a calm, authoritative step towards Farquhar. They made an odd juxtaposition – Ash, lean and supple against Farquhar, pudgy and squat. It made me realise just how much better Ash seemed to be already compared to when we had first met again that morning in the park. The lethargy and defeatism had gone. He wasn't quite back to arrogant, self-possessed Ashwin Laghari standards but I rather liked this new version of him.

Farquhar held up his hands in surrender. 'I'm not here to cause trouble, Mother. I'm only trying to help. You know where I am if you need anything.' He tucked his mobile phone into his pocket and strode out of the kitchen to let himself out.

'You're terrible, Hilda,' I said as I heard the front door click shut.

'I know,' she replied primly. 'Right, back to paint colours.'

'Not quite so fast,' I said, recognising her diversion tactic. 'Do you want to explain what Farquhar was talking about? Why does he think you're staying here? And what's this about the money?' Three thousand pounds sounded like a suspiciously familiar number.

'Ah, that. I was hoping he hadn't blown my cover. I've been staying at my house for the odd night.'

'Your house?' Ash and I both said in surprised unison.

'Yes, dears. It's just around the corner. I go there occasionally to watch *Countdown* in peace.'

With this surprising bombshell, we retreated back to the kitchen, Bill returning to the front room where no doubt he'd snuggle up on the sofa next to Poppy, who was definitely his favourite.

'This colour, I think you're right,' said Hilda, holding up the Farrow and Ball paint chart and pointing to the sage-green colour I'd kept coming back to. 'Mizzle, although I think I would buy Elephant's Breath just because of the name.'

'I think we all would,' I said, before adding sternly, 'so what's this about you staying at your house and why didn't you tell us? And I hope you're not thinking of stumping up for the parkrun.'

'Consider it a loan, if that makes you feel better. Or a community donation.'

'We can raise that money; I know we can.'

'And it will take time and hold things up.' Hilda lifted an imperious chin. She was rocking the Queen that day. 'If you get the grants and monies you can pay me back, but in the meantime this will help.'

'It's very generous of you,' said Ash.

'Pish. It's not as if I can't afford it. I'd far rather it went to a good cause than in death duties. And I'd like to see the parkrun set up before I die.' Her attempt to look sombre failed miserably.

Ash's mouth twitched and his eyebrow rose to its highest point while I pursed my lips.

She grinned with an irrepressible twinkle. 'Well, it was worth a try.'

'Let's see how we get on with the grants and see if we can raise local sponsorship.'

'Yes, dear, but the money's there if you need it.'

'Thank you, Hilda.' Ash laid a dark hand on her white, blue-veined one and the sight of their hands together made my heart hitch with a little pang.

'Thank you, Hilda.' I added my hand to the pile and it felt as if we were making a pact.

'My pleasure, dears.'

'Now, what's this about you staying at your house?' Ash cocked his head as he asked the question, withdrawing his hand to pick up his tea.

For once, Hilda, a little shamefaced, ducked her head before, with a heavy sigh, she lifted it again and said to both of us, 'I miss it… I just wanted to see what it would be like to stay there and I knew Farquhar would play merry hell and say it's far too big for me and what happens if I fall. I just pop in every now and then make sure everything is okay. He's desperate for me to sell the place but I… I can't bring myself to.' For the first time since I'd met her, Hilda seemed to have shrunk a little into herself. 'I know I can't live there anymore but I do miss it.'

'How long did you live there?' I squeezed her hand in encouragement.

'Over forty years. Saw me through a couple of husbands. Farky used to love going to the park. In those days, bands played every weekend in the bandstand.' Her eyes dimmed as though she were lost in the past. 'He was quite a cute little boy, then,' she added with a wistful smile.

Would I miss this house? I looked around the kitchen, remembering the girls helping me make cheese on toast for tea earlier, having pizza with Ash and Hilda last weekend, trying out the new Nespresso machine with Hilda the day I bought it. This room was starting to hold memories; the house starting to work its way into being mine. I had a growing collection of scenes. A house was to be lived in. Shared with other people. Hilda's house must hold a palimpsest of memories built up over the years.

'I'd love you to show me it one day,' I said impulsively.

Hilda's smile was slow but gradually lit up her face. 'That would be my absolute pleasure. Now, what time is this council meeting tomorrow? You'll have to pick me up, Ash, so that I can babysit for the girls and you might as well bring Bill because young Poppy adores him.'

Poppy and Ava were currently in the front room watching television and I was trying to quash the vague feelings of bad-parenting guilt as I wasn't sure what they were watching.

Hilda gave me a shrewd look. 'No word from Alice, yet?'

'No,' I eyed my phone. Still no answer to my calls or the messages I'd left. Worry crawled down my spine like spiders skittering across the floor. 'But she's…' I glanced around, making sure the children hadn't reappeared. 'She's quite unreliable. Knowing Alice, she'll phone when she's landed and expect me to go and pick her up.' Under the table I crossed my fingers. But why, when I called, was her phone still ringing with an overseas dial tone?

'Anyone want another glass of wine?'

'I ought to get Cinderella here back to Drearyside before the manager sends out search parties and I've got...' Ash looked at me. 'Things to do.'

'And I ought to get the munchkins ready for bed and prepare for school in the morning. I need to make packed lunches.' And there was also reading and spelling to do with Ava, and Poppy had homework on electric circuits which we'd abandoned yesterday because I couldn't get my head around it.

'Actually, Ash, I don't suppose... Poppy's struggling with some science homework.'

Ash's eyes rose with surprise and I realised that it was the first time I'd voluntarily asked for help; normally Hilda ploughed in on my behalf.

'Sorry, you said you had things to do.'

'They can wait,' he replied with a shrug, but somehow, despite the laconic body language, I got the impression he was quite pleased to have been asked.

'And I can make the packed lunches.' Hilda had already jumped to her feet. It was as if neither of them particularly wanted to go home.

'Another cup of tea then?' I asked.

'I think it's wine o'clock,' said Hilda. 'I'd probably better not have any more coffee.'

Half an hour later, Ash and Poppy's heads were bent

225

together over a homework sheet. Hilda was cooking pasta carbonara for dinner and Ava was sitting on my knee, dutifully ploughing through her reading book with painstaking but determined slowness.

It wasn't the evening I'd planned and it was all the nicer for it. The girls approved the new paint colour with much enthusiasm and the sight of them pouring over the paint charts, Poppy's science homework complete, Ava's reading book finished, and Hilda and Ash drinking wine, was another scene to add to my memory bank.

Chapter Twenty-One

I dragged myself out of bed extra early the following morning. Ava was fast asleep, rosy-cheeked, with her curls matted around her head like a messy halo. Next door, Poppy, one arm curled neatly under her head, slept like a Madonna. I tiptoed away and down the stairs and blearily made myself a coffee before starting on my calls.

Unsurprisingly, Alice did not pick up and the dial tone was still international.

'Alice, just wondering whether I need to get the police involved.' I hung up. Passive aggressive, I know, but I'd left so many messages now.

To my surprise, when I called my mother, she answered.

'Mum! It's Claire.'

'Hello, dear. Gosh, how lovely. I was going to call you later. It's so difficult trying to work out the times and whether you're at work or not. We're in Cozumel, Mexico. Just docked. It's absolutely gorgeous. Glorious sunshine.'

'That sounds wonderful. Although,' I looked out the

window at the pink and gold tinged wispy clouds against the backdrop of a bright blue sky. 'It's going to be a lovely day here too.' One of those days when you wanted to get your run in early before it got too warm.

'And how are you, dear? Are you enjoying having the girls to stay? I forgot to ask, have you taken holiday or something? They're such a pair of sweethearts. I do love having them to stay when they come for the weekend.'

'Actually, that's why I'm calling, Mum. They're still here. Alice hasn't come back yet and she's not answering her phone. I'm getting a bit worried about her. I wondered if you'd heard from her.'

'Well, she's not due back... Oh, I'm getting my dates muddled. She was going for two weeks. Maybe her flight's been delayed.'

'And she's a liar—'

'Now, don't be mean, Claire. You have to accept that your personalities are very different. Alice isn't as strong as you. She needs a lot more support.'

I almost groaned aloud. I'd been hearing this for as long as I could remember.

'Mum, she told me she was going for a week. That's what she told the girls as well. I'm not being mean, I'm calling it out. She lied. It's not acceptable.' I let my annoyance show because, bloody hell, what was Alice playing at? 'She might think it's funny and clever to get one over on me – I'm a big girl and used to her infantile tricks – but it's not fair on Poppy and Ava.' I knew Mum would be far more sympathetic to the plight of the girls.

There was small pause. 'No, that's true. It's very naughty of Alice.'

'Naughty! Mum, she's not five. She's bloody irresponsible. I have absolutely no idea when she's coming back. She said Sunday. It's Tuesday. Have you heard from her at all?'

'Not this week but she's having a wonderful time. The retreat is up in the mountains. It sounds so beautiful. It's quite remote though.'

'Not so remote that she can't contact you on a ship in the middle of the ocean.'

'She sent an email, Claire.'

'Well can you send her one? Because she's ignoring me. Remind her she has two daughters who are missing her and are a bit confused as to why Mummy hasn't come back yet!' Shouting at my mother was always counterproductive and I should have known that by now, but I was so frustrated with her customary defence of Alice.

'There's no point getting cross. I'm sure there's a very good explanation.'

'Perhaps you can share it, so I could explain things to Poppy and Ava.'

'Oh,' I was glad to hear Mum sound chastened. 'Are they very upset?'

'Actually,' I looked around the kitchen at Ava's pictures on the fridge and Poppy's schoolbag and PE kit neatly arranged on the kitchen table. 'They're okay.' The three of us were working well together. Our own little team. We were doing okay. The realisation gave me a warm buzz of pride.

'But Alice needs to get in touch and tell me when she's coming home. Can you try and call her?

'Of course, dear, and give those babies a big hug and kiss from Grandma. I do miss them.'

'Will do, Mum.'

'Lots of love.'

I hung up and listened carefully as I heard a creak upstairs and then the sound of the toilet being flushed. I put my phone down and began to get the cereal boxes out of the cupboard. The morning routine was about to start. I hoped Alice would call and at least give me an update so I could reassure Poppy and Ava. It would be even nicer if she called and spoke to them herself. Surely, she was missing them?

I picked up a message from the chairman of the Churchstone Harriers, the local running club, as I plonked myself down on my usual bench next to Hilda after my run that morning. Spring was definitely starting to give way to summer and the promise of the sky at five-thirty had delivered a gorgeous bright morning.

'Oh well, that's a start,' I said to Hilda. 'Charles is hoping to get to the meeting tonight, although he may be a bit late, and he says that a couple of members might turn up as well.'

'That doesn't sound too promising,' said Ash. 'We need as many people as possible to convince the council there's local support, otherwise they won't so much as consider the idea.' I glanced up at him and frowned; something was different with him today.

'Well, I'm trying to round up a couple of the old codgers at Sunnyside.' Hilda drew herself up and inclined her chin his way. 'Although they do like to watch *You've Been Framed*, which is on at 6.30pm. Trying to drag them to a council meeting when they've got the delights of idiot people falling over, inadvertently getting wet and capsizing small boats, might be somewhat of a stretch but I'll do my best.' She smiled. 'There's always blackmail.'

And I believed her.

'Fingers crossed we get a few supporters in. If we can't get permission to use the park there's nothing more we can do at the moment.' Now that I was fired up, I was really anxious that the parkrun should take place at Victoria Park. This was an opportunity for the stately old girl to shine.

'Yes, but once we've got it, Thunderbirds are go.' Hilda punched the air in a very un-Hilda-like gesture before adding with a dreamy smile. 'I used to know Gerry Anderson.'

I frowned, not having a clue who that was.

'The creator of the *Thunderbirds*, dear. And *Captain Scarlet*. Gosh, Farquhar used to love those programmes. Dear Gerry always said Lady Penelope was loosely based on me.' She let out a cackle. 'Of course she wasn't; he said that to everyone. It was his wife Sylvia, really, but Parker was definitely my driver to a T.'

'You had a driver?' asked Ash.

'Only while I worked for MI6. He used to take me to Downing Street for security briefings. Although I shouldn't be telling you any of this. Official Secrets Act and all that.'

Ash caught my eye and that familiar eyebrow winged upwards and we shared a brief smile. My heart did a sideways wobble at the unexpected warmth of his expression. I knew it was born of a fondness for Hilda but it brought me a little bubble of happiness.

'And I want to enlist your help, the pair of you. I've decided to move back into my house.'

Before either of us could respond to this, my phone began to vibrate in the depths of my leggings pocket.

'It's Alice,' I said once I'd wriggled it out and with hasty, stabby hands tried to swipe the screen.

'Alice!' I stood up and walked away from the bench towards one of the flower beds filled with the pom-pom heads of dark pink peonies. 'Where are you? Are you okay?'

'Still in India.'

'Couldn't you get a flight back? Do you need some help? Are you all right for money?'

'I'm not coming back.' Defiance and a touch of I-dare-you-to-say-anything rang in her voice.

It took me a moment to add up the sum total of words.

'*What?*'

'I can't do it.'

'What are you talking about, Alice? Why can't you come back? I don't understand.'

'Of course, you don't. You've got everything you want. Your life has all gone to plan. You've got it all. Career. Own home. What have I got? Leftover crumbs from you and Mum and Dad. Stuck at home. Mouldering into nothingness. I'm a non-person. A mother. And a single one at that. A nothing.'

'That's not true,' I protested, feeling the sinuous slide of guilt slither through me.

'Yes, it is. I know what people think of me. You. Mum. Dad. "Poor Alice. She doesn't even work." I have no purpose. Whereas here, I feel alive, in touch with myself. Free. The thought of being back in suburbia with the same dull routine, it kills me. I realise now I was being suffocated. If I stay here, I could become a yoga teacher or something.' The latter point was made with a touch of challenge.

'But what about Poppy and Ava? You have to come back.'

'Don't you dare make me feel guilty. This is about *me*. What

I need. This is *my* time. I'm growing as a person every moment I'm here. Spiritually, I'm re-awakening, feeling the life-force. I think I've been half dead for most of my life.'

'Alice, you can't just abandon them! Who's going to look after them?'

'I'm not abandoning them. Don't bring it down to your simplistic terms. Perhaps I'll be freeing them, allowing them to live. I need to breathe, to be free of the yoke of motherhood.'

'What about what they need? They need their mother.'

'I can't be a mother at the moment.'

'Alice, you can't just stay. And you can't say that. You have responsibilities.'

'I knew you wouldn't understand.' She managed to sound both plaintive and accusing at the same time and it twisted something in my gut.

I sighed, realising I needed to tread carefully. 'Alice, I know it's probably wonderful there but you can't stay; it's not real life. Ava and Poppy need you.'

'I know you think they do but really they don't. Children are more resilient than you realise. They'll be fine. Mum and Dad will be home soon. And it's not forever… I just need more time.'

'But you… you can't.' I pictured Poppy's solemn, narrow face and Ava's trusting, big blue eyes and it felt as if someone had punched me in the stomach.

Fear spiked through me as it suddenly dawned on me that she was completely serious and that no matter what I said, she wasn't going to listen and there was nothing I could do about it.

'Alice, please, think of Poppy and Ava. They'll be so upset.'

'I can't think like that. It will crush me. I've put them first all my life. Don't put pressure on me. Jon says my spirit is fragile and I need to fly. I have to do this, Claire.'

And with that she hung up.

I stared with dismay at my phone and at first tried to call her back but I disconnected the call. It was a waste of time; she probably wouldn't answer. I tried to stifle the sudden wave of panic and the uncomfortable tightness in my chest. What was I going to tell Poppy and Ava? How did you tell a child her mother had turned her back on her? How was I going to manage their heartbreak? Heat stained my cheeks as a small, rapidly growing ball of fury ignited. Both Ash and Hilda were looking at me.

'What's wrong?' she asked. 'Has something happened to Alice?'

'You could say that.' I ground the words out through gritted teeth. 'She's gone stark staring mad.' I pushed harried hands through my hair and tugged at my ponytail, stifling the urge to punch something. 'Basically, she's doing a runner. She's not coming back.'

'Fuck,' breathed Ash. 'That's…'

'How extraordinary,' said Hilda, her forehead concertinaing into a dozen furrows. 'I freely admit I probably wouldn't have won any mother-of-the-year awards…' Her mouth turned downwards. 'Something I regret now, but I would never have waltzed off and abandoned all responsibility. Surely she's coming back eventually?'

'I've no idea. I don't think she knows.'

'What will you do?' asked Ash.

'What can I do?' They would have to stay with me at least until Mum and Dad came back. And Alice had to be back by then, surely.

'Those poor, gorgeous girls… What on earth are you going to tell them?'

I bit my lip hard as I took a couple of steps towards the bench and then wheeled away before turning back again. What *was* I going to tell them? Where did I even start? How did you tell a ten and a six-year-old that their mother had had enough of them, which was the stark reality of the matter? Could I lie and tell them she'd had a nervous breakdown? That she was ill? Nausea burned at the back of my throat. Alice had always been a free spirit but I'd never thought she'd do something like this.

'What do I tell them?' I turned bleak eyes to Hilda and lifted my shoulders in hopeless defeat. 'What a mess.'

'It is,' agreed Hilda, before surprising me by adding, 'And poor Alice.'

'*Poor Alice?*' I echoed in disbelief.

'I'm sure she hasn't come to this decision lightly. She's been putting off calling you for the last few days. You should be proud of yourself for helping her. You gave her a rescue package and she's seized it with both hands. She'll come around eventually; you just need to give her time.'

I stared at Hilda, still too furious with Alice to raise the least bit of sympathy for my selfish, thoughtless sister.

Hilda smiled at me. 'I know. I know. You think she's selfish and thoughtless. It's written all over your face. But there are always two sides to every story. Perhaps she's just not cut out to be a mother. She was very young when she had Poppy. Maybe she does need a break and some contemplative time.'

It was a pinprick in my balloon of fury, letting some of it leak away so I wasn't about to explode but I still didn't buy it.

Yes, Alice had had it tough over the last few years but she'd been supported by our parents, and by me to a lesser extent.

'You'll have to go the meeting without me,' announced Hilda. 'I'll be on babysitting duty.'

'Oh, Hilda, you don't need to do that.'

'I think we need to show the girls that there are people around who they can count on, don't you? Especially with their grandparents being away at the same time. And being purely practical, dear, someone has to and you've already made the contact with the Harriers chap and the Blenkinsop man.' She broke off before musing, 'Hmm, I used to know a Harry Blenkinsop. Lived on Church Street. Not a particularly common name.'

'It would be quite handy for me,' said Ash.

'Oh well that's just dandy,' I snapped wanting to lash out at someone. 'I'm glad someone's pleased.'

'I meant,' his eyes flashed with exasperation, 'I could leave Bill with Hilda and the girls this evening while we're at the meeting. That will cheer Poppy up. I don't like leaving him for too long and I've…' He paused with the sort of shifty expression that left you in no doubt that he was up to something that he didn't want us to know about. 'I'll be out,' he glanced away, 'for the rest of today.'

'Where are you off to?' asked Hilda, completely ignoring his obvious body language, the fidgeting, fixed gaze on the dog's ears and him tugging at his beard.

On any other occasion I might have laughed at Ash's indignant frown. 'Into Leeds.'

'What for?'

Hilda had no shame and I loved her for it.

'Never you mind,' snapped Ash with a flash of the old,

superior arrogance. He rose with fluid grace. 'I'll meet you at Claire's house with Bill this evening at six.'

'Excellent idea,' said Hilda before I could speak. 'I'll cook dinner for Poppy and Ava. I think I'll do my famous French toast and bacon. Have you got any maple syrup, Claire?'

'See you later.' And with that, Ash walked quickly away. I watched him go, not sure if the hollow leaden feeling in my chest came from feeling cheated of the Ash I'd once known or my sister's bombshell. What I did know was that the main thing I needed to focus on was what the hell I was going to tell the girls.

Chapter Twenty-Two

'Come on, you.' Hilda hauled herself to her feet. 'We need cake and neat espresso, preferably with a vodka chaser. Although I doubt Sascha serves alcohol at this hour.'

We found a spot in The Friendly Bean on the veranda at the front where bistro tables and chairs were set up facing towards the bandstand and the formal gardens. 'I'll get these,' said Hilda. 'You sit there.'

'Don't be silly,' I said, although, to be honest, my legs were a little wobbly and I was grateful to collapse onto one of the chairs.

'Claire, you buy my coffee every day, you feed me at your house, and…'

'And you've just donated three thousand pounds.'

'That's for the community, not you.' Her haughty Lady Bracknell rebuff brought a sorry smile to my face. So I sat and did as I was told, nibbling at my thumbnail and studying the splodges of colour in the distance. The municipal nursery men had been busy laying out bright flowers in uniform bursts of colour – red geraniums, orange nasturtiums and yellow marigolds interspersed with borders of white petunias.

I focused on them, the colours and shapes blurring as my eyes filled with tears. Poppy was going to be the hardest hit. She was so bright and intelligent. Ava would be loud and angry and easily distracted. It was Poppy I worried about. What on earth was Alice thinking? If she was even thinking.

'Coffee's on its way.' Hilda announced, putting down two plates each filled with an enormous slice of coffee and walnut cake. I wasn't sure I could eat a single mouthful. 'Well, this is a proper pickle.'

'That's one way of putting it.' I picked up a fork and poked at the cake, taking a tiny bit of buttercream and nibbling at it. Mmm, the comforting taste of sugar settled on my tongue. Sometimes only cake will do. I scooped up a forkful of dark sponge. Sascha's sister had a very light hand with sponge; it was moist with just the right amount of coffee flavour. For a moment, I closed my eyes and focused on the taste and fine texture. Before I knew it, I was slicing off another piece as Hilda watched approvingly. She sat and watched as I chomped my way through the cake almost meditatively, my mind on each mouthful and the bitter, sweet flavours that eased their way across my tongue.

'Better? I always think good cake helps us reset things for a minute.'

With a half laugh I nodded. 'Funnily enough, I do feel a bit better.'

'Good. Now, what do you think we should tell the girls?' She looked at me steadily over the fork and inside I melted just a little.

'You don't need to do that, Hilda.'

'No, I don't, but I think it might help. A united front and all that.'

'It's Poppy I worry about the most. She's not stupid. Anything I say, she'll question.'

'Perhaps the truth? Mum's had a bit of a breakdown and needs to stay away longer to get better.'

'But then she'll worry about her Mum… and quite frankly, bloody Alice does not deserve to have Poppy worry about her. God, I could kill her!' I stabbed at a few loose crumbs on the plate and almost shattered it.

'Probably why she's staying put…' Hilda gave me an irrepressible grin, leaning forward and taking the fork out of my hand with exaggerated care.

'Armed and dangerous with a pastry fork.' I shook my head ruefully. 'I can't think of anything that isn't going to upset Poppy and Ava.'

'She's got chicken pox and has to be quarantined.'

'They both had it and I remember Poppy asking why Alice and I didn't get it. We both had it when we were children.'

'What if she's trapped by a landslide up a remote mountain, there's only bridge over a ravine, and it's been destroyed.'

'It sounds very Indiana Jones but… reasonably plausible.'

'And she's staying to help rebuild the local school which was destroyed in the landslide.'

'Steady on, she's not Mother Teresa. I think that's pushing it a little. But you're probably right; if it sounds as if she's doing something noble to help other people, it will come across a lot better.'

'I was always good at coming up with cover stories.' She

rested her hands on the table with a complacent air and gazed off into the distance as if remembering past glories.

'Bill, Bill.' Poppy knelt down and threw her arms around him as he bounded into the kitchen with a perky trot, sure as always of his welcome, followed by Ash, who had an equally perky trot. I stared at him for a minute, trying to work out what was different, but then turned back to the more pressing worry about Poppy. Bill tilted his tufty head, one ear cocked, and nuzzled into her neck rather than his usual playful greeting of nudging at her knees and sitting quietly, as if he knew exactly how she was feeling. I swallowed back a tear feeling terribly, terribly guilty. Ava's disappointment in her mother's delayed return had been simple and quick, easy tears and breathy sobs before she was distracted with cuddles and false positivity.

Unfortunately, Poppy was a much deeper well and harder to read. Her simple stoicism, the quick indifferent shrug as if that was that, worried me and I ached to comfort her but I didn't know what to say; the truth had stalled my tongue and I hated lying to her.

Hilda gave me an encouraging smile that wasn't reflected in her eyes and she came over and squeezed my hand. I'd been a terrible coward, accepting her offer when she'd suggested she come with me to pick the girls up from school.

I'd told them as soon as we came in and since then, with false jollity, Hilda had been teaching us all how to make French toast which was a welcome diversion. There was now a mound of golden, eggy toast, a plate of crispy bacon and a bottle of maple syrup ready and waiting on the table. My mouth watered and I gave the plates a look of longing while at the same time checking the time on the kitchen clock. I'd have to eat later.

'Ready?' asked Ash, jangling his car keys.

Not really. I wanted to stay and hold the girls. Make sure they were okay. It wouldn't have occurred to me a few weeks ago.

Hilda gave me a quick nod. I smiled my thanks to her.

'Let me grab my folder.' I ducked into my little study and snatched up the A4 wallet, which held all my notes and several copies of statistics I'd downloaded about the parkrun organisation, the numbers of people taking part, the numbers of events around the country, the number of countries now involved and some of the case studies I'd pinched from their blog about mental health and community involvement. I felt like a lawyer about to present my case.

'Good luck,' said Hilda. 'Hope it goes well and I hope you get some support turning up.'

'Thanks, and if you need anything, call.'

'We're all going to be fine. We're going to watch Netflix.'

Ash and I headed out to the car.

'So how was your mysterious assignation?' I asked, as soon as I'd buckled myself in.

Ash gave a low laugh. 'Good.' And he left it at that.

I wasn't going to dignify his secrecy with any further questions; I wasn't that interested in him.

The Town Hall was quiet, not a person in sight in the lobby. My heart sank a little. It would have been nice to have some support, although we were ten minutes early. We followed the signs to the chamber and entered a near-empty room. There was a long table at the front with all its seats occupied – I suspected they were the town councillors. Seated on the wooden chairs in front of them were a few desultory people sprinkled like stray seeds in the rows. Ash and I slipped into two seats near the front, a respectable few rows back. There was a hushed atmosphere and the bunch of middle-aged, stern councillors didn't suggest that there was going to be much light entertainment tonight. They were all studying papers in front of them as if cramming at the last minute for an exam.

A couple of people sidled into the row behind us but it was hardly a crowd. One of the councillors shuffled his papers ostentatiously and squinted up at the clock on the wall. Still another five minutes until kick-off. A group of five sauntered in and snagged places on the front row – two women and three men. I studied them. Runners? But after seeing the Liquorice Allsort sizes of the Tring Park runners, I no longer assumed they might all be string beans.

Behind us, three more people shuffled along the row. Then another four. Laughing and chattering as they came, six more people filed in, followed by seven more. Several of the councillors glanced up, their heads swivelling left and right like startled meerkats. I sat up a little straighter, realising that there was a definite buzz in the room, as if things were afoot. By six twenty-nine the chairs were filled to capacity and there were quite a few people standing up at the back. At the front there was now much paper shuffling, agitated glances towards each other, and muttered sotto-voce conversations amongst themselves. Clearly the swollen audience was unprecedented or certainly unusual. I grinned at Ash as he ducked his head to whisper to me. 'Do you think they're all here about the run?'

'I guess so; there's nothing particularly contentious on the agenda that I can see.'

The man in the middle of the table rose to his feet and immediately the hush of voices died away.

There was an awful lot of official guff about being quorate, terms of reference, and previous minutes being approved. The polite attention of the assembled audience was punctuated with a lot of restless fidgeting and quite a few people were surreptitiously checking their phones.

Various members of the council stood up to give updates on a proposed road closure due to gas works, replacement chains on swings in a park on the other side of town, the results of a tree survey that had been conducted on council property throughout the ward, and finally Neil Blenkinsop rose to put forward the proposal to allow a community group to organise an official parkrun in Victoria Park. He was a tall man in his late forties with a thatch of thick, dark hair, wearing a checked shirt with the sleeves rolled up. He had a mild, slightly myopic manner as he addressed the council and the public.

'We have been approached for permission to run a weekly event, a run in Victoria Park on Saturday mornings from nine o'clock to ten o'clock in the morning.'

Almost immediately one of the other councillors jumped to his feet, a small squat man laced into a dark green three-piece suit which, along with bulbous eyes that roved over the assembled audience squinting with vague suspicion, emphasised his frog-like appearance

'We couldn't possibly allow that.' His pompous voice rang with vehement authority. 'Victoria Park is for everyone to use and enjoy. Every member of the public is entitled to use the park. To allow this group to take over the park once a week would be detrimental to the enjoyment of the park for other users. I think it's a terrible idea.'

A second councillor, a woman in a pale pink suit rose to her feet. 'I'm afraid I'm in agreement. I don't want to be out for a gentle stroll and be steamrollered by a horde of runners.'

Neil Blenkinsop nodded. 'I do understand your reservations; however, it would be for one hour once a week. I think we're grown up enough to accept that this is a small percentage of the hours the park is available and that the runners would be mindful of other park users. I would like to remind the committee that the council does have a commitment to encouraging more people to exercise and Victoria Park is currently underutilised. In addition, this is a non-profit community event which would provide considerable health and mental wellbeing opportunities for local people. The parkrun is a global phenomenon that has encouraged thousands of ordinary people to start running. It is backed by Sport England and meets the nationwide aim of encouraging more people to do sport and to sustain participation levels. The parkrun has been proven to do both and, actually, encouraging and supporting a local parkrun initiative would enable the council to achieve one of its targets at very little, in fact, virtually no cost. Nor would it require any council resources, thus not drawing on our ever-pressed budgets.'

Neil Blenkinsop had played a blinder and there was an outbreak of spontaneous applause from the audience.

In the end, apart from objections from Mr Frog and Deep Pink Suit, the proposal was accepted to a burst of enthusiastic clapping. As the councillors dispersed, lots of groups in the audience began chatting to each other and there was a tap on my shoulder.

'Hi, are you Claire Harrison?'

I nodded. 'Charles?'

'Yes, lovely to meet you and thanks so much for getting this off the ground.' Behind wire-framed glasses, pale blue eyes gleamed and he shook my hand with brisk efficiency. He had the compact, wiry frame of a runner and was appropriately dressed in tracksuit bottoms and an Under Armour running top. 'Quite a turn out.'

'Yes,' I responded with wide-eyed pleasure, 'Thank you so much for mobilising the troops. I was worried it would be me, Ash, three men, and a dog.'

'There's a lot of interest. At the moment, quite a few of us go over to Harrogate or Leeds but it would be great to have our own. Not sure why no one thought of it before.'

'Time, darling,' responded a petit woman to his left. She beamed at me. 'I for one am very grateful that you're picking up the gauntlet. It's no small undertaking but it will be wonderful if you can do it.'

'Do you run as well?' I asked, encouraged by her easy smile and friendly manner.

Charles laughed and she rolled her eyes. 'I am a reluctant runner. I do it because I know it's good for me but… I find it bloody hard work and then when I've done it, I feel so much better. Charles, here, actually enjoys it.' With mock bewilderment she shook her head and held out a small, neat hand. 'I'm Penny. Long suffering wife and married as much to

Charles as the Harriers. We're off for a celebratory curry; fancy coming along?'

'Oh… that would be… thing is, I need to check in with the lady who's looking after my… my children.' It had been easier to say children rather than produce a convoluted explanation but as soon as I laid claim to them, a surge of parental love rose up in me and I imagined what they were up to with Hilda at that moment. Ava, fresh out of the bath, would be rosy-cheeked and her curls damp but wild while Poppy would be prim in her pyjamas, itching to shut herself away in her bedroom and read her book. Except that tonight they might not be okay. My heart ached for them. *Bloody, bloody Alice.*

'I'm sure Hilda won't mind but it's best to check,' said Ash, with his usual clear, incisive understanding. I pulled out my phone to call her

'It will do you good to go out, dear. And Ash, of course. The pair of you are like a couple of hermits. You should be out dancing at your age.'

'But what about the girls, Hilda?' I ignored her comments.

'A little subdued but they're fine, darling.' The rare endearment made me realise she was just as worried about me. 'We're just about to watch *Toy Story 2*. I must say I really enjoyed the first *Toy Story*. It's a big step up from *Thunderbirds*. Go, have fun with Mr Handsome, there.'

'Yes, Hilda and thank you,' I said, touched by her concern while narrowing my eyes at Ash whose mouth quirked in amusement. He could hear every word.

'Tell her I'll run her home when we get back,' interjected Ash.

So it was agreed and Ash and I found ourselves swept

along with the running club – not a phrase I'd ever have thought I'd have heard in relation to myself.

Charles seemed to know quite a lot about the parkrun and he talked to me and to Ash, who sat between us at the curry house, asking us questions, most of which we didn't have the answers to yet.

'Any idea how you're going to recruit volunteers?' Charles asked as plates of poppadums and pickles were delivered to the tables. Nearly everyone had opted for tall glasses of lager.

'That's Claire's department,' said Ash, deferring to me. 'I'm going to be managing the technology side once we're tied in with parkrun.'

The division of labour according to our respective talents and abilities had been agreed since we'd come back from Tring. We were both willing to play to each other's strengths.

'Sounds like the pair of you make a great team.' Charles cast a fond look towards his wife, who was sitting opposite me.

'We do,' murmured Ash in a low voice which I only heard because he'd turned towards me and I saw his lips mouth the words. It was oddly intimate, as if the words were for me alone.

It took me a second to force my eyes away from Ash's golden stare and respond to Charles again; in my bid to sound normal, I came across as overly brusque. 'The key thing was to get permission to use the park. Now we've got that we can really motor on other things. We're going to organise a meeting in The Friendly Bean for people who are interested in helping set up the run and for volunteers. I thought I'd put up a poster in the café.'

'Volunteers are going to be crucial,' Charles agreed.

'Yes, so I'm thinking of designing something that we could post on social media and encourage people to share.'

'Great idea. If you send me something we can get it up on the Harriers page. And are you on the Everything Churchstone Facebook group? You definitely should post there.'

'Not heard of that one,' I said.

Penny opposite me pulled a face. 'Lucky you. A lot of it is about dodgy parking, lots of dog-poo complaints, and "can anyone recommend an electrician" requests, but there are also some useful community posts. Just be warned, people can be quite… shall we say, outspoken on there; be prepared for as many negative comments as positive ones.'

'Ha, you mean absolute toss pots. I don't know what it is about social media; some people shouldn't be allowed anywhere near a keyboard.' A fair-haired woman on Penny's left joined in. 'Bonkers it is. The moral majority come out in their droves wound up more by the piss-takers who seem to delight in stoking up trouble. But, like Penny says, it's a good way of spreading local information. My husband, Matt, is a freelance designer, I could ask him to knock you up a quick design, if you wanted.'

'That would be wonderful, thank you.'

'Don't get too carried away. I have a purely selfish motive. I'm already thinking of the bliss of a couple of child-free hours on a Saturday morning. Can't think of anything better. I'm Janie, by the way, and Penny is lucky enough to live next door to me, where I bring light and sunshine into her life.'

Penny laughed and put her arm around her friend. 'Is that what they call it? Plenty of gin, I'd say.'

'Where do you live, Claire?'

'On Park Road, on the south side of the park.'

'Please don't say on that lovely terrace,' begged Penny. 'I adore those houses.'

'The end one on the right.' I winced in pretend apology but it was exactly the comment I had wanted ever since I first viewed the house.

'Right, I'm coming round. I've always wanted to see what they're like inside.'

'Well, if *she's* coming, I'll have to supervise, and I have gin,' Janie said.

The two of them were completely irresistible and with a smiling shrug, I said, 'Why not?'

And it seemed in Churchstone it was just that simple to make new friends. We exchanged mobile numbers and there and then Janie set up a WhatsApp group titled 'Bitch with Gorgeous House'.

'You do know, Janie, that you could join the kids on the parkrun,' Penny said.

'Why the hell would I want to do that? One, I get to torture Matt and two, like I said, I get a couple of child free hours.' Janie rolled her eyes and turned to Claire. 'Sometimes there is a question mark over why we're such good friends. She has some funny ideas.'

'I also have very good taste in gin.' The two of them began to laugh at each other again.

It suddenly occurred to me that if Alice wasn't home, I'd have to take Poppy and Ava with me.

'Why the hell do you think I started running?' asked Janie,

patting a small firm tummy, laughing again. 'Apart from to try and get rid of the baby fat... eight and five years on, it's still not worked.'

'How old are your children?' asked Penny suddenly

'Ten and six' I said. 'They're not actually mine; they're my nieces but my sister is away at the moment so I'm looking after them.'

'Gosh, you're a saint,' said Janie. 'I don't suppose you want another two?'

'No,' I laughed, enjoying the company of these two women. It was refreshing to see that, despite their diametrically opposite approaches to their children, they seemed to adore each other. 'That's very generous of you but I'm still figuring out how these two work.'

Janie threw herself back in her seat and cackled, pouring herself, me, and Penny another glass of wine from the bottle that she and Penny had ordered. 'Feed 'em, love 'em and sink gratefully into a sofa and a glass of wine when they go to bed,' she said.

'I know that feeling,' I said. 'It's keeping on top of all the paperwork that's a killer.'

'What school are they at?'

'Churchstone Primary.'

'Same as ours,' said Penny. 'Ten and six did you say?'

'Yes, Poppy's in Year 6, Mrs Philips class and Ava's in Year 1, Miss Parr's class.'

'Poppy and Ava.' I could see Penny turning the names over in her head as well as the moment the information clicked.

'Oh my God. You must be Alice's sister.' Then she frowned as if something didn't add up and before she could put a stop on her tongue she blurted out, 'You're nothing like I expected.'

And then she clapped her hand over her mouth. 'God, I'm sorry. That er… sounded a bit rude.'

I laughed at her appalled expression. 'Don't worry. I know Alice isn't my biggest fan.'

Penny gave me a grateful smile. 'I'm really putting my foot in it tonight. But… she's left the children with you?'

'I know. Shocker.' Alice might drive me up the wall and I knew her every fault but blood, it appeared, was thicker and I couldn't quite bring myself to say more, even if she did bloody deserve it. From Janie's suddenly distant expression, I suspected she wasn't a fan of Alice.

Penny studied me as if I were a complex sum that needed working out. 'Alice isn't always…' she winced.

'Alice is a complete cow,' said Janie. 'Sorry, she might be your sister, but she's not well liked.'

'Janie!'

'It's true. I'm not going to sugarcoat it. She dumps those girls on other people whenever she can. Never reciprocates and…' Janie's face was quite purple but whatever she was going to say, she thought better of it.

'Don't worry. I've known her for twenty-six years. I know what she's like.'

'Sorry. That was rude of me. She is your sister.' Janie drank a large slug of wine and although I wasn't supposed to see it, I could tell Penny was patting her hand under the table.

With a placatory smile she asked, 'So where is she?'

I stuck to the version I had told the children. 'She's on a yoga retreat but it's very remote and there have been landslides that have washed the road away so she's stranded for the time being. But it's all fine.' I gave her a cheery grin.

'Oh, poor you. That's tough. How are you managing? Alice

says you have a… big job. What is it you do?'

Her careful choice of words and gentle sympathy made me like her all the more.

'Oh, I work for an accountancy firm.' I gave a quick shrug as if it were no big deal. Not so long ago I'd have said I was Head of Retail Construction Accounting and reeled off the name of the company which most people in the area had heard of. They were the big boys in the north of England. Now though, my title didn't seem that important. 'But I've been on… sabbatical'—okay, so I couldn't quite own the stigma of stress yet—'for a while, which is why Alice left me with the girls, but it was only supposed to be a week.'

'A week? Oh, I thought Alice said she'd be away for two. I must have got that wrong.'

Janie shot me a knowing glance.

'Well, it's been fine up to now. I've rather enjoyed having them but in another week and a half I'm due back at work.' I felt so much better that there was no reason for Dr Boulter to sign me off again and I'd worked out my strategy for going back to work. I was going to manage my time better and if I couldn't do something I was going to say so. Hilda's forthright attitude had taught me the value of that. I would delegate more to the team, especially that lazy git Geoff who I knew had time because he'd boasted, when he didn't realise I could hear, that he deliberately strung things out so he couldn't be given anything else. Well, that was about to change. And I would learn the art of saying no and stop thinking of myself as invincible. I'd accepted that partnership was probably out of reach which took the pressure off. I didn't need to be the best all the time and I was going to be strict with my working hours – which I was going to have to be anyway now that I'd have the girls, although that was something that was worrying me. What was I going to do about childcare?

'If Alice isn't back by then, I'm not sure what I'll do.'

'Oh, don't worry about that. There's a great After-school Club at the school and if you get really stuck I can always help out. Poppy and my Sarah are quite good friends. Poppy's a lovely girl and Ava will fit right in with Thomas.'

I stared at her, amazed at her generosity. Why would she offer to do that? As if she read my mind, she beamed at me.

'And I should have offered before. I feel terrible because now I realise I've seen you a couple of times at school and meant to come over and say hello. Why don't the girls come for tea one night after school, say Thursday, and then you come pick them up at wine o'clock?'

'That's really kind of you.' I blinked, a little overwhelmed at how easily these offers came from her. 'I'll get right on to the After-school Club tomorrow.'

'Rubbish. I should have made a bit more effort. You know what it's like; we all just get so wrapped up in our own little worlds. I mean, Charles and I have talked about how great a parkrun would be here but we've not done anything about it. Good for you for actually trying to make things happen. It's going to be fantastic for the community. What can I do to help?'

She flicked her hair back over her shoulders as if preparing for action. 'I know! Douglas Outhwaite, he's a Harrier. I'm sure he's in the printing trade. If Janie's husband does a design, we could get him to print some leaflets.'

Janie slapped her forehead. 'Doh! Why didn't I think of that? Course he will; Matt quite often uses him. I'll get on to him in the morning.'

'That would be brilliant. I can get the kids to help me distribute the leaflets.'

'We'll help. We could all do a different street each night on the way home from school.'

'If there's a chance we could lose one of mine, I'm definitely game,' said Janie with a broad grin.

'Great. The plan is to hold an open meeting to drum up support for the event and to find volunteers at The Friendly Bean. I can't believe how everything's coming together.'

'Wow, how did you persuade Sascha to do that?' Penny gave me an admiring glance. 'Or are you paying her?'

'No, she offered and it was her idea to supply some cakes.'

'I bet it was.' Janie grinned. 'She's not daft. Much bigger profit margin on the coffee, if everyone pays for those. You feel obliged if you're getting free cake. Smart business woman that.'

'She's been very helpful.' I was quick to defend the other woman; she'd done me no harm and had been quite helpful in her own brusque, businesslike way.

'Sorry, we're not being horrible,' chipped in Penny. 'She has done an amazing job on The Friendly Bean. She's just not that approachable.'

I could see that Sascha's cool reserve might not go down so well with Penny's puppy-like friendliness but I could relate to both women.

By the end of the evening, I'd made a couple of new friends, and somehow Ash and I had been co-opted onto Charles and Penny's quiz team in aid of the Parish Council fund.

Funny how, in such a short space of time, my life in Churchstone had started to blossom.

Chapter Twenty-Three

Meet me on the corner of Park Road and Abernathy Road at 9.15am.
Tell no one. Hx

The text, typical Hilda in Mata Hari mode, made me smile as I dropped the girls off at school on Thursday morning.

'Can I have a quick word, Miss Harrison?'

My heart sank at Miss Parr's quietly spoken words as Ava skipped past her into the classroom. What had I forgotten now? I thought I'd caught up on all the paperwork and paid for school dinners and the outstanding trip money.

'I just wanted to say thank you. It's really noticeable that Ava is finally getting support at home. I can see an improvement in her reading already. I just wanted to let you know.'

'Oh. Right. Thanks.'

And with that she retreated into the classroom, leaving me with a bemused smile on my face.

'Not in trouble then,' teased Penny.

'No,' I grinned at her. 'Not this time.'

'I thought I'd let you know that the leaflets are ready and we can start delivering them this week.'

'Fantastic.'

'I've worked out some routes,' chipped in Janie. 'So if you're up for it, we could start tomorrow night.' She handed over a photocopied Ordinance Survey map of the area between the park and the school. 'I've highlighted two suggested routes each. Yellow for you, Poppy and Ava, Green for Penny and her mob, and Orange for me. You'll see mine takes in the corner shop because bribes may be required to keep the little darlings on track.'

I laughed. I'd quickly learned that despite being so disparaging about her offspring, Janie's children were beautifully behaved and socially confident.

I left my new playground besties and the welcome news that both Poppy and Ava had got places at the Breakfast and After-school Club from the following week and headed off for my assignation, wondering exactly what Hilda was up to. I'd seen her in the park the day before and she hadn't said anything about meeting like this.

I spotted her in the distance, loitering on the corner, swaddled in a big down coat with an enormous scarf wrapped many times around her neck – the Michelin Man meets boa constrictor – as snug as a bug except that it was high summer. In contrast, I was in a running vest and leggings, as I was due to meet Ash for our second morning run in an hour's time. We'd both decided as he drove me home after meeting the Harriers that we needed to up our game if we were to be the official faces of the Churchstone parkrun and had agreed to meet each morning. It wouldn't be good if neither of us could get around a 5k course without wheezing like a couple of geriatric badgers.

'Good morning,'

'Morning, dear.' Hilda, hamming it up dreadfully, glanced up and down the street. 'You weren't followed were you?'

'By whom? I'm pretty sure the KGB no longer operate in downtown Churchstone.'

It was a surprise when her face froze in stern rebuke. 'Don't be so sure of that.' And then, like a magic trick, her face changed completely. 'Now, I've got something to show you.' She held up a set of keys and jangled them. The periwinkle blue eyes brimmed with excitement and she turned and led the way down Abernathy Road, which was home to some of the bigger Victorian villas in the town. She was moving at a brisk trot and I could feel her rising anticipation. We'd gone less than halfway up the street when she stopped abruptly and gestured to a rather grand, double-fronted, cream-painted house with glossy black railings around the large front garden.

'What do you think?'

I frowned, not knowing what to think. 'Is this your house?'

She clapped her hands with delight. 'Yes.'

'Oh my goodness.' I stared back down the street. 'We're less than five hundred metres from my house.'

'I know. Fun, isn't it?' Her whole face glowed with naughty amusement and she sailed past me up the path to the front door.

'How long is it since you were here?' I asked, admiring the original black and white tiled floor in the hallway as Hilda opened up, expecting dust motes to flood the air and the furniture to be covered in Holland cloths like some old stately home.

'Yesterday,' she said with a sheepish grin.

'Yesterday?' I echoed.

'Yes, I told you I like to pop in. Watch the television without the old dears twittering at me. And the cleaner comes every other Thursday. So I drop in to have a coffee with her.'

I shook my head in disbelief. 'I meant how long since you lived here. But how long have you been doing that for?'

Hilda tilted her head, for once sheepish. 'Actually, the first time I came to visit was the day I met you. I felt a little embarrassed after you'd gone. Ranting about Drearyside was all very well but I realised that instead of moaning I ought to do something about it. So I popped in to see the place and because it was quite a nice day, the sun warmed the lounge, so it wasn't too cold... so I stayed for an hour and watched an episode of *Murder She Wrote*.

'And then I started coming in every now and then. Just checking up on things.' With one hand she gave an airy wave down the hall before adding with a touch of defiance. 'And I've stayed over a couple of times.'

'Oh,' I said, wondering what she expected me to say to that.

'I said I was at yours.'

'Ah.' That explained her son's suspicion of me.

'I knew Farquhar would start fretting. I'm a grown woman, for God's sake. He treats me like I'm in my dotage.'

'I think he's just worried about you.'

'I doubt that very much. More worried I'll do something foolish with his inheritance. He's never forgiven me for marrying George. As if I didn't know exactly what he was like.' Her eyes dimmed and I could see she was lost in a memory. 'A complete charmer and a chancer and we had such a lovely time together.' And then she snapped back to the present. 'Come.'

I followed her into the house and she led me into the front room on the right. A huge three-sided bay window with a deep cushion-filled window seat let in plenty of light, making the high-ceilinged room bright and welcoming.

I touched the soft velvet pile of one of two Wesley Barrell sofas in dark cranberry. They were well used and very slightly worn but still comfortable-looking, with the sort of classic appearance that never goes out of style. Floor-length curtains in a plush Arts and Crafts-patterned fabric dressed the windows, adding to the feeling of refined opulence. My eyes were drawn to the beautiful little details in the room like the Art Deco-style bronze lamps that dotted the occasional tables at either end of both sofas.

'This is lovely, Hilda.'

'I know,' she said, her usual blithe self-confidence returning. 'I've been spending more and more time here, heating myself up some soup at lunchtime.'

I could see why; it was a lovely home. There were lots of family photos including several black and whites of weddings in the thirties in silver frames arranged on a table near the window. On the walls there was an eclectic mix of landscapes and still lifes, and a full set of bookshelves took up an entire alcove filled with battered paperbacks interspersed with interesting ornaments – glass vases, elegant china figures and painted porcelain plates – that had clearly come from different parts of the world.

'Daft really, but I just like being here.' She picked up a little Japanese figure and toyed with it. 'I miss my things. After my fall I was a little bit confused.' She frowned and I realised that this was a big admission for Hilda. 'And Farquhar went on and on about how I wasn't getting any younger.' She pursed her lips, exasperation bouncing off her. 'He's a good boy but gosh he winds me up. Sometimes I think he's getting his own back. He never really forgave me for sending him off to boarding school.' With a sigh, she placed the little figure in the palm of her hand and peered at it as she spoke. 'And maybe I shouldn't have done. It was just that, at the time, the business was really taking off. Truth be told, I rather liked jetting off all over the place to auctions with my third husband. Farquhar's dad had been such a dull, old stick and I hated being incarcerated in a stately home. I'd always been used to being so active and busy. I found the whole motherhood thing rather dull. Maybe it might have been different if I'd had two, but I couldn't. I rather put my career before him.' Her fingers tightened on the little Japanese figure, her knuckles whitening. 'Of course, I regret it now. But what's done is done. It's too late, and he's turned into a pompous, overbearing fool. I've no idea where he gets it,' she said as I bit my tongue at the irony.

I'd have said he was definitely an exaggerated version of his mother.

'After I had my fall, before I knew it, he'd organised a place at Sunnyside and when I was discharged from hospital, the ambulance took me there.' Putting the figurine down, she picked up a Chinese jar, fiddling with its lid. 'Of course, being a man, he didn't pack any home comforts or any of my favourite things.'

I didn't say anything for a minute, too bemused by this information. I couldn't see Hilda putting up with such high-handed, however well-meaning, behaviour.

'I know,' her eyes danced. 'Shocking. I think I agreed just to keep the peace.'

Or, I realised with a jolt of sadness, she'd been in worse shape than she was admitting. She always seemed so strong and indomitable.

'I suppose he wanted to know you'd be safe and cared for,' I said slowly.

'You think?' Hilda said wryly, the amused twinkle back in her eyes. 'I suspect it was more that he wouldn't have to worry about getting midnight calls saying I'd had a fall. Someone else could take care of it.'

'That's a bit harsh, don't you think?' Something had struck me about his tapping fingers. I think her son did worry about her; he just wasn't very good at showing his feelings.

'Possibly,' she said, pinching her lips, as I held her gaze. 'Oh, all right. He might have been a bit worried. And I was quite lonely. It was… well, it wasn't a good time. And I admit, at first it was nice to have the company; I'd got used to the bustle of being in hospital and not being so independent but then, after a while, it all became rather routine. I thought people there might have a bit more get up and go. Unfortunately, it's all got up and gone. They're all ancient or not my cup of tea.

'When I saw you that morning, I'd been at Sunnyside for three months. Chatting with you made me realise the people there were starting to make me feel old. And, despite being surrounded by people, I felt lonely. I don't want to feel old. You, Ash, and the girls make me feel young and that there's still a life to live. I was atrophying. That's why I keep running. To keep going. Although, the first time I ran a marathon it was to spite my third husband who said he didn't think I could do it.

'So,' she spread her arms in an expansive gesture. 'What do you think?'

With a grin, which hid my real feelings, I said, 'It's a beautiful home and I can see why you'd want to come back.'

But it was far too big for one person and I could understand exactly why her son had worried about her.

'Study, there.' She pointed to big white-glossed doors as we walked down the wide hallway. 'Dining room, never gets used. Morning room, gets the sunshine first thing, hence the name.' She stopped where the hall widened out into a big square space with a broad-stepped staircase running up the left-hand wall. 'Upstairs, of course. And here, the heart of the house: the kitchen.' I could tell just be the way she said it that this was her favourite room in the house. She led me through into the huge kitchen with an old-fashioned Victorian-style conservatory at the far end overlooking a long garden. It was vast with a mighty eight-ring range as well as two built-in ovens set into a bank of wooden units. There was a marble-topped island inset with a second sink in front of which were four stools. At the other end of the room was a small dining table with eight chairs arranged around it.

'God, Hilda, this is wonderful. Isn't it…?' My voice trailed away.

'I know.' She patted my arm, the light in her eyes fading. 'It's a ridiculous house for one person. Any sensible person can see that. Do you think I'm mad?' Her hand drifted across the marble top. 'We had this imported especially from Italy. George and I went out there to choose it. Ridiculously extravagant but he… he,' her breath hitched, 'he didn't have much time, poor soul.'

She moved into the conservatory with brisk strides to look out at the garden. 'The birds here in the summer are a delight. When he was… George would sit and watch them.'

I went to join her, watching her lift her chin, her throat working. I put an arm around her and she laid her head on my shoulder. She smelled of roses. We stood there for a few minutes in silence before she spoke again. 'It's the memories, you know? I feel closer to him here. I thought moving into Sunnyside would help… but it f-feels like I've abandoned him.' Her voice strained as her face crumpled. 'God, I miss the stupid bastard. He was a complete idiot. Money slipped through his fingers and he was as crooked as they come but he made me laugh. Made me happy. We had such a hoot together. He always wanted to do things. He'd have been a terrible first or second husband; he was definitely a last husband. The fun one, when you've done all the important, adult stuff like jobs, babies, buying houses. He never took anything too seriously. Those last few months we had a ball.' With a sniff she wiped her eyes. 'And then he died.' She sank into a battered armchair by the window. 'Right here.' With old, veined fingers she patted the arm of the chair. 'And then six months later I had a stupid fall. Broke my hip.'

An unhappy twist touched her mouth. 'And then Farquhar decided I shouldn't be here on my own.'

I knelt down next to her and took her hand, gently squeezing her fingers. 'Oh Hilda, I'm sorry.' I could see his point; it was a huge house, but now I realised it was also the repository of Hilda's memories of her late husband and I could see how much it meant to her. It was home. We were lost in thought for a few moments until a cheeky robin bounced onto the wall outside, eyeing us both with curiosity. Hilda laughed and straightened up.

'Freddie's back. George had names for them all. No point being maudlin. Now, what's happening on the parkrun?'

I blinked at the sudden change of tack but there was no arguing with the determined set of Hilda's face and the lines fanning out around her mouth. We were moving on.

'I saw Penny and Janie at school this morning. Janie is emailing the final design for the leaflet and poster today and as soon as I've signed it off, it will go to the printer and he can have them done by Monday next week.'

'That's marvellous news.'

'That gives us a week to distribute leaflets telling people about the meeting which we've agreed with Sascha will take place the following Thursday.'

'You're making excellent progress.'

'I'm getting a lot of support. The Harriers have been brilliant, but I guess they're interested in running, so it's hardly surprising. It's the wider community I'm worried about. Getting people to sign up to help. If we don't have the volunteers, it's a non-starter.'

'Don't you worry about that.' She tapped her nose.

But I was worried. I couldn't imagine why people would sign up and give up their precious Saturday mornings. Didn't most people have better things to do? A little voice in my head scoffed, *what, like you did?* Going to work on a Saturday morning had been a habit for years, the best way to catch up with myself. I wouldn't be able to do that for the foreseeable future, not while I had Poppy and Ava staying with me.

'Now,' Hilda lifted her wrist, 'you're going to be late

meeting Ash and I'd hate you to miss your run. I did mine at seven o'clock this morning,' she added a tad smugly.

———————

'You've shaved your beard off,' I said, stopping dead at the sight of a clean-shaven Ash coming towards me on the path. And then for some bizarre reason I promptly burst into tears.

Ash immediately put his arm around my shoulder and led me to our usual park bench and sat me down as I sobbed. It was the first time in a very long time that I felt crying wasn't a weakness and that I allowed myself to feel the emotion and let go.

'Hey, hey,' he murmured, pulling me into his chest. 'I thought you'd be pleased about the beard. I didn't expect this kind of reaction.'

Dragging in a hoarse breath, I let out a spluttery laugh. 'S-sorry. It's nothing to do with the beard.' At least, I didn't think it was. At the back of my mind I was aware that it was a sign that things were changing. 'I've j-just s-seen Hilda.'

Ash hugged me tighter. 'Is she okay?'

'Yes, I guess.' Sadness overwhelmed me again. 'But not really. I've been to her house today.' I blinked at him and wiped away the last of my tears, my throat choked again. 'It's so sad. It's a beautiful house but she'll never live there again and she knows it.'

Ash held my hand as I spoke, squeezing it gently. 'It's full of memories of her late husband.' I thought of her careful handling of the netsuke ornament. 'Full of things that mean so much to her. There's a whole life packed into that house.' I paused. 'I think Hilda is actually quite lonely. The negative comments she makes about the other people in the home, I think that's frustration that they can't keep up with her rather than from real malice. I think we're helping her as much as she's helped us.' I stopped and cast a quick glance at the empty space on the bench, a smile accompanying the memory of the first time I met Hilda. 'She's good at finding us things to do. She has a very clever habit of telling us what we need to do and then she carries on talking, changing the subject before we have time to say no, so that by the end of the conversation, it's a fait accompli.'

Narrowing his eyes, he considered my words. 'You've got it right. That's exactly what she does.'

'Probably a tactic she learned in her MI6 days.' I sighed. 'Sorry. It just got to me.'

He lifted his hand and swiped a thumb over my tearstains. I stared at his face, all the planes and angles revealed in their full glory. My mouth went dry. 'You look so much better,' I blurted out, except my voice had gone all husky with the sudden bolt of lust. My emotional outburst had left me feeling a little raw, bringing everything to the surface and my tenuous control slipped. Every nerve ending was tuned into Ash. He was back to his old self and he was positively mouth-wateringly gorgeous. For those few seconds I was unable to take my eyes off the lean lines of his jaw and cheekbones.

A slow smile lit his face. 'Like what you see?' There was just a faint echo of his former cockiness in the words and a slight lift of his mouth at one side, a crooked, knowing line of his lips.

And suddenly, just like the night at Darren's, all the sexual chemistry that had been on low charge for weeks came roaring back.

I nodded and reached forward to brush my fingers across the bare skin of his face. His lips grazed my hand and then he leaned forward and kissed me very, very gently on the lips, as if I might break under his touch.

It was a soft kiss, a gentle hello and a promise of things to come, and we both drew back, each of us smiling almost shyly.

'So what brought this on?' I lifted my hand again to feel his freshly bared skin, unable to stop myself.

'I've got a second job interview. That's where I was on Tuesday afternoon. And I have another job interview lined up next week.' Stars of happiness danced in his eyes and it was such a wonderful sight that I couldn't help myself.

'Oh Ash, that's fantastic.' I threw my arms around him and hugged him. 'I'm so pleased for you. Where? When?' As I started to pull away, his hand clamped on top of mine, a sudden sparkle in his eyes, that barely-there lift of an eyebrow. Like a switch tripping, the hormones took over and fireworks fizzed in my chest, my stomach making my toes curl. He could read me as well as I could read him. We'd always been on the same wavelength when it came to the thread of sexual attraction between us.

I flinched as his eyes locked on mine, his steady gaze sending my heartrate into a gallop.

'I think you're more excited than I am,' he stated in a cool drawl with another twitch of that crooked mouth. Despite his sang-froid response, I knew he felt the fizz between us. This time, the kiss was an X-rated sizzler.

When the kiss finally came to an end, both of us slightly out of breath, he leaned his forehead against mine. 'I feel like we're back where we started. I think this isn't far from the very first place I kissed you.' We both turned to look at the lamppost a few metres behind us.

'A lot's happened since then.' I sighed

'Yeah and… I've been a dick.'

I raised an eyebrow.

'Don't get too used to me saying it. I was a self-absorbed prick and I don't know why you've stuck around.'

'To be honest, I didn't really have much choice. Hilda seemed determined to befriend both of us.'

'Her lost souls. But you were kind. You sent that text… and I certainly didn't deserve it.' He reached out and held my hand. 'Shit, I was a mess. I owe her… and you. I've no idea why you stuck by me. I was a miserable bastard. What would either of us have done without Hilda?'

'I dunno.' I lifted my head to give him a frank stare. 'But I think we helped save her too.'

He tilted his head with laughing dismissal. 'You think? I'm not so sure about that.'

'I am.' I spoke with sudden certainty, remembering her at the house earlier.

'It wasn't just Hilda, you know. There were lots of times you could have told me to piss off.'

'I guess I was worried about you as well.'

'You hardly knew me.'

'We slept together. That's quite an intimate way of getting to know someone.'

He winced. 'And I cocked that up, good and proper.'

'Yeah, you did. I don't normally sleep with people that easily.' I paused and looked directly into his eyes. 'You hurt me.'

He lifted a tentative hand to my face. 'And I'm deeply sorry for that. It was a terrible way to treat you and I bitterly regret it now. If it's any consolation, I was so full of self-loathing that I was determined to burn every last bridge. If I hadn't been made redundant, I was going to call you and ask to see you on the Monday night.'

I gave him a sad smile. 'And I probably would have said yes.'

'I'm really sorry, Claire. After I lost my job, yes I was angry and bitter, but also I didn't think I was good enough for someone as amazing as you.' This time his apology was enough, but I wasn't going to be a pushover. He was going to have to prove himself all over again. All I'd ever wanted from him was honesty. It had been the foundation on which we'd started, pushing each other past the façades we'd both built.

'You're forgiven. And talking of sneaky subject changes,' I pursed my lips and folded my arms, quirking my own eyebrow in a replay of his, deliberately bringing the tone back to friendly banter, 'are you going to tell me about this job interview?'

Sudden amusement danced in his eyes and he leaned down and kissed me with a fleeting brush on the lips. 'You're a smart cookie, did you know that?'

I frowned. Where was he going with this?

'Finance Director.' He paused and kissed me again, punctuating his words with more kisses. 'For an engineering company.' Another kiss. 'Offices all around the UK.'

'An engineering company?' I gave him a sharp nudge in the ribs, a cocky tilt to my head, even though inside I was beaming. 'Well, how about that?'

'Yeah, yeah, yeah. You're allowed to take all the credit. And

I don't mind if you say "I told you so," I'm so bloody grateful to get an interview. But... thank you.'

'I didn't do anything. You're the one with the CV, references, and track record.'

'I think you did. As soon as I – admittedly reluctantly because I'm pig headed – changed tack I landed two interviews straight away.'

'That's brilliant, I'm so pleased for you.'

'I haven't got them yet.'

'Yes, but it...' I bit my lip.

He took pity on me. 'Shows that someone wants me despite all my self-pitying navel-gazing.'

'It's a confidence boost,' I said.

'It is, but it's come at the right time.' He shot me a hesitant, sidelong glance. 'I should have been braver, like you.'

'What do you mean?'

'You realised you had a problem. You went to the doctor. I know you didn't like being signed off but it was the right thing. Whereas I knew I wasn't right but I couldn't admit it to myself.'

'I have a confession to make. If I'd have thought for one minute I'd be signed off, there's no way I would have gone to the doctor's. I only went because of that stupid cut and if I'd put Savlon on it like you suggested...'

'Maybe it was subconscious. You knew something was wrong but focused on your arm.'

I realised he was probably right.

'Whatever it was, you still went. Whereas I just hid and drank myself stupid for a week. God knows what would have happened if I hadn't gone out running a couple of times and that was only because I was bored out of my brain. The running has helped. A lot.' He paused and lifted a hand to my face. 'I think dinner is long overdue.'

'Dinner would be nice,' I said with a sigh, almost nestling into his touch.

'The Beech House. Next Friday?'

'Do we want to go back there? I wonder if it's jinxed.'

'It's not jinxed; this time I won't be a dick and I'll call you afterwards.' His smooth-shaven face dimpled with a smile before he added, 'I'm too scared of Hilda not to.'

'Oh God, you do realise she's going to be unbearable.'

'She's going to be bloody thrilled and she won't be able to say no to babysitting.'

I laughed. 'I don't think she would anyway. It feels like she's moved in, although I'm not complaining. She's a fabulous cook.'

'Probably taught Raymond Blanc everything he knows.'

'Wasn't it Mary Berry? Do you think she's really done all the things she's said?'

'Who knows?'

'One of these days, I ought to google her.' I'd thought about it a couple of times.

'Don't do that. Just think how disappointed we'd be if it turned out she'd embellished things.'

'True,' I said, liking the way he phrased the sentence. Embellished sounded so much kinder.

Suddenly everyone else seemed to be moving forward and I was about to step back into the same old groove. I was due back at work next week and in a lightning-strike moment, I wasn't sure it was where I wanted to be anymore. The thought shocked me so much I missed a breath.

The thought of getting on a train every morning and

leaving Churchstone filled me with dread. I loved my morning routine now, taking the girls to school, having a quick chat with Penny and Janie, going for a run and then going home. With sudden insight I realised I didn't want to leave my home every day, I wanted to stay in it and play. Enjoy being there. I derived huge satisfaction bringing the house back to order after the girls had swept through. Making it all neat and tidy again.

The painter was due this week and I'd ordered new furniture for the kitchen-diner to turn it into more of a family living space, as we seemed to spend so much time in there.

My heart banged uncomfortably as it dawned on me that I didn't want to spend hours and hours in an office ploughing through data and figures anymore, almost divorced from real life. I wanted to spend time with people, look after them, cook, clean, make a home. I wanted to solve problems and find solutions for things that mattered, not churn out endless consultancy reports on the possible viability of projects that may never happen.

For so long my job had consumed me… and now I didn't think I wanted to go back. What would I do, though? My job defined me. Without it, what was I? For a moment I was filled with terror; I felt like I'd stepped into no-man's land and on either side there was nothing to rescue me.

Chapter Twenty-Four

Ava was hanging from the fence, like a small, agile monkey, chatting to my neighbour, whose name I'd completely forgotten. She'd introduced herself when I'd first moved in and, I'll be honest, she hadn't seemed like my type so I'd paid little attention and, to my shame, I'd actively avoided her, exchanging probably fewer than six words with her. Ava was more than making up for it now.

'Teatime, Ava,' I said with a friendly nod at the woman, interrupting the little girl's monologue about her soft toys which, it appeared, was being well received with rapt nods and the odd squeaky, 'Well I never!' or high-pitched 'Really?'.

'Hello,' I said, acknowledging the woman but in a cut-off tone that forbade further engagement. There was homework to be done and bath time to be had after tea, both of which Ava was very good at putting off until the absolute last minute.

'Ava's been telling me all about the parkrun. She's a clever little girl.' My neighbour held up one of the leaflets that we'd been out distributing on our way back from school. One through every letterbox on the route home. It was the last leaflet drop; over the last few days, Janie, Penny, and I, and our respective children, had been out every night after school. The meeting next Thursday had been promoted on Facebook, Instagram, and Twitter and the local radio station was interested in doing an interview about our plans.

'It sounds very exciting.'

'Mmm,' I said. Exciting was the not the word I'd have used. Terrifying more like. What if no one turned up?

'Well, different anyway. I've seen you going out running. That's very disciplined. Good for you. Not sure I could run for a bus. Never was very good at sport.' Ducking her head, she scrutinised the leaflet, moving her lips as she read. 'Five kilometres. What's that in real money? Quite a way. I certainly couldn't run that far. Not sure my hips are built for running.'

'People are welcome to come and walk it,' I said.

'Are they? What, not run it? Well, that would be something at least. I hadn't thought of that.'

'Yes,' I said with feeling, realising there might be lots of people like her who needed a reassuring nudge. 'We want everyone to feel they can join in. Walking, running, or volunteering to help. You should come to the meeting.'

'Oh, I don't know about that. I won't know anyone. I'm not sure. All those people. Probably lots of proper runners. You're not going to want people like me there. No doubt it will be very busy.'

'You know me,' piped up Ava. 'And Auntie Claire, now.'

'Oooh, I don't know.'

'Do come. You can come with us.'

I needed every bum on a seat I could get. 'We'll be leaving at quarter to seven next Thursday night.'

'Oh. Right. Quarter to seven. Good. Yes. Well, maybe. Yes. We'll have to see. Bye Ava, nice to talk to you.' Walking backwards as she spoke, she retreated into her house as if she wasn't sure she wanted to end the interaction but wasn't sure how to keep it going either.

I really must encourage her, I decided as I led Ava back into the house for tea. She was exactly the sort of person we needed and who needed us.

The kitchen needed a little navigation. A lot of stuff was packed away, as Hilda's friend's son was coming in the morning and was doing me a huge favour coming on a Saturday. He was going to decorate the whole room and put down a new floor. He seemed to think him, his mate, and his flooring guy could get it all done in one day, which was a great relief as I was due back at work on Monday and I wanted to get as much done before then as possible.

Between us, Hilda, the girls, and I had finally opted for the Farrow and Ball green rather than the grey I'd originally envisioned and a wooden-style Karndean floor instead of the smart, unforgiving black slate I'd planned. With the existing glossy cream cupboards, the colour scheme was going to be smart and homely, especially with all the new cosy accessories I'd already bought.

'It's messy,' complained Poppy, her eyes darting nervously around the semi-bare kitchen as I served tea up on the round wooden table.

'Yes, but it's only for a couple of days and then it will be lovely. And the new sofa will arrive the day after tomorrow.'

The kitchen-diner was about to become the heart of the house and the thought of it filled me with pleasure. Since the girls had arrived, it had already become the room we all used the most and I'd been tempted to move one of my sofas from the front room but then decided that I wanted a big L-shaped sofa that we could all pile on together with a small TV opposite.

We'd settled into a good routine after school and it was difficult to believe that the girls had only been here for nearly three weeks.

'So how was everyone's day?' I asked as we sat down to tea.

Ava bounced to her feet, 'Guess, guess, guess! I got a gold star.'

'Well done, sweetie. That's great.'

'I got eight in my spelling test.' Her eyes shone with pleasure. 'Only two wrong and Miss Parr said my star was for hard work and best provement. And Lucy Chambers didn't get one.'

A little sunshine burst of pride lit up inside me. It was lovely to see her delight in her achievement, especially as she really struggled with reading and spelling. We'd put in a lot of work, practising every day and I'd made sure I read with her every night.

'Huh!' sniffed Poppy. 'Eight.'

I sent her a quelling look and she quietened. 'What about you? What did you learn today?'

'We built a circuit from our homework and the light switched on.' She paused and a smile broke through. 'It was kind of cool. It was the design Ash helped with and ours was the best.'

'Well done, both of you.' I rested my elbows on the table,

suddenly proud of both of them. They were brilliant kids; they'd adapted so well to the news that their mother was going to be away for longer. 'You put me to shame. All I did was pack up the kitchen and go for a run.'

'How far did you run today, Auntie Claire? Further?' Bless her, Poppy liked to keep tabs on my running stats because she knew I was desperate not to show myself up once we got the parkrun set up.

'4.4k without stopping once.' I bent at the waist with a little bow. Both girls began to clap and Ava hopped down from her chair and ran over to the tally chart we were keeping on the fridge door. She tugged it down and brought it over for me to fill in today's total.

'That's good. Only point six to go,' said Poppy with her usual precision.

Only point six. All of us had come quite a long way in a few short weeks.

So it was a heck of a surprise when, ten minutes later, halfway through tea, Poppy suddenly announced, 'I don't like broccoli,' and pushed the vegetable to the side of her plate and let her fork drop with a clatter, folding her arms with mutinous teenage sulkiness.

'I'll have yours.' Ava launched a rescue mission and stabbed at the broccoli with her fork, sending Poppy's oven chips all over her lap and the floor.

In response, Poppy jabbed at Ava's hand with her own fork. Ava screamed, threw her cutlery down, and began to wail.

'Poppy!' I glared at her and put down my own knife and fork, picking up Ava's hand. There were three neat little dents in the pudgy flesh but the skin wasn't broken. 'Calm down,

Ava, she didn't really hurt you, although, she shouldn't have done that.' I rubbed at her hand. 'Poppy, that was unnecessary.' Poppy shrugged and her mouth flattened in a recalcitrant line. 'You need to apologise to your sister.'

There was a small battle of wills as I continued to glare at her.

'Soz,' she said, her eyes meeting mine with a definite now-what-are-you-going-to-do look.

'That's not an apology,' I snapped, irritated by her uncharacteristically unhelpful attitude. 'What's got into you?'

She stared down at her plate. This was unchartered territory and I didn't know what to do. I tried to think what Hilda would suggest. 'I'm very disappointed.' That struck a nerve. I saw her flinch. 'You know better than that. How would you like it if I did that to you?'

Poppy's mouth tightened and she lifted one shoulder. I thought asking for a proper apology was pushing it, so I left it this time.

'Right, let's tidy up. Poppy, you can stack the dishwasher. Ava, go and get ready for your bath and no messing about.'

I ran up the stairs quickly and set the bath going. When I came downstairs, Poppy was putting the plates into the rack but her movements were stiff and awkward and she kept glancing at the counters where I'd stacked all the things out of the way for the painter in the morning.

'Is it bothering you? The mess?' I asked gently.

She lifted her narrow shoulders but didn't say anything. With a flash of unexpected insight, I realised I'd come to know the girls far better than I could have guessed I would. It wasn't just the mess; it was the uncertainty of everything in her young life. She was living in a strange house that wasn't quite home, her mother was absent, and she was living with a woman who had no proper child-rearing experience. My heart clenched at the sight of her pale, stern face and I put my arms around her and pulled her into a hug. 'Come here, you.'

At first she was stiff and then she softened into my embrace and I felt her warm wet tears on my neck. 'N-next w-week… when… w-when you go back to work… we won't have tea here. You won't… you won't want us anymore. We have to go to Breakfast Club and After-school Club and go to bed.'

Oh Poppy, I thought, hugging her tighter, my throat closing. 'Of course I'll still want you. I love you and Ava. You silly sausage, why do you think I'm buying a nice big sofa? It's so that we can all have snuggles together.' I held her close, not knowing what else to say and feeling totally inadequate. I wasn't her mother; what did I know about how an eleven-year-old felt?

Her arms crept around my waist and we stood like that for a minute and I wished I had all the answers.

'Poppy, I'm sorry that I have to go back to work. It's my job and that's what pays the bills. But I promise I'll still be able to look after you. I'm sorry you have to go to the clubs but… I don't know what else to do.' It was worrying the hell out of me and I didn't know how things would work then and I wasn't going to lie to her about it.

Being honest with her seemed to reassure her. I felt her chest heave with the sigh. 'It's all right, Auntie Claire.' Lifting her head she gave me a stoic smile which ramped up my underlying guilt another notch.

'Oh shi—! Shoot! The bath water.' I hugged Poppy quickly and then raced upstairs with her hot on my heels. We made it just in time, the water already lapping at the top edge of the bath. I plunged my arm into the water to yank out the plug, ignoring my clothes.

'Phew,' I said, sinking gratefully onto the loo seat, the sleeve of my hoody dripping wet. 'That was a close call. I'm a bit wet.'

Wide-eyed, Poppy nodded and then giggled at the sight of me, half soaked.

It was a relief to hear the childish release. The next few weeks were going to be challenging and top of my mind was just how long I was going to be able to fob the girls off with the landslide story to explain Alice's ongoing absence. For their sakes, I hoped my sister would grow up and come home soon.

Chapter Twenty-Five

'You're looking well.' Karen the HR Director did a double take. 'You really do look well. Have you spent the last month at a health farm or something?'

'No, just eating properly and exercising.'

'Well, keep it up. I'm supposed to ask you a whole load of questions about how you're feeling.' She grinned at me. 'So how are you feeling about coming back to work?'

'Fine,' I said, although a little knot of anxiety had been burning a hole in my stomach since last night. I'd been super organised over the weekend. All the washing was done and ironed. The girls each had clean clothes for every day of the week. I had bought enough supplies for the three days they had packed lunches. We were up to date on homework. I'd done a menu plan for the week. I was on fire. But I still couldn't help worrying about how it would all work. Poppy had been very quiet going to school this morning. I knew she wasn't looking forward to After-school Club.

'No concerns or worries?' asked Karen. She pounced on my hesitation. 'Anything?'

This was important and I owed it to the girls to be totally honest. 'My circumstances have changed and... well, I'm going to have to be more disciplined about leaving on time. Of course I can work in the evenings to catch up.' So much for good intentions, but I wanted to reassure her I could do the job. That was my emergency back-up option.

'Claire, you shouldn't have to do extra hours. That's what we want to avoid. Times have changed, love.' Her Yorkshire accent deepened along with her sincerity. 'And I know I'm not supposed to say that either, but seriously, they have. We, and I speak for the board, do care that our brightest and best members of staff don't burn themselves out. This company is only as good as the people it employs; we need to look after them. Gone are the days when we expect staff to work all hours. Mental health and wellbeing are high on our agenda.'

'Well... that's good to hear.' I'd heard it all before but this time it did seem to ring true, although I was pretty sure that working nine to five put paid to any promotion prospects. 'I'm now looking after my two nieces; my sister is away at the moment.'

Karen raised one of her heavy eyebrows. 'How long for?'

'That's the gazillion-dollar question. I'm not sure but... it could be for a while.'

'How long's a while? A month, six months?'

It sounded so lame and I shrugged as I said, 'I'm not entirely sure, but I'd say at least a month, possibly longer.'

Karen was visibly restraining herself from asking questions but I could see she was curious. We were friends of a sort, so I gave in. 'My sister went to India on some sort of yoga retreat but apparently she's found herself out there and decided to stay.'

It was quite gratifying to see Karen's mouth drop open in a capital 'O' of disbelief.

'You're not kidding, are you?'

'Unfortunately not. Don't get me wrong, I don't mind having my nieces. They're fab.' My smile was filled with a burst of love for them which seemed to get stronger every day. 'But I'm pretty pissed off that my sister has done this to them. She's not even Facetimed them or anything.'

'Blimey Claire. That's… shit.'

'For them, yes. But for me…' An increasingly familiar glow of warmth settled in its usual place just under my sternum. 'I'm kind of enjoying having them live with me.' My lovely new kitchen was now finished and it looked wonderful. Last night, after everything had been done, the three of us had snuggled on the new sofa under velvety soft blankets and watched *The Dragon Prince*, which, despite claiming it was too young for her, seemed to have absorbed Poppy just as much as Ava. Another memory to be stored in the fabric of the house for as long as it was mine.

'Well, it seems to be doing you good.' She peered at my face. 'I think you're glowing. Or it's make-up and if so I want the brand name.'

'That's just the exercise. I've been doing a bit of running. Me and some friends are setting up a parkrun.'

'Whoa. Who are you and what have you done with Claire?' We'd shared lunch in the canteen often enough that she knew this was not normal Harrison operating procedure.

'I know. Who'd have thought?'

'That's amazing. You do know we have a community policy

here? You can take paid days to do work in the local community. That would probably count.'

'Now, that is useful to know. How would you feel if I left a little early on Thursday as I've got a meeting to recruit volunteers that night?' I might as well push for it now.

'Let me check the policy.' She tapped her pencil in a quick rat-a-tat. 'But I'm pretty sure it's the sort of thing the company would support. Let me know when it starts. I've done the Hyde Park one a couple of times. It's good fun.'

Now, that was a surprise. I couldn't imagine besuited Karen, who wore stilettos every single day at work, in trainers and Lycra.

A dimple appeared in one cheek. 'I wear Lululemon kit and Brooks trainers,' she said, answering my unasked question.

I bit back a laugh. 'Do you break out in a sweat?'

'I try very hard not to. It's so undignified.' She winked and we both burst out laughing.

I settled back into a routine quickly and for once, when five-thirty came, I was more than ready to abandon my computer and dash out of the door to join the rush to Leeds Station. I'd given myself a very strict talking to: I was not going to fall back into my old bad ways. The downside of leaving on time was that I got caught up in the rush hour and commuting back was as miserable as it was in the mornings. I didn't get a seat for several stations. Even with careful time management, Poppy and Ava were some of the last children to be picked up. The club closed at six-thirty and, on Wednesday night, three days in, I arrived at the school at six twenty-seven.

'Claire, Claire!' called Ava, running across the floor when I was buzzed into the After-school Club. 'We had tea. Sausages and beans. And I played with the Lego.'

I helped her put her coat on; although summer was just around the corner, the evening was still cool.

'Come on, Poppy.'

The older girl slouched her way over, dragging her coat along behind her with a heavy sigh. 'How was your day, Poppy?' She'd been sulky and difficult for most of the week. I knew it was just the change of routine and hoped she'd get used to it soon.

'Fine.' She glared at me as she shouldered her bag onto her back. 'Until we got here. It's lame and there's nothing to do. And tea was pathetic. Baby portions.'

'Well, that's all right. You can have something when we get home.'

'Goodie! Can I have some cake? Hilda's lemon drizzle.' Ava yawned sleepily. Poor things, it was a very long day for them. I did a quick tot up of how many hours they'd been on the school premises. Shit. Eleven hours. Longer than my working day and I was a grown-up.

'We'll see,' I said as we filed out of the building.

'That means no, piglet,' said Poppy. There was a vicious gleam in her eyes as she looked up at me.

I closed my eyes briefly as Ava let out the familiar wail of hurt.

'Ava, stop that. Poppy, apologise to your sister.'

'Sorry,' she said in a surly voice which clearly meant anything but, but at least she had apologised, which was a definite improvement. Maybe I did have some authority with her after all.

'When's Mummy coming home?' Poppy's tone rang with belligerence when we halfway home, walking along the road skirting the park, and I could tell she was spoiling for a fight; she had that boxer's bounce in her gait as she walked.

'I'm... I'll phone her this week and see what the latest is. She's very remote and India, where she is, they don't have the same sort of digging equipment we do.'

'Why can't you call her today? We're five hours ahead. Mummy never goes to bed early.'

'Poppy, it's late. By the time we get home, we need to get organised and then it will be Ava's bedtime. Why don't we ring her at the weekend?' That would give me time to text Alice and tell her that she *must* Facetime her children.

I shot a glance at my watch. 'It's already quite late.'

'We're only late because of your job. I want to speak to Mum. You can't stop us.'

'Me too. Mummy!' trilled Ava. Dancing clumsily around my feet, she looked a little punch drunk with tiredness, bless her. 'Let's ring Mummy.'

The jab about my job did the trick as she'd known it would, but when Ava joined in, even though I was tired and desperate to eat – I hadn't had lunch today – I gave in.

'Okay, we'll try and ring Mummy when we get home.'

We were still a few hundred metres from home when I had to scoop Ava up. She was on her last legs and stumbling with tiredness. Lifting her up, I had to struggle with carrying my laptop bag and my handbag as well as a carrier bag of groceries I'd grabbed from the M&S at the station. God, this was so unfair on them. I was knackered, so how on earth did they feel?

'Can you open the door for me, please?' I handed over my keys to Poppy.

She flounced up to the front door and Ava woke briefly as I hoisted her onto my hip, gave me a sweet, sleepy smile that grabbed at my heart, and dropped her head onto my chest. I dropped a kiss on her tangled curls and hugged her, following Poppy up the path.

'She's such a baby.' Poppy's lip curled and as soon as she'd opened the door she marched away down the hall, leaving me to close it with my hip. I watched her go with a heavy sigh. I didn't have the energy to rebuke her.

I climbed the stairs carrying Ava, who was no lightweight, into her bedroom. She roused briefly as I put her down on the bed, undressing her and putting on her pyjamas before tucking her in.

I sat on the edge of the bed and bent to kiss her rosy cheeks. Affectionate as ever, her arms snaked around my neck like a small, determined python and she tugged me down, snuggling into my neck. I smiled. She was an easy child and I relaxed, enjoying the warmth of her arms and her soft snuffly breaths against my skin. If only life were this simple and we could stay here in the lamplit dusky light.

'Night, night Ava da Pava.' The long-forgotten nickname slipped out. Gosh, I'd called her that when she was about three. I swallowed back a lump.

'Night, night, Claire Bear,' she whispered, her eyelashes fluttering against her cheeks as if she could barely keep her eyes open. Stroking her ever matted curls, I watched as she slipped into sleep, her rosebud mouth slackening and tiny snores whistling from her nose. My heart expanded at the sight of her, unguarded and innocent, and part of me wanted to scoop her up, hold her tight and make sure she'd always be safe.

'Oh God, Alice, I hope I'm doing this right. I think Ava's happy,' I whispered in my own personal prayer. 'She's so sunny. Easy. Sometimes she reminds me of you.' Giving Ava one last careful kiss, I stood up slowly and whispered, 'Night, night little one,' before I crept out of the room.

As I came down the stairs with my mobile in my hand, I could hear the television. For some reason, this week Poppy had taken to turning the volume right up. I suspected she did it to annoy me and to drown out the noises of me tidying up the kitchen or cooking or tapping away at my laptop.

I winced at the on-screen shouting. Probably *Hollyoaks*. It was a new treat for her while I put Ava to bed. A compromise on my part because I wasn't entirely convinced it was suitable but I'd needed something that made her feel she was being treated in a more grown-up way than her sister.

When I walked into the room, she was curled up on one end of the new sofa and studiously ignored me. Well, two could play at that game. I was too knackered to care. I'd be in bed not long after her, once I'd cleared out a few emails that I hadn't got to today, but first I had to make myself something to eat.

'Are we going to phone Mummy or not?' The challenge rang in her voice, daring me to say no.

'Well, Ava is asleep now. Why don't we leave it until the morning, then you can both join in?'

'Ava's just a baby. I want to speak to Alice.' Poppy slid off the sofa and lifted her chin with the defiant belligerence I was becoming used to.

I didn't have the energy to fight. Instead I hauled my phone out of my bag and made the call using WhatsApp. The phone rang and rang and rang. Poppy stared hard at the screen, her body rigid.

Please pick up, Alice. Please.

But Alice didn't pick up.

'She's probably in bed,' I said as gently as I could, feeling guilty because I could have handled this better. The rings finally stopped. 'It's after midnight there. Why don't we phone in the morning?' I reached out to try and hug her but Poppy swung away from me, her hands clenched in tight little fists.

Swallowing back the lump in my throat, I let her go and watched as she threw herself onto the sofa and turned the television back on. She reminded me of a hedgehog, prickly and unapproachable, and I decided to give her some time and space. Instead, I busied myself making something to eat.

———

Almost swaying with tiredness and hunger – I hadn't stopped today – I stood in front of the grill waiting for the cheese to bubble. I was already falling into bad habits, working through my lunch hour. I sniffed and sighed. Perfect comfort food. Cheese and Marmite on toast.

'Please may I have some?'

Startled, I turned to find Poppy beside me. Her face was white and strained.

'Of course. Are you hungry?'

'They give you little-kids' portions at After-school Club. Like, a tiny sausage and a spoonful of beans.'

'You should have said you were still hungry.'

Her mouth flattened and she shrugged.

It was as close to an apology as I was going to get.

'You can have one of these and I'll make some more. Can you eat two?'

She nodded.

We both ate the first slice of cheese on toast standing up and I moaned. Nothing quite beats the combination of toast, melted cheese, and Marmite. Poppy gave me an uncertain smile. I raised my eyebrows at her. My stomach let out an unladylike rumble of confirmation.

'Excuse me. I missed lunch.'

Her eyes widened. 'You must be really, really hungry.' She looked down at her slice of toast, catching her lip between her teeth before asking, 'Do you want this?'

'No, no, you have it.' I took another bite of my own toast. 'I'll make some more. You can help slice up the cheese.'

'You should take a packed lunch,' Poppy said. 'It's bad if you don't eat. You'll get too thin again.'

I glanced at her, surprised. It almost sounded like she cared.

'You're right.' Except, the mornings were still a rush, no matter how organised I was or how early I tried to get everyone up. Ava was painfully slow when she didn't want to do something. Like get out of bed or get dressed. No matter what tactics I employed, I had to keep on top of her every minute, chivvying her along. Even Hilda was out of ideas.

Together we made another round of cheese on toast and then sat on the sofa in front of the television to eat it.

'Claire?' Poppy's voice had that leading tone indicating a question was coming.

'Yes.'

'Mum's been away for a long time.'

I stiffened but tried not to show it.

'She has, but hopefully the road will be repaired soon.' God, I hated lying to her. I could kill Alice.

'School are worried.'

'Are they?' I tried to sound nonchalant. Shit. We'd got away with it thus far. I'd hoped by flying under the radar and keeping up with the paperwork, responding to notes, filling in the girls' homework diaries, and doing all the right things, that the school might not notice Alice's prolonged absence. A couple of times in the middle of the night I'd been haunted by imaginary tabloid-style headlines: *Callous Mum of Two Abandons Children to Holiday in Luxury Indian Resort.*

'Do you think…' She paused and turned to me, staring at me with a steady, solemn gaze. Something had been preying on her mind. 'Do you think she'll come back?'

'Of course, she will,' I said, my heart leaping into my mouth. 'Absolutely.'

She lifted her shoulders and her eyes held mine but she gnawed at her lip before lifting her thumb to chew at the nail. I'd noticed her doing it over the last few days. 'What would happen… if… what if you didn't want me and Ava to stay anymore?'

'Oh, Poppy.' I put my arm around her. 'As long as your mum is away, I'll look after you.'

'George Dawkins at school says we'd have to go into care.' I realised that since we'd sat down, she'd sidled closer and was now almost thigh to thigh with me.

'Well, George Dawkins can bog off, because there's no way you two are going anywhere while I have anything to do with it.'

Poppy snorted a little at my vehemence and unexpected language.

'You,' I said, my voice fierce with unshed tears, 'are staying right here, with me.' I put my arm around her and pulled her close. Poor kid. Both she and Ava had had their lives turned upside down and had taken it really well. Alice and I were very different in our approaches. With a flash of realisation, I understood. Poppy needed some surety, some guarantee. I lifted her onto my lap and wrapped my arms around her. 'You're both staying here with me until your mum comes home.'

'Promise?' Her muffled voice came from my chest where she'd buried her head.

'Promise.' I stroked her hair, trying to soothe her, feeling her rigid body huddled against mine.

Chapter Twenty-Six

True to form, Ava hadn't cleaned her teeth and her plait had already started to come undone.

We'd tried calling Alice twice this morning but time was running out and if I was going to get my train, we needed to leave the house in the next ten minutes. Ava had taken not being able to speak to Alice quite philosophically. Poppy had disappeared downstairs, not saying a word.

'Ava, bathroom, now,' I said. 'We're leaving in five minutes and if you're not ready…' She beamed at me, waiting for the empty threat, her big blue eyes guileless.

'I'm nearly, nearly, nearly ready. Just need to put my dolls back to bed. They're very tired.'

So was I. Ava had made a midnight incursion into my bed and done an Exocet heat-seeking missile thing and plastered herself to me. One of us had then slept soundly; the other hadn't. I was knackered. It was a measure of how unsettled Ava was; unlike Poppy, she wasn't able to verbalise it and I wondered if she even realised it herself. In many ways, she was a simple, sunny character.

'They can sleep while you're at school. Bathroom.' I pointed to the frosted glass door, dredging up the French word Dad had always used when Alice and I were kids and he wanted us to get into the car. '*Immédiatement*.' Watching her go, I darted into my room and yanked on my trainers in preparation for my quick hike from school to the station and ran down stairs. It was all about precision timing these days but we were into a good routine. Today was a big day. Tonight was the volunteers' meeting and the good news for the girls was that Hilda was picking them up from school at three-fifteen, so no After-school Club today.

At least I could rely on Poppy to be organised and when I walked into the kitchen, there she was at the table, her uniform neat, her school bag packed and... she gave me a tentative smile and held out a Tupperware box. 'I made you lunch.'

My heart went into freefall as I stopped dead, staring at the plastic box and sudden tears pricked my eyes. 'Oh, Poppy.'

I took the box, my eyes on her narrow, pointed pixie face as her chin lifted in wary defence awaiting my response. I swept her into a hug, feeling her thin frame. 'Thank you.' I sniffed, my voice distinctly wobbly. 'You didn't have to do that. I'm supposed to be looking after you.'

'It's only a cheese sandwich and I put in a Twix and an apple and a cherry tomato.' She shot me a cautious smile as if still uncertain of my reaction.

'I love you, Poppy Harrison.' I gave her a fierce kiss on the forehead. 'That's the nicest thing anyone has done for me for a long time.' I paused. 'I'm sorry we didn't get through to your mum this morning. We'll try again another time.' I'd sent a stinking text to Alice saying she needed to speak to the girls.

'S'okay,' she muttered looking down at her feet. 'Is that Ava ready yet?'

'That Ava had better be.' I grabbed my laptop rucksack containing my heels and my handbag and went into the hall, scooping Ava's duffle coat from the peg.

'Ava, we're going.' A second later, she clattered down the stairs, her white knee socks baggy around her ankles and her hair somehow even more rumpled than before. Sometimes I wondered if her DNA contained scarecrow genes.

'Right, remember that Hilda is picking you up from school tonight.' I stood in the hall by the newel post.

'Yes. And it's the volunteer meeting.'

'An' we can come.' Ava danced around my feet as I checked we had book bags, PE kits, lunches, and water bottles.

'And help,' added Poppy with a little officious nod of her head.

'You can come,' I agreed, although I was a bit worried about Ava having too late a night and being more of a hindrance than a help, but since Hilda had been instrumental in setting up the parkrun, it wouldn't have been fair to ask her to babysit. Poppy had been given clipboard duties and I knew I could rely on her to fulfil them with her usual careful diligence.

'An' when is Hilda coming for a sleepover?'

'On Friday. Tomorrow.' Oh God, it was tomorrow. Friday was tomorrow.

'And you're going out with Ash,' said Poppy, her big eyes strained.

'Yes. We're just going for dinner,' I said in a calm voice,

ignoring the quick flash of excitement at the thought of seeing him on my own, in a restaurant, on a date.

'And Hilda's staying here.' There was deep suspicion in her eyes as they anxiously tacked across my face.

'Yes, but only because if we're late, she can go to bed whenever she wants. It wouldn't be fair to keep her up.'

'But you *are* coming home,' insisted Poppy, holding my gaze with determined doggedness.

'I'm definitely coming home, yes.' I hoped I didn't betray the tiny flicker of thought that I might not come home straight away.

───────────

The rest of the day whizzed by with infuriating speed when I had so much to do at work and had to leave early, and although I could feel my stress levels starting to rise, they were tempered by growing excitement. Tonight's meeting was Phase II of the parkrun programme, bringing us one step closer to making it a reality. Since that life-affirming moment when I passed the finish line in Tring, setting up the parkrun had become a mission, driving me through each week with purpose and resolve. Although I had the girls, my job, Hilda, and a tentative feel-your-way friendship with Ash, the run was the goal that was shaping all our lives. We were all completely invested and the excitement as all five of us, and of course Bill, gathered that evening in my hallway was almost tangible.

'Have we got everything?' I asked, looking around at my assembled troops. Poppy nodded as she clutched a handful of pens in one hand, her arms nursing half a dozen clipboards I'd borrowed from work. Perhaps I was being a little over optimistic as I didn't think more than a handful of people, if that, were going to turn up.

I checked my bag one last time: mobile, notepad, pen, and the usual selection of drinks and snacks to keep Ava going in case she got bored.

'All set.'

'Don't forget Elaine next door,' reminded Ava.

As if I could. As soon as we opened the front door, Elaine yelled, 'Yoo-hoo!' from her own front garden. I think she'd been lurking behind her door for the last half hour. After effusive hellos, she struck up a conversation with Hilda and I fell into step next to Ash, now having acquired Poppy's stationery as she was desperate to hold Bill's lead.

'Evening,' he said in a low for-your-ears-only voice. 'How are you? How's your week been? What's it like being back?'

'Good. Busy.'

He studied my face. 'Not too busy.'

I sighed. The familiar sensation that something bad was about to happen *had* surfaced a couple of times this week. 'I'm coping.' He raised that familiar eyebrow. 'The girls are fed and clothed and I've picked them up on time. Just about.'

'And really?'

'I'm trying really hard to be aware of my stress points. This week I said no to a crazy deadline.'

'Well done.'

I shrugged, not ready to admit that being back at work wasn't giving me the same sense of purpose or of being an important cog in a big, important wheel that it once had.

'If anything, it's the girls I'm worrying about. Especially Poppy. She really hates After-school Club and some horrible child told her she'd get put into care.'

'What a shit.'

'I know. I think I reassured her but poor kid. It's so unsettling not knowing when her mum is coming back. I feel so damned inadequate.' Without saying anything, his hand sought out mine and gave my fingers a gentle squeeze. That unspoken touch offering support and solidarity almost made me cry. Instead, I squeezed his hand back. 'It helps having all this stuff going on outside of work. Having something to focus on like the parkrun, which throws up something new every day. It helps me switch off from work. I haven't got time to worry about my job once I get home. I'd far rather think about what we're doing and the goal... how great it's going to be when we get it all set up.'

'I know exactly what you mean. Instead of worrying about when I'll hear back from a job application, I do a bit on the parkrun. I've worked out how we'll manage the finishing funnel, the tokens, and the timekeeping and I've had a couple of chats with Darren. We're getting there.' His job was working out all the procedures and processes to make it all happen.

'It's all starting to come together.' I squeezed his hand back. 'I'm missing my daily runs.'

'I miss them too.'

We stared at each other for a moment, my eyes dropping to his lips. With a rueful smile, he looked around at our potential audience and bumped my hand against his hip in a quick private promise. Although we'd exchanged plenty of messages this week, it wasn't the same as the daily contact that we'd got used to.

'I'm worried I'm going to lose all the fitness I've built up. I was doing so well with my training.' I'd actually got up 5k.

'But… I can't leave the girls alone in the house in the morning and we're getting up at half six as it is.'

'We could go out on Saturday. I'm sure Hilda wouldn't mind babysitting.' He gave me a quick grin. 'Or perhaps you could ask Elaine.'

I widened my eyes. 'She does like to talk.'

'Maybe she doesn't have many people to talk to during the day.'

'Maybe.'

'It can be tough all day on your own.' There was a thoughtful expression in his eyes as he scanned the path ahead.

'Any news on the job front?'

'I may have news for you tomorrow night.'

'You've got a job?'

He smiled enigmatically. 'Tomorrow.'

'Tease.' I pouted.

'It'll be worth waiting for; it's not long now,' he murmured in an undertone which made my trigger-happy libido jump to attention, releasing excited hormones that skipped through my veins.

'True,' my throaty response brought a slow twisted smile to his face.

For a second we stared at each other, the moment laden with intensity, until Ava skipped up between us, her eyes crinkled in concentration. 'Will there be cake at the café? Sascha's cake? She has nice cake.'

Ash laughed and caught her hand. 'Yes, there will be cake.'

'Are you sure?' she asked with a frown.

'A hundred per cent positive. I saw Sascha's sister delivering cupcakes when I walked over with Bill earlier.'

With a nod of satisfaction, she fell into step beside us and slipped her other hand into mine. 'Ash, do you think Bill likes cake?'

'Bill likes anything but cake is not good for him.'

'But why?'

I grinned at him and listened as he gently explained in great detail how dogs' digestive systems differed from humans and that they were allergic to chocolate and certain fruit. For someone who was in touch with his grumpy side, he could be very patient with the girls.

The park had a closing-down-for-the-night feel to it as we followed the path to The Friendly Bean; a couple of lads were swishing backwards and forwards on the skateboard ramps, a few dog walkers ambled between the flower beds, but the swings were still in the play area and the benches around the bandstand and rose garden were all empty.

The lights in the café beckoned and when the six of us pushed through the door, I was greeted by several friendly faces and a surprising number of vaguely familiar ones. Charles, Penny, and Janie were there along with Neil Blenkinsop and Karen and Dave, the keen runner from work. There were also quite a few other people that I recognised: a woman who worked in Dr Boulter's surgery, the young couple that lived next door but one to me, the man who stood at the ticket barrier at the station every day, the milkman, Greg, who jogged between houses as he delivered pint bottles, and a couple of checkout people from the local supermarket. There were also several fellow commuters, the balding man with a propensity for brown suits who usually sat in the same carriage as me on the seven thirty-seven train, a young permanently cheerful woman with the most gorgeous shade of auburn hair whom I often followed across the park, and a couple of others that I sort of knew but had never actually spoken to.

'Evening,' said Sascha with a very broad grin. 'Busy.'

Wide-eyed, I looked at all the people in the coffee bar. There were easily four times as many as I was expecting and it wasn't even seven o'clock yet.

'I backed a winner.' Her tone was triumphant. 'Good job I got lots of cakes in.' Dotted around the tables were little cardboard cake stands, each filled with mini cupcakes with swirled buttercream toppings of cream, pink, and pale blue. She'd done a far better job of guesstimating numbers than I had.

By seven o'clock, The Friendly Bean was packed. Ash, Hilda, and I made our way to the front of the room to the area we'd decided would be best from which to address people.

'I can't believe there are so many people here,' I muttered to Hilda.

'I have to say, I'm quite surprised too,' said Hilda. 'Although, in the good old days there was always a strong community spirit in Churchstone. Maybe it was the promise of cake. People love a freebie. And also, Sascha has quite a lot of connections.' The turnout was great but I was worried that a lot of them were here to find out more about the run rather than wanting to volunteer.

For some reason, both Ash and Hilda had nominated me chief spokesperson. To my relief, this crowd of smiley people, nodding their heads in encouragement, were clearly going to be a lot easier to please than a hostile boardroom, of which I had plenty of experience. Penny gave me a big double-thumbs-up and Janie waved, as did the man next to her, who I assumed was her husband who had done all our artwork for free. I made a mental note to make sure I thanked him.

'Good evening everyone and thank you for coming.'

Someone lifted a cake in toast. 'Thanks for having us.'

'Thank you to Sascha for letting us use the café and also to Matt who designed the posters, to Neil for supporting the idea with the council, and to Hilda,' I indicated her with my hands, 'who came up with the idea for a parkrun in Churchstone. And to the Harriers who have all been so supportive.

'Thanks to a generous donation from someone in the community to get us started, we have the money to set up the parkrun, although we are researching grants and hoping for local sponsorship to pay this back as we do feel it should be a community-funded event.'

A man at the back of the room put up his hand. 'I run Churchstone Sports on the High Street, I'd be more than happy to sponsor you.'

'That's great, thank you.'

'Me too.' Another man raised his hand. 'Picton's, family solicitor's on Church Street.'

'Brilliant.' I hadn't been expecting people to offer money tonight; this was an unexpected bonus. 'Perhaps we can get together at the end of the meeting? For now, one of the things we are in desperate need of is volunteers. There are 678 parkruns in the UK and we hope to make Churchstone number 679. However, to sustain those existing runs there are over 15,000 volunteers.' I paused and let the number sink in, scanning the faces to vet their reaction. To my relief, half of them didn't jump to their feet to leave. That was a good start. 'In order to make the parkrun happen every Saturday, we need at least twenty volunteers every week. Obviously, we would have a rota so we really need a bank of between forty and fifty people who would be willing to be help. So I'm asking for people who might be interested and who might know other people who would be interested. Some of these roles would also allow you to take part in the run but obviously things like marshals would preclude that. I've drawn up a list of the sorts of roles there are.' I indicated the A3 flipchart which Ash had dropped off earlier. 'We've got everything from run director, marshal, timekeeper, token sorter, funnel manager, pre and post-set-up. There is quite a lot involved but it's only a few hours on a Saturday morning. The aim is to start at nine o'clock so that people have the rest of the day to get on with their weekend. I'm going to hand over to Ash here, who is going to explain what some of those roles are and what they would involve.'

Ash stepped forward and seamlessly took over. I watched as he spoke, his hands punctuating his speech, his occasional steps sure and steady. He exuded charismatic self-confidence and I couldn't take my eyes off him. Despite being dressed in an everyday navy-blue T-shirt and blue jeans, to me he was mouth-watering. Oh yeah, he was back and sexier than ever.

Concentrate, Claire. I forced myself to listen to his words rather than let myself be distracted by thoughts of what was under that T-shirt and just how well his bum filled those jeans.

It had already been agreed amongst us that for the first few months, Ash, Charles, and I would take it in turns to manage the event and rotate the run-director role as this shouldered quite a lot of responsibility. Although, having spoken to the run director at Tring, we hoped that further down the line other people would move up the ranks of the volunteers to take their turn at running the event. The RD was, we'd learned, a big job as this person was in charge of set-up, briefings, health and safety, making sure the course was safe and obstacle-free and ensuring that if there was an accident or anyone was injured that they could be looked after properly. The information pack that had come through from the parkrun organisation itself had been impressive.

After Ash finished, I took to the floor again, thanking everyone for coming and inviting people to fill in their contact details if they were interested in helping or running on the sheets of paper on clipboards with which Poppy, Hilda, Janie, and Penny were now circulating. If anyone was specifically interested in a particular role, they could put their name and number next to the role outlined on the A3 Flipchart.

Elaine, my neighbour, was first to the chart with two other women.

'That was very good, Claire. You're very good at public speaking. I was impressed. This is Marsha. She used to be Head of Maths at Churchstone Secondary – we haven't seen each other for a couple of years – and this is Wendy. She was a science technician in the chemistry labs at the school. Retired like me and Marsha.'

'Hello,' I said to the other two ladies, slightly overwhelmed by Elaine's rapid-fire information dump.

'We've decided to volunteer to be your official timekeepers and token sorters,' announced Wendy. 'It'll be something to do on a Saturday morning and the three of us used to have such a laugh at school. We always organised the school quiz together. I can't believe we've lost touch. And here we are tonight, picking up exactly where we left off.'

'And it doesn't seem like five years since our joint

retirement do,' added Marsha. 'Although that ghastly carriage clock gave up the ghost after five months.'

'I never liked the bloody thing anyway. Who needs to be reminded of how slowly time goes when you're not at work?' Elaine chipped in, the quick smile at odds with the melancholy expression in her eyes. 'Or how many hours it is until wine o'clock.'

'Lord, yes. This will give us a reason to get out in the fresh air on a Saturday morning.'

'And for a weekly meet-up. Sascha makes a damn good cup of coffee. We can sit here putting the world to rights and sort out all your tokens.' Marsha beamed at me. 'Can't wait to get cracking. When do you want us?'

The three of them were as garrulous as each other and, I realised with a sharp pang of guilt as I noticed Elaine's animated face, just as lonely. A touch of shame nudged my conscience at the way I'd avoided the other woman and had taken so little interest in her. I hadn't taken the time or the trouble to find out that, once upon a time, she'd had a busy, useful job and was of value to the community. *Shame on me.* From now on, I would definitely make a lot more effort to be more neighbourly. They were so busy chattering away as they signed up with the big fat marker pens I'd supplied, they didn't notice that I'd been lost in thought for a moment.

'Thanks a lot, ladies. I'll be in touch. Do you do WhatsApp?' I'd already decided that it might be worth setting up a group.

They all nodded and carried on chirruping away amongst themselves like lively canaries. I worked my way through the busy room. Each member of the clipboard team was engaged in earnest conversation. Plenty of people seemed keen to sign up which was extremely gratifying, as was the energetic buzz in the room. Hilda, busy chatting to a group of three older men and two familiar women, caught my eye and called me over.

'Claire, come and meet Bert, George and Harry. They used to run the bicycle shop. And Georgina and Grace both work for Sainsbury's part time and are keen to get involved on their days off.' No sooner had I chatted to all of them than I was called over by Penny to talk to two other men. 'Claire, this is Edward Comely, Sascha's dad, and his neighbour, Adam Fullbanks.' I recognised Adam as the man who'd offered sponsorship from the local sports shop.

'Very impressive turn out,' said Edward. 'And very well organised. I hear you work for Cunningham, Wilding and Taylor. One of their rising stars.' He glanced over to where Dave from work sat with Karen and another woman I didn't recognise. Dave acknowledged us with a brief salute.

'I'm not sure about that,' I said blushing slightly. Edward tilted his head as if sceptical of my modesty and I felt his narrow-eyed scrutiny.

'I'm always interested in good people, if you ever want a change.'

I frowned, trying to think what I knew about him. 'You're an accountant.' I remembered Sascha telling me.

He laughed. 'Well that's put me in my place. I run Comely and Mitchell. We've got a couple of offices in the area but our main operation is in Churchstone.'

'I'm so sorry. Of course I've heard of you.' They had offices in most of the nearby market towns and had a reputation for being a good, solid, reliable family business.

'Why don't you come and have a coffee with me sometime?' he suggested with a very direct expression. The man was nobody's fool and I could see where Sascha got her business acumen.

I smiled at him, savvy enough not to say that I had no intention of leaving CWT; it never did to turn down a contact. 'That would be lovely, thank you.'

I turned to Adam Fullbanks. 'Thank you for offering to sponsor the event. That's very generous of you. Have you any particular ideas?'

'Well, it's the perfect fit, isn't it? Obviously, my shop will benefit. We're the only place for miles that offer advice and expertise on buying trail and running shoes. I was thinking I could offer ten per cent off any purchases in store for anyone who produces a parkrun barcode, same as I offer to the Harriers, and I'd be happy to supply the loud-hailer that you'll need to buy.'

'You've been to a parkrun before then.'

'A few around the country. Occasionally I get to the Harrogate one. Unfortunately Saturdays are my busiest days. But if we're away on holiday I try to get to the nearest one. Last year we did Poole and Edinburgh. But if there's one on my doorstep, I'd hope to take part a bit more often and I could help with the pre-run set up every now and then – although, with the shop I can't do much else.'

'Every little helps, as they say.'

'I'm no runner,' declared Edward, 'but I'd like to help. Sascha is pretty self-sufficient but I could pitch in with the run and then offer her an extra pair of hands. I think she might be a bit busy afterwards if this becomes the designated meeting spot.'

I laughed. 'I think, given the café's location and Sascha's support so far, that's pretty much a given.' At that moment, as if she could tell we were talking about her, she raised her head and gave me and her father a quick wave. The free cupcakes had gone down well and I was pleased to see that plenty of people had bought drinks. It was good to see her support being paid back.

Adam and I agreed to talk more and I moved on to find Ava quietly hoovering up the leftover cupcakes, looking a little flushed. 'You'll be sick if you eat too many.'

'I think I ate too many already. My tummy hurts.' Her lower lip wobbled. I scooped her up onto my hip, hoping that she wouldn't throw up down my shoulder.

'Oh, sweetie, that was silly.'

'But they were yummy.'

'They were. How many did you have?' I bit my lip; I really should have kept a closer eye on her.

'Only two... maybe three.' When I raised a silent eyebrow, she held up one hand extending all her fingers and amended it to, 'P'raps five.'

I swallowed down the laugh bubbling in my throat at the honest jump to five and gave her sturdy little body a hug, even though my own stomach recoiled at the thought of that much sugar. Burying my head in her curls, I dropped a kiss on her head, a surge of love making my heart burst. The cupcakes might be small but they had a good wodge of buttercream on the top. No wonder she felt a bit sick.

Hilda materialised at my elbow like my very own Mary Poppins with Poppy at her side. 'Ava's not feeling too good,' I said. 'She's got tummy ache. Too much sugar.'

Poppy rolled her eyes and muttered something like, 'Serves her right.'

I raised a pointed eyebrow. Poppy smiled sweetly. 'It's nice here. It reminds me of the place Grandad takes us to for ice cream in the Valley Gardens.'

'Don't talk about ice cream,' cried Ava. 'Don't feel well.'

'And a late night, I shouldn't wonder,' said Hilda with a smile, lifting a hand to Ava's rosy cheeks. 'But she's got good colour. Not grey or green. I think she'll be all right. Perhaps some fresh air will help. Shall I take her outside for a little while? It's getting a bit stuffy in here.'

It was unlike Hilda to complain and I realised that her face was a little pale and her eyes not as bright as usual. Because of her sheer energy, I often forgot she was actually quite elderly. 'It's probably time we wound things up. Between us, I think we've chatted to most people.'

'Certainly have, and everyone has signed up.' Her face brightened for a second but I could tell she was very tired. It was definitely time to take her home. I caught Ash's eye and, like a parent, gave a discreet nod towards Ava, Poppy, and Hilda. Immediately getting the message, he nodded and began to wind up his conversation

'Amazing turn out.' Ash came to my side as I glanced around the room, still not quite able to believe the numbers of people who had turned up. For a moment, I felt a little overwhelmed by the outpouring of goodwill and support that everyone had exhibited. It was totally heart-warming.

'I think we're really going to make this happen, Hilda.'

'Well, of course we are. Was it ever in doubt?'

Chapter Twenty-Seven

There was a rustle of feathers as Poppy threw herself onto the bed again, all moody teenager with sprawling, lethargic limbs.

'So, is Ash your boyfriend?' she asked, her eyes measured in the reflection in the mirror as I started to apply my make-up.

'We're friends,' I said, keeping my answer deliberately non-committal and short. I wasn't about to elaborate to a ten-year-old.

'Why's he taking you out to dinner?'

Phew, that was an easy one. 'To say thank you. I helped him get a job interview. And we've got lots of things to discuss about the parkrun after last night. Didn't our meeting go well?'

I was still on a high. After counting up all the people who had signed up last night, we had over forty volunteers.

Unfortunately, Poppy wasn't that easily distracted and I could almost feel her weighing up the next question.

'He likes you.' It was said with a tiny bit of accusation.

'He likes Hilda.' I carried on applying my make–up, refusing to make eye contact with the hard stare I could see in my peripheral vision. 'He likes you. He likes Ava.'

'You know what I mean. He watches you when he thinks no one else is looking. Don't you like him?'

'He's my friend. Of course I like him.'

She let out a heavy sigh and kicked her legs restlessly against the duvet. 'I'm not a baby. I know how things work. We've had our sex-education lessons. I know what sex is.'

What do I say to that? Yeah, okay, I can't wait to jump his bones. Somehow, I was pretty sure it was not the done thing to admit to a ten-year-old that sex had been on my mind quite a lot for the last few days.

'That's a big jump,' I said. 'Ash and I are going out to dinner.'

'Mummy had a boyfriend.'

'Did she?' I turned in surprise.

Poppy wrinkled her face. 'Yeah, he was called Jonathon. He smelled funny. They used to do yoga together and she texted him all the time.'

Jon, Jonathon. Suddenly, a few things dropped into place. Wasn't he the guy that had invited her to the retreat?

I watched as she rolled off the bed and ambled out of my room. As soon as she was out of sight, I quickly opened the dressing-table drawers. A set of black lingerie lay on top of my pile of underwear in readiness… long-overdue readiness. I'd it bought online the Sunday I'd left Ash's flat. Checking the door, I pulled it shut, praying she didn't come back. Since the packed lunch breakthrough – she'd made lunch every day for me – Poppy had been like a faithful shadow, and often, as I'd been working at the kitchen table this week while she watched *Hollyoaks*, I would find her thoughtful gaze on me.

The lingerie whispered across my skin as I slipped it on, deliciously decadent, reminding me that I was an adult again. No responsibilities for the next twelve hours. Hilda was staying over so I didn't have to come home until the wee small hours. And until then, I had no one else to worry about but me. No one to judge me. No one to please but me.

I stared at myself in the mirror. Was this how Alice felt? I bit my lip suddenly, realising how she must have felt. I would never condone what she'd done but for that brief moment, I almost understood.

But I wasn't going to feel guilty about Alice.

Tonight was my night. It felt as if I had this one illicit window that gave me permission to cram in as much as I possibly could.

And that meant sex. Sex with Ashwin Laghari. He was, I'd discovered in the last twenty-four hours, the master of flirty, innuendo-laden texting.

With a little shiver of anticipation, I pulled out the new little black dress that I'd also ordered online and had delivered to the office. I'd wanted to wear the same outfit as I had on our first date but unfortunately it was too big. The weight I'd lost had come back on but I felt fitter and a lot healthier, which was probably down to new muscle tone developed by all the running.

Ash was bringing Hilda over at seven-fifteen… I glanced at my watch. Oh God, in exactly six minutes' time. All the butterflies in my stomach rose as one and I almost gasped with sheer excitement.

'So, come on, tell me. How did the interview go?'

Ash's eyes glowed with sudden superiority. 'Well done. You kept it in for...' he lengthened his arm to pull his watch out from beneath his shirt sleeve, '...sixteen minutes and nine seconds.'

'Or I could pretend not to be interested at all,' I said, and we were right back to the crossfire of the first date when we had played with each other, trying to work out who had the upper hand. I smiled at the memory. At the time we'd come out on a level playing field.

Tonight we were at the same table and I was pretty sure it was by design. The waiter had already taken our orders and brought over an expensive bottle of Chablis. Ash had dressed up – a dark grey shirt with black wool trousers rather than the nonchalant, devil-may-care T-shirt and black jeans he'd worn the first time we'd gone out – as if this time he was making an effort.

Rearranging my cutlery, I avoided looking his way for a moment but eventually, as the silence grew, I lifted my head. The satisfied glow in his eyes had intensified and he was all predatory tiger once again.

'You got the job.'

With a nod, he picked up his glass and lifted it in toast to me. 'I was offered the job. The formal confirmation came through this morning.'

'And... are you going to take it or wait for the other interview?'

With a quick frown, full of thought, he paused. 'I've never been a great believer in gut instinct... but this feels right. I liked the guy that interviewed me. I like the company culture. There was something about the place.'

'Don't they say that gut instinct is our sixth sense, a primeval ability that we've overlooked as we've developed?'

'Would you take a job on instinct?'

'Hard to say. I've been with Cunningham, Wilding and Taylor for ten years; I can't imagine going anywhere else.' I'd always liked being there but now I wasn't so sure. I didn't wake up itching to get to work anymore. My focus, for so long, had been on the next promotion. Even when I'd been signed off, the goal had been to get all my ducks lined back up as quickly as possible. Ash looked excited and animated about his new job and the new direction he was taking. I felt a touch of envy.

'I really liked the people. It's a very different environment to what I'm used to. The old dog-eat-dog. This is… well, it seemed almost like a family. They genuinely liked each other… I met the board. There didn't seem to be any jockeying for position.'

'Maybe they were on their best behaviour.'

Ash shook his head. 'No, I don't think they were… there was more.'

'You might as well go for the other interview, though. No?'

'I feel like being rash. Taking a risk. Going with my gut.'

'You've changed.'

'You think? Losing my job made me reassess a lot of things. Including relationships. They always came bottom of my pile before.'

'Oh.' His words made me feel nervous.

'I never allowed them to take up much space in my life. I could only allocate so much time for dates and invariably girls got pissed off. You were the first girl I dated who didn't mind that I wasn't prepared to see you for nearly two weeks.'

'Probably because I was too busy. I'm not much of a bet now with two kids in tow.'

Ash reached over for my hand. 'Yes, but that's not for ever is it? One day you'll be footloose and fancy free. And then we can enjoy ourselves.' He let out a rueful half-laugh. 'Although I think we might be stuck with Hilda.'

'Where would we be without Hilda?' I said.

'I'd still be a pathetic wreck, feeling sorry for myself and possibly drinking my way into oblivion. I'll never forget that first run she dragged me on… I threw up at the end and she told me off for being so unfit and out of shape and for letting my body down. Not one word about pulling myself together. She's a wise old owl. She focused on the physical, knowing it would help my mental state.'

'Same with me. Gentle advice and suggestions all the time, or browbeating us into doing her bidding which miraculously helps with other things,' I said as the waiter appeared with two steaming plates of pasta. Seafood linguine for me and spaghetti carbonara for Ash. 'Mmm, that smells gorgeous.'

'Sure you don't want a dessert?' asked Ash as the waiter cleared away our plates, exchanging a look laden with intent. We both knew that dessert of an entirely different sort was on the table. We'd been building up to tonight ever since he'd asked me for dinner. Now, almost by tacit understanding, the wait was worth taking the time to enjoy. Tonight there was no hurry; the prize was in sight and not an obstacle in our way. I think we were both savouring the anticipation.

'Yes,' I murmured as his fingers entwined with mine, giving them a gentle squeeze. 'Another thing we owe Hilda for.' I thought of her possibly already tucked up in my spare bedroom in the bed Ava and Poppy had once shared.

'We owe her big time,' he agreed.

'I'd like to do something nice for her. I was thinking about inviting her to come away for a few days in the summer with me and the girls. Somewhere by the sea.'

'You think they'll still be with you, by then?'

'I was thinking that even if they weren't, it would be nice to take them on holiday. I've kind of got used to them being around.' I tried to make it sound humorous but the thought of my house without the girls made my stomach hurt.

'That's a lovely idea,' he said softly. His thumb rubbed over mine. 'If you're inviting Hilda, have you got room for one more?'

'You want to come on holiday with us?' I smiled. 'Really?' Once upon a time, I bet sophisticated Ashwin Laghari would not have been seen dead with a bucket and spade, two little girls and an elderly lady in tow. How times had changed.

'Why not? I like the kids. I like Hilda. Especially now I've convinced myself she was once a spy. And you're all right.'

'Thanks.' I acknowledged the barely-there compliment with a wry twist to my mouth. 'But what about your mates? Don't you have anyone you want to go away with it? Don't you have mates who have palatial pads?'

'No one I'd rather spend time with than you.'

Ash tossed his hair, making me smile. I really did prefer his longer hair and the way it softened the sharp angles of his face.

Now I'd started thinking about it, I *really* liked the idea.

'Where do you fancy? Devon? Cornwall?'

'Don't know either particularly well. I'll leave it to you. I'm very good at carrying suitcases. And navigating. Although we might have to hire a car because I'm not sure where we'd put Bill.'

It all sounded very domesticated and I giggled unexpectedly. 'None of this sounds like Ashwin Laghari, International Arms Dealer.'

He grinned. 'I promise you, it's an awful lot better than being Hilda's shopping bitch.'

'What?' I stuttered and almost spat out my wine. 'Seriously?'

He grinned at me and pulled my hand to his mouth giving it a quick familiar kiss on the knuckles as if we'd been going out for years. 'Hilda's commandeered me to take her on a shopping expedition. She wants me to take her to Leeds because I mentioned I needed to buy a new suit. I start work the week after next.'

'I hope you're going to Marks & Spencer,' I said, suddenly prim.

He burst out laughing. 'Well, the Armani doesn't fit anymore and the dry cleaners never did get those stains out. I was thinking Hugo Boss perhaps. My waist size has gone down a bit.'

'All that running.'

'And not going to bars and drinking overpriced fizzy beer.'

'I can't even remember what a wine bar is like.'

'Want me to take you to one?' The predatory gleam was back and there was a more than pregnant pause as he held my gaze. I caught my breath. Was it obvious that the only thought searing through my brain was, *just take me to bed*. I shook my head saying regretfully, 'We sound terribly grown up.'

'Do you mind?'

'No,' I said with a touch of sadness. 'Yes. Sometimes. My life has changed dramatically in the last few months and it's hard work with the girls but... I love them both and it's not like it's for ever.' I looked at him, the touch of his fingers sending gentle vibrations through my nerve endings. Desire ran through me as I thought of the silk lingerie under my clothes. 'We've got tonight.'

'We do.' His eyes narrowed as they swept over me, appreciation and something much darker in them.

'Would you like a digestif? Sambuca? Cointreau? Tia Maria?' The discreet waiter loitered, waiting for an answer.

Ash's eyes darted to mine in silent question, his fingers stroking the underside of my wrist, sending little tremors of awareness fizzing along my skin. I stared back at him and gave a tiny nod. He knew I wasn't referring to the drinks.

'I think we'd just like the bill,' said Ash with regal aplomb, which was commendable when any second now we were both going to bolt from the restaurant and burst into a run down the street back to his apartment. Either or both of us might spontaneously combust from sheer lust on the way.

Just as I shrugged my way into my coat, my mobile phone rang. Ash raised an eyebrow.

'Oh, crap.' Reluctantly, I glanced at the screen. Hilda's name flashed on the screen. I pulled a face.

'It's Hilda. I hope the girls aren't playing up.'

'Or she's unwell,' suggested Ash, concern clouding his expression.

'Hey, Hilda,' I answered.

'Claire, I'm really sorry,' Hilda's voice was laden with apology. 'I'm really sorry... I wouldn't have called but...' Immediately a dozen panicked thoughts raced through my head. Hilda wasn't feeling well, she needed to call an ambulance, there was an intruder, she'd lost power... they went on and on.

'Are you okay? Is everything all right at the house?'

'I'm fine. It's not me. It's... Poppy.'

'Poppy!' I had wondered if Ava might be a bit unsettled. She was still a regular visitor to my bed and I had worried that she might wake up in the night and be scared if I wasn't there. But Poppy was always so sure of herself and determinedly grown-up.

'Oh God, what's she done?' She normally behaved herself with Hilda; they got on well.

'She's not done anything... not naughty.'

'What's wrong with her? Is she ill?'

'No, she's just very... she won't stop crying and asking for you. I'm sorry, I really didn't want to disturb you but she's really not herself. I've tried but... it's just not like her. She's beside herself.'

'Oh, bless her. She's been a bit...' Un-Poppy-like was the only way I could describe it. 'Well, she hasn't been right all this week. We're just leaving the restaurant; I'll be right there. Do you want me to talk to her now?'

'No, I sneaked out. She's in the lounge. I'll just tell her you're on your way back.'

I sent an apologetic grimace Ash's way as I tucked the phone back in my pocket. 'Sorry Poppy's...'

He squeezed my hand. 'It's okay. I get it. It's not like Poppy; there's something wrong.'

'She's been funny all week. One minute really stroppy and the next almost glued to my side. I can't even go to the loo without her suddenly appearing by the door when I come out.'

'Sounds like some sort of separation anxiety. Especially if you haven't been able to speak to Alice all week.'

'Dr Laghari, I presume.' I smiled at him. 'But it sounds entirely plausible.'

'Comes of growing up with a medical professional. I remember my sister when she was doing a stint in paediatrics specialising in mental health. There was a girl in there who wouldn't go to school. Her mother had been ill and was recuperating at home. The child was terrified her mother would go back into hospital and leave her.'

'Thinking back over some of the things Poppy had been saying this week, that would make a lot of sense. I thought I'd reassured her but obviously not. God, just when I think I'm getting the hang of this parenting lark, it all goes tits up again. I'm a bit worried what the school might say when they finally realise that Alice still isn't back. I've no idea what the legal position is with the girls.' I tugged at my lip. 'What if social services take them away?'

'They're not going to do that, Claire.' He put his arm round me. 'Come on, let's go and reassure her now. I'll take Cinders back.'

'I'm sorry.'

'Me too, but...' He shot me a wicked grin. 'That lingerie doesn't have an expiry date, does it?'

I folded my arms. 'What lingerie?'

He looked smug.

Goaded, I asked, 'Who says I'm wearing any?'

'Tell me you're not.'

'You're such a cocky git.'

'I know. You love it.'

No, I love you.

The sudden thought took my breath away. No! That wasn't part of the plan. When I'd first met him, it had been a game. A challenge for both of us. Each of us vying for top-dog spot. Then it had never even occurred to me that things would last with Ash. He was too dangerous, too much of a flight risk. Somehow, over the last few months, he'd become much more approachable and less brittle. He'd become lovable.

Chapter Twenty-Eight

As soon as I walked into the living room, Poppy, curled up at one end of the sofa with her arms around Bill, began to cry inconsolably.

My heart almost burst at the sight of her distress.

'Poppy, Poppy, darling, whatever is the matter?' Within seconds, I was on the sofa beside her, scooping her up into my arms, while Hilda and Ash stood in the doorway.

Weeping, she clung to me, her arms tight around my neck, her words incoherent. There was nothing I could do but stroke her back, murmur words of reassurance and wait for the storm to pass. Hilda and Ash crept away and I could hear their low voices disappear to the kitchen.

With Poppy settled on my lap, her wet face cuddled into my neck, I spoke softly to her, my heart aching at her anguish, holding her tight as if that might keep the demons at bay.

'Poppy, darling. It's okay. You're okay.' I kept whispering words of comfort and eventually she calmed, her sobs subsiding in little snuffly hiccoughs and her arms releasing the death grip around my neck.

All I could do was hold her, make her feel safe, and wait until she could tell me what was wrong, all the while dropping kisses on the top of her head. Finally, she looked up at me, her eyes filled with heart-breaking sadness and her cheeks tear-stained and mottled.

'Sweetheart, what's the matter?'

'I w-was scared.'

'Scared of what?'

'That you wouldn't come back.'

'Of course I was going to come back.'

'But you don't have to. You could send us away. You're not even our mum and she's gone.'

'Poppy, I promise you, I won't send you away.'

'But you might.'

'Who would look after me and make me packed lunches every day?'

'But we're not yours. You don't have to stay. Why doesn't Mum come home? Or even answer her phone or send us messages?'

'I...' I wasn't going to lie for Alice. 'I don't know, darling, but I do know that I will never send you away.'

'Even if she doesn't come back?' Poppy's candid stare made my heart bump uncomfortably.

'I promise I will never, ever send you away.'

'She's not coming back, is she?'

I felt my teeth catch my lip and I stopped myself; it was becoming a habit.

'Do you think it's because I'm horrible sometimes? I make Ava cry.'

'Poppy, *I* make Ava cry too.'

'I know, but sometimes I'm not very good. Sometimes I'm horrible.'

'Yeah, you are,' I said making it sound as light-hearted as possible. 'But we all are, sometimes. You think I'm this perfect all the time?'

She let out a little half-snuffle-giggle.

'It takes a lot of work. I've had thirty years of practice. You've got a way to go. You're only ten.'

'That's silly, Auntie Claire.' After a pause, she said, 'I don't mean to be horrible. It just comes out sometimes. I'm sorry I've been mean this week. I thought you put us into After-school Club because you didn't want us anymore. Because you liked your work more than people. Mummy always said you…' she faltered, 'didn't have time for us. That's why you never came to visit very often.'

With a wince, I pulled her closer. 'I was busy… but so were you. At the weekends you had birthday parties, football, swimming lessons, dance classes.'

'We never did football,' protested Poppy, wrinkling her nose at the very thought.

Maybe I'd got that wrong, but there'd always been something when I'd offered to come over to see them all. And when I'd offered to babysit, Alice had brushed me aside saying she never went out. So I'd offered again, so that she could. Alice had put up the barriers, not me, but how could I tell Poppy that? Or that her mother usually called me or invited me over when she wanted something, most of the time money?

'Do you feel better now?' I hadn't answered her original question but thankfully the moment seemed to have passed. I'd have to have something for her next time.

She nodded. 'Can I stay up with you for a bit longer?'

'Course you can. Why don't I make us both a hot chocolate?'

'Can Bill stay too? In my room?'

I looked down at the dog who was snuggled into Poppy's side, one of her hands fondling his ear. His big brown eyes blinked up at me before he sighed and nestled his head back onto Poppy's lap.

'As long as it's all right with Ash.'

Bill spent the night in Poppy's room and Ash did not spend the night in mine. He went home alone, which had not been in either of our plans.

'I could kill Alice,' I muttered fiercely to Hilda on the landing as we said our goodnights. 'She's not responded to a single one of my messages. I don't know what to do. I'm worried that the girls might get taken into care. Like I said to Ash earlier, I don't know what my legal position is.'

'Ah, well, there's something I can help with there. We'll phone Farquhar in the morning. He's a barrister. Family law is his speciality. Difficult to believe, I know. You expect someone like him to be dealing with criminals or corporate sharks but no, family law.'

'Will he mind?' I thought of our last meeting.

'He won't have a choice. If he doesn't help, I'll disinherit him. Now, there's nothing more you can do this evening. I suggest we all get some sleep.' With a quick pause, she patted me on the arm before adding, 'I'm sorry I had to interrupt your evening. Just when things were going so well.' She shot me a naughty grin and I almost expected her to rub her hands together Bond villain-style.

'And just when I was thinking of asking you to come away for a few days with me and the girls,' I teased.

'Oh, that would be a capital idea. I have a lovely house in Norfolk, right above the beach. Kevin McCloud said it was one of his favourites. Although we'd better not tell Farquhar before he's advised you as it might set him off again. He might think you've got designs on his inheritance.'

'Where does Farquhar live?' I asked suddenly. Although Hilda talked about him disparaging terms, he was still her son.

'Not that far away. Near Ripon. He has a little Lord of the Manor place, although he'll inherit the entire estate in Scotland when his father dies.'

'Perhaps we should invite him for tea one day.'

'Why on earth would we want to do that?' Hilda's regal tone didn't fool me.

'Because,' I said firmly, 'it would be a nice thing to do and you are his mother.'

'I suppose when you put it like that...' With a regal nod she turned and glided off in marabou-feather-trimmed slippers towards the spare bedroom.

I watched her go with a fond smile. For once I'd managed to take the wind out of her sails.

It felt good the next morning to get my running kit on and Bill bounced around my feet as I left the noisy kitchen where Hilda was teaching Poppy and Ava how to make pancakes.

'Will you bring Bill back with you?' Poppy darted down the hall as I opened the front door.

'Yes, sweetie. Hilda is going to cook breakfast for me and Ash when we've done our run but I think Bill could use the exercise.' And she was going to phone her son and hand her mobile over to me. I chewed my lip at the thought of that conversation; I hoped, despite our earlier meeting, he'd be helpful.

'I could take him for a walk.'

'Maybe we can ask Ash if we can borrow him tomorrow and go for a walk up on the moor.'

'Okay,' she agreed, giving Bill one last pat.

Ash was waiting for me at the entrance to the park. This morning we were going to map a route that he'd been working on during the week using a phone app.

'I've been thinking,' he said as we set off at a gentle pace, Bill trotting along beside us with the closest thing to a doggy grin on his hairy little face that I've ever seen, 'we don't want to make the run too easy, do we?'

'No… but not too hard either.'

'It would be nice to feel a sense of achievement at the end.'

'And you don't think running 5k is an achievement?' my voice pitched in laughing protest.

'Yes, but I think we could put a little hill in to make it more challenging. If we take the path around the western edge of the park right up to the end and then veer north east through the wooded area, we could climb up Beacon's Knoll for the fourth kilometre and then it's downhill for the last kilometre and we could finish just up from the bandstand where there's plenty of room to stake out the funnel, and it's only two hundred metres from the start point.'

'Sounds like you've given this a lot of thought.' I shot a suspicious glare at him. 'Have you mapped the route already?'

'I might have done.' He patted the phone in his pocket.

For a moment I considered the route in my head; despite the hill, I rather liked the sound of it. We were already running towards the west side of the park. 'I hate to say it because you'll be all cocky, but it sounds quite good. Even with the hill, there will be plenty of flat and we'll stay out of the way of most park users if we go up into the woods, plus there is the reward of the great view from Beacon's Knoll.'

'You know it makes sense.'

'Hmm. I'll let you know when I've got up the hill.'

Although running came a lot easier now than it had when I first started, I still wasn't up to speeding up the hill. I watched Ash tackle the incline at a steady pace, Bill leading the way with the occasional diversion to sniff at exciting prospects in the shrubs on either side of the muddy track as I slowed to an almost walk but I was determined not to stop. *One foot in front of the other*, I told myself. My calves were aching and my thighs burning when I reached the top but it made the downhill slope to where the finish line would be all the sweeter and I pushed myself hard for that last kilometre.

Chest heaving, I sank onto the grass and put my head on my knees. Ash was sitting sprawled on the floor with Bill prowling backwards and forwards next to him looking as if he would be happy to do it all over again.

'Well done! You were flying down the path.'

'Mmm,' I managed. 'Wanted to up my pace.' That was the problem with having an app that broke down your run and told you your pace for each kilometre. Bizarrely, given that I'd never been that sporty, I seemed determined to rise to the challenge and beat myself. Suddenly I was obsessed with my times and comparing each run I did.

'So what do you think?'

'I think you've got yourself a 5k route.'

'Even with the hill.'

'Even with the hill,' I agreed.

Ash grinned. 'I knew you'd love it.'

'Hmph.'

'Come on, I'm ready for breakfast.' He hauled me to my feet and gave me a quick, sweaty kiss.

'I've certainly earned it. And Hilda was promising poached eggs, smashed avocado, and bacon.'

'What are we waiting for?'

'You do realise that in a couple of weeks' time, this will be us. We'll be packing up. Sorting out the times for everyone.' We smiled at each other. 'We're nearly there.'

'We certainly are.' Ash closed the gap between us and kissed me firmly on the lips. In just over three weeks, this would be our Saturday mornings for the foreseeable future. I couldn't help reflecting just how far we'd all come, although there was still one thing I wanted to do for Hilda and hopefully speaking to her son this morning might help me bring it about.

———————

Hilda and I discreetly withdrew from the kitchen, leaving Ash in charge of washing-up, ably assisted by Ava, while Poppy sat with her new best friend, Bill. After Hilda had explained the situation, she handed the phone over to me and sat down on one of the pale blue sofas and pretended to be fascinated by the view out of the window.

'Well this is an interesting one,' mused Farquhar, 'but you don't need to worry in the short term. Social services are all about the best interests of the child. Leaving children with immediate family is always preferable to taking them into care… always assuming you're happy to keep the children.'

'Well, of course I am.'

'What about your parents?'

'I think they'd be willing to take the children but…' I stalled for a second. Much as I loved my parents – and they weren't particularly old – I felt I could care for the girls better. 'I think I'd be a more appropriate carer. For the long term at least.'

'I'm inclined to agree. Do you think it might become a permanent arrangement?'

'A month ago I'd have said no but… my sister hasn't been in touch at all.'

'Are you able to contact her?'

'Yes. I'm assuming she's getting my messages. She has a phone and it rings out and I can see from Messenger and WhatsApp that the phone's still active.' I'd left messages on every damn platform going in the vague hope she might respond.

'Hmm… this is a tricky one. It sounds like abandonment. If you feel that Alice is derelict in her duty and that you want to make a provision for the children, my best advice for their sakes would be to apply for a Special Guardianship Order. That then gives you some legal rights and enables you to make decisions for the girls about their health, medication, education, all sorts of things. At the moment, as it stands, you have no legal rights with regard to the children at all. And if the authorities felt that Alice had abandoned her children without proper arrangements, they would get involved. To apply for a Special Guardianship Order you will need Alice's consent and you'll need to make an application to the court, which of course I can help you with. Alternatively, if you feel strongly enough and that it's in the best interests of the children, you could formally adopt them.'

'Adopt?' That wasn't something that had even crossed my mind. Hilda didn't even pretend not to be eavesdropping. She raised both eyebrows.

'It would be relatively easy if you have Alice's permission.'

'God, I hadn't…'

'Something to think about. Remember, you always have to think about what's right for the children. You could adopt without permission but that would get messy and unpleasant and you really don't want that.'

'No.' My parents would be so upset. Although, at this present moment, if Mum had any idea what Alice had done, she'd be furious. I hadn't dared contact her since our last conversation and Alice's subsequent phone call. I was hoping that if Mum did get hold of Alice she might talk some sense into her.

'Make sure you get this number from my mother and if you have any concerns, just call me. I've dealt with lots of cases over the years. Families are complicated and there are lots in far worse situations than this, I promise you. You're providing a stable, loving home. As long as you do that, you'll be fine.'

'Thank you,' I said meekly.

'No trouble… How is my mother? Still hanging out at your place?'

'Yes,' I said carefully.

'Don't worry. I know the old bat will be earwigging. You might as well be as blunt as she would be.'

'Okay,' I said, amused but not surprised. He was definitely of the same mould as his mother. 'She's thriving... now.'

Hilda shot me a puzzled look.

'Not lonely then.' There was a definite touch of concern in his voice.

I paused and looked pointedly at the older woman beside me. With a huff and a roll of her eyes that Poppy would have been proud of, she walked out of the room.

'If you have to talk about me, make sure you say nice things. I'm a wonderful woman really.' And with that she shut the door with a loud sniff.

I laughed. 'Your mother has just left the room. She's not impressed that we're talking about her.'

'I just care about her wellbeing. I realise that perhaps the nursing home was a bit of a knee-jerk reaction but... the house...'

'I agree, it's far too big for her. Perhaps a smaller one nearby might be a solution. She's very fit and active. I think she was very lonely at the home at first but... since she's adopted us, I'd say that's not the case anymore. We see quite a lot of her. She babysits and quite often spends the weekend with us.'

'Well she must be fond of the children if she phoned me. It's not like she has grandchildren of her own. Ought to get that sorted really. Might make her think of me a bit more fondly.' There was an almost wistful sigh.

'Perhaps if you came to see her a bit more often, that might help.'

'I'm busy. Just like she was when I was a child.'

'Maybe you can understand now why she was busy,' I suggested gently, hearing the petulance of a child in his tone. 'I think she regrets that. But there's still time for you. Why don't you come for tea on Saturday? Hilda loves an excuse to bake.'

'She used to make a mean Victoria sponge.'

'She still does. I'm sure she'd love to see you.'

'Hmm, not so sure about that. She'll wonder what I'm doing there.'

'That's easy. You can come and check that we're not half-inching the family silver.'

'Are you?' he asked with a quick bark of a laugh.

'No. The market for second-hand silver has sunk, although the Baccarat crystal she has in the house would go for a fortune.'

This time Farquhar's laugh was deep and hearty. 'I think you've been spending too much time with my mother. That's the sort of thing she would say. Get her to give you my number. Keep me posted.'

———————

'Was he helpful?' asked Hilda as I went back into the kitchen. Ash had taken the girls into the garden and they were all playing with Bill, throwing a tennis ball up and down the lawn.

'Yes, and very reassuring.'

'He's quite good, I believe,' she said with practiced nonchalance that didn't fool me for a second.

'Proud of him?' I asked with a wry smile.

She gave a non-comital lift of her shoulders. 'He was one of the youngest to be called to the bar.'

'So you're proud of him.'

'Might be.' She sat back, an unrepentant grin crinkling her face with laughter that spread like cracks across her papery skin. 'Of course I am.'

'You. Are. Incorrigible.'

'I know,' she said with a beatific, prim smile that had me laughing again.

'I do love you, Hilda,' I said, the words spilling out and surprising me. 'There's never a dull moment.' The rush of emotion flooded over me and I leaned forward and gave her a hug. 'I don't know what I'd have done without you over these last few months,' I muttered into her rose-scented silk blouse as she embraced me.

'You would have been fine,' she said, rubbing soothing little circles on my shoulder blades. I pulled back a little.

'I don't think I would. Thank you. For being such a support.'

'Don't be silly, dear. That's what friends are for.' Despite her brusque dismissal, there was a faint shimmer in her eyes.

Chapter Twenty-Nine

'**O**kay,' I called over the chatter, 'down to business. Tonight we need to agree where we're going to need marshals and the sort of briefing pack they'll need. And a big thank you to Neil for coming to join us.' The councillor was going to advise on the route, emergency access, and let us know if we could have keys to some of the vehicular access points alongside the usual footpath gates which were normally closed so that we could widen the access.

When I'd started this, I'd had no idea so much would be involved but now, as I gazed around my overcrowded kitchen, I still would have done it. My life was so much better for it, despite the long hours we were now putting in.

There were a few polite claps from everyone. Over the last three weeks, a parkrun sub group had sort of formed itself as everyone stepped up to help arrange the final details. It consisted of me, Ash, Hilda, Penny, Janie, Charles, Elaine, and Marsha. This was our fourth meeting and the designated day was looming fast. We'd agreed to have a trial run on the following Saturday with all of our volunteers and twenty members of the Harriers so we could test the route and iron out any problems that arose. What they might be, my brain was too discombobulated to think about. Thank goodness for Ash who, in the last few days before he started his new job, had been considering all the probable catastrophes that could strike.

'So, Neil, we're thinking of having four marshals on the route positioned at approximately each kilometre, but obviously where they're placed will depend on terrain and emergency access if there is an accident.' Ash peeled back the front sheet of the flip chart to reveal an enlarged map of the proposed area. I grinned at the sight of it – another team effort, and so what if it might be dotted with a few crumbs of Hilda's chocolate cake. The route itself was marked in thick, dark red marker pen and I could picture Poppy, her tongue between her lips, meticulously colouring in the line. Keen to join in, Ava had drawn a few scrubby trees to illustrate Beacon Knoll and with considerable and unexpected skill, Hilda, having delegated flapjack making to me, had abandoned her apron and inked, in painstaking detail, some of the landmarks in the park. The route map was now beautifully embellished with the bandstand, the folly in the woods, and with somewhat of a flourish, the finish line, which was decorated with colourful bunting. 'We would suggest one here, one here, another one there and one here.'

Neil stood up and peered at the map. 'If you have one here, you're closer to the road, so if you needed emergency vehicle access, they could drive right into the park at this point. It would make sense to put one of your marshals here. I can let a responsible person have the key for that gate.'

'That would be the run director on the day.'

'And how would you alert anyone if there was an accident?'

Ash explained the protocols he'd worked out that involved walkie-talkies for each marshal and a designated parkrun mobile that the run director carried each week. I watched as he spoke, almost bursting with pride at his easy confidence. Since starting the new job earlier that week he seemed to have blossomed and he wasn't the same man I'd first met or the man that Hilda had met. He'd grown into something so much more, and in that moment I knew that what I felt for him was much deeper and richer than anything I'd felt for anyone before and, while the smooth, enveloping sensation didn't have that fast, fizzy burst of emotion that had exploded when I first realised I was in love with him, this warmed my soul from the inside out. As he came to the end of his piece he looked up, straight at me, and smiled, his mouth slightly crooked, those beautiful eyes full of warmth. It was a private exchange in a room full of people and it hit me straight in the heart.

Forcing my attention back on the room, I checked the next point on the agenda. Briefing Packs. As the meeting progressed, Elaine and Marsha scribbled frantic notes as they'd both volunteered to put the marshal briefing packs together. What a find they'd been. Talk about invaluable. During the day, when the rest of us were at work, they typed up minutes and action plans, circulating them daily for everyone's approval. Elaine was a demon with a laminator and had proved, despite my first impressions, to be a very good neighbour. She was also a big favourite with Ava. They hung out over the garden fence and Elaine appeared to be genuinely interested in the names and doings of Ava's soft-toy collection.

Hilda stood up as the meeting reached half-time.

'Tea? Coffee? And I've made a nice lemon cake.'

Janie groaned. 'Oh, I love your cake, Hilda. I need the recipe. I also need the parkrun to start so I can run off all the extra calories I've put on.'

'No one's forcing you to eat it,' teased Penny from her right, rising to her feet. 'Let me give you a hand, Hilda.'

I was already pulling mugs out of the cupboard as Hilda put the kettle on and Penny took everyone's orders.

'The cake is on the side there,' directed Hilda. 'Baked today and it's decorated with smarties.'

'Ava?' I asked.

Hilda grinned. 'Well, why not?'

'Thank you.' Hilda was now picking the girls up from school three nights a week, for which I was extremely grateful. It made family life so much easier, especially as Poppy much preferred this solution. She'd been a lot less moody and withdrawn for the last two weeks and we'd got into a new and much happier routine. Hilda collected the girls from school on Tuesdays, Wednesdays, and Fridays and by the time I came home from work, dinner was under way. Ash invariably came round after work with Bill, and Poppy, designating herself chief dog walker, got her puppy fix by taking him for a walk in the park while Ash and I went out for a run. After that we would all sit down together for dinner like one big, happy family.

Hilda had also got into the habit of staying overnight,

which meant that Ash and I got some much-appreciated time together taking Bill for a last pre-bedtime walk. It was fair to say that our frustration levels were rising and my new sofa had seen some serious necking.

'I don't know what I'd do without you, Hilda.'

'Well it's quite mutual, dear. I can't remember when I last enjoyed myself so much.' She lifted the lid from the cake tin to reveal a rather lurid cake. The colours from the smarties had bled into the white, lemon-flavoured icing. Glancing down at it she chuckled. 'Ava's such a card.'

'Looks like someone's been murdered,' I murmured.

'Yes, but it will taste bloody lovely,' chipped in Penny from over my shoulder, 'because Hilda made it. Honestly, I've never known anyone with such a light touch with sponge. You should go on *Bake Off*, Hilda.'

'I was all set to go on. I got through to the round before you go on television but then I had my fall. I'll have to make you my signature cake one day.'

'You were going to be on *Bake Off*?' Penny's eyes widened. 'Did you meet Paul Hollywood?'

'No, they don't come to the early rounds. Of course I know darling Mary; we go way back, long before the *Bake Off*.'

'Really?' Penny squeaked.

I smiled to myself, by now used to Hilda's stories.

As mugs of tea and coffee were dispensed along with generous portions of cake, we sat back down at the table, everyone dividing into smaller groups and chatting away to each other. Neil, Ash, and Charles were deep in conversation, Penny and Janie were bickering light-heartedly together as they usually did, Hilda was listening to Marsha and Elaine, and I sat back and let the general noise waft over me, with a lovely sense of wellbeing – although that might have had a lot to do with the cake. It was rather uplifting to see the disparate group in the room, all working towards a common cause. The sight and sounds filled with me happiness.

I belong. These are my people.

Chapter Thirty

F eeling ridiculously self-conscious, I pressed the button of the walkie-talkie. 'You there yet, Jim?'

'Just arrived, Claire. Over and out.'

The first marshal at the furthest point of the run was in place. We were good to go. For the last three quarters of an hour, Ash and I had been dashing here, there, and everywhere, consulting our lists, and checking laminated sheets. Runners had started arriving and wandering about looking for somewhere to put their sweatshirts and fleeces. I grabbed my notepad and scribbled quickly.

I walked over to them. 'Sorry guys. Next time there'll be a tarpaulin where you can leave things. That's why we're doing a trial run. For today leave your things on the run director's table.' I pointed to the trestle table set up just beyond the staked-out and taped-off area which denoted the finishing funnel. Marsha and Elaine, our official timekeepers, were already in place with their stopwatches guarding the finishing line and Wendy, now official funnel-manager, was prowling up and down with a proprietary air. I didn't mind one bit; the three of them were my secret weapon as, between them, their roles were crucial to ensuring that everyone who took part received the correct time for their run. At the other end of the funnel would be another two volunteers who handed out position tokens which had to be scanned along each runner's personal barcode. It was all quite complicated but, thanks to the patience of our parkrun ambassador, Helen, I had a pretty good grasp of how the magic worked. I was looking forward to meeting her next week at our inaugural Churchstone parkrun when Ash would be run director. Today he was running but next week it would be my turn and although the two of us had run the course together a couple of times, I couldn't wait to do it for real. I envied him today but someone had to be in charge.

Now that real people were starting to turn up and all of our volunteers were in place, it was all starting to feel official. Hopefully, next Saturday we'd have a few more runners. All this week we'd been putting up posters, sharing the date on social media, and had also sent out invitations to the other nearby parkruns in Leeds and Harrogate. We were hoping to get a few visitors coming to check out the new course.

'You all right?' asked Penny, appearing beside me and jogging on the spot, warming up.

'Yes, just a bit knackered from juggling this and work. But I'm quite proud of myself. I told my boss no twice this week'—because that on-edge feeling had started to creep back—'and they gave me the afternoon off for "community investment", which was handy. I never realised this was going to involve so much.'

She studied my face thoughtfully before saying with a sympathetic smile, 'I don't know how you do it all.'

'Some days, neither do I. Thank goodness for Hilda.'

'Where is she this morning?'

'You mean you haven't seen her?' I pointed across the park.

'Yikes. How did I miss her?'

Hilda was sporting a brand-new running kit in honour of the event – apparently Poppy and Ava had helped her choose it online. I suspected Poppy hadn't had that much to do with it; she had more taste than to choose the ultra-violet purple seventies-style tracksuit with its lime-green stripes down each arm and leg. It made the sunshine-yellow one look positively conservative.

'Yoo-hoo!' Hilda waved and we both laughed. Although not up to running the course, she, Bill, and Poppy were going to be our tail walkers today. Their job was bringing up the rear of the run to make sure that no one was left behind on the course. Poppy was desperate to have a go at the run while Ava was equally keen not to have to walk too far. This morning she was on a playdate with Janie's youngest, for which I was quite grateful.

'How are we doing?' asked Ash, coming up behind me and dropping a kiss on the back of my neck. I turned, desperate to kiss him back and walk into his arms, but we were on duty. I missed him. But I knew how this worked. The job came first. I'd been like that once and I completely understood.

With a sudden flood of happiness, I just knew that for me, my job was no longer everything. I had a home, a ready-made family, and the parkrun, and it felt... enough. My life was full of things that I enjoyed and loved.

Ash might have only started his job in the last week but already our routine had changed. He'd had to put dog-care plans into place and Hilda, egged on by Poppy, had volunteered to collect Bill at two each day for a walk around the park before going to pick up Poppy and Ava from school on Tuesdays, Wednesdays and Fridays. On Mondays and Thursdays, Poppy would collect Bill from Ash's ground-floor flat and take him straight out after school before bringing him back to our house. So Ash still called each day but it wasn't the same. No run, no family dinner. He was in work mode, distracted and distant. Last night he'd been due to stay for dinner but had been late back from work and Poppy had begged for Bill to stay overnight and meet him here this morning.

'We're ready.' I felt a fizz in the pit of my stomach as I grasped the loud-hailer. 'This is it.'

With Ash following me, I walked over to the official start line and, as I began to move, the runners realised that this was it and began to make their way over.

Lifting the loud-hailer to my mouth, I scanned the faces in front of me. Ash gave me a big smile and a thumbs up. 'Thanks everyone for coming for our trial run. I'll keep it short and sweet today. If anything's not clear or there are any problems or things you think need to be done, please come and see me or Ash or Charles at the end.' I went on to describe the course, thank the volunteers, and tell everyone we were meeting afterwards at The Friendly Bean. 'And finally, it's really important at the finish to cross the line, stay in the funnel, and stay in your finishing position to receive your finishing token. If you don't you'll have Wendy to answer to.' I pointed to her standing at the back of the crowd. 'Don't forget to get your tokens and barcodes scanned and make sure you return the tokens. That's all folks. Good luck. Enjoy the run. On three. One. Two. Three. Go.'

At my words, the runners streamed away along the path, spreading out quickly. I could see Charles already working his way to the front, while Penny was running at a steady pace near the middle. I lifted my camera and snapped a few pictures, smiling so hard my face felt like it might split. This time next week, who knew how many runners we'd have. I crossed my fingers. *Please let us have a good turnout.* We'd worked so hard to get this far; I really wanted it to be a success.

Hilda clapped me on the arm. 'We'll be off then.'

I kissed Poppy on the cheek and ruffled Bill's ears. 'Enjoy the walk.'

With everything now done, loud-hailer hanging loosely in my hand, I walked the two hundred metres to the finish line, the sudden quiet ringing in my ears. Now all I had to do was wait – I glanced down at my watch – for approximately twenty minutes for the first runner to come back in.

At nineteen minutes past nine, there was a ripple of excitement as the first runner came into view, a young lad who seemed to be absolutely sprinting towards the finish line. The next runner was a good three hundred metres behind him and a hundred metres beyond him a third man. After that, the runners were more bunched together and all pushing hard for the line.

All the volunteers swung into action and everyone seemed to know exactly what they were doing. 'Well done!' I said, beaming at the first over the line, even though the poor guy was gasping like a landed salmon.

'Well done, Claire, Ash, Hilda, Poppy,' called Penny, waving goodbye as she and Charles headed out of the door of The Friendly Bean. They were the last to leave. With only twenty runners, the inputting of all the times had been relatively quick and easy and Elaine, Marsha, and Wendy were all finished by ten-thirty with test emails sent out to all our runners. Ash's had pinged into his phone as we sat there.

'Phew,' I said, leaning back into my chair. 'Aside from the tarpaulin, no glitches at all.'

'We're all set for next weekend,' said Ash.

'Let's hope lots of people turn up.' Hilda drained her coffee before adding briskly, 'Now, some of us need to get back; I have a cake to bake. Claire has invited people for tea.' She peered over the top of her coffee cup at me with schoolmistressy disapproval. I ignored her; she been quite exacting about ingredients when I'd gone to do the shopping. This Victoria sponge wasn't going to be any old Victoria sponge. Apparently only Baxter's raspberry jam would do.

———————

'Poor Farquhar. I was a terrible mother.' Hilda paused as she sifted flour into a bowl. We'd been home for an hour, showered, changed, and the girls were outside primed and ready for the minute the invitation to come and lick the bowl was extended.

'I'm sure you weren't. You've given me tons of good advice.' Out of the window I could see Poppy sitting on a blanket on the grass in the sunny garden with her faithful pal curled up next to her while Ava was administering to the patients of her make-believe hospital ward of soft toys tucked up in shoe boxes that she'd unearthed from my wardrobe, after clopping about in my heels for ten minutes. 'Look at the pair of them; they're both happy, thank goodness. I don't think they're missing Alice too much. Although I still worry about Poppy sometimes.' I sighed. 'I sent Alice another message this week. I don't know what else to do. I can't keep saying she's stuck on a mountain for ever.'

'You're doing a wonderful job. They know they're loved and that's the most important thing. I learned that lesson too late. I think I could have done more to let Farquhar know that when he was a child and now it's far too late. My son has got his own life and I don't blame him. I wasn't around that much. It's karma.'

'I don't think it's ever too late. He clearly remembers your Victoria sponge.'

'He does?'

I nodded. 'And he worries about you.'

'Well he needn't,' said Hilda, although her sharp words were softened by her wry smile. 'He always did prefer Victoria sponge to any other cake, funny boy. Even on his birthday, he wanted a plain sponge. No frills, no fuss. That's my boy.'

'Wonder where he gets that from? The two of you are quite similar.'

Hilda drew herself up with horrified indignation. 'I don't think so. He's like his father.' Then she smiled and with a shake of her head, added, 'Not a spontaneous bone in his body. But, like his father, he's also determined, loyal and, I will say this for him, the boy does have bags of integrity. He'll always do the right thing. Where's Ash this afternoon?'

'He had things to do but he's coming over later to pick up Bill.'

'I don't know why you don't just leave Bill here. Poppy's so attached to him and now that Ash is at work it would be fairer on the dog.'

'Don't put ideas into Poppy's head, for goodness' sake.' I checked anxiously that she was still outside. Sure enough, she and Bill were still entwined.

'Why not? It would make sense.'

'Because…' I pinched my lips together and studied the sunshine dancing on Ava's unruly curls as she chattered away to herself and Poppy's absorption in her book as one hand absently stroked Bill's head. I couldn't imagine life without the girls. Lovely as he was, Bill would make a poor consolation prize. 'Because, what happens when Alice comes back? If she baulks at the responsibility of her own daughters, she's hardly going to want to add a dog into the equation.'

'You could keep him.'

'I think Ash is quite fond of him now.'

'Perhaps you could all share him.' She ignored my comment.

'Isn't that what we're doing at the moment?'

'Mmm,' she said absently, suddenly very busy cracking eggs into a bowl. 'Can you grease the sandwich tins for me?'

By the time Farquhar arrived, the kitchen was spotless and the table was laid with the Victoria sponge on a cake stand (which I seemed to have acquired) in the centre, along with some rocky-road brownies that Ava was eying hungrily, as usual, and some homemade lavender and vanilla star-shaped biscuits (again, I seemed to have acquired new biscuit cutters). Ash had rolled in five minutes before, his hair still damp from the shower and smelling of expensive, subtle aftershave which left my stomach curling with frustrated longing.

Farquhar clutched a bottle of Veuve Cliquot and a dozen yellow roses and faltered on the doorstep like a schoolboy caught out. With his hurried glance from me to Hilda, I realised that he wasn't quite sure who should be the recipient of his bounty and which of us was his hostess. Poor man appeared positively torn. I took pity on him and with a discreet tilt of my head indicated Hilda.

'Mother,' he said as he handed them over.

She beamed with pleasure. 'My favourites. Come in.'

Behind her back as she led the way, nursing her bouquet like an actress on opening night, he mouthed, 'Thank you.'

'Well hello! Who's this handsome chap?' Farquhar made a beeline for Bill, which immediately put him in Poppy's good graces and broke the ice as she explained how he'd been found.

'We had a couple of lurchers, don't you remember, Mother?' he said as he crouched at Bill's side, giving the dog a good rub. 'At the estate. Gertie and Bertie.'

'Oh gosh, yes, and do you remember when one of the little blighters finished off the roast beef when we'd retired into the drawing room? What a handful they were, but so adorable. So inquisitive. Into everything they were. But lovely calm creatures. That's why I chose Bill; I knew he would be perfect for you all.' She encompassed Ash, the girls, and me in her bland smile as she surveyed us.

I pressed my lips together hard and did my best not to catch Ash's eye, trying not to snort at this blatant but typically Hilda-esque high-handedness.

'I wanted to call him Hairy Carpet Dog,' explained Poppy earnestly.

Farquhar let out a proper upper-class guffaw. 'Priceless, sweetheart. That's an excellent name.'

'But they wouldn't let me,' said Poppy with a mournful twist to her mouth.

'That was a bit mean but Bill's a good solid name. I mean, imagine shouting Hairy Carpet Dog across the field when you want him to come back. It might have embarrassed the poor chap.'

'I never thought of that.' Poppy, somewhat mollified, smiled at him. He'd definitely won her approval. 'Would you like some tea?'

'Yes. Because we weren't allowed to have any cake until you came so that it's still nice. So can you have some Victoria sponge, please, because then I can have some and I haven't had anything to eat for hours,' complained Ava. 'And I'm starving.'

'Good gracious.' Farquhar clasped his hands. 'That won't do. I'm very sorry. I think we'd better have some cake straight away then.' He raised mischievous, laughing blue eyes my way, echoing the expression I'd seen so often in his mother's eyes. 'My mother does make the best Victoria sponge.'

'What? Ever *ever*?' asked Ava, intrigued by this.

'Well, I think so.' Farquhar gave her a very solemn nod. 'But perhaps you'd better try some and let me know what you think.'

Ava bounded to her feet and darted to the table, pulling out a chair for herself. She needed no second invitation.

Hilda gave an approving nod towards her son, who was gallantly helping Poppy to her feet. Ash was still frowning at him as if trying to puzzle him out. Once Farquhar had escorted Poppy to her chair, he pulled one out for his mother, who, with a regal incline of her head, sat down.

'The Veuve is chilled if anyone would like a glass,' said Farquhar.

'That would be delightful. The flutes are in the cupboard there.'

My eyes widened. I didn't even know I had any flutes. When I opened the infrequently used cupboard, I found six of Hilda's Baccarat crystal champagne flutes.

'Who knew?' I muttered to myself, removing each one with great care.

The tea party went off far better than I could have ever imagined and at one point, Farquhar even volunteered to come along to the parkrun one Saturday.

'You could come to the cinema with us on Friday, if you like,' said Poppy suddenly. 'Ash is taking us to see *Swallows and Amazons* at the Regal. He thinks we'll like it.'

I hid a smirk. Ash had volunteered a couple of weekends ago to take the girls to the recently restored Art Deco independent cinema for the teatime matinee because he really wanted to see it again.

'Is he now?' Farquhar smiled. 'That's a real shame as it's one of my favourite books and I particularly like visiting the Regal but unfortunately I have a court date in London that day and I don't think I'll be back in time.'

Surprisingly, his old fashioned manners, thoughtful and attentive to every member of the party, made him very good company and although he was a little stuffy, he completely won over the two girls, listening with great attention to everything they had to say. Funnily enough, they blossomed by being treated like little adults. Watching all this, Hilda softened towards him; even Ash – who'd been a little bit suspicious of him at first – unbent when Farquhar started asking him questions about his new job and seemed to know a little about the industry.

'Can I just say that I had no idea that your mother had brought those glasses here?' I whispered urgently to Farquhar on the doorstep when he came to leave.

'My dear, I know that. She was testing me, wanting to see if I was going to make a fuss.'

'Oh.'

'Thank you for inviting me today. You have a lovely family... Oh, I quite forgot. Have you heard from your sister?'

'No. I sent her a message asking her to get in touch and explaining that I don't have parental responsibility and if she intends to stay any longer I need to apply for a Special Guardianship Order and that I need her consent. She still hasn't come back to me. And the school's asked me to see the headteacher.'

'Have you been?'

'Not yet. I'm going on Tuesday.'

'Hmm. Well, here's my card. If you need anything, call me. And don't worry. You're doing a wonderful job with the girls. I honestly would have thought you were their mother. They're clearly happy and settled with you and that's what social services will be checking, if they get involved.'

I twisted the card between my fingers. 'Thank you. That's very kind of you.'

'And don't hesitate to call me. This is my field.'

'Yes but—'

'Don't even think about money. I'm very grateful that you're keeping an eye on my mother. She can be rather difficult. Not everyone… well, the manager at Sunnyside isn't a fan.' With a deprecating tug at his mouth he admitted, 'Unfortunately we're both a bit headstrong. But she's definitely mellowed since she met you. In fact, you seem to have given her a new lease of life. I only insisted on her going to Sunnyside because… well, she was going into a decline. After her fall she was very… well… more difficult than usual and despondent too. Although, I realise now that she was a touch depressed and lonely.' With an apologetic smile, he added. 'We've never got on terrifically well. Fault on both sides. And her terrible taste in men. Her late husband, George, was an out-and-out crook. I caught him selling some of her jewellery.'

'I think she knew,' I said, remembering her throwaway line about giving him permission to sell her ring. 'But he made her happy. It sounds like they had a lot of fun together.'

'A bit too much fun.' Farquhar's mouth pursed. 'But… she did seem a lot happier with him.'

'I think she has some regrets about the past,' I offered. 'Especially about your childhood.'

'No point looking back.' He surprised me. 'Now I'm an adult at the peak of my career, I have a better understanding. She had work she enjoyed. Not supposed to say anything,' he tapped his nose in a sitcom way that made me want to laugh, 'but I think she might have worked for MI6 at one time. Something m'father once said.'

'Really?' I said, stifling the urge to giggle.

'But thank you for today. I'd like to come again, if that

would be all right. I think perhaps we all need to sit down and have a bit of heart to heart and sort a few things out. I feel a lot better knowing that she has friends who care and can keep an eye on her.'

'I don't want to interfere but I think she would be happier in a home of her own rather than in the nursing home. She's still very independent.' I put a hand on his arm as I saw him stiffen. 'I know that house is far too big for her. But she loves cooking and baking. She likes having nice things around her and I think she'd like a garden of her own. Perhaps we could find a smaller one for her. A bungalow or something?'

He sighed. 'I appreciate that but at her age she could go downhill so quickly…' He suddenly frowned. 'You do know how old she is, don't you?'

'No.'

When he told me, I was too stunned to say a word.

Chapter Thirty-One

'Does anyone have any further questions?' I glanced around the boardroom. Each seat was filled with a besuited executive all studying my final slide with great attention.

'Well, I certainly don't,' said Alastair Taylor, our managing director. 'Very detailed and diligent as always, Claire.'

'Yes, another excellent job,' added Bob Wilding. That was because I'd insisted on focusing on it and not getting dragged into several other projects.

Both were founding partners and their opinion had previously been very important, with a capital V. I gave them a professional, modest, little smile. I felt strangely indifferent. I'd done the job I was supposed to do to the best of my ability but I hadn't felt any sense of challenge or excitement.

One by one, everyone from the meeting drifted away and as the last one disappeared through the heavy wooden door, I dropped into one of the leather boardroom seats and rubbed my fingers against my pounding temples.

Karen caught me as I returned to my desk clutching my laptop to my chest. 'I hear the presentation went extremely well.' Her eyes twinkled with an unspoken message she was bursting to share. 'Alastair Taylor wants to see you at half past four this afternoon.' She finished the sentence with a decided flourish and an extremely unsubtle comedy-moment wink.

'Half four?' Ironically my immediate thought wasn't, *what time shall we crack open the prosecco?* It went straight to, *shit will I get out in time to pick up the girls?*

Anxiety twisted in my guts as I weighed things up. I'd have to keep the meeting short and sweet without being too obvious about it and I still had a ton of pressing work to do by the close of business.

'Yes. I checked your diary; you're clear all day.' She nudged me as if trying to unearth my missing enthusiasm.

'Right.' I dredged up a smile.

'You do know what this means.'

'I think so.'

'First woman partner,' she whispered. 'I'm so proud of you.'

'You don't know that for sure,' I whispered back, still not taking it all in. I'd been convinced that my unplanned absence and the stigma of stress-related absence would have put the kibosh on any promotion to partner.

A few hours later, I left the office in a state of shock. Alastair Taylor had indeed offered me a partnership, something that I'd been working towards for the last ten years. All those extra hours I put in, all the missed weekends, the late nights... they'd all paid off.

First female partner and youngest in the history of the company.

I still couldn't quite believe it.

I stared at the screen for ages before I texted Ash from the train with the news, ignoring the little voice at the back of my head asking if this was really what I wanted.

Guess who made partner!!!!!!!

I sat watching the screen of my phone, waiting for his response. Now that he was working again, I knew he'd be pleased for me. A minute later my phone pinged.

And Coffee Girl is back! Well done you. The International Arms Dealer has strong-armed Hilda into babysitting. Dinner. Beech House. Celebration. Xxx

Dinner with Ash, well that definitely was the icing on the cake for the day. I wondered if I could ask Hilda to stay the night and we could finally collect on our rain check.

I rushed from the station, arriving at six thirty-two at the After-school Club. The manager stood at the door, Poppy and Ava beside her, her mouth squished into a disapproving moue as if she'd just sucked the sourest lemon on the planet. In the face of such abject censure, I didn't dare respond to the ping of a new text message on my phone or even take it out of my pocket to take a quick peek. 'You're late, Miss Harrison. I'm afraid we'll have to fine you.'

Even her fearsome, Miss Trunchbull scowl couldn't dim my

glow. 'I'm very sorry. I got held up at work.' *I'm going to dinner with Ash!*

'Off you go, girls.' She ushered them towards me and then made a great show of switching the lights out and setting the alarm as she closed the door behind her.

'Sorry guys. Mad day.' I wasn't sure how impressed either of them would be at my promotion, I shepherded them out into the cooling evening. 'How was your day?'

'Rubbish,' said Poppy. 'And *she* has been really horrid, checking her watch all the time, making us wait by the door and saying she had more important things to do and places to be, like it was *our* fault you were *late*.' Her eyes narrowed, accusing and angry.

'I really am sorry, Poppy. Something happened at work.' My encouraging come-along smile had no effect; she simply lifted her shoulders in one of her dismissive shrugs.

'I only got one sausage,' piped up an aggrieved Ava, 'and Lucy Chambers got two. It's not fair.' Her round cheeks puffed up in indignation. 'I hate nasty, old After-school Club.'

Boy, they really knew how to bring me down to earth. I raised an eyebrow. Ava didn't normally complain about After-school Club. 'No, you don't. You normally like the tea.'

'Yes, I do. It's just me and Lucy Chambers from my class that go. And her mum picks her up at half past five. We have to wait for ever for you to come. We're always last and mean Mrs Winter goes on about it.'

'Well she shouldn't do that.' The After-school Club's advertised hours were 3.15 to 6.30pm and I was always there by six thirty. This was the first time I'd actually been late. A whole two minutes late.

'Well she does,' snapped Poppy.

The three of us trailed into the house and I unloaded book bags and PE bags onto the table. 'Would you like some beans on toast or cheese on toast or a fish finger sandwich?' I asked, hoping to mollify their crankiness with good, old-fashioned comfort food.

'Fish fingers, fish fingers!' cried Ava, throwing herself onto the sofa.

I cocked an eyebrow at Poppy and she gave me a wan smile. God it was hard work being the grown-up all the time and trying to stay upbeat when someone, or two people, had sucked the joy out of your good news.

As I yanked a box of Findus' finest out of the freezer, I checked my phone.

Sorry, can we take a rain check on tonight? I need to work late. I know you'll understand. Dinner tomorrow? I've cancelled Hilda. Call later x.

The sad thing was that I was relieved. Now I was home and back in the real world of after-school pick-up, homework, and tea, I realised that I was far too knackered to go out. Grabbing the loaf of bread, I cut another two slices. *Looks like I'm having fish finger sandwiches too.* With a sigh I buttered the bread; at least I could get on with some of my own work once the girls were settled and then, if I put in a couple of hours, I could get to bed at a reasonable hour.

My phone rang at ten past ten. 'Hey, Ash.'

'Hey, Claire. Congratulations.'

'Thanks.' I pushed my laptop aside and moved over to the sofa, rubbing my tired eyes. 'Feels like I've reached the top of the mountain at last.' I felt like a Sherpa – one who had carried a very heavy load all the way up the north face of Everest.

'Must be wonderful. You've done really well, Coffee Girl.'

I thought back to the day we'd met. Coffee Girl was from another lifetime. She would have been thrilled with this promotion, probably still out swilling prosecco with her work colleagues, whereas I was rushing to After-school Club and worrying about what being a partner would mean in terms of extra workload and childcare and whether, after everything, it was really what I wanted. I'd got more of a work-life balance back, but the work itself didn't give me that buzz it once had. When I'd first started I'd been helping businesses get set up and solving problems. Now I was doing reports on the viability of huge projects with faceless executives I rarely met. I wasn't sure this was what I wanted to do anymore. And what about the girls? Did I want them to be the last children to be collected every night? The children that never had anyone at assembly? The ones that only got two out of ten in spellings or that were falling behind in reading because no one ever read with them?

'Claire?' Ash's voice pulled me from my thoughts.

'And how's Ashwin Laghari doing?' I asked with a teasing note in my voice because I didn't want to dwell on everyday stuff. For now, I wanted to enjoy fairy-tale Ash and me, the high-flying couple we'd once been on that very first date.

'I'm doing okay. Although…' There was lengthy pause. 'I've got some bad news.'

'What's that?'

'Er… it's about Saturday.'

'Don't tell me you can't make the parkrun?' I laughed, knowing it to be impossible. We'd worked too long and hard for that even to be considered but when the silence down the line seemed to get heavier and heavier, my skin goose bumped in sudden awareness.

'Ash?'

'I'm really sorry. It's work... I can't... not when I'm still so new with the company.'

'But... you're run director.'

'I know but you know I wouldn't let you down if it wasn't important. There's a sales conference this weekend down in Gloucestershire. I've been invited to present a session on the Friday and I'm expected to do a board-address thing on the Saturday morning.'

I was too disappointed to respond. He'd clearly forgotten he was supposed to be taking the girls to see *Swallows and Amazons* at the Regal. I wasn't going to make him feel any more guilty than he already did.

'Claire? Don't be cross. I know it's a big deal because it's the first one but if you think about it, the important thing is that we've built a legacy. It's the first one of many. And after three, four, five, six, you'll look back and it won't be such a big deal.'

What he was saying made perfect, logical sense, and if I took a couple of deep breaths, I could be equally understanding and logical but something else bothered me. A niggling thorn that dug its way in.

This is the beginning of the end.

Coffee Girl and Ashwin Laghari might have sparkled and flown high in a relationship that would have glittered with explosive chemistry like fireworks in a November sky, but it would never have lasted. Our careers would always have come first.

Claire and Ash… well, it had been good while it lasted but we were headed in different directions now. Our blossoming relationship was about to hit its autumn before the petals had properly unfurled. I doubted they would get the chance now; I couldn't see it surviving much longer. Maybe, to use a pertinent pun, I should nip things in the bud now, but a lump in my throat stopped me saying anything.

'Claire?'

'Mmm, you're right.' I forced the words out. The parkrun was more than one run and no matter what, I was proud of what we'd achieved to get there.

'I'll make it up to you. Maybe dinner one day next week.'

Yes, but what about making it up to the girls? He still hadn't realised that he was letting them down as well.

'This week is already… well, it's just unravelling fast. God, I'd forgotten what it's like. And it's even worse starting a new job. So much to do just to get up to speed. But it's great to be working again. I didn't realise how much I'd missed it. The routine. Being valued. Having stuff to do.'

Ashwin Laghari was back and I couldn't begrudge him feeling good about himself and his new sense of purpose. I thought of the sad figure he'd cut before I'd realised he'd been made redundant, before Hilda had taken him in hand. Ash needed work; it defined him.

'You sound happy,' I said, genuinely pleased for him. 'And I know the feeling. I've got a ton of work stuff to do tonight. Good luck at the conference. I hope it all goes well and you blow their socks off.'

'Thanks and… I'm really sorry about Saturday. I'm going to miss you.'

'Yeah, me too.' But I didn't think that would last very long. 'Welcome back to real life.'

He laughed, and I was grateful that I was able to sound like Coffee Girl, the sort of woman who would accept that careers came first because inside I didn't feel like that anymore.

Chapter Thirty-Two

'Morning,' Sascha appeared carrying two big thermos flasks and a basket over the crook of one arm which was full of plastic cups, a plastic bottle of milk, and some wooden stirrers. 'Thought I'd help you kick off the event.'

'That's brilliant.' I almost snatched the coffee from her hands. It was ten past eight on a gloriously sunny Saturday morning – *the* Saturday morning – and the butterflies in my stomach were preparing for mass migration. Coffee was exactly what I needed.

Last night I hadn't got much sleep and I was quite grateful for the trip to the Regal, which I ended up doing in Ash's absence. I lied to Poppy and Ava, telling them he'd paid for the tickets as a treat because he couldn't make it.

'I was too nervous to have one at home earlier. Thank you.'

'Nervous, what on earth for?' She spoke with the blithe confidence of someone who didn't do nerves. 'Shall I set up here?' With a tilt of her head, she indicated the trestle table near the finishing funnel. 'I'd say you've got it all sorted.'

'We're getting there,' I said. She put down the flasks and, efficient as ever, poured two cups of coffee. 'Wouldn't catch me up at this time running around a park. Can't see the appeal but to each his own. Hope it goes well.' She lifted her cup in a quick salute.

'Thanks. Nothing I can do now. Just pray people turn up.'

She shrugged. 'There's always next week. Rome wasn't built in a day.'

'That's what I've been telling myself the whole way through this.'

'You've done a good thing. Good for the community. Most of those volunteers that turned up... I'd never seen them before and I've lived in Churchstone nearly all my life. This park should be used more and before you say it, not just because I'm going to benefit from the custom. I know people think that I'm a bit of ballbreaker and I'm only interested in my profits, but this park is special.' She stared off into the distance and then her mouth softened. 'When I was seven my gran used to bring me here every Saturday morning, rain or shine. When it rained she bought a picnic rug and we sheltered in the bandstand and ate banana sandwiches out of tin foil and drank black tea from a thermos flask. You know the old-style ones with the tartan pattern on the outside? Bless her. She was a lifesaver. My parents were going through a shitty divorce and I was caught smack bang in the middle. Those Saturday mornings were a reprieve. The only time in the week when I didn't have to feel guilty for being with one instead of the other. My gran loved this park. I miss her. She died last year.'

'I'm sorry. She sounds like she loved you.'

'Oh God, yeah.' Sascha rubbed at the chrome valve of one of the big thermos flasks and I suspected she was avoiding catching my eye. 'She wasn't the sort that spoiled you, wasn't backwards about clipping you round the ear if she thought you deserved it either, but I always knew she was in my corner. Hilda reminds me a bit of her. Kind but firm, and speaks her mind.'

'Talk of the devil,' I said, spotting Hilda in another new tracksuit. I blinked. She'd outdone herself today. She marched across the park resplendent in a shiny fuchsia-pink shell suit that rustled along with her self-important steps.

'Freakin' hell! Where did she get that little number?' Sascha put her hand over her mouth, hiding the snigger I could hear. 'Is it vintage?'

'I think she gets them online,' I murmured.

'And that's why some people should not be allowed an internet connection,' muttered Sascha.

Following in Hilda's wake was a man with a large camera around his neck, who was obviously Adam, the photographer from the local paper, and a second older man tagging along behind him.

'I'll leave you to it,' murmured Sascha, sidling away.

'Morning Claire, this is Mr Benton and his father Mr Benton, senior. Ooh is that coffee?'

'Do call me Harold,' said the older man, who swept off his panama hat and nodded to me with old-school courtesy. 'I'm not here in a professional capacity. I'm just being nosy.' Hilda was already helping herself to coffee and offering him one.

'And I'm the son of the nosy one, here in a very professional capacity. Adam Benton, photographer with the Churchstone Advertiser.' He held out a hand.

'Hi, nice to meet you and thanks so much for coming.'

He gave me an amused smile and glanced back at his

father, who was chatting to Hilda over their steaming drinks. 'I'm not sure I had an awful lot of choice. My dad met Hilda in the library this week. She's... very persistent.'

'Oh God, I'm sorry,' I looked over his shoulder. 'Although, to be fair, this *was* her idea so she deserves most of the credit, and,' I laughed, 'if it's any consolation, I'm a victim of that persistence too... but look where it got us.' I waved my hand around the park and the busy team of volunteers who were setting up.

'Quite an undertaking.' His admiring grin and swift, flirty glance wasn't entirely unwelcome. 'I wasn't sure what to expect but it all seems very organised.' He turned his head to take it all in.

'That's thanks to the parkrun organisation, who've given us lots of support, but mainly to our fantastic team of volunteers.'

'How many people are you expecting to turn up and run today?'

'I'm not sure but I'd be pleased with forty.'

Charles had promised that most of the Harriers would be coming along, Penny and Janie had persuaded the school to put leaflets in all the children's book bags, and Elaine had taken two cartons of leaflets up to the secondary school. There'd been a lot of interest on Facebook and Hilda had been telling everyone about it, pressing leaflets into the hands of every shopkeeper on the High Street.

'Seems like a lot of effort for forty people.' He shrugged and I wondered if he was being deliberately confrontational to get a story.

'Not at all. It's about taking part and making a free event available to the local community. The smallest parkruns average about thirty to forty people. Did you know, there are even parkruns in prisons?'

'No, I didn't.' Now I had his interest.

'Yes, there are over twenty parkruns in prisons and young offender institutions throughout the UK. Don't you think that's amazing?'

'You sound positively evangelical,' teased the photographer.

'You know what, I am. This,' I held out my hand to indicate the park full of people, 'has changed my life. I've got to know more people in the last six weeks than I have the whole six months I lived here before then. I've made friends, met people I'd never normally have met, and I think we're going to make a difference to a lot of people's lives.' I thought about Elaine, Marsha, and Wendy reconnecting.

'Don't you think you're attributing quite a lot to… well, a run in the park?'

'No, not at all. There's been a lot of interest and support from the community.'

'So how does it all work?' he asked with another one of those flirty smiles which gave my ego a welcome boost. Aside from a few texts, I'd barely heard from Ash. Not even a good-luck text this morning. With a smile warmer than he perhaps deserved, I gave Adam a very quick explanation, apologising for its brevity as I had a volunteer briefing to do in the next five minutes. 'And that's about it. Actually, if you're staying for the run, it would be great if you could let us have some photos. I'm supposed to appoint a volunteer photographer but that one fell by the wayside this week. Just too much to do.' I might as well take advantage of his flirty interest.

'I'll definitely do it today but I can do better than that. Hey, Dad. Fancy a job?'

Harold lifted his head as Adam explained that we were a photographer short. 'I'd be delighted, especially if I get to spend some time with this lovely young lady.'

To my surprise, Hilda simpered – or something very close to it. Oh God, was this husband number five coming up?

'That would be fabulous, if you could. But do you know what?' I turned to Adam. 'Hang around, talk to people. Then come back next week and take part. There are lots of stories here, lots of human interest. Isn't that what local papers want? Now, please excuse me; I must go and brief the team.'

As Adam stepped back I saw that I'd piqued his interest. 'I think I will stick around. Interview a few folk. Thanks Claire, hope it all goes well. Perhaps I can give you a call… do a follow-up piece?'

I just nodded. He had my number but, nice as he was, he'd make a poor substitute for Ash.

As it was the same team as last time and they all knew the ropes, the briefing didn't last very long and the marshals with their lanyards and walkie-talkies set off to take up their positions. Charles and I had walked the course earlier to make sure there were no issues and aside from a large fallen branch that we'd picked up from the main path and tossed into the shrubbery, there were no hazards or obstacles. Elaine, Wendy, and Marsha checked the stopwatches and the scanners and made sure the funnel was set up to their liking while I paced about, trying not to mind too much that I wouldn't be running today. It was going to be difficult watching them all set off and disappear into the trees and then have to wait for at least twenty minutes before we caught the first glimpse of the lead runner.

'Claire,' Penny came dashing over, Hilda hot on her heels, still rustling like a paper bag. 'We've been talking. And we think it's only fair that Charles acts as run director for you today, or at least during the run.'

'What?'

'He ran the course last week. He's co-director anyway and we all feel really strongly that you should run the first one. You've been an absolute hero setting all this up.'

Hilda nudged my arm. 'Just say yes, dear. You know you want to. And isn't Harold charming?' I eyed her and gave in to a sudden urge to hug her. 'Thank you, Hilda.' I could tell that she'd been instrumental in arranging this.

'It's only right, dear. You're the one who's made this happen. Honestly, if I'd known what was involved, I'd never have suggested it.'

'Now she tells me,' I said, as we both began to giggle.

'It's been a ride though, hasn't it?' Hilda winked.

'It certainly has. I wouldn't have missed it for the world.'

'Me neither. And look...' She pointed to the growing crowd of people gathering around the edge of the big ground sheet we'd spread on the other side of the path for runners to leave their things.

'Blimey!' I'd been so busy with other things, I'd not realised how many people had begun to gather but there must have been at least a hundred runners and it was only quarter to nine. 'Build it and they will come,' I murmured, shaking my head.

'And they're coming.' She lifted a gnarled old hand to fist bump mine. 'We did it.'

'We certainly did.' I straightened and a burst of pride fired up the blood cells in my veins, pushing through a zing of electricity. 'We certainly did.'

'And I for one would be disappointed if you didn't run it today... and so would you.' She glanced over to where Poppy and Ava were bundled up in coats against the early morning chill. 'I'll keep an eye on both of them.' Poppy was playing with Bill as always and Ava was guarding the small pile of tins of brownies, cakes, and cookies that some of the volunteers had brought along.

'That's very kind of you. Although Bryan – he gets my train every morning – has said she and Bill are very welcome to join him on the tail walk.' Bryan Fellbrook, it turned out, had once been a keen runner but had got out of the habit. His wife had died recently and this, he thought, would give him something to do on Saturday mornings. I hoped so. Since that first volunteer meeting, he and the other lady with the gorgeous auburn hair had come and sat with me a couple of times and the three of us had developed a little commuter friendship, chatting all the way into Leeds.

In the end, I didn't take much persuading and I was very grateful to Charles.

And so I found myself in the thick of a crowd of runners facing Charles on the start line, my heart pumping with nerves and excitement. This was it. The Churchstone parkrun.

'Welcome everybody!' yelled Charles, using the script I'd

put together, 'And thanks for joining nearly one hundred and forty thousand runners this morning who take part in over 600 parkruns every Saturday morning in the UK alone. It's great to see so many of you here.' He went through the standard announcements about the course, the finishing line, barcodes and scanning process. 'And finally, I want to say a big thank you to Claire Harrison and Hilda Fitzroy-Townsend, who have been so instrumental in setting up this run. And also, Ash Laghari, who unfortunately can't be with us today. Can you ladies give us a wave and can everyone give them a bit of a clap and a cheer.'

Feeling very self-conscious, I put up my hand and was almost deafened by the cheer that went up around me. A couple of people standing nearby, complete strangers, clapped me on the arms and the back.

'Well done.'

'Good job.'

'Thanks so much.'

I just grinned at them, not sure what to say. I wasn't sure I deserved this much credit. Suddenly, I wished Ash were here and I felt in my pocket for my phone.

Don't break a leg. Thinking of you. Wish I could be there. Go for it xxx

He hadn't forgotten us after all.

'On your marks, on three. Three, two, one!'

And we were off. I was swept along with the crowd and a tide of euphoria. Running in a crowd was so different to running on your own and I had to force myself to slow a little when I realised my breath was coming too hard and fast. This pace was much faster than my usual plod and if I kept it up I'd run out of steam. Unlike a lot of people alongside me, I knew about the forthcoming hill. I needed to save some gas for that.

It didn't take long for the field to even out and I settled into an easy pace, running for a while alongside a couple of the Harriers who all sported broad grins and each gave me a thumbs up as they noticed me. All the training had paid off and it made me smile to myself as I remembered those early days when I puffed and panted my way around the park, gasping for air. It was still tough and my lungs were working overtime but I had a rhythm, and each inward breath didn't feel like a burst of fire in my chest. My legs stretched and flexed, hard at work, and I certainly knew about it as we started the climb up to Beacon Knoll. The front runners were long gone but I was pleased to see that a couple of people like me had slowed to a walk. I was never going to get up this stretch without stopping but I'd definitely improved since I'd first started running. Then, I wouldn't have been able to run up any of it. I picked up my feet and forced myself to run up the last third of the steep hill, knowing that once I'd crested the top I only had one downhill kilometre to the finishing line.

Hunched over, carrying tension in my neck and shoulders, I finally reached the top, my thighs burning. I hauled in a desperate breath and plunged downhill, allowing my arms to swing wildly, letting relief and gravity carry my body. My feet thudded on the soft, grassy path as I focused on the red top of the man in front of me. He was wearing a '50' T-shirt, denoting that he'd run fifty parkruns, and I had nearly caught up with him. I forced my legs to go a little faster, I was going to overtake him. I think my head must have been flooded with hallucinogenic endorphins because the *Chariots of Fire* music was playing in my head and every competitive bone in my body had suddenly sat up and taken notice. I streaked down the hill, passing the other runner, hell bent on reaching the finishing line that I knew was just round the next bend, hidden by the shrubs crowding the entrance to this wooded avenue.

I burst out into the sunlight, the finishing line just a hundred metres in front of me and ran so hard I thought my knees might give way.

'Go Claire!' yelled Elaine, who was a mere blur in my vision as I reached the end of the funnel. I heard the click of her stopwatch as I crossed the line.

'Well done!' called Marsha.

I staggered up the funnel bent double and trying to catch my breath.

I'm going to die. Or throw up. Or both.

'Great finish,' said the man with the '50' T-shirt from behind me.

'Thanks,' I gasped. 'Don't know what got into me.'

I held out my hand to the young volunteer dishing out the finishing tokens. 'Thanks.'

'This is a *good* course,' said the man behind me. 'Really enjoyed that. And so glad you've started one here. I've been driving over to Harrogate for the last two years. This one's a bit more of a challenge.'

'Mmm, I'm not so sure,' I wheezed. 'I knew putting that hill in was a mistake.'

He roared with laughter as we joined separate queues to have our barcodes scanned and hand in our tokens.

Chapter Thirty-Three

The mood in The Friendly Bean was triumphant, especially after Sascha announced that the coffee was on the house. 'For this week, only,' she added with stern admonishment. 'Don't think I'm going soft or anything.'

Her father, who, as promised, had marshalled for us this morning and was now helping behind the counter, rolled his eyes and carried on doing sterling work at the big espresso machine. I'd had a very useful chat with him on the walk back to the café after we'd tidied up after the run.

'As if,' muttered Penny under her breath and I gave her a nudge. Sascha had been nothing but generous to me.

'Can I have that?' asked Ava, reaching forward to my plate where the last third of the brownie I'd treated myself to sat.

I frowned. 'I'll cut it in half and you can share it with Poppy.' I glanced across the table where Poppy was sitting next to Penny, scrolling through her phone, a sharp-eyed expression on her face as she concentrated on the screen. She was hunched over her mobile a little too secretively to my mind. The school was very good at sending reminders about keeping children safe online which gave me cause for a whole new set of worries. Was I being diligent enough with the Wi-Fi settings? I trusted Poppy to be sensible but smarter girls than she had been caught out online.

'Everything okay, Poppy?'

Alarm skittered briefly across her small, sharp features and then she straightened and shoved her phone in her pocket. 'Yes.'

I narrowed my eyes, wondering what she was doing. I didn't like the idea of snooping on her phone; she was a good kid. For all I knew she was texting or messaging some boy. 'Want some brownie?'

She shook her head and lifted her chin. I noticed she was a little pale, her mouth set in a stern line. 'Ava can have it.'

I lifted a brow. It was rare for her to let Ava get away with having more than her fair share.

She shrugged. 'I'm not hungry. Can I go outside?'

'Yes, we shouldn't be too much longer. Don't go too far away.'

Like a bird released from captivity, she sprang up and dashed outside.

Penny caught my attention and we started chatting. When I next checked, Poppy was leaning with her legs crossed at the ankle against a low wall over by the swings, fully absorbed in her phone.

'I can't believe we had three hundred runners,' exclaimed Elaine for about the fifth time from the table where she, Wendy, and Marsha were compiling the times and results for all the runners.

'Neither can I,' I said, still blown away by the incredible turnout. 'Are you going to be okay with all that inputting?'

'Piece of cake,' said Wendy, slightly outraged that I had dared to doubt them. 'We wanted something to get our teeth into.' The three of them cackled away like Shakespearian witches and carried on typing into the laptop.

'Don't you fret, Claire.' Marsha beamed at me, some of her wiry grey hair standing on end where she'd pushed her hands through it as she concentrated on checking that all the times and tokens were in the right order. I didn't envy her; this was the point at which the technical wizardry happened. 'We'll get these results out by half past eleven.'

As if by magic, each runner would receive their time and various personal stats about the run including their overall position in the run, position by age category, their age-graded percentage and their personal best time all in one personalised email. It seemed that overnight I'd become a proper runner because I couldn't wait to see how I'd done.

When the door pushed open, with the ting of a bell, some sixth sense made me glance up. Ash stood in the doorway, his eyes immediately seeking me out.

My breath hitched at the sight of him, broad shouldered in an expensively tailored suit that definitely hadn't been anywhere near a Marks & Spencer. The striking eyes held mine and part of me wanted to throw myself into his arms and another part wanted to protect myself. Over before it had started. I didn't blame Ash for not being here for the run; I understood it, but I knew that this was just the start. There'd be lots of occasions where he wouldn't be here for me or the girls or Hilda.

I stood up and weaved my way through the tables to greet

him, taking his arm and leading him back out into the sunshine, my heart heavy with what I was about to do.

'Hey, how did it go?' he asked softly.

'It went brilliantly. Over three hundred runners.'

'Wow. God. Sorry. I should have been here. I left straight after breakfast.'

I led him over to one of the benches, just sliding out of reach when he went to put his hand in the small of my back.

'Ash, don't beat yourself up. It's just one of those things. Like you said, we're building a legacy here. And today was amazing. I really feel we've started something and I'm proud of what you, me, and Hilda started. We were all in bad places and now look at us.'

He leaned forward to take one of my hands but I moved it out of reach.

'Claire?'

'Ash. I don't expect anything from you. When we met, things were different. Things have changed for me but they don't have to for you.'

'What's that supposed to mean?'

'This last couple of days, I realised that things have to change now and I think we've reached the end of the road.'

'What are you talking about?' I sensed his genuine confusion.

'You've got this great new job. You need to focus on that.'

'I'm working extra hours at the moment while I get my feet under the table but it's temporary.'

'Is it?' I searched his face and saw that momentary flicker of doubt.

'Of course it is. I... need to the put hours in now but... you know I care about you. We're mature adults. Okay, I've cancelled a couple of times recently but... you know what it's like.'

'I do. I completely get it and I'm really not blaming you or being a spoiled brat.' I gave him a sad smile. 'When we first met, we had everything at our feet. The attraction was instant.' Our eyes met and my heart gave a little jolt at the memory of the first time I'd seen those amazing golden-green eyes. 'On that first date'—I couldn't bring myself to say that the air had fizzed with sexual chemistry—'we were on the same page. We both knew our careers came first; they defined us. Both of us. I thought I'd die of the shame when I was signed off. Then I saw what happened when you lost your job. You need to make this job work and it won't be long before you move on. I'm just trying to save some time.' *And some heartbreak along the way.*

'Save some time?'

'We're going in two different directions. You've got a new career and you're going to want to put your all into that.'

'But what about you? The partnership?'

My laugh was hollow. 'It's funny... now that I've been offered it, I realise I don't want it. I've come to see that there are more important things in life. My job has changed over the years and what I do now, it doesn't give me any particular satisfaction. I realise that as I've climbed the ladder, I've got further away from the small-business work that once interested me. But the good thing is, it doesn't matter so much.'

'Wow, I didn't know you felt that way.'

I laughed without mirth. 'Neither did I, until they offered me the promotion. I thought I wanted that more than anything else in the world. But it turns out I don't. I want to spend more time at home and not have to commute every day. I want to enjoy my time with Hilda, with the girls. I want to make the parkrun even more of a success, go out for a gin with Penny and Janie every now and then... I want to cook dinner every night. I don't think that domestic set-up is for you.'

'And you're not going to give me a chance to prove otherwise.' He sounded bitter.

'Ash? Seriously? You'll put work first. You already did with the parkrun and I don't blame you, I really don't, but that's going to happen more and more. Work will come first because that's how you're built and I'm not going to slow you down.'

'Big of you.'

'Don't be like that, Ash. You'll thank me later.'

'Must be good having all the answers. Being right all the time.'

'I only wish I did,' I said, hit by a wave of dejection. I liked Ash more than I'd liked any man in a long time but he was about to return to his former glory; he had the chance to go back to being Ashwin Laghari, sexy, arrogant go getter. It wouldn't be long before he was back up to speed and we'd be a distant memory in his wake. It was better to do this now before the inevitable happened. 'I think we should concentrate on being friends rather than anything else at the moment. You need to focus on the new job. We need some space.'

To my surprise, Ash gave me a pitying look and pushed himself to his feet. 'What you're really saying is that you're not prepared to give us a chance.'

No, it's not what

I want you, but I'm being practical because one day you'll walk away because you don't have to stay. They're not your children.

'That's not what I want but it will make it easier.'

He paced a couple of steps and then turned. 'What about Bill?'

'What about Bill?'

'You'll break Poppy's heart.'

I hadn't thought about that and I shot him a mutinous glare.

'I can hardly ask you to dog-sit all the time if we're not'—he made irritating quote marks with his fingers—'friends anymore.'

Chapter Thirty-Four

'Y ou're kidding me? What about the partnership?'

Karen put down the letter I'd just handed her and stalked about her office with her hands on her hips. I gazed beyond her out of the eleventh-floor window down over the Headrow to the majestic Town Hall guarded by its stone lions. Despite its grandeur, with its baroque dome and clock face, it wasn't a view I was going to miss.

'I've realised I don't want it.'

She whirled around, studying me as if I were some exotic species in a zoo that she might never get to see again. Her eyebrows beetled upwards and were lost in her heavy fringe.

'What did Alastair say?'

'He was very understanding.' In fact, I was still reeling from how unexpectedly candid he'd been when he told me I was doing the right thing and that I ought to get a life while I was young enough to enjoy one. *'I've put my heart and soul into this place, it's cost me two marriages, and I've not seen my kids grow up. I'm not sure lowering my golf handicap when I finally get to retire will make it all worthwhile,'* he'd said.

His words had helped, reinforcing the decision I'd already made.

'And you've got another job?' She wheeled around again, turning on her heels, accusation ringing in her voice. 'Are they going to pay as much as we do? I didn't even know you were job-hunting.'

'I wasn't. And it's not about money. I just happened to meet Edward Comely. It was at the volunteer meeting. In fact, you could say it was your fault because you and Dave were telling him I was some wunderkind. Turns out he runs a local family accountancy practice.'

'Comely?' And then her eyes widened with sudden recognition. 'Grey-haired guy, well-dressed, nice brogues. Damn, and I thought he was so nice.'

'He is nice and also very astute.' I thought back to the two-hour-long meeting we'd had on Monday after work. I'd spoken to him at the parkrun on Saturday morning and he'd been keen to meet up as quickly as possible.

'And what's he got to offer that Cunningham, Wilding and Taylor can't?'

'More client-facing consultancy with local businesses. Less pressure. Senior partner role. Four days a week. Nine to five. In Churchstone. I can walk to work.' Edward Comely had agreed to every one of my requests. And he was offering good money too, but as I'd said, it wasn't about the money. It was about being valued, being a part of something smaller, and besides, I'd really liked him.

'Well good for you, I guess.' The downturn of her mouth suggested she was being diplomatic. 'I suppose it will save a lot of hours commuting and having a day off is a bit of a luxury. Although I'm sure we could have matched that. And we do have flexible working arrangements.'

'It's more than that, Karen.' I didn't think I could explain to her that I didn't want the hard-edged politics of a big firm, the high-octane, demanding clients who assumed that big fees bought your soul and every hour of your day. It just wasn't me anymore. There were also the simple practicalities: being able to drop the girls at school on my way to work, which would be so much better for all of us.

'When are you planning to leave?' She sank into her chair behind her desk. 'You know we don't want to lose you. Are you sure you don't want to change your mind? You've got a three-month notice period; you can always decide to stay.'

'I've made up my mind. Besides, Alastair's agreed to put me on gardening leave as of the end of this week for a month.'

'How the hell…?' Karen blinked in amazement. 'That's… jammy.'

'I'm going to a competitor.' I shrugged.

'Hardly,' Karen dismissed Edward's extremely successful business with a wave of one hand, which I think would have amused him. He had an excellent, solid practice that did good work and didn't need or want to compete with the likes of Cunningham, Wilding and Taylor.

'Don't ask, don't get.' Alastair had been more than generous in our discussion. I think he'd been impressed by my candour. 'He even said he was planning to come to the parkrun one Saturday.'

'Bloody hell. I don't suppose you fancy popping back in there and negotiating me a salary rise, do you?' She stared down the corridor towards the MD's office and put both hands on the table, stretching out the fingers in sudden defeat. 'Bugger it, Claire. I'm going to miss you.' She got up, came around the desk, and gave me a hug. 'Really miss you.'

'I'll still be in Churchstone and you live just outside. You'll have to come round one evening. Come to dinner.' We should have done it before and I wasn't sure why we hadn't. I realised that Karen was another person I really liked. 'Or we could go for coffee after the parkrun.'

She grinned. 'Dinner sounds like a plan, especially as you're going to have all the time in the world to cook. I'll bring the prosecco. I love pasta, by the way.'

Once I'd handed in my notice, things started to change at a pace, and not just at work. I'd had a very uncomfortable meeting with the headteacher at the school on Tuesday when I explained that Alice wasn't coming home any time soon. Inevitably, social services had to be involved; she had no choice and I understood that, but she was also very supportive. 'Both Poppy and Ava's teachers have commented how much more settled the girls have been in recent weeks and how much progress they've made, particularly Ava. I will, of course, make this known to social services. Don't worry. The school will back you and it's always in the best interests of the children to keep family together.'

'Thank you,' I whispered gratefully, worried I might cry. 'I'm going to apply for a Special Guardianship Order. But I'd be grateful if you didn't say anything to Poppy or Ava at the moment. They still think their mum is stranded… I'm going to have to tell them the truth.'

At which point the headteacher began to cry, which really disconcerted me. 'It's so sad. I don't know your sister very well... we did try to have her in a couple of times but she... was quite evasive.'

'Alice doesn't like authority.'

'Yes. I can see that now. There were a few concerns about the girls' lack of progress, especially Poppy. She's a very bright girl and she needs stretching. I realise now that perhaps your sister wasn't coping. It's not easy being a single mother.'

'No,' I agreed dryly, resolving to phone Farquhar as soon as I got home. I'd been trying to put off the application for the Special Guardianship Order for as long as possible but now I realised that both the girls and I needed a sense of permanence in our lives and that I was going to have to sit them down very soon and tell them the truth.

I left the head's office and went to collect the girls from outside their classrooms.

'Why are you here?' asked Poppy, her tone a touch belligerent. 'Where's Hilda?'

'I worked from home this afternoon and I thought I'd pick you up for a change. Hilda's gone to a tea dance and then she's walking Bill.' I didn't want to let her know that I'd been to see the head. She'd only worry and then start asking questions. Poppy wasn't stupid.

Ava held my hand and chattered sunnily about her day, giving inconsequential details about who'd been weather monitor, how many meatballs she'd had for lunch, and what colour skipping rope she had at breaktime. 'And I got another sticker for reading today.'

'That's brilliant, sweetie. We'll do some more this evening.

Hold up, Poppy,' I called to the older girl who'd put quite a distance between us. 'Wait for us.'

Poppy turned around, sent a ferocious glare my way, and then threw herself against a wall, folding her arms across her chest with all the sneering arrogance of a fully-fledged teenager.

Because she'd done as I asked, albeit with a bagful of attitude, I decided to leave well alone and not push her to find out what was wrong. She'd been difficult since the weekend and I wondered if it was hormones starting to make themselves felt; she was eleven, so the timing was bang on the button.

We caught up with her and then she decided she would trail behind us. By the time Ava and I reached the road on the other side of the park, with my house in view, she was four metres behind us, walking deliberately slowly.

I clenched my fists and tried to be patient, knowing that my own anxiety was starting to rise at the thought of having to face Ash in the next couple of hours as he'd be coming to pick up Bill as per our usual arrangement.

Hilda arrived back not much later than us and, thankfully, the sight of Bill's shaggy head seemed to cheer Poppy up until teatime.

'What's wrong with her?' asked Hilda in a quiet aside as we stacked the dishwasher together. 'And since when hasn't she liked tomatoes?'

'Hormones, I think.'

'Hmm, I was always quite glad I had a boy.'

'I remember Alice being hell on wheels'—I winced—'from about fourteen to sixteen… and then she got pregnant. My poor parents. She's been hormonal ever since.'

'Have you heard from them?'

'Yes.' I raised my eyes heavenwards. 'They're in denial. I had a long email from Mum. She believes Alice is having a protracted holiday and will be home soon.'

'And no word from her.'

'No.'

'I didn't like to ask how it went with the head, *pas devant les enfants*.'

'We've hit crunch time. She's going to inform social services and I'll have to have a meeting with them so I need to get the ball rolling with Farquhar to apply through the court for the Special Guardianship Order. I'm going to call him later.'

'Hmph. You two seem like bosom buddies all of a sudden.'

'He's very kindly helping me – free of charge, for which I'm very grateful. Farquhar isn't as bad as you painted him and he does care about you.'

'Hmm. The boy wants to see a couple of bungalows this weekend. Says he's coming to the parkrun and why don't we view the one on Long Acre Road and one on Abernathy Road – actually, that one's a ground-floor maisonette but it's all right. It's a conversion, so has the high ceilings that I prefer and a bit of grandeur about it. I'd be happy entertaining in a place like that. I don't want to live in a soulless box. And what's this I hear about a dog-sitter? Ash tells me Bill's having a trial tomorrow.'

I winced and glanced over at Poppy who was once again stabbing at her mobile and viciously scrolling.

'Ash and I are cooling off a bit,' I said in a quiet undertone.

'Cooling off?' Hilda's fierce whisper attracted Poppy's attention. 'What on earth does that mean?'

'Shh.' I grabbed her arm and steered her into the lounge.

'What?'

'I don't want the girls to know.'

'To know what?'

'That Ash isn't going to be around as much.'

'Whyever not?'

'I told you, we've decided to… to be friends.'

Hilda snorted rudely. 'There's enough heat between the two of you to start an inferno. I think the pair of you should just have sex and be done with it. I'm surprised your ruddy knickers haven't caught fire; when the two of you are in the same room they're practically smouldering.'

'Hilda!'

'Well, you know what I mean.'

'Sadly, I do and that's part of the problem. There's plenty of chemistry but no substance.'

'What poppycock.' She slammed her coffee down on one of the little side tables, ignoring the liquid slopping over the sides. 'I've never heard so much rubbish in my life and I've heard a lot, I can tell you. My second husband could… well, that's for another time. Why on earth would you want to do that?

'Hilda, Ash is building his career. In no time he'll be back to being Ashwin Laghari, International Arms Dealer, not Ash who's got a dog, two kids in tow, an honorary grandma and a formerly high-flying girlfriend. He's going to move on and I don't want to be left burnt out in his wake.'

'Claire, that's absurd. The two of you are… well, I wouldn't say perfect – that's too twee for you two – but you make a great team. I suppose that is what "perfect for each other" means. You're both always on the same page. I don't understand.'

I raised an eyebrow. 'Ash will be back to his workaholic ways in no time. We were on the same page when we were both like that.'

'Hmph. Well, I think you're cutting off your nose to spite your face.'

'It's called self-preservation.'

When Ash turned up half an hour later, Hilda lifted a snooty nose and said she and Ava were going to play with the ducks in the bath.

'What's she in a snit about?' asked Ash, placing his laptop bag on the kitchen table and crouching to accept Bill's happy welcome while also giving Poppy a warm hello. 'Hey pipsqueak, how was the maths homework?'

'I got them all right.' She beamed at him, the happy grin lifting her pale face. It was the most animated she'd been since I picked her up from school. 'Ten out of ten.'

'Phew!' He wiped his forearm across his forehead in mock relief.

Darn, who was going to help with her maths and science homework in future?

Poppy handed him Bill's lead. 'See you tomorrow, Bill.' She bent and ruffled his ears.

Ash and I both froze, our eyes meeting over the top of her head.

'Actually, Poppy, Bill's not coming tomorrow.'

Poppy glanced up at his face, curious at first and then alarmed. 'Why? What's happened?'

'I'm sorry, Pops, but Bill's getting very confused about

where he lives and because he's a rescue dog, he's getting a bit anxious. This is best for him.' He explained that from next week, dependent on tomorrow's trial, Bill would be going to a dog-sitter who would take him out for a nice long walk every day.

'But when can I see him?' Poppy asked with an anguished cry.

Ash swallowed but, to give him credit, he didn't look my way. Even so, I felt horribly guilty. This was my fault but it was protecting all of us in the long run.

'You can still see him at the parkrun every Saturday.'

'But…' Poppy's lip quivered. 'Why are adults always so mean? You tell lies. You don't stay. And you pretend. Why won't you just tell the truth?' She stood up and stormed out of the room and slammed her bedroom door so hard that the whole house shook.

'Well that went well,' said Ash, glaring at me.

'She's been in a difficult mood since Saturday,' I said. It seemed the slightest thing triggered her instant flare ups and champion-standard door slamming these days.

'What, since you dumped me?'

'Ash,' I threw my head back and huffed out a long sigh. 'I didn't dump you. I'm just making things easier for you.'

'Or for you, perhaps.'

'How do you figure that?'

He pushed a hand through his hair. 'I don't know. Not having to explain to them when I have to let you all down. I forgot about taking them to the cinema. I feel really bad about that and you didn't mention it.'

'Exactly,' I said crisply. 'No point upsetting everyone.'

'Were they very disappointed?'

'Poppy more so than Ava. I told them you paid for the tickets and that it was your treat even though you couldn't come along. You also bought them Maltesers and Minstrels. You owe me £4.60.'

He winced. 'I'm sorry.' His eyes showed genuine regret. 'I get your point now. And now I feel like a real shit, especially as I'm going to ask one last favour and then I really will stay out of your hair. This Thursday, I have a really big meeting with the board. An all-dayer. I'm leaving early and I'll be back late. Can I ask you to have Bill all day Thursday and overnight until Friday? I shouldn't ask, should I? It's not fair on Poppy, is it?' Guilt softened his eyes. 'Everything you said. You're right. Shit. I'm sorry, Claire.'

Tears welled up in my eyes and I swallowed hard. 'You see.'

'I do. I'm sorry. I'll find an alternative arrangement.'

I was touched that he was so worried about Poppy's feelings.

'Don't worry. We'll get over it. Children are very resilient. And no doubt she'll use every bargaining chip she has to get me to let Bill sleep on her bed.'

'You sure?'

I nodded, trying hard not to give in to temptation and meet his eyes. Instead, I gave him a perfunctory smile. Being in the same room was too much like temptation. I wanted to lean in to that broad chest and let him fold his arms around me. It would have been so much easier to give in and keep seeing him but I knew it would only prolong the heartache at a later stage.

Thank goodness we didn't sleep together again.

And then I wished I hadn't let that thought come to fruition because now I'd have a lifetime of regret. I would never get to sleep with Ashwin Laghari again.

'Is it okay if I drop him off at seven?'

'What?' My mind was still caught up in the fantasy of his golden chest and those predatory tiger eyes. 'Sorry, yes. He can walk to school with us and then I'll bring him back here, get the later train to work and then Hilda can come in at two.'

'Thanks Claire. I want to kiss you… but I guess that's out of the question now.'

My heart clenched. ''Fraid… so.' I had to force the words past the huge lump in my throat.

'Right, well I'll be off then. See you Thursday.'

He gave me a glum smile, called to Bill, and left.

I watched him stride down the front garden, the dog at his heels. He didn't look back once, thank goodness. Not that he could have seen my tears from that distance.

Chapter Thirty-Five

On Thursday morning, Poppy was overly bright and cheerful during breakfast, as if she was trying to make amends for the last few days' sulks without actually saying sorry. I recognised the tactic. It was the exact same one I'd used with my mother.

'Go up and clean your teeth, both of you. I can see Ash and Bill.' I waved through the kitchen window. Poppy, instead of going upstairs, diverted to the front door to welcome Bill.

'Morning,' I said to Ash over Poppy's crouched body where she was fussing with her pal. 'Poppy, teeth. You can see Bill in a minute and he's coming on the school run this morning.'

'Okay,' she huffed and dashed up the stairs.

'Thanks for this, Claire. I really appreciate it.'

'No prob—' I made the mistake of looking at him properly and the words died in my mouth. Oh my, Ashwin Laghari, firing on all cylinders. All that sexy charisma slammed into me and I felt like I'd taken a hit.

'N-nice suit,' I managed. Silhouetted against the sun, his

broad shoulders filled the doorway and the perfectly tailored suit emphasised what was under it a little too well.

'Thanks.' The warm, almost shy, smile made my knees go weak and my pulse take off at an untenable pace. Would I ever get over that initial lightning bolt of lust and attraction every time I saw him?

'Good luck today,' I said, trying to sound brisk and businesslike. 'I hope it goes well. What time are you on?'

'I'm presenting the budget to the board at eleven but we're starting the meeting at nine.'

'I'm sure they'll be extremely impressed with their new financial director.' Unable to help myself, I reached out and touched his arm. 'Knock 'em dead, Ash. I know you'll be brilliant.'

'Thanks, Claire. I'd better go. Be good, Bill.' He turned and then paused with his back to me. I swallowed, studying the line of his suit.

With a sudden turn he faced me again, leaned forward and pulled me towards him. The kiss surprised me and I was just getting used to the idea when he stepped away, shot me a crooked smile, and said, 'Gotta go. Think of me.'

And then the bastard strode down the front path without a backward glance, leaving me touching my lips and sighing like some forties ingenue. Inside, I was all fired and ready for action and he'd just left me hanging.

I stepped out of the front door as he swung into the Porsche and spotted Elaine next door, who crossed her hands over her heart and gave me a big smile. 'So romantic.'

'Hmph,' I grunted, wanting nothing more than to slam the door. Instead I shut it very firmly and carefully. Bloody man. What did he go and do that for?

'You can't bring Bill onto school property.' Poppy stood barring my way on the path at the school gate.

'Oh, that's right. I'll just tie him up here.'

'No!' Poppy almost sounded panicked.

'It's all right. He'll be okay for a minute.'

'I'll take Ava.' I smiled at her uncharacteristic bossiness; she was definitely growing up. 'I can take her to her classroom. I don't mind.'

'Fine. Yes, if you want to.'

'You'd better go. You don't want to be late for your train.' She almost turned me around and packed me off.

Thanks to her consideration, I caught the train before the one I had planned and had a lovely chat with Bryan, who was also running late, and consequently was only a little later than usual to work. The morning had gone so smoothly that it never occurred to me something wasn't right.

Alarm bells began to ring when I received an automated text from the school advising me that my child was absent and I should ring to explain the absence. I'd had one before and it had been an error. Ava's teacher hadn't marked her in. Since I was about to go into a meeting, I very nearly ignored it, knowing that I'd dropped off both girls myself but some sixth sense made me stop.

'I'll be there in a minute,' I said to Dave. 'I just need to make a quick call.'

'Hi, it's Claire Harrison. I had a text saying one of the girls is absent,' I said, as soon as the call connected.

'Yes, Miss Harrison. Thanks for calling. We just need to know why Poppy isn't in school.'

'But she is. I dropped her off myself.'

The lady on the other end of the line tutted. 'Well, she's been marked absent in the register. I'll just send someone down to let the teacher know and change the register.'

I could hear muffled voices, as if she'd put her hand over the receiver, despite which I heard her asking one of her colleagues to go down to Mrs Philips's class and see if Poppy Harrison was present. I tapped my fingers on the table, a little irritated. Kind as she was, I felt like she was fussing. I knew Poppy was there because I'd taken her.

Then she came back to me. 'I'm sure it's just an error but we always check. Do you want to hang on a minute until Mrs Turner gets back?'

I waited, giving a thumbs up to Dave who'd popped his head out of the meeting room mouthing, 'Do you want coffee?'

'Erm, Miss Harrison,' the school secretary's voice sounded strained, 'can I call you back?'

I sat up, jolted into alertness by the unexpected words. 'Why? What's happened? Where's Poppy?'

'She's not in class but some of them have gone to the church... and we're just checking as she might be with that group. We're just trying to get hold of the TA who's with them.'

'But she must be there. I dropped her...' Poppy's face, as she helpfully pushed me away, popped into my head along with the careful calculation in her eyes.

'I dropped her and Ava at the gate. I had a dog with me. They walked up the path together. Ava's there, isn't she?'

'I'll... I'll just check. Do you want to stay on the line?' She put me on hold and I put my phone down, staring at it.

Poppy had to be at school. Where else would she be?

Finally, a new voice spoke down the phone. 'Hello, Miss Harrison? This is Mrs Cummings, the headteacher; we met on Tuesday. I'm sorry about this but the teacher hasn't seen Poppy today. She's not in class or on the trip.'

'Well, where is she then? She must be somewhere in the school? Have you checked everywhere?' But where else would Poppy be? She was a conformist sort of child, not the kind that would run away or hide in school. 'She must be there.' She had to be because if she wasn't... where was she? I stopped and leaned over the table, my forehead touching the surface.

Calm down, Claire. She'll be there.

'Poppy must be there. I saw her walk into the grounds of the school.'

'Is there any chance she might have gone home? Does she have her own key? Sometimes children who are unsettled... have you told her about her mum yet?'

'No, not yet. And she doesn't have a key.'

'Are you at home?'

'No, I'm at work.'

'Do you have a friend or neighbour who could go there and check, to see if she is there. Oh... hold on a minute.'

More muffled talking.

Please let them have made a mistake. Please let them have found her.

'It turns out that one of the girls in her class did see her in the playground this morning but hasn't seen her since. We're going to conduct a thorough search of the school and check our CCTV footage. In the meantime, perhaps you could get someone to check on the house?'

I nodded numbly, before realising she couldn't see me. 'Yes. Erm… I'll do that straight away.' But what if she wasn't there and she wasn't in school? What then? What did I do?

'I'm afraid if she's not there, we'll have to call the police.'

This can't be happening.

Where is she?

Hi Sweetie. Please text me. Let me know you're safe. Love you xxxxxxxxx

What else could I say? But if she texted back I could go from there.

I stared at the screen, willing to see the dots to indicate that Poppy was typing.

Please Poppy. Let me know you're okay.

Nothing.

With shaking fingers, I called Hilda and explained the situation.

'Can you go to the house? The school says Poppy isn't there. They're searching the building but just in case she went home…'

'Don't worry. She's a sensible girl.'

'But why isn't she there? And where would she go?' My voice squeaked and Karen, who was walking past, stopped in the doorway with a quizzical frown. 'It's not like she has any… Actually, Hilda, when you're in the house, can you check in her bedroom? In the top drawer beside her bed, there's a little beaded purse covered in ladybirds. Can you see if it's there?'

Poppy had always been good with money. She was a regular little hoarder of her pocket money and birthday money.

'I'll call you as soon as I've checked the house. But don't go borrowing trouble.' I tucked my phone in my pocket, praying that Poppy would be at home.

'Everything all right?' asked Karen.

I stared up at her, the enormity of it sinking in. 'No. One of my nieces has gone missing.'

I snatched up my mobile fifteen minutes later, most of which had been spent pacing and feeling sick while Karen kept offering me coffee and glasses of water. 'Hilda? Is she there?'

'Sorry, Claire, she isn't and'—Hilda's voice dropped—'the purse is missing.'

'Oh God.' I clutched my head with my other hand. 'Where could she have gone?' It just wasn't like Poppy. She wasn't a street-savvy kid. She didn't catch buses to places. She wasn't one of those kids who hankered to go into the city. She was a homebird, happy with her books and her own space. Where would she have gone? The library. The park. Those were the only places she went to on her own. It wasn't as if she was used to using public transport. You could walk everywhere in Churchstone.

'Have you let Ash know?'

'No.' Even to myself I sounded defensive.

'I think you should.' Her calm, even tone made me answer with less belligerence.

'What can he do?'

'He's close to Poppy. She talks to him when they walk Bill. He might have an idea. Besides, he'd want to know.'

She was right; Ash would want to know. He deserved to know. Guilt punched hard with the realisation that I was the one pushing him out of our funny little family and also the sudden awareness that I was doing it because I was scared. Scared that he would move on when I'd fallen hard.

'In the meantime, I could round up a few people and we could search the park. She might have gone there; it's a familiar place. Somewhere she might go if she's feeling upset or sad.' Though her voice was strong, I could tell Hilda was as worried as I was but I knew she wouldn't want me worrying about her, about her age, or whether she should be doing this. It would be insulting to her so instead of saying, *please sit down and take care of yourself*, I said, 'That's a good idea. If you give Janie and Penny a ring, they might be able to help and round up some people to search for her. Try the library, as well.'

Deep breath, Claire.

'I'll call Ash. Then I'll let the school know she's not at home.' I glanced at my watch. It was nearly eleven o'clock; he was already in his meeting and he was about to do his big presentation. He probably wouldn't answer. Maybe a text would be better.

My fingers were too fumbly for a text. I called him, overwhelmed by the rush of relief when I heard his voice.

'Ash! I didn't think you'd answer.'

'Hang on,' I heard voices in the background and then a door close. 'You wouldn't call unless it was important. What's wrong?'

'It's Poppy. She's gone missing—'

'Missing?'

'Yes, I dropped her off at the school gate this morning but she isn't at school. Hilda's at the house. Her purse is missing. She had about thirty pounds. I don't know what to do. I know she talks to you. Have you any idea... has she said anything?'

'No... nothing in particular. I know she's been fretting about Alice not being in touch. Remember, she used my phone hoping that Alice might pick up a call from a strange number.'

'Thirty pounds isn't going to get her to India.'

'If she is in India...' Ash said slowly.

'What do you mean?'

'Hang on a minute. I'll call you straight back. I need to check something.'

'Check what?'

He hung up.

I threw my head back in frustration but he called back almost immediately.

'Alice isn't in India.'

'What?'

'I just called her number. It's not an overseas ringtone. Where are you?' There was sudden urgency in his voice.

'I'm at work but I'm going to go home right now.'

'Stay there; I'm coming to get you.'

'But—'

'I'll see you in ten minutes. Be out front?'

'But your presen—'

'Claire, give me some fucking credit.' And with that he cut me off.

The Porsche screeched to a halt outside Cunningham, Wilding

and Taylor. Karen gave me a hug and then squeezed both my hands. 'Let me know when you find her. And if there's anything I can do.'

'W-Will do,' I said, desperately trying not to cry.

When I scrambled into the low-slung seat, Ash unpeeled his hands and opened his arms. 'Sorry I yelled.'

'Oh Ash...' I did my best to hold it together while he held me against his chest. 'I d-don't know w-where she could be. And she's so y-young and... and...'

His hand cupped the back of my head, rubbing a soothing hand down my back, pressing a kiss onto my forehead.

I hauled in a snotty, tearful breath. 'Sorry... it's just... I feel so helpless. I don't know what to do. Or what made her run away. Is this my fault? Is it about Bill?'

Ash kissed my face again and put his hands on my upper arms, as if to anchor me.

'It's okay, Claire. I've got an idea where she might have gone and none of this is your fault. I'm pretty sure it's all down to your bloody sister. I've never met her and I want to wring her neck.'

I pulled back and looked into his face, my eyes blurred with tears. With a knuckle, he brushed away a tear. 'We'll find her.'

'Where do you think she is?'

'Harrogate, is my guess. Are you friends with your sister on Facebook?'

'No, she blocked me a long time ago.'

'Poppy is. I think she's gone to find Alice.'

'Oh.' His words hit hard. Even though I knew Poppy was a young girl so of course she wanted her mum, it still hurt. 'She's spent an awful lot of time poring over her phone these last few days. And acting up.'

'Does your sister have friends in Harrogate?'

I pulled a face. 'I'm not sure. Maybe. Possibly some old school friends. We grew up there. My parents live there. Why Harrogate?'

'Poppy asked me how far away it was.'

I sat back in my seat. 'That would make sense.' I bit my lip. 'My parents' place. That's where Alice would go. They're not back for a while yet. She knows where they keep the spare key. Yeah, that's where Alice would go.'

'So that's where we're headed. We'll find her, Claire.' He laid a hand on my clenched fingers.

'Do you think I need to let the police know? They called me and asked me to meet them at the house. I said I'd be there in an hour.'

'Harrogate's only half an hour away. It would take you longer to get back to Churchstone by train. And this is a guess. Is there any point saying anything? I can get you back home in an hour.'

'It's a good guess. Poppy's not an adventurous or particularly bold child. Going somewhere that's slightly familiar – she's been to her grandparents' hundreds of times – that makes much more sense.' I sucked in a harsh breath. 'But how would she get there? And how would she know?'

'Bus. There's a bus that leaves the market square every two hours. There was one at ten past nine this morning. She could have easily looked it up on the internet. She's a smart cookie.'

'Yes, but not street smart. What if someone… offered her a lift or something?'

'Don't think like that. It's highly unlikely.'

Despite his words, I did think like that for the next half hour.

***

'Take the next right. And then left.'

We finally pulled up on the leafy street outside my parents' rambling detached 1930s home. They'd lived here for over thirty years and had planted the wisteria that now climbed up the front porch and curled around the window of the master bedroom on the first floor. I leapt out of the car and raced up the gravel drive, ringing the doorbell like a crazy woman, Ash hot on my heels.

The house seemed empty and for a moment I thought we'd come on a fool's errand but then the door peeled open and Alice peered out. She was all mascara-smudged eyes, tousled hair, and she was wearing a cotton kimono-style dressing-gown.

She blinked in the sunlight.

'Alice!' Until she opened the door, I hadn't really believed she'd be there.

'Claire! What are you doing here?' Her words were slurred with sleep and possibly something else. 'You'd better come in.' She stepped back to invite me in.

'Is Poppy here?'

'Uh, God.' Her eyes closed and it seemed to take an awful lot of effort for her to open them again. She pulled a weary face. 'She was.'

'*What!* Was? Where is she?'

'Dunno. She woke us up, shouted a lot, and then ran off. God, I need another coffee.'

'Alice!' I grabbed her shoulders and shook her, blanching at the stale breath that hissed out of her mouth. 'This is serious. Poppy is ten. Where did she go? What did you say to her?'

Alice stepped back, her eyes sliding away from mine.

'What did you say?'

'Stuff.' Her eyes still wouldn't meet mine. 'Things. I can't really remember. What was she doing here? You're supposed to be looking after them.'

Typical Alice, pushing the responsibility back onto someone else.

I saw Ash clenching his fists by his side and thought for a second that Alice was very lucky that he hadn't punched her – although, there was still time yet and I was first in line. I knew I was taking the wrong tack with her, but I was so angry I couldn't help myself.

'Yes, because you're allegedly in India!'

She waved a hand and swayed on the spot before turning and weaving her way into the kitchen. 'Problem with visas and shit. We had to get out for a while.'

I followed her, knowing that she was quite capable of weaselling away at any minute. Anything to avoid facing up to her problems… which, I realised with a flash of insight, was why I was so good and so keen to solve them all the time, because I'd seen what happened when you ducked them. It made things far worse.

'Oh my God,' I blurted out, at the sight of my mother's normally pristine kitchen. Every surface was covered in dirty dishes, foil takeaway trays, and spilled food. 'Mum will kill you.' How could she show so little respect? This was our parents' home.

'Chill, sis. I'll clean up before they get back. They'll never know we were here,' she pushed her face into mine, 'unless you, steady Eddie, tell them.'

I stared at her and for the first time saw her as she really was. For years I'd thought she was a bit spoiled, a bit of a free spirit, and probably a product of my parents letting her get away with things. I'd thought she needed help, so I'd helped. Bought the girls' uniforms, cut garden hedges, taken her to the supermarket when the girls were little, all the while hoping that she'd grow up one day and start taking some responsibility for herself and for her children's lives.

Looking at the state of the kitchen, I realised that Alice neither wanted nor needed help.

The trashed kitchen. This was deliberate desecration. There was a touch of spite about it. It was a deliberate kick back. She knew how much Mum loved this room.

'You really don't care, do you?' I thought of Janie and Penny's opinions. The headteacher's diplomatic comments.

Alice lifted her thin shoulders and stared back at me, defiance and mockery twisting her lips.

'Not much, no.'

Ash exchanged a quick, shocked glance with me, his eyes full of pain.

I felt cold and numb inside but I had to ask, 'What about Poppy and Ava?' Her eyes narrowed to gleaming, malicious slits. 'Oh Claire, you're so fucking *holier than thou*. "What about Poppy and Ava?"' Her tone was a cruel mockery of mine. 'What *about* them? What about *me*? Yeah, what about me? I didn't ask to get pregnant. Imagine the best years of your life wasted in breast feeding, nappies, sleepless nights... and where were you? Swanning off to work in your natty suits thinking you were better than me. Popping round and babysitting so that I could get some fucking sleep. Being the saviour… oh you bloody loved that, didn't you. Helping. Being the superior one as usual. Showing me what a fuck-up I was.'

I lost it then, realising she was twisting things to suit her version of reality. 'No! That's not true and you know it,' I yelled, feeling an odd sort of freedom in letting it all out. 'You always asked for help. Whenever you messed up, you asked someone else to sort it out. When you were pregnant, you asked for my help. Remember the morning of my first A-level exam? You had choices then. Adoption. Abortion.' I tossed the words at her lightly although my heart clenched at the thought of never having Poppy in my life. 'You asked me what to do. And I told you: tell Mum. You didn't… you left it and left it and left it and then it was too late to do anything. And then Mum offered to help if you decided to have the baby. And you took the easy way out. You chose to have those babies. And now you don't like it.'

'*I want a life!*' she screamed back at me. 'I deserve one. I'm sick of having to do stuff. The school's always on my case. The other mums look down on me. It's shit and I hate it. There's never any time to myself. It's like being on duty your entire life… and *I've had it!* I want my life back.'

'What about their lives?'

'I'm sure you'll be much better at playing mum than I am,' she sneered. 'Rushing here and being all like, "Where's Poppy? Where's Poppy?"'

I thought I might be sick but her words were a salutary reminder.

'Oh God, what did you say to her?'

Alice pursed her mouth and her eyes slid away from mine again.

'What did you say?'

Next to me, Ash stiffened and his hand squeezed mine. That silent, strong solidarity. A man I could rely on. My heart filled with gratitude and love, so much love.

She huffed and turned her head away, pulling at a pack of cigarettes on the side before tugging one out and lighting it. Taking a deep drag, she blew out the smoke in a long, slow puff. 'Kid told me off. Said I was mean and a liar. Why wasn't I in India rescuing people? Grateful there, Claire, that you made out I was Mother Theresa or something. I told her I needed some time away. Like being at school… I was taking my six-week holiday. She asked when I was coming back.'

I winced, feeling sicker than ever. 'What did you say?'

Finally, Alice looked ashamed. 'Look, there's no point pulling punches. I'm not coming back any time soon. She needed to know the truth. You can hand them over to Mum and Dad. They'll be better off with them.' Her face flickered and I saw something else, something that broke my heart. 'Let's face it, Claire, I'm not a good mother. The school, they were talking to social services. Neglect, for Christ's sake. They'll be better off without me.' She lifted her chin but, behind the façade, I saw the bravado. I stepped forward, instinctively wanting to help. To offer to work out a solution, so that she could stay with the children but make her life easier. Ideas were flashing through my head: maybe I could have the girls every weekend to give her respite, maybe I could…

And then I realised it was the same old pattern.

I softened my voice, realising that, deep down, she did care and that she was a little bit broken at the moment. 'Are you sure?'

Her voice wobbled. 'Sure as I'm sure about anything at the moment. I just know that in India I was a little bit happy.'

I nodded, too drained to say any more. We were done. 'We need to find Poppy.'

'Yeah, I'm sorry I upset her. It was… just a shock seeing her.' Alice's lips curved into a mirthless smile. 'Never thought she had it in her to run away. More Ava's style. They're like you and me. Don't let Ava be the fuck up, Claire, will you?'

Tears stung my eyes. 'No, I won't.' I shook my head, trying to blink them back. 'Do you know where she went?'

Ash's thumb rubbed over my knuckle, reminding me of his stalwart, steady presence.

'No, she ran off but I'd guess she's gone down to the Valley Gardens. It's the only place she'd know how to walk to from here. Dad takes them a lot. Gets an ice cream at the pavilion.'

'Do you know the way?' asked Ash.

I nodded and led the way out of the house, not saying another word to Alice.

'Let me know if you find her,' she called after us. Ash, still holding my hand, growled under his breath.

As the door closed behind us, I stood for a moment staring at the solid panelled front door with its cast-iron knocker and black letterbox and sighed. It felt as if I'd reached the end of a very long journey and there was no going back.

Ash kissed me softly on the cheek. 'Come on, sweetheart. You can think about it all later but we need to find Poppy. She needs us.'

I swallowed back the lump and smiled a little stupidly at him. 'Sweetheart?'

His smile was gentle. 'Seemed appropriate.' And then he smirked, with that classic Ashwin Laghari lift of his eyebrow. 'Don't get too used to it. Come on, let's find our girl.'

I directed him down the hill towards the nearest entrance to the park, the route one I'd walked a thousand times in my own childhood and could probably have done blindfolded. I knew every tree, hedge, and crack in the pavement along the way.

There were plenty of mothers and toddlers dawdling along in the sunshine, a few of them with ice creams. Grandad brought Poppy and Ava for ice creams, just liked he'd bought them for me and Alice.

'The pavilion's this way,' I said. 'It's an ice-cream café but it's in a pavilion, just like The Friendly Bean. It's familiar. I bet that's where she'd go.'

I walked quickly, too exhausted by the emotional storm to run, and sighed with hope when I saw the cupola on the top of the pavilion. I looked left and right along the wide path and put a hand out to Ash's arm when I spotted a familiar flash of red school-uniform sweatshirt. My heart stopped at the sight of Poppy huddled, her knees up to her chin, on a wooden bench just a few strides ahead. She was sobbing her heart out.

On shaky legs I ran over to her, Ash close behind.

'Oh, Poppy, darling.' I scooped her up and somehow hauled her leggy body onto my lap, hugging her tight. She cried harder and I hugged her tighter, tucking her head under my chin as Ash sat down next to me, putting his arms around both of us.

'It's okay, sweetheart,' I murmured, tears pouring down my face. 'We've got you. We've got you.'

Lifting my head, I gave Ash a relieved, watery smile. We'd found her. My bones felt like water and I had to hang on to her otherwise I thought I might collapse. Ash hugged us both and kissed the corner of my mouth, his eyes shimmering with his own tears.

Eventually, Poppy's sobs subsided but we clung together after the storm as if none of us could bear to let go. When Poppy finally lifted her head, one of her hands came up to touch my tear-streaked face. 'I'm so sorry, Auntie Claire.'

'Shh, darling. I'm not mad at you. I'm just so relieved you're okay.'. Hell yes, she'd frightened me, and there would be recriminations later, but they'd probably just be threats that I was never going to let her out of my sight again until she was at least twenty-nine.

With a sniff, she straightened and I arranged her body more comfortably on my knee, with Ash's arms around both of us.

'I went to see Mummy.' She gulped and her mouth trembled.

I cupped her cheek and smiled sadly at her, doing my best not to cry again. 'I know, darling.'

'She's not in India.' The lump in my throat was so huge I had to take a second to breathe.

'I promise, I didn't know until I went to Nanny and Grandad's just now. I'm really sorry. I honestly thought she was still in India.' Inside, I felt sick for her and defeated by how she must be feeling.

'Alice doesn't want us anymore.' Her lower lip began to quiver in earnest and tears filled her eyes again. Try as I might, I couldn't hold back the sob and it came out a half-swallowed hiccough.

Bloody, bloody, Alice. How could she?

I'd never wanted the girls to know that. It would have been

413

easy to explain, to create excuses, but for Poppy's sake, I wasn't prepared to lie on Alice's behalf.

'But *I* do.' I clutched her fiercely. '*I* want you.'

She began to cry again and Ash, who hadn't said anything, dropped a kiss on my cheek.

'Me too,' he murmured.

Poppy looked up and her gaze went from me to Ash and back again, her eyes narrowed in sharp assessment. Thoughtful, clever Poppy.

'You should be at work.'

Ash snorted. 'I don't think so. Not when there's a Poppy on the loose. Who else but me and Claire was going to come and find you?'

Again, she looked from him to me and back.

I kissed her nose. 'You're far more important than that. Than anything.'

She swallowed and sniffed bravely. 'Not to Mummy.'

'To us. I love you, Poppy Harrison. More than anything.'

'More than Ava?'

'Well…' I hesitated and kissed her again. 'The same as Ava.'

'That's okay. I don't mind that.' She paused and with a tiny spark of her natural cheekiness, asked, 'More than Ash?'

My heart stalled and I looked at his warm eyes reflecting love and hope.

'The same as Ash.'

He laced his fingers through mine.

'And I love you, Poppy… and Ava, *and* Claire. Nothing in the world is as important as you three.'

'What about Bill?' Poppy's eyes glowed with outrage which made Ash and me laugh. 'And Hilda.'

'I love you, Ava, Claire, Bill, and Hilda,' declared Ash, stroking her face with his hand.

'That's okay then.' She gave him a trusting smile and I had to swallow hard again. 'Can we go home, now?'

'Home?'

'To your house.'

'*Our* house,' I said firmly.

The three of us stood up, Ash took one of Poppy's hands and I the other, and the three of us walked slowly up the path back to the car.

Ash sent me a gentle smile over the top of Poppy's head and I smiled back, secure in the knowledge that we were on the same page after all.

Life ahead of us was going to be tough but we were a team and between us, between me, Poppy, Ava, Ash, Hilda, and Bill, there was enough love, friendship, and community to build lasting foundations for the future. Poppy and Ava would not be short changed in love.

And – my eyes met Ash's – neither would I.

Epilogue

'Morning everyone. I'd like to welcome you to our one hundred and fifty-eighth parkrun. Today's our third anniversary.' I paused and sought Ash out in the crowd. 'Hopefully it will mean that *someone* will never forget the date.' I shot him a meaningful look and a loud cheer went up followed by a storm of clapping. Ash, in a black '100' T-shirt, grinned back and Poppy, now nearly fourteen, in a red '50' T-shirt, clapped him on the back and gave me a grinning thumbs up. At the back, in a tail-walkers hi-vis vest, Ava was hanging on to a straining Bill and waved madly at me with her spare hand, while next to her Hilda was busy chatting to Harold. The two of them, very much an item – although she'd decided that she quite fancied living in sin rather than making him husband number five – were taking it easy today and were in charge of cutting up the multi-tiered cake that Hilda had spent a couple of months planning, baking, and decorating in her newly modelled kitchen in her maisonette just around the corner on Abernathy Road.

We took it in turns to have tea at her house or at mine on Saturday afternoons, often joined by Farquhar and his girlfriend, Antonia. They were a perfect match, and she had an even more cut-glass booming voice than he did. I owed Farquhar a huge debt that I wasn't sure I'd ever be able to repay. He'd helped me through the endless paperwork to ensure that legal responsibility for the girls was mine and would remain so until they were eighteen.

Both girls saw their mother on the fleeting occasions she returned home. She was now an experienced yoga teacher who taught at the retreat in India. Ava, being younger and of a more laid-back, sunny disposition, was more easily reconciled to the ever-youthful Peter Pan figure who turned up unannounced every six or seven months. Poppy was troubled by her mother's infrequent visits but a good counsellor, recommended by Ash's sister, was gradually helping her come to terms with the rejection she felt. Ash and I did everything we could to make sure she knew she was loved unconditionally by us.

Today we were having a bit of a celebration in the park after the run. Not that the last three years had all been plain sailing. We'd had to reroute the run a couple of times in the winter because ankle-deep mud and running are not happy partners; there'd also been a couple of dicey moments when complaints from the general public about us using the park free of charge had set off a spate of emergency council meetings, but thankfully Neil Blenkinsop continued to champion us and, with the help of his dad, had dug out some old covenant which revealed that the park had been gifted to the town by one philanthropic Victorian, Thomas Outhwaite, who happened to have competed in the first Modern Olympics in 1896 in Athens in the 100m race. With far-sighted design, he had stated very specifically that the park was to be used for the promotion of a healthy lifestyle.

Good old Neil Blenkinsop. I sought his tall frame out in the crowd. Next to him was the auburn-haired girl from my old commute, Sally. I'd got to know her a lot better over the last three years and she had got to know Neil a lot better too. They were now engaged and officially our first parkrun couple.

I wondered if on the morning of her wedding she'd also be crazy enough to do the run in a second-hand wedding dress. I smoothed a hand down the gauzy fabric of the ballerina-length white dress, the floaty fabric creating an interesting juxtaposition with my pink trainers.

Charles wrenched the loud-hailer from my hand, forcefully taking over his role as run director, and I worked my way back through the crowd, receiving lots of congratulatory back slaps and smiles, to join Ash and Poppy.

'Ready, Mrs Ashwin Laghari to be?' Ash's magnificent eyes twinkled.

'Yes, although I still wish we hadn't put that sodding hill in.'

'It's been three years; get over it.' He winked and grabbed my hand. 'But I'll help you up the hard parts today, and the easy bits, and the not-so-straight-forwards bits.' I smiled mistily at him. He wasn't just talking about the run.

We'd decided to do the parkrun hand in hand today and to celebrate with all our friends in the park after the run before going home to change (into a straight sheath number that there was no way I could run in) to arrive at the registry office for two this afternoon.

'You'd better. That hill never gets any easier.'

'It will be today. I'll pull you up.'

'And I'll push,' chimed in Poppy.

I smiled at the pair of them. 'I guess when you have the support, it's like life: it's easier with family and friends.' I looked around at the nearly three hundred people waiting for Charles to send us off. Some I knew, some I didn't, but they all belonged to the Saturday morning parkrun and we were a community. I smiled at Ash.

'Three, two, one. Go.'

Acknowledgments

You might have guessed I'm a bit of a Parkrun fan, although I definitely fall into the category of plodder rather than runner. I'm never going to beat any records or impress anyone with my times but it's become an essential part of my weekly routine and even on those days I come home dripping with wet, the colour of my trainers scarcely discernible under the inches of mud, I feel a huge sense of achievement and, moreover, that I'm part of something.

The sense of the community that I describe in *The Saturday Morning Park Run* mirrors that of my own local Parkrun in Tring but isn't unique to that event. I've found the same wonderful welcome, friendliness, inclusivity and belonging when visiting other venues, as a 'tourist', whether at St Andrews, Delamere Forest, Luton or Aylesbury. There are over 700 Parkruns in the UK all of which are 'free forever for everyone' thanks to the teams of volunteers that turn out every Saturday. Parkrun is a fabulous organisation which has done a wonderful job in encouraging more people to improve their health and well being by taking up running and I could bang on about it for some time but do check the website www. parkrun.org.uk to find out more.

At every Parkrun there are lots of wonderful stories and characters and I've stolen quite a few from my own Parkrun, including Jim, the wonderful marshal (sadly the boom box has now been banned) who cheers us on with enthusiastic smiles week in and week out; the amazing Luciana, who really has lost 12 stone and is an absolute inspiration; the former Olympians who flash past in a blur; and the couple who met and subsequently got married. I have to thank my friend Vicki Wilson who encouraged me and my husband to go on that first run, although I'm not sure thanks were at the forefront of my mind when she and I had to take shelter in a bush prior to the start of one of the wettest, windiest runs of the winter last year. On those days I do think I might be a bit mad. But all that is more than made up for by the friendliness of the volunteers and other runners and I have to give a shout out to some of the people who I have mentioned in the book including Luciana Walker, who has inspired me so much and often keeps me going; the lovely Katie Haines, who answered my initial questions; and to Andy Evans, who set up the Tring Parkrun and also helped with my early research.

I'm afraid to suit the story I have to confess there are some areas where I have taken poetic licence with regard to the setting up of a Parkrun and I hope readers will forgive me. In fact it takes considerably longer than my characters did to set up a brand new event.

Sadly as I write this the Parkrun in the UK has been shut down by the pandemic but I sincerely hope it will be back up and running in the very near future to welcome yet more runners. Why not give it a go, either as a runner or volunteer? It might just change your life, it's certainly changed mine!

I wrote this book not long after I gave up my day job, and as a tribute to some of my former colleagues, I have shamelessly plundered their names and surnames for this books. Biggest thanks go to the real Claire Harrison, who has been a staunch fan since I was first published; and also to my lovely senior management team colleagues Louise, Claire and Gilly, whose surnames were stolen for my heroine's work place, Wilding, Taylor and Cunningham. Love to all at the Grove Junior School where I spent eight very happy years with the best team you could possibly wish for.

As always writing any book is a collaborative effort and the birth of each one differs; this one was definitely a breech! But after a long labour, thanks to the persistence and dedication of my brilliant editor, Charlotte Ledger, we finally got there. And huge thanks to my superagent, Broo Doherty, who keeps me smiling and positive, even when that little voice inside is whinging 'this is too hard'. I'd also like to thank some of the unsung heroes who work away in the background at One More Chapter to make everything happen, including Bethan Morgan, Mel Price and Claire Fenby, as well as the awesome HarperCollins Rights Team, Aisling, Emily, Iona and Zoe.

And behind the scenes, as always, urging me on, are my faithful friends: Donna Ashcroft, the absolute queen of pep talks and prosecco brainstorms; and my Messenger crew, Sarah, Bella, Philippa and Darcy, who all have the capacity to cheer me up with a single gif.

Special thanks go to my friend, Paulene, for her uncanny ability to spot those pesky missing words which I could have sworn I'd typed!

I'd also like to say a 'wow' and 'aren't you fabulous' to the book blogging community who are so generous with their time, providing book reviews and sharing the love on social media. I value you all but a special shout out to Jenn Webley, Rachel Gilbey, Julie Morris, Kaisha Holloway and Kate Mclaughlin, who have been especially supportive. Many thanks ladies, reviews count and I appreciate every last one.

Last and most importantly, thank you for choosing to read this book. I've had some wonderful comments over the years from readers and I treasure them all. If I can take people on a life-affirming, uplifting journey for a few hours, then it makes every hour spent writing more than worthwhile. I hope that you enjoy reading *The Saturday Morning Park Run* as much as I loved writing it.

YOUR NUMBER ONE STOP

ONE MORE CHAPTER

FOR PAGETURNING BOOKS

One More Chapter is an
award-winning global
division of HarperCollins.

Sign up to our newsletter to get our
latest eBook deals and stay up to date
with our weekly Book Club!
<u>Subscribe here.</u>

Meet the team at
<u>www.onemorechapter.com</u>

Follow us!
@OneMoreChapter_
@OneMoreChapter
@onemorechapterhc

Do you write unputdownable fiction?
We love to hear from new voices.
Find out how to submit your novel at
<u>www.onemorechapter.com/submissions</u>